Bloodline

A DAMIEN KAINE THRILLER

Victoria M. Patton

Dark Force Press – www.darkforcepress.com

Dark Force Press
City of Publication: Piedmont, OK
www.darkforcepress.com

Book Layout © 2016 BookDesignTemplates.com

Bloodline/ Victoria M. Patton. -- 1st ed.
ISBN 13: 978-1-946934-28-4
ISBN 10: 1-946934-28-3

Library of Congress Control Number
2022901137

For Zachary
I know you got this.

For Ariel
You amaze me every day

CONTENTS

CHAPTER ONE

Monday evening 8:30 p.m.

Peter gripped Frank in a bear hug. He buried his face in his shirt, inhaling his woodsy scent.

"Dude, you trying to kill me?" Frank laughed, stepping back.

"I'm sorry." Peter gazed at his feet.

Frank squeezed his shoulders. "It's going to be okay. You're going to marry Chrissy and live happily ever after."

"I wish you could be there. Maybe we could move the wedding up."

"No. We talked about this. You will not rearrange your life for me. I love you too much to let that happen." Frank nudged him off the stoop. "Go. Remember, I love you. And these last few months have been the best few months of my life."

Peter looked up from the bottom of the stoop. "I'm the one who is thankful. I wouldn't be the man I am today without you." He wiped the moisture from his cheek. "I'll see you next week. I love you, Frank."

"Go." Frank turned, entering his house. Watching through the small window next to the front door, his gaze followed Peter as he walked away. He wished he had more time with the most important person in his life. The only person in his life.

***

Corbin watched him walk away from the older man. His fingers tightened around the steering wheel. "I can't believe I ever trusted that bastard. Chrissy deserves better." Driving slowly, he followed behind. Before Peter reached the corner, he sped up, rolling down his window. "Peter? Peter?"

Peter turned at the sound of his name. He glanced back at Frank's stoop. His brow wrinkled. "Hey, what are you doing here?"

"Visiting a friend. You want a ride?"

Peter shook his head. "No. I parked in the car park a few blocks down the street." He took another few steps.

"Jump in, man. It's the least I can do."

Peter hesitated, glancing up and down the street. The back of his throat ached, making it hard for him to swallow. He shifted his weight, fighting the urge to run. He gave one last glimpse towards Frank's house, then walked to the truck and opened the door. "Sure. I guess. Why not?"

Corbin smiled as his passenger strapped in. "Hey, I'm sorry about the phone call the other day. I shouldn't stick my nose in your and Chrissy's relationship."

Peter glanced out the passenger window. "It's okay. I need to explain something to her. I'm sure that's why she is so upset. It's my fault." He wiped his palms on his jeans. Peter pointed towards a small SUV at the back of the dimly lit lot. "There's my car."

Corbin positioned his truck, blocking the view of any passerby. When Peter exited, he waited, letting him get to his vehicle.

Peter unlocked his car using the key fob as he walked to the driver's side. "Hey, thanks for the ride," he said as he waved.

"Hey, heck, man, I almost forgot." Corbin left his vehicle door open as he walked towards the other man. He pulled the switchblade from his front pant pocket, glancing around.

"Forgot what?" Peter turned towards his friend.

He placed his left hand on Peter's shoulder. "I'm really sorry." Before the last word left his mouth, he stabbed Peter in the stomach, twisting the blade and pulling it upward.

Peter tried to yell out. His hands grabbed the knife, trying to remove the blade. "Why?" the word came out as a gasp.

"You're fucking with Chrissy's heart, that's why. Telling her you love her, then hanging with this other guy. You think I'm stupid. I know what you're doing." Corbin pulled the knife out, closed the switchblade, and placed it back in the pocket of his jeans.

He held onto Peter's shirt collar as he fell to his knees. Corbin peered over the roof of the SUV as Peter fell on his side, he gasped, trying to say something. "Save your explanation for the Devil." Rearing his leg back, Corbin kicked Peter in the stomach.

Peter grunted, trying to speak. Garbled words and blood spewed out of his mouth.

"Fuck you." Corbin kicked him again in the stomach, then shifted his stance and kicked his head. As the anger and hatred bubbled over, he stomped on Peter's pretty face. Bone and cartilage splintered under the weight of his heavy biker boots. After several blows to the face, he used the grassy area to wipe the blood and brain matter off his boot.

Corbin strolled to his truck. Reaching into the flatbed, he grabbed a rag. After wiping his boot clean, he dropped the rag on the ground, then entered his truck. Looking in the rearview mirror, he fixed his hair. Adjusting his shirt, he smoothed down the front, tugging on his sleeves. He surveyed the area with a pleased expression as he drove out of the lot.

CHAPTER TWO

Tuesday 7:30 a.m.

Detective Jim Fogle sat on the toilet in the men's restroom. Choosing the stall with an out-of-order sign, he sat in silence, away from the prying eyes of Division Central. Renovations were being done all over the building, including this bathroom. But some stalls were still in use. He'd turned his phone on silent and texted his soon-to-be ex-girlfriend.

Stop texting me.

Why?

I don't want to talk to you. You've been pestering me since early this morning. I'm now at work.

I don't give a shit. This relationship is over for me.

Fine. I'll pack your shit and leave it on the porch.

Jim sniggered. He planned to have her stuff packed and locks changed by the time she got back in town.

You better not touch my shit.

Bitch, it's my house.

Jim heard the restroom door open, and a muffled conversation grew louder.

"Are you sure no one knows about the stolen drugs?"

"Yes. I'm sure."

"What about the evidence officers?"

"Wait," one man said. "Hold that thought."

Jim heard each stall door slam open. His jaw clenched as he braced himself with his hands flat against the sides of the stall and his feet against the door. His heartbeat thrashed in his ears.

As the steps came closer, Jim breathed as quietly as he could. He squeezed his eyes together. He'd left his weapon in ECD and knew he couldn't take on two men. *Shit.* His pulse echoed in his head. *The one time I need my damn gun.* He pushed harder against the door. He could hear heavy boots coming closer. The thud of each door slamming open made him jump.

"There's no one in here."

"Yeah. Okay." The boots turned and walked back towards the front of the restroom. "Cutter was on duty. Don't worry about him. I got him covered."

"I don't even want to know."

"Yeah. That's for sure. Look, I checked the drugs in after the Metacruze case. I sealed a box with weights in it. Enough to mimic fifteen kilos."

"What the fuck! Man, I don't like this. What if someone else opens the box?"

"Calm down. Only someone with clearance can get to it. And there are very few. Plus, I put them in the locked storage."

Jim heard the click of a lighter closing. The faint smell of cigarette smoke wafted in the air.

"Don't light up in here. Shit, you'll set off the fire alarms."

"Fuck you. Why are you so jumpy?"

"I don't want to get caught. I think they are suspicious as it is."

Jim strained to recognize the voices. One sounded vaguely familiar.

"Suspicious about what?"

"The FBI has been asking for all of Damien's files. Looks like he's under investigation."

"I heard. He's a fucking asshole. Him and his bitch of a girlfriend."

The other guy chuckled. "You're pissed she chose him over you."

"Fuck you."

Jim heard the familiar voice laugh.

"Seriously, they're pulling all his files. Along with a few other detectives in his unit. I'm worried they might use it to look into other units."

"No one knows you did anything wrong. You weren't even involved in the drug case. As long as you keep your mouth shut, you will be okay." The man took his cigarette, pushed it into a small puddle of water in one sink, and threw it in the trash. "Listen. I'm the one who will have to get the drugs for the Metacruze trial. By then, I'll be long gone with my share of the money. All you have to do is keep working like normal."

"I know. I mean, I wasn't involved, but my unit was. You and I covered our tracks pretty well. I want this to go away. I only helped you cover it up because you helped my brother."

"You need to remember that."

"Don't threaten me."

Jim heard boots laugh.

"I'm not threatening you. Quit worrying. And if Damien and his faggot ass partner stick their nose in my business, they'll have more to worry about than an investigation."

Jim heard the restroom door open.

"Don't go causing any more shit with him or Dillon. You'll bring unwanted attention to us. To me."

Jim heard the voices fade as the door shut. His legs trembled when he placed his feet on the floor. Gripping his phone in both shaking hands, he blew out several breaths before standing. Bracing himself until his legs held his weight, he listened to the silence. The restroom door opened as he walked out with his phone in his hand. Jim quickened his pace, nodding to the man who entered. "Hey, Jeff. How's the day going?"

Jeff Anvil smiled at him. "Great." He waved a newspaper in the air. "Taking a break from the office. This is still the best restroom to hide in," he said, smiling as he entered and locked a stall.

"You got that right." Jim exited the bathroom, glancing up and down the hallway. He breathed a sigh of relief as he entered the elevator heading to the Electronics and Cyber Division. His heart rate slowed as the elevator doors shut. Jim didn't want any trouble. He didn't want to be in the middle of anything. For now, he would keep his mouth shut.

CHAPTER THREE

Tuesday, 7 a.m.

Damien leaned against the kitchen doorway. Dillon stood at the counter. Her Iowa State t-shirt hugged her curves. Her long hair pulled up in a messy bun. Strands hung loosely around her face. He admired her shape as she finished cooking breakfast. His heart rate sped up at the thought of taking her on the counter.

And then he saw her sweatpants. Old dingy gray littered with raggedy holes of various sizes. He stepped around her as she talked on the phone. Coach and Gunner sat at her feet, waiting for a piece of bacon. "Get. Scram. You guys are worthless."

Coach huffed at him, and Gunner growled softly.

Dillon shooed him away as she handed a piece of bacon to Gunner and a smaller piece to the cat.

Damien sat quietly, listening to the one-sided conversation with her lawyer. He contemplated if this was the right time to talk about something. Things changed once she came back from her grandparent's farm and the reading of the will.

They went from having very little sex after her grandparents' murder, to Dillon being hypersexual. He chuckled inward. Not really something to complain about, but he knew it wasn't Dillon. She used sex to keep from dealing with the loss of her only family and the emotional issues that brought her.

He knew her well enough to know when she finally dealt with those feelings, it would not be easy, making him the prime target for her anger. She still harbored resentment, even though she said she didn't. Blaming him was easier than blaming her mother, who set the chain of events in motion when she had an affair so long ago.

"Andrew, I really appreciate this. I know Taylor will too. Call me later with a day and time, and I will have her on the phone with me." She nodded as she handed Damien a plate of food. "Okay. Give my love to everyone." She placed her phone on the counter, grabbing her plate.

"You have to stop feeding them. They are going to weigh hundreds of pounds and not be able to walk to the bathroom." Damien gulped his orange juice down, refilling his glass.

Coach jumped up and sat in an empty chair.

"See," he said, pointing at him. "It's bad enough he thinks he's a person. I'm sure Gunner would sit in the other chair if his butt wasn't already too big."

Dillon scoffed at him. "You are so mean." She gave each of them a piece of toast. "Mama loves you. Yes, she does."

Damien laughed, shaking his head. "You're looking like a hot mess. Do you have to go in today?"

She sighed. "No. I have one more meeting with the psychologist. That's later this week. I think on Thursday, or maybe it's next week. Until then, they want me to keep a low profile. You know the whole thing about your favorite person, DEA Johnson."

"He's an asshole. I hate him. Can't they send him somewhere?"

"If only. They want to get him on the drug charges and for being dirty. If they send him to another unit, they will lose the chance to stick his ass in jail. Can you imagine his fat ass in jail?" Dillon shared part of her eggs with the cat. Then gave a bite to Gunner.

"They're going to be so fat. Gunner is a lab, but he is looking like a brown hippo." He took a sip of orange juice. "What are you going to do today?"

Dillon smiled at him. "I don't know. Do you have a case you need help with?"

"We always have cases. Clear it with Director Sherman, and then come down to Division Central. I know we have about three cases we aren't getting anywhere on. Maybe you can help." Damien put his plate in the sink. He turned to give her a kiss when his phone rang. "Damien."

"Yo, come get me." Joe's voice boomed over the phone.

"Why can't you drive? What am I, your chauffeur?"

"Yes. Yes, you are. And my truck is in the shop."

"What's wrong with it?"

"Nothing, getting new shocks and jacking it up one inch."

"Pretty soon, you're going to need a damn ladder to get into it."

"Just get your ass over here."

Damien held the phone away from his ear when Joe burped. "Seriously, you're an Irish pig. I'll be there in twenty." He put his phone in his pocket. "Well, where was I?" Grabbing her, he pulled her next to his body, covering her lips with his, softly kissing her. He leaned back. Her eyes were laced with desire. "Don't look at me like that."

"Like what?" she kissed him. Heat fueled the kiss.

He melted into her. His hands roamed up her waist, under her t-shirt, following the curve of her breast. He stopped abruptly. "Oh, no, you don't. You did this to me yesterday. Made me miss my Monday morning lieutenant's meeting. I can't let you make me late again."

She laughed. "I can't help it. Mornings are my favorite time."

"Then we need to work on getting up earlier." He grabbed his jacket and wallet. "When will you come by the unit?" he asked, standing next to the door leading to the garage.

She considered her current state of dress. "A few hours. I need to shower."

"Yes. Yes, you do. And please don't wear those to DC." He pointed to her pants. "Can we burn those?"

"No. I don't ask you to get rid of your holey t-shirt you wear every weekend."

"That's different. It's a Notre Dame shirt. You can't throw it away. He's sacred." He laughed at her scowl.

She raised up on her toes to give him a kiss when his phone beeped. "Uh oh."

He glanced at the screen and sighed. "Looks like we may have a fresh case for you to help with. There's a dead body near Greektown."

"Nice area."

"Not nice enough to not have a murder at 7 a.m."

"Can't you get someone else in the unit to cover it?" she asked, wrapping her arms around his waist.

"No. Joe and I are up on rotation. Plus, Davidson started his vacation yesterday, making us a man down. Shower. Don't look too pretty when you come to DC. You know how much you distract Detective Hall." He opened the garage door, heading to his SUV. Her renovated sports car shimmered under the lights. "I can't believe you bought this car." Damien stared at the newly rebuilt and remodeled Porsche 911 Carrera coupe.

Dillon's eyes lit up as she walked around the vehicle.

"You just had your Vette restored. I mean, you get a little money in your pocket, and you go hog wild." Damien stepped back out of her arm's reach.

Her lip curled as she glared at him. "You're turning green."

He laughed, hugging her. "I'm teasing. I know that car is connected to memories of David and what he did to you and your grandparents. But you need to get something for the winter months. You're going to tear the hell out of this if you don't."

"I know. It's early March. By the fall, I will have something for the winter." She took the edge of her t-shirt and wiped a speck of dust off the hood. She squatted, inspecting the rest for smudge marks.

"You're worse than Joe. And I never thought those words would come out of my mouth." Damien opened the door to his SUV. "I guess you're in luck. The next few days, it is supposed to be warmer than normal, with no rain in sight."

She walked to him, closing the driver's door. She bristled as the cool air swirled in when the garage door opened. "Warmer than what, twenty-five degrees? That's what you call a heatwave?"

Damien laughed. "Better than fourteen degrees. It is Chicago, after all." He leaned out and kissed her. "Please drive carefully. And no speeding."

She stepped back with her hand over her mouth and her eyes wide. "What? I never speed. That would break the laws of this land. I don't do that." She waved as he backed out.

"You need to go to confession for lying."

"I'm not Catholic. I love you."

She waved at him as he waited for the garage door to close before he drove off.

CHAPTER FOUR

Tuesday morning 8 a.m.

Damien pulled into a commuter parking lot off Van Buren. A CSU van and two squad cars blocked off a perimeter around a small SUV. Parking his vehicle, he turned towards Joe. "This is a popular place to live. Expensive."

"I wouldn't want to live near here. Too many uppity types." Joe opened his door.

"Uppity?" Damien squinted at him.

"Yeah, you know, the artsy-fartsy kind." Joe closed the car door and walked around the front of the vehicle standing near a squad car and pointed towards the lamp posts. "There are only two lights. Helps when murdering someone."

Damien pointed to the small SUV. "I bet our dead guy is over there. Our killer had the perfect cover with the wall and low lighting."

They walked around the CSU van. A marker sat on the ground next to a discarded rag. Both detectives ducked under the crime scene tape.

Damien blew out a breath. "Wow." He stared at the side of what he assumed was the victim's SUV. Brain matter and blood had spattered onto the driver's side door and front panel. The victim lay in the grass with his face and head nearly obliterated. Markers blocked off an area directly in front of the body, moving outward to a perimeter of four or more feet. A set of keys lay near the body.

Joe kneeled next to Roger Newberry, head Crime Scene Tech, careful to stay out of the pooling blood. *"Bloody cac."*

"What the hell? Bloody—what?" Roger asked.

"What blood?" Joe zeroed in on Damien.

"Roger doesn't understand you." Damien laughed.

"Oh, means shit," Joe said.

"Can't you just say shit?" Roger asked.

"No." Joe pointed to the victim. "Not much of his head left. The killer did a number on this guy's face."

Roger smiled at the two detectives. "Got a guess what the weapon was? Either of you."

Damien tilted his head to the side, then studied the droplets of blood on the SUV. "Whatever he used, he didn't swing it upwards. No cast off or arcing pattern."

"No cast off or arcing pattern," Joe mimicked his partner. "What are you, a blood spatter specialist now?"

"No. I'm just not an idiot. Like some of us standing here." Damien winked at him.

Roger laughed. "What are you guys like, twelve?" he stood, stepping around the body. "Damien's right. He didn't swing the weapon upward." Roger lifted his foot back as if to kick the victim. "I think he used his foot."

Damien's brow drew together. "Where is the doc?"

"He's running behind. Car wreck." Roger snickered. "Not his."

"Gotcha." Damien squatted next to the victim's head. "I'll be interested to see if Forsythe thinks the same thing. But I think you might be onto something." He pointed to the head. "If the killer kicked him to death, he had to be wearing some heavy-duty shoes to cause this amount of damage."

"Maybe boots?" Joe said.

"Yeah. Biker or work boots," Damien said.

All of them stood at the sound of an approaching vehicle.

The medical examiner's van pulled around one of the patrol cars and parked near the victim's car. Dr. Forsythe exited the vehicle dressed in sweats.

"Are you wearing approved attire for the ME's office?" Joe asked, chuckling.

"It is when I wasn't supposed to be the ME on duty today." Dr. Forsythe donned one of the plastic jumpsuits and a pair of booties over his tennis shoes.

"Who should be here?" Joe asked.

"The new ME." Dr. Forsythe snapped his fingers. "Parker. Beth Parker."

Joe glanced over at Roger. "Who is this Beth chick?"

Roger shrugged. "Some hotshot out of Oklahoma or Texas." He lifted his chin in Dr. Forsythe's direction. "Right?"

"No. She's from Seattle. Do you pay attention to anything I say?" Dr. Forsythe carried his ME bag towards the victim, carefully stepping around the marker. "That's a lot of blood."

"Wait, you can't just leave us hanging. Who is this Beth character?" Damien crossed his arms. "Are you leaving?"

Dr. Forsythe didn't look up from the body. "No. But I need another ME. Since the state's part-time ME can't cover this area anymore. I swung enough in the budget to hire someone." He opened a fresh swab and rubbed it across a black mark on the victim's cheek. The only part of his face still intact. He placed the swab back in the original paper container and handed it to Roger.

"Is she good?" Joe asked.

"Why are you so concerned with who I hired?" Dr. Forsythe took a small glass jar and scraped some of the brain matter and flesh from the side of the victim's head.

Damien frowned. "We don't want to work with anyone else. We like you."

Roger snickered as he took samples from the side of the vehicle.

Damien cocked his eyebrow at him. "Do you have something to say?"

Roger laughed. "You just don't want someone making you wait for answers."

"I can't believe you're implying I use my relationship with Dr. Forsythe to get—things." Damien moved to the right, glancing over the hood of the small SUV. A crowd had gathered outside the entrance to the lot. "We're going to have several people pissed soon." He motioned towards the road.

"Ooh. Morning commuters need this lot," Joe said. "Crap."

Dr. Forsythe stood. He surveyed the area. Turning towards Roger, he motioned towards the parking area. "Have you looked through the lot?"

"Yeah. When I first got here. I took photos and bagged anything I thought might be remotely needed. The only thing I didn't touch was the rag on the other side of this vehicle. I placed a marker next to it and took photos. I was waiting to move it until you guys showed up." He nodded towards Damien and Joe.

"Was there any evidence of another vehicle having parked near here?" Damien asked. "I mean, I'm guessing our killer left in another vehicle."

Roger shook his head. "Aside from the rag, I found nothing leading to another vehicle. Maybe the rag will give us something."

Dr. Forsythe pointed at Joe. "I don't have a problem opening some of the parking spots. Take some cones and block off a few rows for a bigger perimeter. We may have a riot on our hands if we don't let people park in here."

"I'm on it." Joe headed towards an officer.

"Tell me what you think, Doc?" Damien asked.

The ME shrugged. "Not a lot here to go on. When I get him on the examining table, I'm sure I will find out more." He glanced at Roger. "Do we know who he is?"

Roger reached into his kit. He handed Damien a plastic bag with the guy's wallet and a pair of latex gloves. "Peter Martin."

Damien put on the gloves and inspected the victim's wallet. A picture of a young girl and some coffee coupons were stuffed in one area. Another picture was hidden between two credit cards. Damien unfolded the picture to find the victim standing bedside an older gentleman. He took his phone from his pocket and snapped a photo of Peter's license, the photo of his girlfriend, and the photo of him and this other man. "Thanks," he said, handing the bag back to Roger.

Joe walked back over. "I told the officer to take a picture of each license plate as the car pulled in. We can at least cross-check if we need to."

"Good thinking. Doc, let me know when you have something. Please."

"I will," Doc said.

"The new ME won't be doing the autopsy, will she?" Damien placed the gloves he had removed in an evidence bag and handed it to Roger.

"I will assist her. She should be here in the next few hours, and she is quite capable of working this case, or any case." Dr. Forsythe sighed. "I promise, she is one of the best pathologists in the country. I was lucky to snag her. Just trust me for crying out loud."

Damien chuckled. "Okay. If you say so."

They were heading to Damien's SUV when loud yelling came from the entrance of the parking area.

CHAPTER FIVE

Frank exited his house. He needed to get his morning walk in before he headed to the clinic for his chemo treatment. The walk helped clear his head and prepared him for the horrible next few days. This chemo treatment was his last. Not meant to save him, he just needed a little more time. Time with Peter.

Stepping off his stoop, he headed towards the main street. His block had a few more cars than usual. Glancing up and down, he wasn't sure where all the traffic had come from. He frowned as he neared the end of the block.

A massive traffic jam locked cars in place in all directions. Most waited to enter the small commuter parking area near the end of his street. Frank made his way over to where a few of his neighbors stood.

"Jeff," Frank called out.

Jeff Barker turned around at the sound of his name. "Hey, Frank. How you feeling?"

Frank smiled. "Better. What's going on?" he asked.

"Not really sure. My daughter usually parks here when she comes over to our house. But today, we had to move one car to the backyard so she could park in our driveway. She said it was blocked off, and the police were everywhere. I came out to see what was going on." Jeff took a step towards the front of the line.

Frank followed, pushing his way to the entrance to see what all the commotion was about. "Well, I guess it can't be good." He pointed to the crime scene van.

Jeff Barker, a former NYC police officer, motioned to the police officer blocking the entryway. He snapped pictures of cars as they entered. A few other officers directed them where to park.

Frank listened in on the conversation. He strained to see around the vehicles. His heart rate sped up as he pushed his way a little closer to his friend and the police officer. Frank's eyes widened when a truck pulled out of the way and parked. Peter's small SUV sat at the back of the lot. "Peter!" he screamed as he bolted past the officer and ran towards his friend.

CHAPTER SIX

Damien watched the man running towards them. He heard him calling their victim's name. When two officers caught the guy and handcuffed him, Damien jogged towards them. "Wait." He motioned for the officers to stop.

They held the man by his arms.

"Let him go. It's okay. Let him go."

Joe stepped up next to his partner. "Who are you?" he asked the man.

"Frank. Frank Spencer. What's happened to Peter?" Frank couldn't catch his breath. His wheezing made him cough.

Damien reached out and grabbed him. He recognized the man from the photo in Peter's wallet. "Come sit on the back of my SUV," he said, leading him to his vehicle and opening the back end. "Sit. Catch your breath."

Joe opened the rear passenger door and grabbed an unopened bottle of water, handing it to the man.

Damien waited a moment, allowing the man to take a drink. "Tell me who you are and how you know Peter?"

Frank's hand shook as he set the water bottle down. "Then it is Peter, isn't it? That's his SUV."

"Who is Peter to you?" Joe asked.

Frank blew air out through pursed lips. Nausea swept over him. He slowed his breathing to keep the water from spewing out. "He's like a son to me. I was his history teacher in high school. His mother died when he was young, and his father died shortly before the end of his senior year. We became close." His voice quivered. "Please tell me what has happened."

Damien sent a sideways glance to Joe, who shook his head as he raised a brow at him. Damien ignored him. "When did you last see Peter?" He removed a small notebook from the back pocket of his jeans.

"Last night. He came by the house." Frank hesitated. Not sure how much to tell.

"Mr. Spencer, what else?" Damien asked. He waited for the man to respond.

Joe shifted his stance, crossing his arms across his chest. "You need to tell us what you know."

Frank's shoulders sagged. "He's been helping me. Several times a week. He comes over and helps me." Tears crested over, running down his cheeks.

"Help you with what?" Joe asked.

"I'm dying. I have stage four colon cancer. Along with a lot of other problems." He halfway laughed. "I'm on borrowed time. Peter took me to my chemo these last few months. I've been having some serious complications, and the chemo is no longer working. Nothing is working."

Damien sat next to the man. "I'm sorry. Can you tell me when Peter left your house?"

"Around 8:30 p.m. Maybe a few minutes before. He usually parks here. I just live a block down the street." Frank motioned towards his house.

"Did you see anyone talking to Peter when he left? Maybe you saw him get into someone's car?" Damien asked.

Frank shook his head. "No." He wiped his cheeks with the backs of his hands. Wiping the moisture on his pants. "Someone has to tell Christine."

Damien raised an eyebrow at him. "Who is Christine?" he pulled out his phone, opening the picture he had taken a few moments ago. "Is this her?" he showed the picture to Frank.

He nodded. "Yes. They are getting... were.... They were supposed to get married in a few months."

"Do you know her last name?" Damien asked, scribbling in his notebook.

Joe watched the man as he spoke. His skin tingled as he watched the man's color become increasingly paler.

Frank tried to breathe. The air whistled out with each exhale. Frank swallowed. "Christine..."

"He's going down!" Joe grabbed him before he slipped off the back of the SUV. "Damien, call an ambulance."

Damien called dispatch. "Doc!" he yelled for Dr. Forsythe. "Doc, get over here!"

Dr. Forsythe poked his head out from around the ME van. "Damien, what is it?"

"We need your help."

Dr. Forsythe ran over. "Oh my. Lay him on the ground." He dashed back to his van and grabbed his bag. "Who is this guy?" he placed a stethoscope on his chest, listening. "His breathing is labored. His lungs sound congested."

"He knows our victim. He also has stage four colon cancer." Damien watched as Doc tried to ease the man's breathing issues.

"He's crashing." Dr. Forsythe began CPR. He motioned for Joe to begin chest compressions. The sirens of the ambulance grew increasingly louder.

Joe immediately started the compressions, timing them with Dr. Forsythe's breathing. As the ambulance pulled up, Frank began to breathe on his own. They loaded him up in the ambulance and watched as their only lead in this case left, taking any information with him.

CHAPTER SEVEN

Damien pulled out of the parking lot. Both sat in silence. As Damien turned in the direction towards Division Central, Joe glanced up. "Are you okay, Joe?" Damien asked.

"Yeah. Aren't we going to the hospital?" he asked.

Damien sighed. "I don't think he has much else to tell us. We have Peter's information, and we know his fiancé's name. We should be able to track her down."

"I guess you're right." Joe sat still for a few minutes.

Damien turned onto the main thoroughfare. "You sure you're okay?"

"You think Frank has anyone else?"

Damien glanced at his partner. "I don't know."

Joe nodded and remained quiet the rest of the way to Division Central.

***

As Damien pulled into the parking garage, his phone pinged.

"What?" Joe asked.

"Dillon is on her way in. She wants to help us with this case."

Joe chuckled as they exited the SUV. "She's bored as shit, isn't she?"

"Yes. And a pain in my ass. I like it when she is preoccupied. With work."

They both nodded at Officer Jennifer Ward in the small shack just outside the doorway.

Joe scanned his ID, unlocking the door. He smiled as he held it open. "Ugly old man before me."

"Bug off." Damien smiled as they entered DC. The parking garage was in the basement of Division Central. The evidence locker and holding took up most of the floor, with a few outlying offices. As they rounded the corner, Robbery Detective Freddie Ardroin stepped out of an interview room.

"Hey, Joe, Damien. How's it going?" Detective Ardroin asked.

"Good. You?" Damien held the door leading to the main hallway.

"Not bad." He followed the two detectives towards the elevator.

"You interrogating someone?" Joe asked as they stepped into the lift.

Detective Ardroin shifted his feet. "Yeah. I'm letting him stew for a bit."

Joe didn't like the detective. Ardroin seemed shifty to him, but he couldn't convince anyone else to feel the same way. "How's your brother?"

"Um, yeah, he's doing okay. Why?" the detective asked.

Joe shrugged. "Just wondering. I know he was having a hard time there for a little while. Seeing if things have gotten better."

"Yeah. Thanks for asking." The doors opened onto the second floor. Detective Ardroin stepped off.

"Um, aren't you going to Robbery?" Damien asked him.

Detective Ardroin glanced up and realized he had stepped off on the wrong floor. He motioned behind him, towards some offices. "I need to take care of something in Human Resources."

"Gotcha. See you around." Joe said as the elevator doors shut. He raised an eyebrow at Damien. "He's up to something."

"You say that every time you talk to him." Damien laughed as they exited onto their floor.

They walked down the main corridor to the Vicious Crimes Unit. Several other divisions were on this floor, including Vice, Robbery, and Electronics and Cyber Division. VCU and ECD were the first set of offices in the main hallway. As he walked past ECD, he waved to Travis.

"You guys think I'm crazy. But I swear he's up to something. Fishy Mods dot com...man. I'm telling you. Something is up with him," Joe said, following behind.

"Maybe he's just private. Doesn't like sharing his family business."

"I don't know. He's hiding something," Joe said.

As they entered the VCU, Damien's crew huddled around Detective Hall's desk. "What are you hoodlums up to?"

Everyone turned towards them.

Hall smiled at his boss. "Just showing off a picture."

"Yeah, of who?" Joe asked as he sat at his desk.

"My new baby," Hall said with a beaming smile.

"When did you have a baby?" Joe asked.

"I didn't have a baby, you idiot." Hall walked over to Joe's desk. He swiped through a few photos. "This is my new baby."

Joe squinted at the screen. "It's a fucking cat."

Detective Jamal Harris laughed. "That's exactly what I said. It's a fucking cat. The way he went on and on about this all morning, I really thought he had a damn baby." Jamal sat at his desk. His wide shoulders extended well past the sides of his chair.

Damien motioned towards Detective Mike Cooper. "Where you and Jamal at on your case?" he glanced at the case board hanging off the back wall of the unit. It showed five open cases. Detectives Hall and Alvarez were assigned to two. Detectives Harris and Cooper had two, and Detective Timothy Jenkins had one. Detective Davidson had two open cases that had yet to be reassigned.

Detective Jenkins interrupted. "Hey, Davidson found a lead on one of our suspects before he left for his vacation. I was going to take one of our assigned police officers with us. Do you care who?"

Damien rubbed the back of his neck. "No. Take whoever. Baker could use the time. The detective's exam is in a few weeks."

"Sweet," Detective Jenkins said, grabbing his coat. "I think she's down the hall. I'm going to get her."

Damien sighed. "Also, between you guys, do some follow up on Davidson's open cases. Coop, have you and Jamal made any progress?"

Detective Mike Cooper leaned back in his chair. "I'm doing all the work. That's foremost."

"Shut the hell up," Detective Harris said, throwing a pencil at him.

"I want to file a charge against this man." Mike ducked when Jamal threw one of his squishy stress balls at him. "Maybe you should use this instead of throwing it at me."

"You're an ass." Jamal turned towards Damien, laughing. "We got so little. No one in the homeless encampment where he was found will speak with us."

"What do you expect?" Cooper asked. "Shit, man, you're as big as a house and scary as shit looking. I told you not to go in all serious and shit." Cooper nodded at his boss. "We just need a little time."

"What about the other case?" Damien asked.

"Now that one is a little different." Jamal handed his lieutenant a folder. "This kid's family is pointing fingers at everyone."

Mike Cooper set his soda on his desk. "Our victim is twenty-eight, hardly a kid. But the way the family talks about him, you would think he was a high schooler."

"Yeah, it's weird. We think one of his coworkers may have killed him. From what we've gathered, our victim was about to blow the whistle on a few people at his firm. They were stealing from the company. ADA Flowers is pulling a bunch of warrants for the company. As soon as we can tie up a few loose ends, we think we can get one guy to roll on the other."

"Keep me posted. Dillon can always help if you need it... I think. She isn't cleared to go back to work yet." Damien stood. He turned when movement in the corridor caught his eye. His jaw tightened as DEA Johnson strolled by with a couple of Vice members.

"Who is with Lieutenant Diego?" Joe asked.

"Some new Lieutenant. Transferred in from Rockaway. I think he made lieutenant, and they didn't have any place for him, so they transferred him here." Damien watched the men as they continued down the hallway.

Joe leaned into Damien. "Didn't the captain say they weren't sure if someone from Vice was involved with Johnson?"

"They aren't sure who or what department. But I can't imagine Diego is involved with this. I don't see him as a crooked cop. All I can say is I hope Johnson is gone before Dillon shows up." Damien stood with his arms crossed as Johnson saluted him.

Joe leaned in, covering his mouth with his hand. "Do you think he has any clue about the investigation?"

Damien shook his head, glancing at Alverez when she whistled. He shook his head, laughing at the hand gesture she gave to DEA Johnson.

"Do you even think he knows what that means?" Detective Hall asked his partner.

She scoffed. "I don't care. He's an asshole. And it makes me feel good doing it." Detective Alverez made the same gesture to Hall.

"Girl, I will whip your ass." Detective Hall laughed.

Alvarez nodded at Damien. "We could actually get some work done on our case if this new dad could get his face out of his phone."

"You're just jealous." Hall pointed to the case board. "Our case should be cleared in a day or so. We can help Jenkins, since Davidson is gone."

"I like it. Keep me posted." Damien walked into his office. A smaller version of the same board hung on his wall. He made a few notes with a marker on the side of the board, glancing up as Joe walked in.

"Hey, I called the hospital to find out about Frank. He's in the ICU. They wouldn't tell me much of anything else." Joe sat.

Damien sat in his chair. "Why are you so concerned about this guy?"

Joe shrugged. "I don't know. I feel for this guy. No one should die alone." He leaned back, rubbing his hands on his jeans. "I just got a bad feeling about this case."

Damien leaned back in his chair, rocking slightly. "We will leave early and go to the hospital. Okay?"

Joe nodded. "Thanks." He took a handful of jelly beans from the jar. "What do you need from me?"

Damien pulled his phone from his pocket. "We have our victim's name. We know he was engaged to this girl. Now we need her last name. Chrissy." He sent pictures from his phone to his printer.

Joe waited as they printed out, then reached over and grabbed them. He stared at the photo of the girlfriend. "This isn't going to be fun."

"What won't be fun?"

"Telling her what happened to Peter."

"It is the worst part of the job." Damien took the photos from Joe and placed them on a whiteboard hanging on his wall.

"After I get the information, we can grab some lunch on the way to tell the bad news."

Damien checked his watch. "You just ate."

Joe shrugged him off. "So. That was hours ago."

"Okay, Fatty McFatButt." Damien printed a few crime-scene photos CST had loaded into the system.

"Wow," Joe said as he took one from the printer. "Man. Whoever did this was really mad at Peter."

"You know, the photo of Frank in Peter's wallet?"

"Yeah, what about it?"

"It was hidden between two credit cards. Like he was hiding it from someone." Damien stacked the photos in a file and labeled it with Peter's name and the date.

"You think he was hiding the relationship?" Joe asked.

"I don't know. It struck me as odd. That's all."

Joe frowned. "Why would he need to hide it? I didn't get the impression they were anything but pseudo father and son. Nothing, you know, different."

Damien laughed. "You mean like they were having a sexual

relationship?"

"Yes. Asshole." Joe grabbed more jelly beans. He picked several of the same colors and then put them in his mouth at once. "I mean, it could be a reason to hide it. But I don't see it. I sensed a more paternal love from Frank."

"Maybe the girlfriend can tell us." Damien's phone rang. He smiled as he answered. "Hey, babe."

"Hey. I'm on my way. My director gave me permission to help as long as I don't do anything in an official capacity."

"What, you mean, like you don't shoot anyone?" Damien asked.

"Haha. Yeah. Probably. I think he means I can't take point on this."

"Well, now. Then, you will have to check your bossy pants at the door." Damien laughed at Joe's reaction to his one-sided conversation.

"Funny," Dillon said before hanging up.

He laughed at the dead air on his phone. "I think I poked the bear."

"Why?" Joe asked, standing.

"It's so much fun." He waved his partner out of his office. "Go. Do some work. You lazy *vacca grasso*."

Joe flipped him off as he walked out.

Damien studied the photos from the crime scene. Like Joe, Damien also had a bad feeling about this case.

CHAPTER EIGHT

Dillon parked in a visitor parking spot. She stood at the side of her car, hesitating. She hadn't been back to DC for a while. *Why am I so fucking nervous?* she thought as she shook off the feeling of dread and walked to the guard at the door.

"Dillon?" Officer Jennifer Ward said as she stepped out of the guard shack.

"Hey," Dillon paused for a minute. "Jennifer, right?"

"Yeah," she said. "I'm surprised you remembered."

"I remember. You sent me a card. I really appreciated it." Dillon smiled as she signed the log. "I should have sent a thank you. I'm sorry I didn't."

"No worries. You were going through a lot. I'm glad you're back at work. It's great to see you." Officer Ward buzzed her in.

"Thanks. It's definitely nice to be out of the house." Dillon headed towards the elevators. A few officers waved or nodded in her direction. Some didn't even make eye contact. She squeezed her hands into fists, opening and closing rapidly. "Don't say anything. And don't punch anyone." She muttered under her breath.

Standing at the elevator, heat spread across her shoulders. Entering, she turned around. Lieutenant Thomlinson, from robbery, stood, staring at her from behind a glass wall. She kept eye contact with him until the door shut.

She let her shoulders relax and made a mental note to find out all she could about him. She heard the director's voice in her head. *Stay out of the undercover investigation.*

The elevator door opened to a small group of high school students on a field trip. Turning the corner into the main hallway, DEA Johnson was fifty-feet in front of her. She tamped down the anger. Cracking her neck, she stood outside the VCU door as Johnson and Detective Ardroin walked towards her.

"Well, look who it is. I thought you weren't allowed to work until you were cleared?" DEA Johnson asked.

Dillon didn't say a word and maintained eye contact. Her hands tightened into fists.

"What, you can't speak to me?" DEA Johnson stopped, waiting for her reply.

"I'm sorry. I rarely pay attention to assholes." Dillon cursed inwardly. She tried. She really did.

Damien came out into the office when Joe whistled for him. "What the heck..." his voice trailed off as Joe pointed to the hallway and the other side of the glass. He watched as Dillon and DEA Johnson walked towards each other. Grimacing, he hoped this encounter would stay calm.

Dillon smirked. "I'm surprised they let you in here."

Johnson stepped a little closer to her, staying just out of arm's length. "I see you are all healed up." He sized her up. "You look like you're doing okay."

"I'm doing fine, Agent Johnson. How nice of you to be concerned," Dillon said.

DEA Johnson laughed. "How's your family? Oh, wait, you don't have any left, do you?" He made a pouty face. "So sorry."

She took a step closer, closing the gap and pushing the anger down. "I've been meaning to ask how you keep your girlfriend satisfied... oh wait, you don't have a girlfriend. She left you for Agent Paschal, right? Silly me, I should ask how hard it is to have a tiny dick." She licked her lips as she leaned closer. "Damien has enough to spare." She stepped back, smiling.

Johnson's nostrils flared. He drew his fist back, ready to strike.

Detective Ardroin stepped in between. "Stop. Just move on, Agent Johnson. You don't want this."

Dillon saw Damien out of the corner of her eye, giving him a quick side glance before turning back to Agent Johnson. "Yeah. You don't want any part of me." She turned the knob, opening the door to VCU.

Agent Johnson continued down the hallway. "One day, Dillon, you won't have anyone around to protect you." He winked at her.

Stepping inside, Dillon smiled at the detectives. She hadn't seen them in so long and didn't realize how much she had missed them.

"Yo, girl," Detective Alvarez said, walking towards her. "What did asshole Johnson say?" Detective Alvarez gave Dillon a warm hug.

"He tried to convince me he had a dick. I told him he was delusional." Dillon smiled at the former vice cop. "How you been?"

"Not bad." Detective Alvarez gave a half glance towards her partner. "I would do better if I could have a dependable partner."

"Screw you, Alverez. You know you love me." Hall winked at her, making smoochie sounds with his puckered lips.

"Isn't that sexual harassment?" Alverez asked Damien as he walked towards them.

"He isn't worth the paperwork. Just punch him when you leave here." Damien smiled at Dillon, kissing her on the cheek. "Your director gave you the all-clear for you to work with us?"

Dillon shrugged. "Sort of."

Damien stepped back, frowning at her. "What does that mean?"

"I can help. I can go out in the field with you. But I can't do anything in an official capacity. I'm not even cleared to carry my weapon." She patted her empty hip. "At least not while I'm helping."

Joe stood next to Damien. "Afraid you will shoot someone, huh?"

"Yes." Dillon laughed. She glanced around at the unit. "What cases are open?"

Damien pointed to the board. "We have a few. They all seem to be moving along pretty good. I think you can help us. Once ours is cleared, we can help close some others."

Dillon followed Damien into his office with Joe quick on their heels.

Once sitting, Joe looked at her. "What did Johnson really say?"

Dillon glanced between Damien and Joe. She thought about lying, but why? "He made a comment about all of my family being dead."

Damien cocked his head to the side. "I'm going to kill that fucker."

Joe snorted. "No, you're not. We are going to let his ass go to jail. Hopefully, his cell mate will be some fat fuck named Bubba."

Dillon giggled. "Oh great, now I have that vision in my head."

Damien didn't laugh. He didn't like this guy, and he didn't like the way he targeted Dillon every chance he got. "I hope this case against him moves quickly."

She nodded towards the photos on his desk. "Are those from this morning?"

He handed them to her. "Yeah."

Joe munched on some jellybeans. "Whoever killed this guy had to have a beef with him. There was no robbery or theft. But the damage to this guy's head and face was overkill."

Dillon scanned the photos. She stopped on one picture and then continued.

Damien watched her as she digested what she saw. He hoped working this case would help ease some of her tension. "Do you see anything?"

She shrugged, laying the photos on the desk. "I agree with Joe. I think the damage is overkill. Do you know anything about this guy?"

"Just started digging into his life." Damien nodded towards Joe. "Did you find anything?"

"Give me a sec. I'll go grab some notes from my desk."

Dillon watched him leave, then turned to Damien when she was sure he was out of earshot. "I want to ruin Johnson's life." Her fingers tapped on the arm of her chair.

"You and me both. I could help that along." He raised an eyebrow at her.

"I'm so tempted to let you use your dad's connections and equipment to do just that." She sighed, slumping in her chair. "But you and I both know it wouldn't be the right thing to do."

"I think sometimes doing the right thing sucks," Damien said.

Joe walked back in. "I found the girlfriend. Or at least I think so." He handed over a printed page from their victim's Facebook profile. "Peter mentions his fiancé and links to her profile on several posts. Her name is Chrissy Stanchion."

"Did you get her address?" Damien asked.

"Yup. She lives in Bridgeport." He handed Damien a piece of paper with her address.

"Nice. What else?"

"Her family owns Tiger Cycle Shop."

Damien watched Joe's eyes twinkle. "Don't even think about it."

"What?" Joe asked, chuckling.

Dillon's brow wrinkled. "Is that the shop that raffled off the specially built bike?"

Joe smiled. "Yeah. For the World Series in 2005." Joe whistled. "Man, it was one sweet bike, too. The show on TV, the cycle shop show, came out to film some of the build."

"I remember. Raised like millions for several charities," Dillon said.

"Pretty much put the bike shop on the map." Joe took a handful of jellybeans from the jar.

Damien glanced at his watch. "How about we go talk to the girlfriend and her family, and then we can get something to eat?"

"Sounds great. I need to go pee. Then we can go." Joe headed towards the restroom.

Damien and Dillon stood in his office. He wanted to reach out and hold her, but she didn't like public displays of affection, especially at DC. He put on his jacket when he heard yelling from the pen. "What the hell."

They both walked out to see Camilla yelling at Detective Alverez.

CHAPTER NINE

"I want to speak to Damien. Now!" Camilla said.

"Miss, please quit screaming." Detective Alverez maintained her composure.

"I can fucking do what I want. Do you even know who I am?" Camilla crossed her arms, huffing at the detective.

"Oh yeah. We all know who you are." Alverez took a small step towards Camilla.

Detectives Hall and Cooper flanked Alverez.

"And we don't like you," Alverez said with a big smile plastered on her face.

"Like I give a shit about some loser female detective. Please," Camilla said.

Detective Jamal Harris stood by his desk. He made eye contact with Damien as he walked towards them.

Damien gave his detective a slight nod. "Camilla." Damien stood a few feet from her.

Dillon's mouth curved slightly upward. "My, it's so nice to see you, Camilla. You're such a pleasure."

Camilla glared at her. "I don't care about you." She waved her hand around in the air. "Or these other losers. I need to speak with Damien." She squinted at Dillon. "You are of no importance to me." She focused on the man she still loved. "I told you someone is stalking me. I need you to help me."

"Camilla, we don't handle this kind of case."

"If your stalker kills you, we can take over." Alvarez smiled.

Damien shot his detective a quick glance. "You need to go down to the front desk and file a complaint. Give all the details to the sergeant on duty, and he will get someone to help you," Damien said.

"If I wanted some fucking unimportant loser to help me, I would have already done that. I want you to help me." Camilla took a half step towards Damien.

He stepped back. "I will not help you."

"You will try absolutely anything to get him back, won't you?" Dillon asked.

Camilla turned on her six-inch stilettos, narrowing her eyes as she stared at Dillon. "You don't matter. You are the in-between girl. You need to just go away." She focused her attention back on Damien. "Someone has been in the parking garage of my work, watching me. Plus, you owe me."

"What the hell are you talking about? I don't owe you shit." Damien said.

Joe walked around the corner and slowed to a stop. "Uh. Hey, Camilla."

She huffed, ignoring him. "If you don't help me. I will tell everyone all your secrets."

"Camilla, don't blackmail me. I know more about you than you think I do. So don't go there," Damien said.

"My sleeping around? Big deal. If a guy sleeps around, they're a stud. If a woman does it, she's a whore." She took a step closer to him. "Your secrets could ruin your career. Could even get you thrown in jail. Are you sure you want to push me?"

Damien glared at the spiteful woman. He caught the look from both Joe and Dillon. "Go ahead. Just remember, all your dirty secrets, all the men, and all the cases you handled will come into question. What about your boss? You think he wants his dirty laundry out there?"

Joe took a step towards Camilla. "Hey, listen. How about if I walk downstairs with you and help you file the complaint? We couldn't do anything anyway unless you put something on an official record."

Camilla's jaw tightened. Her head snapped to the side. She glared at Joe. "I don't want to file a complaint. I just want help." She looked at Damien. "I know someone is after me. I just want help. Your help."

Damien took a small step back. "Go with Joe and file the complaint. Give the sergeant the details. Joe will make sure someone in the Domestic Violence division gets the case."

Camilla's mouth hung open. "I—I don't need domestic violence to help me. It isn't someone I know."

"Stalking usually is someone you know." Dillon watched her reaction. "I know you don't want to hear this, but with your history, it more than likely is someone you know."

"My history? Really? So, you're saying I'm to blame for some crazy person stalking me?" Camilla's nostrils flared.

"No. Not what I said at all. But let's be honest, Camilla. We all know what you did to Damien. We know you slept with several people you work with. You can't think you can sleep with married men and not have repercussions for your actions."

"I can't believe you," Camilla said.

"I don't like you. Never hid that. But, as much of an asshole as I think you are, I don't think for one minute you should be stalked." Dillon pinched the bridge of her nose. "If you can make the report, explain on paper what is happening, then a detective can look into it. It could be someone from your office. It could be a wife or other family member of someone you have had an affair with."

Damien glanced at his crew. Locking eyes with Joe. "Camilla, just go with Joe."

Camilla studied his face. She missed him. Only now did it hit her how much she regretted her actions. "Fine." She turned towards Joe. "Let's go." She walked away, then turned around to face Damien. "Don't think I won't use the information I have."

She smiled at Dillon. "Don't get too comfortable, Dillon." She walked toward the hallway, turning when Joe was not behind her. "Hello, let's go. I have a life, you know." She snapped her fingers at him.

Joe looked at his boss. He glanced around, staying out of earshot, leaning into Damien. "I fucking hate her. I'm only doing this to get her out of here. And it will definitely cost you."

Damien chuckled. "I will gladly pay your price." He watched the two leave, then turned to his crew. "How did she get in here in the first place?"

"One of the new officers walked her up. I'm betting she sweet-talked him," Alvarez said.

"Makes sense. Let the desk sergeant know to not let that happen again."

Alvarez nodded at Damien.

"Okay. The excitement is over. Back to work," Damien said.

Hall shook his head. "I can't for the life of me ever understand why you dated her."

Alvarez snorted. "That's because you stare at photos of a damn cat all day."

The other detectives laughed as they returned to their desks.

Damien nodded for Dillon to follow him. Once in his office; he closed the door. "I can't stand her." He growled as he gripped the back of his chair.

"You and me both." Dillon sat across from him. "Do you think she will say anything about the incident at the hotel?"

Damien shrugged. "I don't know. And I don't care. I don't regret catching her with her other boyfriend. I regret going into the man's past and using it to keep him from filing a police report. In all honesty, I don't think he ever would. How would he explain being in a hotel room with one of the company's lawyers? I'm pretty sure he didn't want his wife to find out."

"And, of course, letting him know you would tell her and share where he was hiding money helped keep him quiet." She winked at him. "For what it's worth, I would have done the same thing."

"Still doesn't make it right. I don't like who she made me become. When I found out about the cheating, I wanted to kill her. I almost did. I was so close," he said. "In the end, she wasn't worth it. But I understand those feelings and why some can't stop themselves. Doesn't make it right, but I sure can empathize." He glanced at his watch. "As soon as Joe comes back, let's get out of here."

Dillon took a few jellybeans. She picked out the red ones and put the other back in the jar.

"That is so unsanitary." Damien frowned.

Her jaw slacked. "You can't be serious. You let anyone put their hand in this jar... especially Joe." She shook her head. "I don't even want to think where his hands have been."

He pointed to the folder holding the photos of the crime scene. "What do you think of this case?"

"Not much to go on. Do you have Joe's information from the social media accounts?"

"Yeah." Damien opened the folder from Joe. He placed a few of the papers in front of her.

She scanned the information. "Can you pull the Facebook profile up?"

"Sure." Damien turned his computer screen, allowing her to see it.

Using the mouse, she scrolled through the young man's profile first. "He shared a lot of his outings," Dillon said, chuckling. "Why do people think everyone wants to know what they ate for breakfast?"

"I don't understand it either." Damien opened the girlfriend's profile in another window. "Here's his fiancé."

Dillon scrolled through the feed. "She has a lot of wedding stuff." She looked at Damien.

"What?"

She opened her mouth to say something, closed it, then spoke. "I don't want a big wedding."

He tried to hide the smile. "I don't want to ever get married."

She squinted at him. "Really?"

He nodded yes. "No. I want very much to marry some really hot chick with a lot of money."

"Ah, the truth comes out." She looked over the Facebook profile. "Wait, who's this?"

Damien looked at the young man in the photo. He clicked on the link, which opened the bike shop business page. "Looks like a family member." He scrolled through. "Yeah, look. He mentions his sister and her upcoming marriage."

They both read the post.

"Wow. If my brother posted those comments about my soon-to-be husband, I might be a little pissed." Dillon clicked on the brother's personal profile. "Look." She pointed to a few heated conversations. "I don't think the brother approved of his sister's choice of husband."

"I'd say so. Maybe we need to speak with him." Damien scribbled his name on the folder. "I think..." the door to the office opened, interrupting him.

Joe walked in and melted into the seat. "That woman is infuriating."

"Did she fill out the report?" Dillon asked.

"I have no fucking idea." He waved his arms in the air. "I left after about fifteen minutes of listening to her complain about you," he pointed to Dillon, "Damien, this office, and then she ripped into the sergeant. I walked away."

Dillon stood. "Let's get out of here before she comes back up."

"That's a great idea." Damien grabbed his coat.

Joe moaned as he walked to his desk and grabbed his ID and gun from his desk drawer. "So glad I wasn't wearing this when I walked her downstairs. I might have shot her." He slipped his gun into his hip holster.

"I'm not sure anyone would fault you if you did," Dillon said. "Maybe my director was psychic."

"What makes you say that?" Damien asked as they stepped into the elevator.

"He told me not to carry my weapon. I definitely would've shot her." Dillon smiled as they walked to the garage.

CHAPTER TEN

Tuesday - late morning

The parking lot of Tiger Cycle was packed with motorcycles, cars, and food trucks.

Joe whistled. "Oh, we have to look around."

"Another time." Damien parked next to the building.

A young kid approached them. "Hey, man. You can't park here. Don't you see the no parking sign? I'll have your vehicle towed."

Damien flashed his badge. "This gives us permission. We need to speak with Chrissy. Is she here?"

The teen stammered. "Uh yeah. She's in the store."

When Damien opened the door, music played as several customers stood around with food and drinks. A young man demonstrated how to change spark plugs on a bike. He noticed several customers glance at his weapon, as well as Joe's.

A young man stepped out from around the counter. "Hey, we don't allow weapons on the premises."

Damien and Joe both showed their badges. "We are here on official business."

Joe glanced around. "What's going on here?"

"Bike rally." The young man responded.

Damien motioned towards him. "What about Chrissy or her brother? Where are they?"

"I'll go get them." The young man disappeared behind a door.

Joe walked around, looking at some bikes. A fat guy blocked him as he neared an area. "You the bouncer?"

"Yeah. We don't like cops." The guy said.

The guy reeked of beer and onions. Joe leaned in and sniffed. "Well, I don't like fat, stinky men. And what the hell happened to your hair? Looks like you got in a fight with a lawnmower."

Damien turned around, waiting for all hell to break loose. He caught Dillon's eye.

They took a few steps towards Joe.

The fat guy squared up with Joe. "You're one ugly cop." He ran his eyes up and down his body. "Still a little on the heavy side," he said as Joe stepped next to him.

"I can't believe they let you in here. Doesn't this place have standards?" Joe cracked a big grin. "Why are you even here? Don't you have a job?"

The fat man hugged Joe. "Shit. You're the one they shouldn't be letting in here. How the hell have you been?"

Joe patted Dale Haskins on the back. "Damn good, man. Haven't seen you in way too long." He turned around to see Damien and Dillon were ready to break up a fight. "Relax. This fat fucker is Dale."

"Hey, until you lose that big Irish butt of yours, you can't call anyone fat." Dale reached out his hand. "You must be Damien." He shook Dillon's hand. "Nice to meet you."

"Yeah. I'm Damien. This is Dillon." Damien frowned at his partner. "I really thought you two were about to start swinging."

Joe laughed. "Not at all. This guy does all my truck detailing."

"Hey, I hope everything is okay. Why are you guys here?" Dale asked.

"Unfortunately, I can't tell you. It's official business," Joe said.

The door to the back opened, and Chrissy and her brother, Corbin, walked towards them.

Joe nodded to his friend. "I'll call. We need to go out for a beer. It's good to see you, man."

Dale waved as he walked off, giving the group some space.

Damien stepped up to Chrissy. He and Joe showed their badges. "I'm Lieutenant Kaine. This is my partner, Joe Hagan." He pointed to Dillon. "This is FBI Agent McGrath. We need to speak with you," he looked at her brother, "both of you. It's a delicate matter. Is there somewhere we can go?" Damien noticed the shift in the brother's stance. He gave a quick side glance to Joe.

The brother squinted at the trio. "What's this about? Why the hell are you and the FBI here?"

"Corbin," Chrissy said as she reached out to touch her brother's arm. "Yes, let's go out into the shop." She motioned for them to follow her as she pushed open the door leading to a private area.

Damien, Joe, and Dillon followed her to an outside covered patio. Heat lamps had been placed around the chairs and small tables.

She pointed to a few chairs. "Will this work?" She adjusted the heat on the tall lamps, making the sitting area cozy and warm.

"Yes. This is great." Damien waited for her and her brother to sit. When they were settled, he turned to Chrissy. "When was the last time you spoke with Peter?"

Chrissy sat up straight. She twisted in her seat, staring at her brother, before turning back to the detective. "What's happened to Peter?"

"When did you speak with him last?" Damien asked again.

Dillon watched as Chrissy searched her memory for the last conversation with her fiancé. The brother stared blankly at his sister. His emotionless demeanor surprised Dillon.

Chrissy wrung her hands in her lap. "I—I don't know. I guess yesterday sometime."

"Do you know where he was going? What were his plans for yesterday?" Damien jotted something in his notebook. He noticed Joe staring at the brother's shoes. Heavy steel-toed boots. When his partner caught his look, Joe leaned his head towards the shoes. Looking closer, he could see red discoloration on the toes of one boot.

"Why are you asking about Peter? Did someone hurt him?" Corbin asked.

Damien cocked his head to the side. "Why would you ask if someone hurt Peter?"

"Why else would you be here?" Corbin snapped at him.

"Maybe it was an accident." Damien glanced over at Dillon and Joe.

Corbin huffed in disgust. "I think you should tell us why you are here. Did he do something?"

"What would Peter do?" asked Dillon.

The brother's glare narrowed in on the agent. "Why is the FBI here? Don't you investigate white-collar crime?"

"I really don't understand. Why are you asking about Peter?" Chrissy's voice broke.

"Can you just tell me where Peter was supposed to be yesterday?" Damien waited for her to respond.

"I'm not sure. He said he was helping a friend. And then he would be home late. We were supposed to meet this evening for dinner and to go over the final plans for the wedding."

"Did you see him?" Damien asked.

Chrissy shook her head. "No. I was at home yesterday. Wasn't feeling well. I spoke to him on the phone." She turned towards her brother. "Did you see Peter yesterday?"

Corbin shook his head. "No," he answered sharply. "I was in and out of the shop yesterday. Peter didn't come by here at all."

"Do you know who the friend was?" Joe asked.

"Um, Frank. A teacher he knew." Chrissy sighed. She opened her mouth to speak, but her brother cut her off.

"You know about Frank?" Corbin asked, flinching back.

"Yes. They have been friends for a long time. Frank was like a father to him." Chrissy focused on the detective. "Please tell me. What has happened to Peter?"

Damien leaned forward. "I'm sorry. We found Peter murdered early this morning."

Chrissy gasped, placing her hand over her mouth. "You—you must have made a mistake. No one wants to kill Peter. He was a good man." She looked at her brother. "Corbin. Tell them. No one would hurt Peter."

Corbin shook his head. "Yeah. Are you sure? Maybe you identified the wrong guy."

"Can you tell me about your relationship with your future brother-in-law?" Damien asked.

"What do you mean? You think I had something to do with this?" Corbin jerked back, standing up.

"Corbin. Calm down." Chrissy wiped the tears from her face. "I don't understand. Where did you find Peter?"

"They found him in the parking lot near Frank's home. He may have been mugged while walking to his vehicle." Damien noticed the brother eased and sat down next to his sister. "Corbin, I only ask about your relationship with Peter, because we can see from your social media posts, you and Peter didn't have the greatest relationship. Your conversations led us to think you didn't like Peter."

Corbin huffed. "I have nothing against Peter. I made those posts in anger over stupid stuff," he said in a flat tone.

"Calling someone a faggot and a loser homosexual doesn't strike me as just being angry. Did you have reason to think Peter was gay?" Damien asked.

Chrissy glared at her brother. "Why would you think Peter was gay?"

Corbin shuffled his feet around. "I didn't. Shit, I was just angry.

Haven't you ever said something stupid when you were angry?"

Chrissy looked sheepishly at the detectives. "I'm sure Corbin got mad at Peter over something. He has a quick temper." She feigned a smile. "Corbin is protective of me since our father died. You can't tell, but we are twins. He thinks he has to police my life. Every chance he got, he tested Peter. I'm sure he meant nothing by those comments." Chrissy took Corbin's hand in hers.

The tears overflowed again. Streaking her makeup. "He wouldn't do anything to hurt me." Her brow furrowed. "I'm confused. I thought Frank lived in a good neighborhood. Peter has been over there several times and never had any problems." Her breath hitched. She couldn't maintain her composure and broke down.

Her brother put his arm around her. "Can you ask us questions later? Give her some time to work through this?"

"I understand how hard this is, but we need to rule out as many things as we can in order to find his killer. Corbin, can you tell me the last time you saw Peter?" Damien asked.

Corbin shifted his gaze between the detectives. "I'm not sure." He wiggled in his chair.

"Um, okay. Was it within the last day or so?" Damien asked.

"Yeah. I'm sure. Might have been the day before yesterday," Corbin said.

"Can you tell me where both of you were yesterday, say, from 5 p.m. until midnight?" Damien waited for their response.

Chrissy wiped her cheeks with her sleeve. "Last night, I was with my mom. I live with her. We were going through the seating chart. A few of my bride's maids were there. I can get you their names."

"Thank you. You?" Damien said to Corbin.

"Am I a suspect?" he asked.

Joe raised an eyebrow at him. "These are routine questions."

Corbin nodded. "I was helping a few customers here until late. I can get their names."

"That works." Joe stood.

Damien rose, giving Joe a quick glance. "We may have more questions."

"That's fine. Please find out who did this. Find his killer." Chrissy broke down again and ran into the building.

Corbin stuck his hands in his pockets. "If that's all, I need to check on my sister."

Joe nodded. "Yeah. Hey, one more thing. Totally off subject, but your boots. I've been looking for a good pair. I'm about to ride down south with some friends."

Corbin frowned as he held his foot out. "I had these specially made for me. They're based on the Aether Moto Boot. I couldn't find some I liked, so I had some custom-made."

"Those are sweet. Do you mind if I take a picture? I'd like to get some like this." Joe pulled his phone from his pocket. He waited a few seconds for Corbin to say no.

"Um, yeah. I guess so," Corbin said.

"Thanks." Joe snapped a few photos. "Can I get your guy's name?" he pointed to the boots. "The boot guy. I want to have him make me a custom pair."

"Yeah. His name is Camden Sparks. He's got a shop called Bootmania." Corbin watched as the detective wrote the name.

"Thanks. We'll be in touch with follow-up questions or any information we find." Joe waved as he led the way out to the front.

Once in Damien's SUV, both Damien and Dillon stared at Joe.

"What?" Joe asked.

"That was rather odd," Dillon said.

"Did you guys pick up on the brother's vibe?" Joe asked.

"Yeah. Didn't seem too surprised and seemed slightly defensive," Dillon said.

"I saw how surprised he was that his sister knew about Frank." Damien started the SUV.

"His boots had red colored stains all on the right toe. Could be blood." Joe took a piece of gum from the pack in the middle console. He lifted his phone. "Now we have photos."

"It could also be paint or anything else. A photo won't tell us what it is," Dillon said.

"Yes. True. But I think with all this, and his sketchy behavior gives one pause, and maybe enough to get a search warrant for the shoes." Joe smiled at the two. "Now we can go to the bootmaker and get more information."

"Definitely worth a look at the brother. Let's see if Travis can find any CCTV coverage from the area. We might get lucky." Damien pulled into traffic. "Where you want to eat?"

"I'm fine with anything," Dillon said.

"Chinese." Joe texted Taylor. His phone pinged back. "Taylor can meet us at Chang's."

"Tell her we should be there in about twenty minutes," Damien said.

CHAPTER ELEVEN

Taylor rushed out of her office. She needed the break, and meeting the gang for lunch was the perfect distraction. As soon as she sat in her car, a barrage of text messages flooded her phone. Ping after ping.

"What the hell? Who is texting me?" she thought about her schedule and was desperately trying to remember if she missed a meeting or a deadline. Starting the car and letting it warm up, she checked her phone. "Oh, no." Her heart sank.

Her brother sent her over thirty texts. She had gotten a new number since the first text he sent her, and now he had this number. "How? How could he get this number?" she scrolled through the messages. They started with, "Why haven't you answered me?" and ended with, "You can't hide from me."

She blew out a curt breath. Highlighting the messages about to delete them when she remembered what Dillon had told her. Keep every correspondence from him. No matter what it is, keep it. Her hands shook as she laid the phone in the dash cubby.

Driving out of the lot, her phone rang through her Bluetooth. Set to automatically connect when in her car, she didn't have time to screen the call. "Hello?"

"Taylor."

She bristled. She didn't have to look to know it was her brother. She stopped at a light and fumbled for her phone. She clicked the icon allowing her to record the call. "Adnon."

"Why are you trying to avoid me? I just want to talk. You are my sister."

"Adnon, we really have nothing to talk about. Our relationship was over long before I left for school."

"With our parents dead, I would think you would want to be family. We are all we have left."

"You didn't care about family when your mother was being abused by her husband. Your father. Why would I want to be family with you?" Taylor tapped the steering wheel. As soon as it turned green, she gunned the gas.

"Our mother..." Adnon paused. "Our mother killed our father. You should be angrier with her."

"Our father abused her. I am not sorry he is dead. I'm only sorry I didn't help my mother. I'm sorry you are my brother. I don't want anything to do with you."

"Taylor, this is not how women from our culture speak to the men in their lives. You know, without our father alive, I am the head of the family. You must do as I say. Or there will be repercussions for your behavior."

"You don't scare me. You can't have my share of the inheritance. I will fight you for everything."

"It is mine! I deserve it! I am the head of this family. You will give me what I want, or you will die. It's your choice."

Taylor pulled into the parking lot of the restaurant. Her entire body shook. She took a deep breath. "Adnon, you need to hear me. I will kill you if you come anywhere near me. I will kill you if you show up at my home or work." She gathered herself. "I will see you in court."

"You won't have to wait to see me. And your veiled threats don't worry me. I will sell you to the highest bidder, and he will teach you how to submit."

The phone went dead. Taylor's eyes filled with tears. She missed her mom, and now realized how much her mother sacrificed for her to get away from her family. She wasn't about to let her brother take away everything she had built in her life. Not without one hell of a fight.

CHAPTER TWELVE

Chrissy clung to her brother. "I can't believe this. How could this happen to Peter?"

Corbin patted her head. "I know how hard this is. I don't understand it, either. But maybe things happen for a reason."

Chrissy stepped back. "Are you kidding me?" she pushed him away, recoiling. "I can't believe you would say that. What is wrong with you?"

"Hey, I didn't mean he deserved it. But he was never the man for you to marry. I know you know that deep down inside." Corbin stepped towards her. "Look at all the fights you have been getting into. That has to mean something."

"First, you think Peter is gay. Then you say this. I don't want to talk to you right now." She raised her hands as she stepped even further away.

"Chrissy. Be realistic. Did you know everything about Peter?" Corbin reached out to grab her arm. "Are you sure you knew him?"

"What does that even mean? Yes, I knew him. I knew he was a kind, loving man. No other man cared for me like he did. He was creating a tech company. He was the man I loved and wanted to marry." Chrissy covered her face with her hands. "Someone took him from me. For what, for a few dollars?" Chrissy left the store.

Corbin watched as she drove off the lot. He glanced around to find several customers looking uncomfortably at the conversation they had heard. He stormed off to the back office. As he sat in the chair, he figured if the cops were looking at a robber or mugger, he should have nothing to worry about.

CHAPTER THIRTEEN

Dillon's smile faded as Taylor entered the restaurant. "What happened?"

Taylor kissed Joe as he stood and pulled out her chair. "What do you mean, what happened?"

Damien glanced from Dillon to Joe, then to Taylor.

Joe scrutinized his girlfriend. "Something happened."

Taylor sighed. "My brother called me."

"What?" Joe asked, facing her.

"I thought we got you a new number?" Dillon asked.

"We did. I did. I have no idea how he got it." She pulled her phone from her pocket. "When I got into my car, I turned on my phone, and a bunch of texts pinged. They were all from him." She fiddled with her screen. "I was smart enough to turn on the app to record the phone call." She held her phone out and pushed play.

They listened to the conversation.

"Andrew is going to let me know when we can talk to him. We will have him push this through as fast as possible." Dillon took a drink of her water.

"Maybe I should just relinquish my inheritance." Taylor looked at her hands in her lap.

"No." Joe reached over and took one of her hands in his. "It's not about the money. It's about controlling you. And if you give in now, he will have power over you."

"I agree, Taylor," Damien said as the food was delivered.

"I know you guys are right. I just don't know what lengths he will go to." Her gaze fell on each person. "Do you guys really think he will try to hurt me? Or do you think it's all a ploy to get the money?"

Dillon's shoulders sagged. "I think he will kill you if he gets the opportunity. This is why I want you to keep all phone calls and texts. We will give them to Andrew, and he can hopefully use them to get a restraining order against him."

"Yeah, by filing a restraining order, you create a record of Adnon harassing you. Then if he shows up and you shoot him, you will have all the threats he made." Joe took a bite of his noodles.

"I don't like this. I feel like I'm going to be looking over my shoulder all the time." Taylor picked at her food. She took a bite of beef broccoli, but it didn't taste good. She pushed her plate to the center. "I'm too anxious to eat."

"Taylor, I can take you to and from work. I think that may be best anyway," Joe said.

"No. I don't want to live like a prisoner, scared to go about my daily business. I refuse to let my brother do that to me. I will be diligent. I will pay attention to my surroundings and have the security guard at work walk me to my car, just in case he figures out a way to get on the property." Taylor tapped the screen of her phone.

"I have that new security system in place at my house. My landlords love the video surveillance. So, they let me put in the whole house system." Joe grinned at Damien. "Thanks for the discount."

"Discount? You paid nothing for it." Damien laughed.

"I know. That's because you love me." Joe leaned into Damien and batted his eyes.

"No. No, I don't." Damien leaned away from him.

Taylor pulled her plate towards her. As she listened to the banter between the two men, she pushed her food around.

"Hello, Taylor?" Joe waved his hand in front of her face.

"What? I'm sorry. What did I miss?" she smiled at everyone.

"Taylor," Damien said, "I will call and get a phone from my dad. I should have done it a few weeks ago. It will track you."

"You mean like everything, right?" She glanced at Dillon. "Like the one you carry?"

Dillon nodded. "Yes. I promise you Damien's family won't read your private things." She chuckled. "I would suggest you don't send any photos to Joe. And watch your sex talk."

"But if they aren't going to look at it, why do I have to worry?" She wiggled her eyebrows.

Joe reached over and took her hand. "It won't be forever. But until we get this stuff straightened out with Adnon, I want to know I can track your whereabouts."

"It also has a panic button on it. If you feel threatened but can't make a call, hit the button, and Nicky will get an emergency notice, and he can begin tracking you," Damien said.

Taylor sighed. "I appreciate it. All of it. You and Dillon are doing so much for me."

Dillon wanted to hunt down Adnon and bury him somewhere. Instead, she would do what she could to protect her best friend. Pretty much her only girlfriend. "Guess who showed up at the office today?" Dillon asked, wanting to change the somber mood.

"I do not know. Who?" Taylor's brow wrinkled at the smirk on Dillon's face. "Who?"

"Camilla." Dillon looked at Damien, then back at Taylor. "She was in rare form today."

"Oh, my gosh. What happened?" Taylor picked at her food, nibbling here and there.

"She went on about being stalked." Damien took a long sip of his soda.

"She still claiming she's being stalked? Do you guys believe her?" Taylor opened one of the fortune cookies sitting in the middle of the table.

All three shrugged at the same time.

"I'm not sure anymore." Damien leaned back in his chair. "On one hand, I think she may be telling the truth. But I think she is using it to drive a wedge between me and Dillon."

Dillon snorted. "More like a semi-truck than a wedge." She sighed. "I think she is being stalked. But I really think it is a wife of one of the men she has slept with."

"I can't believe you ever dated her. She doesn't seem like the kind of woman you would normally date." Taylor stared into Damien's blue eyes. He was more than handsome. He dripped sex. She turned her focus to Joe, equally sexy in his own right. His emerald green eyes, dark red hair, and Irish accent made her melt. She couldn't believe how lucky she was to have him in her life.

"I can't either." Dillon laughed at the dirty look Damien flashed her.

Damien paid the bill when his phone rang. He glanced at Joe and Dillon. "It's the ME." He stood as he answered. "Dr. Forsythe, what do you have?"

Dillon, Joe, and Taylor followed him outside. They all stood at the SUV, waiting for the call to end.

"The doctor has something for us. He told us to come by autopsy." Damien hugged Taylor. "Pay attention. Call Joe, me, or Dillon anytime you don't feel safe at work."

She hugged him back. "I will." She kissed Dillon on the cheek and walked to her car with Joe.

"Listen, babe, I know you are worried, but we can stay a few steps ahead of Adnon." He took her in his arms and gave her a passionate kiss. "I won't let anything happen to you. I promise you."

She wrapped her arms around his waist. The smell of his cologne comforted her, made her feel safe. "I know you will." She squeezed him before letting go. "I will text when I am leaving and heading home."

"I don't know what time I will get home, but it won't be late. I have to pick up my truck, then I will be home. Lock all the doors and set the alarm when you get there." He kissed her head and waited for her to enter her vehicle, waving at her as she drove off. There was no way he would let anything happen to her. Even if it meant sacrificing his own life.

CHAPTER FOURTEEN

Early afternoon

Damien pulled into the ME's parking lot. As they entered the building, Maggie, the girl at the desk, waved them on through.

"He's expecting you," she said as she buzzed open the door.

Silence surrounded them as they walked down the hallway.

Damien couldn't help but feel as if a hundred hidden eyes watched his every move. The echoes of his shoes on the tile floor seemed louder than usual. He felt like he disturbed the dead with every step.

Nearing autopsy, soft sounds of jazz drifted towards them.

Pushing open the doors, Dr. Forsythe glanced up from his table. Damien smiled at his favorite ME and friend. "Hey, Doc, what do you have?"

"Ah, look who you brought with you." He removed his gloves and moved towards Dillon. He stopped a foot away from her, grabbing her shoulders with both hands. "You look beautiful. How are you doing?"

"I'm good. I'm doing good." Dillon held her emotions in.

"Well, I am glad you are back. I've missed you." He didn't hug her because of the blood on his apron, but he squeezed her shoulders. "If you ever need me, you only have to call."

"I will, Dr. Forsythe. Thank you." She focused on her feet when she saw Damien staring at her.

"What do you have?" Joe asked, staring at a young lady on one table. "She's not our victim."

Dillon scanned the body of a woman on another table. Besides the long gash across her throat, something else caught her eye. A mark on the torso. Not a birthmark, something made by the killer. She leaned down and inspected it more closely. Something seemed familiar, but she couldn't place it.

"No. She isn't. They found this girl near Starved Rock State Park. On one of the trails. Some of the park's rangers found her. The local sheriff's department in the area started the investigation, and their local doctor asked us to take a look." Dr. Forsythe donned another pair of gloves as he spoke.

"Not sure what we have here. I just started on her. As for your guy," he walked towards the cabinet of drawers. The drawers that held the dead. "Come over here." He pulled out the drawer containing Peter Martin's body.

Dillon frowned at the woman on the table. She followed the doctor to the cabinet of the dead, but she glanced back over her shoulder at the young woman.

Joe winced. "Man. I just can't get over the damage done to this kid."

Dillon stepped closer to Peter's body. His face was bashed in, and several teeth were missing or broken. "Wow. This is—horrible." She stared at the young man. "Have you figured out what did all this damage? Like what weapon he used?"

"I think a shoe was the weapon of choice. I know Roger mentioned this to you guys at the scene this morning. He was one hundred percent correct.

The doctor pointed to the gap in teeth. "If you look at the broken teeth, you can see an almost perfect shape." He dragged his gloved finger along the gap in the top row of teeth. "To me, I see a curved slot where the toe of shoe, probably a boot, knocked out the teeth."

Damien's lips pooched out. "Did you find anything caught in the teeth? Maybe something telling us what kind of shoe?"

Dr. Forsythe nodded. "In between two teeth, I found a long strip of leather. It was super small, almost fiber-like. I had Trace look at it, and they confirmed my suspicions."

"Every boot or shoe is made of leather." Damien scanned the rest of the body.

"This is true. But in this case, this is super high-end leather. This won't be on a shoe you can get from one of the discount retailers. No, sir. This is specialized leather. Custom made."

"Corbin wore a pair of high-end leather boots. Custom made. You think the leather could've come from those?" Joe asked.

"It's possible. Get the shoes, and Trace can confirm." The doctor pulled the sheet down a little further, then pointed to the knife wound. "This was made with about a six-inch smooth blade. Extremely sharp. It passed through tendon and muscle like it was butter."

"Do you know what kind of knife?" Joe asked.

"I don't have enough to tell me the type of knife. But the blade was rather thin." Dr. Forsythe pulled the sheet up. He patted the young man's head before he closed the drawer.

"I'm waiting on the rag Roger found at the scene. There was some kind of substance on it. The odd thing is the same substance was inside of Peter's mouth. It was what I swabbed off his cheek when I first got on the scene." He pulled down his bottom lip and pointed to the inner ridge of the lip. "Here," he mumbled. "It had to be a transfer from the shoe. As soon as Trace has the results, I will call you."

Damien sighed as he dragged his hand down his face. "I appreciate the help, Doc, as usual."

Just then, they heard singing nearing the autopsy room. When the doors pushed open, a middle-aged woman stepped in. Smiling at the small crowd, she held out her hand. "Hi, I'm Beth Parker."

Dillon took her hand. "Are you new here?"

She nodded. "Yes, I am. I was supposed to be at the scene this morning, but I had a minor mishap."

Dr. Forsythe eyed Damien. "This is the new ME. Beth, this is Lieutenant Damien Kaine, his partner Detective Joe Hagan, and FBI Agent Dillon McGrath."

"Nice to meet all of you." Beth stepped up to the table, holding the young woman.

Dillon moved to stand next to Dr. Parker while Joe and Damien chatted with Dr. Forsythe. "Have you started this one yet?"

"No. I will start on her soon." Beth smiled at the pretty agent. "I've heard about you."

Dillon stared at her. "Really? From the doc?"

"No. I heard about the case you covered in California a few years ago. The serial rapist who began murdering his victims days after he raped them." Beth raised her eyebrows at the agent. "Your brief on the case was fascinating. The way your mind worked to put the cases together. It impressed me."

"I had a lot of help from a detective on the San Francisco PD," Dillon said.

"Dillon, you ready?" Damien asked from across the room.

"Yeah." She faced Beth. "Can you send me the report on her when you're finished?" Dillon asked.

"Sure. Do you see something?" Beth asked.

"I'm not sure. Something seems familiar, but I don't know why."

Dillon turned on her heels. "Thanks, the doc has my number," she said, walking away.

CHAPTER FIFTEEN

"I guess everyone is out," Joe said as he hung his jacket over his chair in the VCU. He motioned to Dillon to check out Detective Travis Black from ECD and Officer Katie Baker.

Dillon studied the two love birds behind the glass of ECD. Ever since the Metacruze case, they had been hanging out as Katie liked to call it. But Dillon knew better. It was way more than a simple friendship and hanging out. Their giddiness made her happy. "Let's get all the photos of the crime scene. Lay them out in the conference room."

Damien stopped short of entering his office. "Okay. You got an idea?"

"Not sure." Dillon walked towards the restroom.

Joe made sure he had the folder with the notes from the Facebook accounts. He quickly grabbed a soda from the new soda machine in their unit before walking into the conference room. He motioned to Damien. "I think the brother is guilty as hell."

"Because?" Damien texted a message to Travis, asking him about the CCTV footage from the area near the crime scene.

"I can't tell you." Joe sat at the table.

"Can't tell me because you don't know?" Damien opened the folder on the table. "Listen, I think he's hiding something. But murder? Seems a stretch." He stared at his friend. "Maybe your soft spot for Frank has you jumping to conclusions."

"No. I'm right. I'm willing to bet on it, too." Joe leaned into him. "Are you?"

"Bet? Bet on whether her brother did it?" Damien leaned back in his chair. "You're kidding, right?"

"No. I'm not." Joe popped the tab on his soda, taking a big gulp.

"I'm not sure I want to bet on anything. You cheat, and I always lose." Damien's mouth watered as he watched condensation bead down the can.

"I don't cheat, you're just *sicín*." Joe broke out in laughter at the glare his partner gave him. "Bwak, bwak, bwak," Joe danced around, clucking like a chicken. "You scared, bro?"

"You're an asshole." Damien chuckled at his partner.

Dillon walked in and stopped. "What the hell are you doing?"

Joe straightened. "Um, nothing."

"Doesn't look like nothing. Looks like a *sicín mór saille*." Dillon plopped into a chair.

"He is a big fat chicken." Damien died laughing. "I'm going to call you big fat chicken from now on."

"He's just mad because he knows I'm right." Joe took another long sip of his soda.

"Right about what?" Dillon asked, glancing over at Damien.

"He thinks the brother did it. Killed Peter."

"I'm right, too," Joe said.

"He just may be. I mean, there is something off with the brother. I noticed it from the start." Dillon grabbed the folder with the pictures. "I agree with both of you. This was a furious attack. Nothing was stolen. Not even the car. If I killed someone and he was a random stranger, I would take the money from his wallet and his car."

Joe slapped the table. "Exactly. See." He leaned forward, placing his forearms on the table. "I think, if not the brother, it is definitely someone who knew Peter."

Damien's shoulders slumped. "I hope it is anyone else but the brother. That's going to crush his sister. But I have to agree with you guys." He held up one of the crime scene photos. "If the killer knew Peter, then he had to know he would be in this area and he saw Frank regularly."

"Yup. That's why I think it's the brother. When Chrissy said she knew who Frank was, the brother's reaction showed me her revelation surprised him." Joe finished his soda. "And you have to ask why?"

Dillon shuffled a few pictures around, then laid them out in the center of the table. "Look at the scene. Nothing was disturbed except for where the assault took place. This killer had one purpose; to kill Peter." She shifted her attention between the two detectives.

"I had the impression when we first started interviewing the two, that the brother knew something," she said, glancing at Damien. "When you asked him about the Facebook posts, he back peddled. And his sister seemed horrified he thought Peter was gay. Why would he think he was gay, anyway?"

Damien sat for a few minutes. "If it was the brother who made those posts about Peter, we could assume, for argument's sake, that he knew Peter was going to Frank's house. He may have followed him before or seen them together and thought they were lovers."

"He has to know he made a huge mistake. I mean, killing him was a big enough mistake, but killing Peter because he thought he was gay, to find out he wasn't... that's going to tear this family apart," Joe said.

Dillon sighed. "We can't prove any of our assumptions until we get something to tie to the brother. And a good defense attorney could spin this by saying the sister thought he was gay and killed him. We need some proof."

"I asked Travis to search the CCTV. It could take some time to see if there was a camera in the area. Even then, we don't know if it will show the lot." Damien rocked in his chair. "What about neighbors?"

Joe and Dillon glanced at him.

"Um, what about what neighbors?" Joe asked.

"Frank's. Maybe one of them has a security camera," Damien said.

Dillon rubbed her temples. "What the hell are you talking about? Why do we care if the neighbors have a security...," she paused. "Oh. I see."

Joe squinted. "What am I missing?"

"We could see if any of the neighbors have a security camera and see if they picked up a car or person of interest. We know the time Peter visited Frank," Damien said.

"I could go check." Dillon smiled. "I promise to behave."

Damien and Joe laughed.

"What? I can be nice." Dillon crossed her arms as she huffed out a breath.

Joe chuckled and smirked, backing up when she glared at him. "I can call the boot guy. See if he can tell me anything about Corbin and his sister. Kind of feel the guy out." Joe snapped his fingers. "Wait, my buddy Dale. I could call him and see what he thinks of the brother."

"Good idea. Do it." Damien watched as Joe left the room.

Dillon squinted at him. "What are we going to do about Camilla?"

"What can we do about Camilla? Nothing. So why worry about her?"

Dillon leaned on the table with her elbows. "She's going to cause trouble for us."

Damien leaned his head back against his chair, sighing. "I still can't do anything about her. I can't arrest her. I can't say or do a damn thing. If she is going to bring up what happened in the hotel, she is going to bring it up."

Dillon sat quietly.

Damien leaned back again, staring at the ceiling. "The guy in the hotel with her has more to lose than me. I know he won't press charges." He sat up straight. "Not with what he knows I know about him. I doubt Camilla would do anything to lose her job or her standing. She's all bark when it comes to blowing up my life."

"Do you think she is really being stalked?" Dillon asked.

Damien shrugged. "I don't know for sure. At first, I thought it was a ploy. Something she was doing to mess with us. With me. To be honest, I don't know." He stood, stretching. "I don't care either."

Joe sauntered back into the room. "Spoke with Dale. He said the brother was very protective of the sister. He never thinks anyone is good enough for her. He mentioned another guy Chrissy dated before Peter." He checked his notes. "A guy by the name of Hershel Marcum."

Dillon glanced between Joe and Damien. "Why does that name sound familiar?"

"Hershel Marcum was a linebacker for the NFL." Joe waited.

"Oh, no." Dillon shook her head.

"Wait, you don't think?" Damien asked.

"I do." Joe leaned against the table, crossing his arms. "Hershel died in a car wreck. It seemed odd, but he had been drinking, so the wreck went down in the books as an accident. But Dale mentioned Corbin had a real problem with his sister dating a black guy."

"So now we think Corbin is killing his sister's boyfriends?" Damien paced around the room. "No."

"I don't know. But it seems awfully suspicious two men tied to Chrissy have died," Joe said.

"There's no way we can get anything going on the Marcum case. Let's leave it alone for now." Damien cocked his head to the side as he watched Joe. "You got somewhere to go?" he asked.

Joe scowled at him. "What? Why are you asking me that?"

"You keep messing with your watch." Damien frowned. "What's up?"

"I want to go call the hospital." He turned towards Dillon. "You think you can assert your authority and get information from the hospital regarding a patient? Or possibly get me in to see the patient?"

"I doubt it. I could scare them into giving us something." Dillon followed Damien and Joe out of the conference room.

"I don't think it's a good idea." Damien walked into his office. He checked his email, looking for something from the lab regarding the case.

Dillon flopped into the chair.

Joe grabbed a piece of gum from the pack sitting on Damien's desk, then sat in the other chair. "I think it is a great idea. You're great at scaring people."

"Of course, you think it's a good idea. It wouldn't be your ass on the line." Dillon picked several red jellybeans out of the jar. "Who is the patient at the hospital, anyway?"

"Frank Spencer," Joe said.

"The victim's friend?" Dillon asked.

Damien nodded. "Yeah. Joe wants to go by there after work."

"Why?" She popped a few jellybeans into her mouth.

Joe shrugged. "I don't know. This guy doesn't have anyone. He lost someone special." He stared at his hands in his lap. "Just seems like the right thing to do."

Dillon sighed as she pulled her phone from her pocket. "Which hospital?"

Joe beamed a huge smile at her. "You love me, don't you?" he leaned in, batting his eye at her making kissing sounds.

"Just stop," Dillon said, pushing him away. "Save it for Taylor."

CHAPTER SIXTEEN

Late afternoon traffic had picked up as Dillon drove down Frank's street. An old man sat on his stoop two houses down from Frank's. Pulling her sports car into the man's driveway, she placed her FBI placard on the dash.

She monitored him as she removed her weapon from the glove box. "I'll pay the price if I have to shoot him, but I'm not questioning anyone without my weapon," she mumbled to herself as she stepped out of her car.

"Hello, there." The old man walked towards her. "Looks like the FBI has upgraded their cars." He smiled as he studied the Porsche.

"I had to kill a cartel guy for this." She winked at him.

He placed his hands in his pants pockets. "Why do I believe you?" he laughed as he stretched out one hand. "I'm Winston."

"Churchill?" she said, taking his hand.

"Pfft. I'm not old, lady." He stepped around her car. "This is nice."

"It is." She stared at her prize possession. "Can I ask you some questions?"

"Sure." He motioned for her to follow him towards his stoop. "I might not be as old as Churchill, but my body doesn't know that." He sat down on the top step, breathing a little too hard for such a short walk.

"I'm looking for information regarding one of your neighbors. Frank Spencer." She took out a small notepad from the back pocket of her jeans.

Winston's head hung low. His shoulders sagged a bit. "It's a damn shame."

"Are you good friends with him?" Dillon asked.

"I've known him for a long time. We both have lived here for years. I'm supposed to make sure his will gets taken care of. He gave my information to his lawyer." Winston sighed as he pulled a vape from his pocket.

"Do you know what he had planned for his will?" Dillon glanced over her shoulder when Winston waved at a jogger.

"It was supposed to go to Peter. He loved him like a son. Frank doesn't have anyone else he considers family." He smiled at the pretty agent. "He didn't have much. I'll sell everything and donate it to cancer research. In his name."

"I bet he would like that. Do you know if anyone has a security camera covering the area in front of his house?"

"Yeah. Actually, I don't know if it is working. Jess, next door, has one." Winston stood. "Come with me." He led her to the house in between his and Frank's. "She might not have gotten it fixed. Her son knocked it off its perch when he was playing basketball a few weeks ago. Winston knocked on Jess Rankin's front door.

A rather feisty-sounding dog barked and howled on the other side.

"I'm coming." A voice yelled through the closed door. "Stop... get back." The front door flew open, and the woman stepped out. "Oh gosh. I'm so sorry. My dog is a few bricks shy of a full load... he goes ballistic when someone knocks on the door." She wiped her hands on her jeans. She smiled at Winston. "Hey Winnie, what's up?" she glanced at the lady standing next to him.

"Jess, this is Agent...," he looked over at Dillon. "I don't know your last name."

"I guess I forgot to tell you. I'm Agent Dillon McGrath with the FBI." She held out her hand to Jess.

"Nice to meet you, I think. Why are you here?" Jess folded her arms across her chest.

"Don't get worried. She's here about Frank and what happened to Peter." Winston smirked at Dillon. "Jess is sure the government is out to get her."

"Stop. I am not." Jess' face softened. "I'm sorry about what has happened. But what do you need with me?"

"Did you fix your security system?" Winston pointed to the camera facing the driveway and the street.

"Yes. Why?" she glanced between the two.

"Do you have any footage of the last few weeks? It would really help us." Dillon pointed over her shoulder. "Your camera looks like it might capture this area in front of Frank's house."

"Oh. You think I might have the killer on my security?" Jess took a small step backward.

"We are hoping someone might have seen Peter the night he died." Dillon smiled at her.

"I see. I don't have a very sophisticated system. But I can download my videos for the last thirty days and save them to a jump drive. If you give me a few minutes, I'll do it." She opened her door and stepped inside.

Winston's eyes narrowed in on the agent. "You're looking for the killer, aren't you?"

"I can't really say. But we are hoping we see someone who has been in the area before." She glanced up and down the street. "Have you noticed anyone who doesn't live here hanging around? Maybe watching Frank's house."

Winston took a puff on his vape. "Maybe." He pointed to a few spaces down the block. "Now and then, I would see a big black truck parked. Sometimes on this side, sometimes on the other side of the street." He shrugged. "I never thought much. We have a lot of families on this street and lots of people coming and going." He stared at Dillon. "I'm thinking it's important."

"It might be. Can you tell me anything about the driver? Did you ever get a license plate number?" she scribbled in her book.

"No. I never thought to write it down. As for the driver, the windows were tinted dark. I couldn't tell you if it was a man or woman in the cab." Winston started to say something when Jess stepped out of her house.

"Here. I only had about twenty days on there. We just got the thing fixed a few weeks ago." She handed the agent a small jump drive. "You can keep it."

Dillon put the jump drive in her jeans pocket. "Really appreciate this. Can you tell me if you ever noticed a big black truck driving around here, or parking on the street?"

Jess sighed. "I can't say I have. I work all kinds of hours, and if I'm not, I'm running kids all over the place."

"If you think of anything or remember something, please call me." She removed two business cards from her small wallet before replacing it in her back pocket. She handed a card to each.

Jess glanced at the card. "I will. I will ask my kids. They are out here more than me. If they say anything, I will call you."

"Thank you." Dillon started towards her car when Winston called out to her.

"Agent," he waved at Jess and dashed towards her. "Hey, do you know what is happening with Frank? By chance."

"I know he isn't doing well," she said glancing over at Frank's house, before turning towards Winston. "I don't think he is going to make it through the next few days. Call his lawyer and get things in order. You will have power of attorney, and you can get the hospital to tell you things."

"I will do it now. You know, Frank was the nicest man I ever met. He always had a pleasant word for anyone on the street. He let all of us use his driveway when we had parties or family functions." Winston wiped his cheek. "To have it all end like this. It just shouldn't happen this way." He walked back towards his house. "I'll call if I remember anything else."

Dillon stood at her car as the saddened man walked into his home and shut his door. A slight shiver ran through her as she opened her car door. The crisp cold air and the dreary skies only added to the sadness which seemed to engulf the street.

CHAPTER SEVENTEEN

Early evening Tuesday

Camilla stormed out of her office. "Thanks to you, I have to go to a client and try to fix your mistake," she said, glaring at the receptionist.

"I'm sorry, Camilla. I didn't mean to ruin your evening plans." The receptionist glanced at her feet.

"Forget about my plans. I just hope we don't lose the client." Camilla marched towards the elevator. Stepping inside, she sneered at the woman as the doors closed. Her phone pinged as she stepped out and into the parking garage.

She fumbled with her keys and a folder when her phone rang. "Hello?"

Silence.

"Hello?" she shuffled her handbag and briefcase to her other shoulder while she held the phone in her other hand. "Hello?" When no one answered, she hung up.

Squeezing the folder under one arm and balancing her briefcase and purse with the other, her keys slipped from her hand as she stood beside her car. "Crap." Her phone rang again.

"Hello?" she barked out the word.

"Hey, are you okay?" the voice asked.

"Yes. I just dropped my keys," she said, picking them up. "I'm getting ready to leave..." she stopped talking. Holding the phone away from her head, she peeked over her shoulder. Scanning the area near the elevator, she swore she heard someone call her name.

"Hello?" she called out.

"Um, I'm right here," said the voice on the phone.

"Not you, Jeff. I thought someone called me." She pushed the key fob to unlock her rear door. When another noise startled her, she dropped the folder on the ground. Glancing over her shoulder, she saw a young couple enter the elevator. "Stop it."

"Stop what?" Jeff asked.

"Not you. Listen, I should be at the restaurant in about twenty-five minutes. I'm going to get off this phone." She hung up before Jeff could answer. Her hands shook as she reached for her car door. Placing her briefcase and her handbag on the backseat, she bent down and picked up the scattered papers.

"Camilla," a soft, whispery voice called out to her.

Standing up straight, the hair on her neck bristled. She peeked over both shoulders. No one. She flung the folder onto the back seat and slammed the car door. As she reached for the driver's side handle, she felt an arm grip her around her waist. Just as she screamed, a hand covered her mouth.

Her phone and keys dropped onto the concrete floor. A whimper escaped when a soft voice whispered in her ear.

"Don't fight it."

She struggled a moment longer, clawing at the hand over her mouth.

"Shh. There, there. I've got you. And what fun we shall have."

CHAPTER EIGHTEEN

Tuesday evening

Damien and Joe walked into the hospital. They took the elevator up to intensive care. At the main desk, they showed their badges.

A nurse nodded. "The FBI called. You know about that?" She glared at the two detectives.

"Yes Ma'am," Damien said.

"I don't like being threatened. Normally I would fight you on this. But I feel this guy is special."

Damien lowered his head. "I'm sorry. We don't mean to make your job harder than it is."

Joe stepped closer and flashed his best smile. "I'm very grateful you have allowed me to be here with him."

She rolled her eyes at him. "Go in. I've put a chair in there. You can stay as long as you need." She motioned towards the room where Frank lay unconscious. "He's condition deteriorated quite fast. We don't expect him to make it through the night." She slid open the glass door to his room. "The heart attack did too much damage. On top of his cancer, it's just too much for his body to recover from." Her expression softened. "He shouldn't be alone." She sighed. "It's nice of you to do this."

Joe and Damien stepped inside.

The man had cables and cords and way too many machines attached to him. Even though he breathed on his own, it was labored.

Joe walked towards the chair. "Why don't they have him on a ventilator? He sounds like he is struggling."

Damien read the chart at the foot of the bed. "He has a DNR." The board clapped against the bed.

"Makes sense." Joe moved the chair a little out of the way. He leaned towards Frank, taking his hand in his. "Hey, Frank. You're not alone. I hope you don't mind if I keep you company."

Damien stared at his partner, who never ceased to amaze him. "How long do you plan on staying?"

Joe shrugged. "I don't know. Taylor is at the office late tonight. She's going to text me when she is done," he said looking over at Damien.

"You don't have to stay."

"I know." Damien pulled another chair from the corner next to Joe's. They sat in silence for a few moments.

A nurse came in and changed out a bag hanging on his IV stand.

"What is that?" Joe asked.

"A saline solution." She checked his temperature.

"If he has a DNR, why is that hooked up?" Damien asked.

"We can't take heroic measures to save him, but this makes him a little more comfortable. The medicines we gave him are pretty strong and have some serious effects on the body. Keeping him hydrated keeps him more comfortable." She stopped at the foot of his bed. "It isn't really going to help keep him alive. Just because someone is dying doesn't mean they should suffer." She patted Frank's foot as she turned to leave. "I'll be back, Frank."

"I need to make a living will." Joe scooted his chair a little closer to the bed.

"I never want to be hooked up to anything." Damien glanced around the room. "I can't imagine dying here. In this place." He reached out and squeezed Joe's shoulder. "What you're doing for him, by being here, is a really great thing."

Joe patted the top of his hand. "Thanks for hanging with me for a bit." He checked his watch. "I should've grabbed something to eat."

"Go down and get something. I'll stay here."

Joe stood. "You sure?"

"Yeah. Go." Damien shooed him out of the room. Once gone, Damien scooted his chair closer to the bed and reached for Frank's hand. He closed his eyes and remembered when his *Nonna* died.

He silently prayed for Frank. Mumbling in Italian, he didn't hear the door slide open. A beeping noise startled him. He smiled at the nurse, who changed out another IV bag. "Hey."

"How do you know him? I didn't think he had any family."

Not the same nurse from earlier. Damien wasn't sure how to answer. "I'm a detective investigating an event involving someone he knew." He angled his head towards Frank. "We, my partner and I, just wanted to come see him. Check on him."

"How nice. Few people choose to sit at the side of someone who is dying, especially if they don't know him." She fiddled with something on a machine. "I have seen people with family in the area die alone." She stopped at the door. "You know, when he first came in here, he kept calling out for a young man named Peter. Can he come here to be with him?"

Damien's shoulders sagged. "No. Peter was murdered late last night."

"Oh my. That makes perfect sense now."

"What do you mean?" Damien stood.

"I thought he was just mumbling. He kept coming in and out of consciousness." She took a small step towards Damien. "He kept saying, 'Peter, I'll be there soon.' Of course, I thought he was talking about seeing him when he left the hospital. Now I realize Frank knows he is dying. He was talking to Peter."

She slid the door open. "I hope you catch whoever killed Peter. I believe Frank knows you are here. Tell him what you are doing. Give him some peace to go on."

As she walked out, Joe walked in. He had several cans of soda, chips, cookies, and a tray of food.

Damien frowned at him. "Did you leave anything for other people?" he waved at the amount of food.

"Dude, I'm hungry. What did the nurse say?" Joe set his food on the tray near the bed. "Something happen?"

Damien shook his head. "No. Not really."

"Not really means something happened."

"She said when Frank first came in, he kept mumbling 'Peter, I'll be there soon.' When I told her we were investigating Peter's murder, she said she believed Frank knew he was dying and was talking to Peter. She also encouraged us to tell him what we have found out so far. To give him peace."

Joe held a french fry inches from his mouth. Using it as a pointer, he nodded in agreement. "I believe we should. Frank needs to know we think Corbin did it, and we are closing in on him."

Damien frowned. "We don't know for sure he did it. Yes, it is looking very much like Corbin killed Frank. I don't..."

Joe raised his hand, stepping closer to Damien and leaning into his ear. "Don't say why we think he killed him, and don't argue. Frank just needs to hear we are going to get Corbin. Even if things change, Frank needs to hear Peter's murder will be solved."

Damien sighed, rolling his eyes at the same time. "Fine. Frank, I'm

Damien Kaine, the investigator you met earlier this morning. We believe we have found Peter's killer and are working to get him into custody."

"Frank, this is Joe. We will give you and Peter peace. I promise." Joe sat in his chair, pulled the hospital tray over, and lowered it. "See, was that so hard?"

"Okay. What do you think our next steps should be?" Damien sat in his chair, scooting back a little from the bed.

Joe swallowed his bite of food. "We have to get Corbin to crack or get his sister to apply pressure."

"How? We would have to show her he killed Peter. We don't have much except our guts. And we all know how much trouble we get in when we rely on our gut intuition."

Joe laughed. "You mean how much trouble you get into? You're the one who always does what he wants and then asks for forgiveness later."

Damien scowled at him.

Joe smirked. "You know I'm right." His phone beeped. "Taylor will be another hour or two." He texted a reply asking her to pick him up at the hospital.

"When will your truck be ready?" Damien asked.

"They had some trouble with one rim. Tomorrow or the next day." Joe finished his first soda and cracked open another one. "Back to Corbin. If we can get video evidence of him being in the vicinity, I think if we apply pressure, we can get him to confess. I might have a plan."

"No. You should not be in control of any plans." Damien laughed at Joe's stink eye. "Your plans don't always go over very well."

CHAPTER NINETEEN

Tuesday 5:00 p.m.

Dillon drove into the garage. She didn't want to go to the FBI office, and she didn't want to go to Damien's office to view the USB drive. The last place to go was home.

Gunner and Coach greeted her at the door. Coach meowed, and Gunner growled and whined at her.

"Hey, babies." She reached down and scooped up Coach, giving him a big kiss on the nose.

He purred and head-butted her chin.

"Did you miss me?" she kissed him again and placed him on the floor. Next, she turned her attention towards the big brown dog. She bent, giving him several kisses on the nose, and scratched his ears. "You guys hungry?"

Coach meowed and spun in circles.

Gunner raced her to the kitchen and pawed at the door with their food.

Dillon removed the child lock and pulled out his dry food and a can of wet for both. "I bet you hate that lock, don't you?" she asked Gunner as she emptied the canned food onto his dry and mixed them.

He barked in agreement.

"Well, if you weren't such a smart boy, we wouldn't have to lock you out." Filling Coach's bowl with his favorite canned food, she placed their bowls on the floor. As she removed a beer from the fridge, she texted Damien.

"Where you at?"

"Hospital."

At her desk, she turned on her laptop. Plugging in the jump drive, she accessed the videos. Starting with the day of the murder, she scrolled through the video until she was within a few hours of Peter leaving Frank's house.

"If I were following someone, I would want to see how long they stayed somewhere." At four hours out, she saw Peter walk up to Frank's door. The video was grainy, but she could make out Peter, and she knew

Frank's front stoop.

She slowed the video, hoping to see the black truck Winston had described earlier. Not even sure it was Corbin's truck, it at least gave them a place to start. The time stamp on the video showed that a black truck drove by the home an hour after Peter entered Frank's house.

Dillon rewound the video and advanced it slowly. The truck came from an area off-camera. She couldn't tell if it was driving by or if it had been parked. Advancing the video, the truck appeared twenty minutes later. This time, it drove down the street and parked in front of Winston's house.

The angle of the camera couldn't pick up the license plate. She jotted down details of the truck, then sped through the video, slowing it down when she saw Peter leave Frank's house. The time stamp matched within minutes of the ME's time of death. The silent video clearly showed Peter hugging Frank on the steps.

Their body language made it clear they shared a loving bond between them. She paused the video. Breathing slowly, she calmed her emotions. Her thoughts went back to the last time she spoke to her grandparents before they were murdered.

What she wouldn't give for one more conversation. One more hug. Her chest tightened. Using her sleeve, she wiped the moisture from her cheeks. "Push it down, Dillon. Nothing you can do now."

Gunner walked in and laid his head on her knee.

She patted it, bending to kiss the top. "You miss them too, huh?"

He nudged her when she quit scratching his ears.

She lifted his head and stared into his brown eyes. "At least I have you. You and me, Gunner. You tried to save them. And you have definitely saved me." She kissed him on his nose.

He sighed as he sunk down and laid at her feet.

Shaking off her emotions, she started the video again. Peter walked away from the stoop when the black truck pulled into view and stopped. Peter glanced in the truck's direction, then glanced over his shoulder at Frank's house.

"Get out," Dillon scoffed as she watched Peter walk around the truck to the passenger side and get in. Even though the grainy video made it impossible to see much in the way of details, if they could get pictures of Corbin's truck anywhere else in the vicinity, this video might hold up in court.

"Well, hot damn. If this isn't the killer, this person definitely saw Peter just before he was murdered." She opened the FBI database and plugged in Corbin's information. He had a few vehicles registered to him. But DMV records didn't show a black truck.

"That can't be." She tried the sister's name. Nothing. She was about to call Damien when she remembered the name of the cycle shop. Entering the business name into the database, several vehicles and properties tied to the cycle shop flooded the screen. Reading through the list, she smiled. There it was—a black Chevy pickup truck.

"Bingo." She ran out the door and headed to the hospital.

CHAPTER TWENTY

Tuesday 7:00 p.m.

Joe's eyes were closed. He heard Damien's light snoring as he rested his head on the edge of the bed. Joe had told him to leave an hour ago. But Damien wouldn't do it. Taylor had texted earlier and said she was running late.

The room was quiet. He scooted his chair closer, putting him almost next to Frank's head. Lowering the side rail, he placed his hand on the man's shoulder. "I can't imagine how scary this is."

Joe leaned closer, glancing over at Damien, making sure he didn't bother him. "I wouldn't want to die in the hospital alone. I want you to know something. Everything we have gathered on Peter tells us how important you were to him. Lots of people have said he thought of you as a father."

Joe waited before continuing. "I know you cared for the young man. I'm really sorry it went down this way." He gripped Frank's hand with his other hand. Leaning even closer to the bed, he placed his mouth as close to Frank's ear as he could.

"I want you to know. I will make sure Corbin pays for what he did. I promise you. I will get you and Peter justice." Joe gave a sideways look towards his partner. "If you are holding on, waiting, you don't have to. I promise I won't let him get away with this. Go to Peter. You don't need to suffer anymore, Frank. I got it covered here."

Joe leaned back. He didn't know if Frank heard him or not. He jumped when one machine began beeping. Within seconds, another machine beeped.

Just as alarms on two other machines went off, Taylor and Dillon walked in, followed by a doctor and two nurses.

Damien stood up and pushed his chair out of their way.

Joe moved his chair, but held onto Frank's hand.

"I need to get in here." A nurse pushed him to the side.

"I'm not letting go of his hand. Do what you need. But I'm not moving." Joe stood as close to the bed as he could get.

The nurse glared at him but didn't force the issue.

A doctor read through the chart. "He has a DNR. There isn't much we can do."

Dillon stood next to Damien, taking his hand in hers.

Taylor took the spot vacated by the nurse, wrapping her arm around Joe's waist. "Hey, baby," she whispered.

He leaned in and kissed the top of her head. "It's time for him to go." He reached out and touched the top of Frank's head. "It's okay. We got this covered. You go. Peter needs you. You need him."

The machine monitoring his heartbeat flatlined.

The doctor waited for a few minutes. He flipped off the machine and checked for a heartbeat and other vitals. "Death occurred at—7:38 p.m." He scribbled on the chart. He turned to the full room. "You guys can have a few moments. Then you will have to leave."

The nurses followed him out, closing the door behind them.

Joe wasn't sure why this stranger's death hit him so hard. He tried to stop the tears, but he couldn't. His skin broke out in goosebumps as all eyes fell on him. "Shut up," he said, turning towards everyone.

"I don't think anyone said anything." Damien smiled at him.

Dillon and Taylor's eyes glistened with moisture.

"You did a good thing. Being here." Dillon patted his back. "You're a good man, Joe."

Taylor leaned in towards him, squeezing him with both her arms.

He turned towards her, taking her in a big hug. When he released her, he motioned towards Dillon and Damien. "Now we need to nail Corbin to the wall."

Dillon snapped her fingers. "I think I got him."

Both Joe and Damien stared at her.

"You're shitting right?" Joe asked.

"Nope. I went to Frank's neighborhood, spoke with a few residents, and found the house right next door had a security camera. The owner gave me a jump drive with about twenty-two days on it." Dillon made sure no nurses were about to walk in.

"One neighbor had mentioned a truck had been around a few times. The day Peter was murdered, I found him on the security camera, getting into the same truck Frank's neighbor described," Dillon said.

Joe moved closer to her. "Do we know if the vehicle belongs to Corbin?"

Dillon smiled. "I checked. The cycle shop owns the same make and model."

"Hot damn." Joe almost squealed.

"Not so fast. The video is very grainy, you can make it out, and you know it's Peter. But there is nothing definitive about the truck. We still have to put Corbin in the truck and over there at the same time." Dillon turned towards Damien. "Have you heard anything from Travis on the CCTV?"

"I haven't yet. I need to see if he found anything." Damien paced.

"If we can get a camera angle showing his license plate and we can put him in the area using the video, it should be enough for a warrant on the truck and possibly his boots and personal areas such as home and the shop," Dillon said.

Joe looked at his watch. "Damn, I didn't realize how late it was."

Damien stopped pacing. "Tomorrow morning, I'll pick you up early. I want to get into the office and call the lab. See if they have anything else. I need to get Travis to find some CCTV footage. Let's go home. Nothing much we can do right now."

Everyone focused on the door when it slid open.

The nurse from the main desk earlier in the evening stood in the doorway. "It's time for us to move the body," she said, waiting for them to leave.

Joe stopped in front of her. "I can't thank you enough."

"You're welcome. Next time, don't threaten. Just ask." She watched them leave. Even though it went against protocol, she knew it was the right thing to do. No one should ever die alone.

CHAPTER TWENTY-ONE

Damien followed Dillon into the house. He carried the food from Vinnie's Sub Shop. "I can't wait to eat."

Gunner sniffed the air as he followed them into the kitchen.

Coach lay on his sofa. He opened one eye.

Damien placed the sandwiches on two plates, along with the two bowls of soup. "Grab something to drink, please."

Dillon opened the fridge and grabbed two beers along with the pitcher of water.

Damien filled two glasses with ice and set them on the table.

At the sound of clinking glassware, Coach ran into the kitchen. He perched himself on a chair at the table and waited.

"Oh, hell. See what you have created." Damien glared at the cat and pointed at him. "You are not human."

Coach huffed at him, squinting. The cat turned his attention towards the sandwiches.

"Leave him alone. He can sit there." Dillon filled the glasses with water.

Damien grabbed two spoons from a drawer. "This soup smells fantastic."

"It's minestrone." Dillon tasted it. "Oh man, this is so good."

Damien watched as she shared some of her sandwich with the cat and dog. When Gunner turned towards him, waiting for him to share, Damien shook his head. "No. Don't look at me that way."

"Just share with him. And Coach too."

"Fine." He tore off a piece of cheese and meat from his sandwich. And gave Gunner a piece of the bread. "There. Now leave me alone."

"Okay. We need to put Corbin's vehicle in the area. With what we have from the homeowner's security camera, we can build a pretty good case against him. I think it will stick, too." Dillon blew on her spoon. "This is so good. Hot, but good."

Damien washed down his bite of food with a gulp of beer. "I hate to think this guy really killed his sister's fiancé. I hope we are wrong. I hope we travel down this road and find out we missed the mark."

"Why?"

"Joe said he had a bad feeling about this case. The more we seem to close in on the brother, the more I have a sense of doom." Damien scoffed at Coach, who reached out to his plate, trying to steal a piece of meat from the sandwich. "Stop."

Coach hunkered down. A little squeak came out.

"You've hurt his feelings," Dillon said.

"Oh, poor baby." Damien taunted the cat. Sighing, he agreed and gave him the piece of meat. He then had to give Gunner a piece of something, or he feared he would send him into some kind of psychotic break.

"Why do you think Joe wanted to be at Frank's side so much?"

Damien shrugged. "I really do not know. I know this case has affected him. Something about the entire case has gotten under his skin."

Dillon giggled. "Usually, it's you with the bug up your ass."

"Oh, thanks."

She laughed. "You know what I mean. Quit pouting."

"I'm not pouting." His phone pinged.

"Who's that?"

"I don't know." He pulled his phone from his back pocket and let out a sigh of relief. "It's my mom. She wants us to come over for dinner sometime next week."

"You thought it was Camilla, didn't you?"

"I have to be honest; I was a little worried. I don't want to deal with her. Not now."

Dillon reached over and grabbed his hand. "Listen. She can't hurt us. Even if she tells the world you held her and her lover at gunpoint, so what? You didn't shoot them. And you were acting on impulse."

"I shouldn't have done it. It was wrong, and it was against the law." He swallowed a spoonful of soup. "She's like a rash that just won't go away."

"When she sees her lame attempt at trying to get you back doesn't work, she will give up. If not, I will help nudge her in the right direction."

Damien laughed as he stood and put his plate in the dishwasher. "Don't nudge. Your nudging is more like pushing her over the edge of some cliff."

Dillon helped clear the table.

Gunner and Coach sat, waiting for scraps.

Damien pointed at them both. "You fed them earlier today, right?"

"Yes. But they are always hungry." She picked up the cat off the table, along with another beer, and headed towards the office. Placing him in his bed, she then turned on her computer. She scanned the file from the neighbor's security camera, logged into the secure home network and put the videos on the big screen on the wall.

"Look." She motioned towards the LCD. "Here is the night of the murder. You can see Peter leaving Frank's house." She pointed as she slowed the video. "I know it's grainy, but you can see Peter stop on the sidewalk and talk to whoever is in this truck."

Damien stood in front of the large screen, watching the last moments of Peter's life. "It feels as if Peter knows this person too. At least from his reactions." Damien turned towards Dillon. "You said the neighbor had seen this truck before?"

"Yes. Several times. He never got a license plate, but he remembers it. Gave the same description the DMV has of Corbin's truck. Or the shop's truck, anyway." Dillon took a sip of her beer.

Damien's mouth puckered. "I have an idea."

Dillon sighed. "Your ideas usually get you or us into trouble. I'm not sure we have too many favors to cash in to keep our butts out of the doghouse."

"True. But no one will know." Damian sat at his computer. He logged into his father's security company's server. "I won't know if Travis found anything on the CCTV until tomorrow. But maybe we could get a head start."

"Oh, no."

"What?"

"Don't what me. I know what you are going to do."

"Listen, no one can track this. I can get into the CCTV system and pull up records from the day in question." He used his father's software to hack into the city's CCTV. "I know we can't use this. However, we could at least give Travis an area to look in if he doesn't find it himself."

"Travis is pretty sneaky, too. I'm sure he will find it. You just don't want to wait."

"True."

Dillon moved towards his desk. She positioned herself behind his chair. She watched him put in the coordinates of Frank's house and let the computer find all the CCTVs in the area. A list propagated, showing all the cameras near Frank's address. "What address is that?" she asked when he pulled up another list of camera stations.

Damien found it hard to concentrate. Dillon leaned against his chair. With her every movement, the soft scents of vanilla and citrus filled his nose. He fell in love with the way her hair smelled the first time they met. "That's the cycle shop's address."

"Oooh, nice."

"Yeah." He smiled up at her. "Let's track Corbin."

"Totally illegal without a warrant. But good idea." She squeezed his shoulders.

"Like I said, no one can track this. They won't even know I pulled down the videos." He scanned through footage of a camera near the entrance of the cycle shop. The day of Peter's murder, Corbin pulled into the shop around 9:00 a.m. Fast forwarding through the day, the truck left multiple times, usually returning within an hour.

"Well, shit." Dillon moved to stand in front of the big screen. "Is that Peter?"

Damien slowed the film. "It sure looks like it."

"The time stamp says 4:00 p.m." She whipped her head around. "Didn't both of them say they didn't see Peter that day?"

Damien nodded. "Yes. Chrissy said she wasn't at the shop, and Corbin said he didn't see him at all." Damien slowed the film. Peter walked into the shop. Within fifteen minutes, he left.

"Look." Dillon pointed at the screen.

"That's Corbin." Damien stopped the film. "Looks like they are having a disagreement."

Dillon shrugged. "Won't hold up. Any court would say you could infer anything. But what it shows is Corbin is a big fat liar. Now we just have to find a way to get this information out without letting anyone know how we did it."

"Let's follow him." He sped up the film. Corbin could be seen leaving the shop in the truck. Damien typed on the keyboard. He scanned the next CCTV camera station. Following his grid, he tracked Corbin's truck.

They watched as the software scanned the CCTV grid and followed Corbin's truck. "Look." Damien stopped the film. He typed out a few coordinates and pulled the CCTV from the same street near the parking lot where Peter was found. "This is the only view I can find near Frank's house." The entrance to the parking area wasn't in view, but the parallel street was. Damien pointed to the screen. "This is Frank's street."

"Travis should find this." Dillon sat in her chair and spun around.

Damien chuckled. "You and that chair."

"And you bought it for me." She smiled at him.

"Yes. Best gift I ever gave you."

Dillon laughed, snorting. "Actually, it is." She turned back towards the screen. "Now we just need Corbin's truck."

Damien sped through hours of film in a few moments. "Wait. There." He slowed it down about twenty minutes after Corbin's truck left the shop. "I can text Travis to see if he can find any CCTVs near the cycle shop. That should give him a jumping-off point. And if he can find what we see now, we can use it."

They both watched as Corbin's truck drove down Frank's street. They couldn't see Frank's house from the angle of the camera. But the street was in full view. Several times, Corbin's truck circled the block until he parked.

"There. Where he is parked is just a few houses down from Frank's place." She spun around and stared at him. "That puts his truck there."

"Yes, it does." Damien closed the connection to the CCTV network. Scrubbing his tracks as he went. He logged out of his dad's software and shut down his computer. "Now, we need Travis to find the cameras in this area. Which I'm sure he has already. If not, we steer him to it." He tapped out a message on his phone. Glancing at his watch, it wasn't too late.

"Did you tell him where to look?" Dillon asked as she shut down her computer.

"I did." He walked out of the office. "Gunner!"

Gunner ran out after him, following him to the backdoor.

Damien let the dog out. They had opened the backyard area to make one large run for Mrs. C.'s dog and Gunner. He watched as the big brown lab ran to Mrs. C.'s backdoor, sniffing. He sat for a few minutes, waiting for her to open the door. "Gunner, she isn't home. Remember?"

Gunner cocked his head to the side. As if he remembered her giving him a goodbye kiss a few days ago, he bolted off, checking the parameter.

Damien closed his eyes, inhaling the crisp air. The developer sold him the undeveloped land next to his unit and on the other side of Mrs.

C.'s unit to keep other homes from being built, and forcing him to deal with neighbors. He hadn't told Dillon about his expansion plans yet, but he didn't think she would mind them. Neither of them wanted to move.

The builder had signed off on his architect's plans as long as Damien kept the outer façade the same as the other units. This gave him the go-ahead to make one large home from the two units.

Damien chuckled as he watched Gunner run back and forth. From the moment he met Dillon, he was drawn to her. He thought of her in the hotel bar that first night in Springfield. Closing his eyes, the case slammed into him.

It had been a long time since he had thought of Jason Freestone. Finding all those girls buried on his property almost made him walk away from his job. In the end, this job was his life. And even though he had other options, this job was the only thing he knew how to do.

He and Dillon had the money to leave all this behind, but neither of them could walk away from law enforcement. Giving closure to the dead was their job. A job he didn't think either of them could live without.

Gunner ran past him, chasing a squirrel along the fence line.

"Gunner, let's go," Damien yelled at the dog.

With one last look around, Gunner ran up to him.

Entering the condo, music played through the sound system. He glanced at his watch—9:00 p.m. "What is she doing now?" he checked the living room and the gym. Both were empty. He followed the music up the stairs. Their bedroom was empty. But he heard the shower running.

He stopped at the bathroom door, about to enter. Reaching for the doorknob, he yanked his hand back. He couldn't shake the feeling there was something to Camilla's claims of being stalked. As much as he wanted to say his ex-girlfriend was making up shit, the situation nagged him. "Amazing how years later, you are still messing up my life," he whispered. He pushed Camilla out of his mind as he pushed open the bathroom door.

Dillon stood under the oversized rain showerhead. The massive plume of steam almost hid her silhouette. He could see her hands braced against the wall as the water cascaded down her body.

Her long golden blonde hair almost reached the middle of her back.

Damien stripped as he watched her. He wondered what she was thinking. Where her thoughts were taking her. Opening the door, a rush of hot air hit him in the face.

She turned towards him, not speaking a word or breaking eye contact. He was beautiful. His dark hair and blue eyes made her melt. His naturally dark Italian skin color made him look like he had a year-round tan.

Her breath caught in her throat. She fell more in love with him every day. Something she thought would never happen. Not one to give her heart away, Damien had imprinted himself on her soul.

Her legs quivered as he stepped next to her. She closed her eyes as his arms wrapped around her waist. He said something, but Dillon grabbed his hair and pulled him close. Her lips melted into his. The warmth of his mouth mingled with hers and her tongue wanted more.

Damien let everything go. His lips trailed from her mouth down her neck. His hand caressed her voluptuous breast. He bent down, teasing it with his tongue. A purr-like sound rumbled in her chest, driving him crazy.

Dillon reached down, taken his length in her hand. Hard. Yet silky soft. He moaned as she squeezed. She let her hand drift downward. Letting her fingers tease the soft skin between his legs.

Damien couldn't wait any longer. He lifted her, wrapping her legs around his waist. Bracing her against the wall of the shower, he slowly entered her. The warmth of her body surrounded him. His lips covered hers, swallowing her moan.

Dillon wrapped her legs tighter around his waist. Threading her fingers through his hair, she tugged on the ends as her climax intensified. Her body trembled against his. Panting into his kiss, she bit his lip at the moment her orgasm exploded.

Damien buried his face in her neck, biting her as he released. He used the wall to keep both of them upright. 70s rock music filled the bathroom. He leaned back to find her eyes closed. "You okay?"

"Yeah." She sighed. "I'm perfectly fine. I don't know if I can stand. But I am perfectly fine."

He chuckled as he lowered her to the floor, making sure she had her balance before letting go. Damien adjusted the flow of water to the jets lining all sides of the shower. Using the keypad on the shower wall, he set the jets to pump out water at different rates and speeds. Dispensing her favorite shampoo from the wall-mounted container, he lathered up her mane. "I love this smell."

"I do, too." She rinsed her head, then slathered him in his woodsy soap. She inhaled deeply, letting his scent fill her as if it would be the last time she smelled it. "I remember the first time I met you and the way you smelled." Dillon stepped back. Her eyes turned into slits as a smirk crossed her lips. "If you had asked to come to my room that night, I would have said yes."

Damien roared back in laughter. "You are so full of shit."

Dillon smacked him. "I would have let you come up to my room. I didn't say I would let you fuck me."

"Oh, really?" Damien rinsed the soap off. "You wouldn't be able to resist me. I would've had your panties off in no time."

"Ha. Don't flatter yourself." She pushed the buttons on the keypad, turning off the water and turning on the blowers. "I love this feature."

Damien stepped out, grabbing a towel from the heated rack. "I am glad I let you talk me into the shower upgrade. But I still don't like the blowers."

Dillon stepped out, wrapping a towel around her head. Standing naked in front of the mirror, she smiled. "I hate dripping when I get out of the shower. The tub is a different story. The shower is too much work."

"Only you would think toweling off is too much work." Damien brushed his teeth as he watched her do her nightly ritual of creams on her face.

She reached over, putting a few dollops on his face. "Rub those in. You need to do this at night. It will help keep you wrinkle-free."

CHAPTER TWENTY-TWO

Wednesday 12:30 a.m.

Brycen drove the van through the dilapidated gates. He'd used his mentor's journals and found an old maintenance entrance to this state park. It was no longer in use and, therefore, no risk of security cameras. Parking on the side of the overgrown road, he opened the rear doors, where Camilla rested in a crumpled mess. He pulled another pair of surgical gloves from his pocket and put them on.

He'd learned his lesson with the first girl. A mistake that almost got him caught. His mentor wasn't happy. And although he said nothing, Brycen saw the disappointment in his eyes. He had promised him it wouldn't happen again. It took a couple more for him to find his rhythm, but he finally did.

Before he lifted Camilla out of the van, he removed a small vial from his pocket. A few drops would allow Camilla to be conscious but unable to move. Pulling down on her chin, he separated her lips enough to get the liquid in her mouth. Her body's instinct took over, and she swallowed.

He pulled Camilla closer, letting her feet dangle just off the edge of the van. "Pure perfection," he said as he dragged his fingers down her well-toned and shapely leg.

As pretty as she was, she wasn't anyone's favorite person. Camilla had a mean streak. Yet her behavior didn't dampen his desire for her. He couldn't help his attraction to her. Even though she didn't know he existed, he still felt a connection to her—one he could no longer control.

Removing his phone from his back pocket, he snapped a before picture. The before picture was for him, not his project. He needed to take a picture once he had her in position. Once he finished with her.

Camilla whimpered softly.

"Shhh. There now, sweetie," he said as he rubbed her skin.

The drug would keep her from moving, but he needed to pick up the pace. He had to get her to the designated spot and prepare her. Although he didn't worry about someone out here at this time of night, he never wanted to take chances.

He removed the headlamp from the box in the back of the van. His go box, as he called it. If someone saw it, his profession could explain away most of the items. Switching the lamp to the brightest setting, Brycen grabbed the small bag next to the box and hoisted Camilla over his shoulder. Using the fireman's carry, he headed down the trail.

Brycen thought back to when his mentor showed him how to carry someone. As a young child, he soaked up whatever his mentor told him, more like a father figure than anything else.

His mentor had written about his time in the military, explaining how he had to save his strength and energy for those moments when he needed it most. He often carried his fellow wounded soldiers like this. It wasn't about having muscles, he wrote. It boiled down to positioning. Even the smallest stature of a man could carry twice his weight if done correctly.

As a child, Brycen was impatient. He had a hard time controlling himself. Over the years, Terrance helped him. But when the illness took over, it was Brycen who had to help his mentor. The man, who was once larger than life, slowly withered away.

Brycen stumbled over the uneven path. Stopping, he adjusted Camilla on his shoulders. Once he secured her, he continued. He laughed inwardly. If Terrance saw him now, he would tell him he was doing it all wrong. "Just because I'm not doing it your way doesn't make it wrong."

When he started out, he couldn't do it exactly like his mentor did. He had no desire to rape anyone. Even when his mentor berated him for his lack of dominance, Brycen didn't change what he did. Raping wasn't his style, and he didn't need it to make him feel dominant.

The first few girls gave him clarity. However, there was one thing he had to do, just like Terrance. Brycen had to put his on his own spin on it, of course. And Terrance had reluctantly accepted the changes.

Camilla's moans brought him back to the present. "Damn. Maybe I should've waited to take you." Brycen considered his actions until this point. "I shouldn't have followed you, Camilla. But I couldn't help myself." His desire for her made him do the one thing his mentor had said never do. Do not get attached. Attachment leads to mistakes.

In the end, his obsession with her became too much. He lost control. Replaying everything he had done in his mind, he was sure he had made no missteps. "No. I won't second guess my decisions. It was her time. I can make this work." A pang of regret nestled in his belly.

Brycen's pulse sped up as he reached the end of the path. Entering the clearing, he kneeled as he lifted Camilla off his shoulders, easing her down to the ground.

Camilla groaned, wheezing lightly with each exhale of breath.

"Try to relax," Brycen said as he wiped some of her makeup from her face. "I don't know why you wear so much of this stuff. You have such natural beauty." He leaned back, letting his light hit her face, moving her chin from side to side. "Perfect."

Removing her clothes, he dressed her in the outfit he brought for her. Similar to the previous girls. The ribbons had to be just right. The corners of his mouth curved up. "It's almost time to start."

Removing his phone from his jeans, he scrolled through the pictures of the last few girls. He checked Camilla's position. It had to be just right. It would mess up the entire chain if she wasn't positioned properly.

Camilla ached. Her head pounded. She blinked. At least, she thought she did. "Where—where am I?" She said the words, but her mouth didn't move. "Am I talking? Can anyone hear me?" Not sure if she was blindfolded, she focused on the blurry pinholes of light. "I don't understand. Why can't I see anything?"

Her racing heartbeat caused pains in her chest. "What's happening? What if I'm having a heart attack? Someone, help me," she cried out. Camilla wasn't sure if the words came out of her mouth or not. "Please help me," she screamed louder.

Trying to sit up, she felt her stomach clench down, but her body wouldn't cooperate. Her pulse thumped against her skull. With every breath she took, it sounded like a freight train echoing in her ears. She tried to focus her eyes, blinking several times. Camilla felt moisture against her skin. "Am I crying? Someone? Anyone, please help me."

He shined his light on her face, wiping her cheeks. "I know you can hear me. You can't move or speak if you are trying to. I suggest you let yourself go. Don't fight it."

"Who said that?" she felt a pressure on her chest as if her heart was about to explode. "Help me!" she screamed. "Help me."

He watched her eyes as she stared straight up at the night sky. "I hope you can see the stars. Sometimes this drug affects the optic nerve. Things are too blurry." Brycen glanced up. "They are beautiful. The sky is dark, almost black. The stars look like thousands of tiny flashlights."

Camilla heard someone. She couldn't make out what they said, but she knew they were close. "You have to help me. Please. Please help me. Call for help, please."

He watched her as she stared blankly at the night sky. Brycen struggled with wanting more time with her and knowing he had to get on with it. "This won't hurt. You might feel pressure. But that's it," he said as he positioned himself across her chest, putting most of his weight on his knees. Checking the picture one last time on his phone and moving her right arm down a bit, he leaned back and surveyed his work. "That's better."

Easing the knife from its sheath on his belt, he lowered his chest, positioning his face above hers. "I wish you could see me." Using his free hand, he caressed her cheek. An overwhelming desire flooded him, and he lowered his lips to hers.

A light, airy kiss. Just one. That's all he needed. He'd never felt the urge to do this with the other girls. But he needed to feel Camilla's lips against his. His chest ached at the realization these were his last moments with her. "It's time. I'm sorry, but I can't wait any longer." He raised the knife to her throat. "Camilla, take a deep breath."

Something brushed against Camilla's lips. She tried to reach up and swat it away, but her arms were too heavy to lift. "Time? Time for what? I don't understand. Please, help me." The lights seemed brighter. The pin holes looked bigger. Maybe that's what the man meant. It was time to save her. She forced herself to calm down, knowing help was on its way.

"This won't hurt. Just breathe," Brycen said as he slid the knife across her throat.

Whatever was happening didn't hurt. Camilla felt pressure on her throat, but no pain. A warming sensation covered her skin. The fear which had engulfed her a few moments ago seemed to lesson. A slight shiver ran through her as she let go. As her mind drifted, the last person she thought of was Damien.

He watched as the blood drained from her body. This was always the best part. The blood spread on either side of her head. Her arms created a barrier or dam of sorts, allowing the crimson liquid to form a glassy pool. Her face drenched in peace, and she looked even more beautiful.

Brycen had to work fast. He'd promised his mentor he would leave the mark. Using the tip of his knife, he slowly carved a symbol into her abdomen. Same as he had done with the others.

Standing, he made one last check, making sure the position was correct. "Perfect," he said as he snapped a few photos before placing the knife back in its sheath.

He gathered his things but left Camilla's clothing. With one last look, he headed back to his van. Placing everything back in the go box, he closed the van doors. As he walked to the driver's side, he scrolled through the photos on his phone of all his girls.

Smiling as he drove out of the park, a sense of pride filled him. Continuing what his mentor had started all those years ago was his way of thanking him. He was there when no one else was. When no one else wanted him. Brycen's hands tingled with electricity. He couldn't wait to share what he'd done with Terrance.

CHAPTER TWENTY-THREE

Wednesday morning

Damien entered his office. He came in after an early morning call from Travis asking him to meet at ECD. After hanging his jacket, he went to the work area. As he walked past the glass wall of ECD, he saw Travis talking animatedly to his coworker, Detective Jim Fogle. When they saw Damien, Travis buzzed him in.

"Hey, Damien," Travis nodded towards detective Fogle. "Stop. You aren't going anywhere." Travis hit the lock on the keypad, keeping everyone out, even someone with a key card. He motioned to Damien. "This room is soundproof. What we are about to tell you doesn't go anywhere else."

Damien leaned against the counter. "Okay. So, this doesn't have anything to do with my current case?"

"Yes, and no. First, Jim has something he needs to share." Travis waited. "C'mon, Jim. Tell him."

Detective Jim Fogle glanced around. He glanced out into the VCU, making sure no one was around.

"C'mon Jim. No one can hear us, and they will just think I am going over Damien's case." Travis turned to Damien. "This is big."

Damien focused on Jim. "Detective? What is it?"

Jim fidgeted with his sweatshirt sleeve. "Man, I don't think this is a good idea, Travis."

Travis turned towards his coworker and friend. "Jim, you can trust Damien. I promise you." Travis reached out to him, touching his arm. "I promise. He can help."

"What's going on, Travis?" Damien asked.

Jim took a deep breath. "I overheard a conversation the other day. And now I know who was in the conversation."

Damien glanced between the two men. "And? What is so important about a conversation?"

Jim paced in the small area. "Fuck. Man. This will not end well. If he finds out, I know I'm dead." He looked right at Damien. "I don't know if even you can keep me alive."

"Okay. Let's start from the beginning." Damien waited. "It's okay. I promise we can keep you safe."

Jim sat in a chair and told him about the bathroom incident. "I was in the canteen last night. I worked late, and Marcia sometimes stays open for the late shift. Two men were talking with other detectives. I recognized one voice. I tried to play like I was stupid.

"One of the Vice detectives asked me something before I could leave. Another guy asked me a question, and I knew immediately he was one of the guys in the bathroom." He rubbed his temples. "Shit, I can't prove it, but I know it was him. The guys in the bathroom were talking about the Metacruze case."

Damien watched as Jim took several deep breaths. "Okay. Who do you think the two guys were?"

"I don't think, I fucking know who at least one of them is," Jim said.

"Okay. I believe you. Who is it?" Damien asked.

"Tell him, Jim." Travis pushed his friend.

"Fuck. It was," he stopped short.

Damien saw the fear in the man's eyes. "Jim. Who was the man?"

Jim looked at the floor. "Promise me you will keep me safe." He looked Damien in the eye. "I know you can help do that. Promise me."

"You have my word. Who was the other man?" Damien asked.

"DEA Agent Johnson." Jim felt the pressure ease in his chest. Just saying the name out loud felt like a weight had been lifted.

Damien's jaw dropped open. He shouldn't have been surprised, but having someone hear such damning evidence against Johnson could be the break they needed to catch him.

"Did they say anything else while in the bathroom? Something you may not think is important?" Damien waited. His foot tapped on the floor.

"Yeah. First, Johnson said he made sure Cutter wouldn't spill the beans about the box in evidence. Then at some point, the other guy, the one who sounds familiar, mentioned he helped Johnson because Johnson got his brother out of trouble," Jim said.

Damien crossed his arms over his chest. "And you aren't sure who the other guy was? You can't say whose voice it was?"

"If I heard it, I would recognize it."

"Okay. Was there anything else said?" Damien asked.

"Umm, I didn't mention this to Travis," he glanced at his friend, then back at Damien. "DEA Johnson mentioned you were under investigation, and if you and your faggot-ass partner stick your nose in his business, you would have more to worry about than any investigation." Jim sheepishly smiled. "His words."

Damien waved him off. "No worries, sounds like him." He thought for a moment. He couldn't tell either of these guys anything about the investigation into Johnson. "Listen, say nothing. Not to your family or girlfriends. Not even Katie," he said, glancing at Travis.

Travis zipped his mouth shut. "Not saying anything."

Damien turned towards Jim. "You're sure you didn't recognize the other voice?"

Jim shook his head. "He wasn't in the group in the canteen. I'm sure if I heard his voice, I would recognize it."

Damien stood. "Jim, don't worry. DEA Johnson doesn't know you were in there. Just act like you normally would. Don't act weird or suspicious." Damien pulled a business card from his pocket. He scribbled a number on the back. "If you ever feel threatened, or think someone is following you, anything. You call that number and ask for Nicky. Tell him you know me, and I told you to call. He will get you help and call me."

Damien reached out and grabbed the man's shoulder. "You did the right thing telling me. You can trust Travis. He won't tell a soul. I need you to be normal. Do you understand?"

Jim nodded.

"I need to go to my office. Travis, did you get anything on the CCTV?"

"Yeah, I did. It was enough to get a search warrant. I took the information you gave me and I could see Peter enter the cycle shop. Hey, how did you know to look at the cycle shop footage?" Travis asked.

"Something Dillon said after interviewing Frank's neighbors. It made me think to look at the shop," he said, grinning. "Glad it paid off. Did you contact ADA Flowers?"

Travis gave him a cockeyed look. "Hmm, I think there is more to that answer." He chuckled, shaking his head. "Yes. Early this morning. I sent the ADA an email asking for a search warrant for the shop and to see if she could stretch it to include Corbin's home and his sister's as well." He shrugged. "It may be a stretch, but it doesn't hurt to ask."

"I appreciate you going the extra mile. Send me the footage." Damien headed towards the door. As he walked past the glass, he pulled his phone from his pocket and texted Dillon. He then put in a call to his captain.

At his desk, his phone pinged. Dillon said she would call in an hour. He sat thinking about his next move. He had to concentrate on Peter and his murder. It was going to be hard to keep his hands off the Johnson mess. The only thing he knew for sure was that his captain and Dillon's director had to be told ASAP. He just wanted to talk to Dillon first. He sent her a text saying for her to call him now.

"What is so damn important you can't wait?"

He closed his office door and turned on his radio to block out his voice. He told her about the conversation with Detective Fogle. There was a long silence on the phone. "Dillon?"

"Holy shit."

"Yeah, I know."

"What are you going to do?"

"I'm going to talk to the captain, and I'm sure he will call Director Sherman. I just wanted to talk to you first. Give you a heads-up. Here's the thing. I need to figure out who here has a brother who got caught up in something requiring DEA Johnson's help."

"That would definitely give us the other person. I bet he would turn on Johnson in a heartbeat," Dillon said.

Damien heard something outside his office. "Hang on..." he rose and stepped quietly to his door. He yanked it open to see no one there. He glanced down the hallway—nothing. "Okay, I'm back."

"What's going on?"

"I thought I heard something outside my door."

"Shit. That's not good."

"There was no one there when I opened it. No one is even in the pen." Damien glanced out through the open door. "I'm sure I just imagined it."

"Let's hope so."

"Listen, stay at the house. Call me if you go anywhere. Do you have anywhere to go?" Damien asked as he moved to his open door.

"No. I was going to come to your office in an hour to finish helping you guys with the case."

"Just stay at home. Joe and I will come get you. I'm sure the captain will want us out of here when he hears what I know." Damien scanned the hallways. He walked to the other side of the pen and glanced towards the hallway leading to the elevator area.

He was about to turn around when he saw Officer Cutter from the evidence locker walk out of the men's bathroom. He nodded at him. Cutter waved but headed in the opposite direction.

"Damien? Hello?"

"Hey, sorry. Just stay put. I'll come get you."

"What just happened?"

"Nothing. I promise. I'm going to call the captain again. I don't want to wait. Dillon, I love you."

"I love you too. I'll be ready in an hour."

The line went dead. He put his phone in his pocket and headed towards Officer Cutter. Damien entered the stairwell, pausing on the landing. He heard a muffled conversation coming from below.

He put his back against the wall and tiptoed down the stairs. As he descended, he heard a man and a woman.

"I didn't hear everything. Just something about him being investigated. He must be in some kind of trouble," the man said.

"I wonder if he really is on the take. I just always thought he was a straight arrow," the woman sneezed. "I think I have a cold."

"Don't give it to me. Maybe we have it all wrong. Maybe he is a straight arrow, and someone is trying to frame him. You know DEA Johnson hates him."

The woman laughed. "Oh yeah, he does."

Their conversation stopped when a door below him opened. Damien moved quickly to exit the stairwell when he heard footsteps coming towards him. Once inside the hallway, he darted into the bathroom. Not sure if Cutter heard anything, Damien decided he wasn't taking any chances and needed to set up the meeting with the captain away from DC. He dialed the captain's number.

"Well, since you can't wait for me to call you, and now you call me on my private number, it must be important."

"Sorry, Captain, it is. Can you meet me at my house in an hour?"

"Are you serious? What's going on, Damien?"

Damien glanced around. A few of his detectives were now in the pen. He acknowledged them as he made his way to his office. "I can't say much, but it has to do with my biggest fan."

"DEA Johnson?"

"Yes, sir. You need to come to my house. I'm calling Director Sherman and having him come over as well."

"Okay. One hour."

The line went dead. Damien immediately dialed Joe.

"What do you want?"

"I need you to be at my house in an hour. Can Taylor drop you off?" Damien grabbed his jacket and headed for the elevator.

"Yeah, she can on her way to work. Is it bad?" Joe asked.

"Not sure. It could be." Damien was about to leave the area when Detective Travis called out to him. "One hour, Joe. Be there." He hung up his phone as he walked towards Travis. "What's up?"

"Flowers called me. She said she should have the search warrant by lunch."

"Hey, that's great. I might call you and have you email it to me, if I don't get back here." Damien turned towards the elevator and felt a hand on his arm.

"Listen, I think Jim is terrified." Travis glanced around, making sure no one was in earshot.

"I know he is. I promise you; I will do my best to keep him safe. But I need you to make sure he keeps this to himself."

"He isn't telling anyone."

"He told you," Damien said.

Travis snickered. "Only because he was scared to death to tell you." Travis glanced at his phone when it pinged. "I got to go. I'll call you when I get the warrant."

Damien waved him off as he stepped into the elevator. As he exited and walked down the hallway towards the garage, he noticed all eyes seemed to be on him. He chuckled inwardly at the gossip Officer Cutter must have spread. Word travels fast at DC.

He nodded at the evidence officer as he walked by. "Hey, Cutter." He had to work extra hard to hide his smile. As he passed a few detectives from the Burglary unit, one of the canteen ladies hollered his name. He turned to wave. Lowering his hand, the hair on the back of his neck stood on end. Stopping, he spun around.

About twenty feet down the hallway, Lieutenant Ratcliff from Narcotics stared at him from the doorway of one of the interrogation rooms.

Damien locked eyes with the man. He held his stare for a few minutes before Lieutenant Ratcliff disappeared into the room.

As Damien headed to his SUV, he glanced back over his shoulder. He didn't know Lieutenant Ratcliff except for the fact that he was trying to get his Captain's position when he retired at the end of this year and that the lieutenant was a lifer and had every intention of dying in this job. Damien also knew he was good friends with Johnson. And that alone was enough to put him on Damien's radar.

CHAPTER TWENTY-FOUR

Joe kissed Taylor as she stood at her truck, holding the door open for her. "Thanks for running me to Damien's. My truck should be finished today."

"Of course." She climbed into the driver's seat, closing the door as Joe walked to the other side.

Climbing in, Joe buckled his seat belt. "Please don't leave work today. Order lunch. Have it delivered."

She reached over to him and ran her fingers through his hair. "I like the longer locks on you."

"Quit deflecting."

"I'm not. I just don't want to think about Adnon."

"Well, you need to. Your brother has it out for you. I don't know how far he will take this. I think it goes far beyond the money." Joe pulled her close to him.

"Family members do strange things for inheritances."

"Yeah, but it isn't millions like Dillon's family. We are talking about a few hundred thousand dollars. I know he already had money before your parents died. I think it's about control. He wants to control you. He thinks of you as his property."

Taylor started the truck and pulled out of the driveway.

"Taylor, promise me."

Looking over at him, she nodded. "I promise. I won't leave the facility. I will also tell my boss and let security know what is going on. They can make sure anyone with his description is questioned if they try to enter the area. You have to go through two guard shacks, and the facility is locked down. It is the crime lab, after all."

"Still, when someone is determined, they can get past anything to get what they want."

"I'm not sure how late I will be. I will call you throughout the day. Make sure you tell me if you are leaving early or if you are going to be home before me."

"I will."

"Do you have your gun?" he asked.

"Of course. It's in my bag, but I brought my holster. I will clip it on when I get to work."

Joe stared out the window as Taylor whizzed past the morning traffic.

"Joe, I promise to be extra diligent. Please try not to worry. You have a case to concentrate on."

"I can't help but worry." He took her hand in his and kissed the back of it.

CHAPTER TWENTY-FIVE

Wednesday 8:30 a.m.

Damien pulled in front of his home, not bothering to park in the garage. He had no idea the course of action his captain or the director would want to take knowing the information, but he had a suspicion this would shift the undercover sting into high gear.

Stepping onto the porch, a car pulled in behind him. Damien smiled at Director Sherman as he walked to his car, meeting him at the end of the walkway. "Hey, Phillip." He reached out to shake the man's hand.

"Hey, Damien. I'm gathering you didn't feel safe saying anything while you were at DC." Sherman followed him up to the front door.

"Not at all. Hey, you haven't let it slip about the party for Dillon?" he asked at the edge of the porch. He glanced at the front door.

"No. And Laura needs Taylor's number to coordinate."

"I will make sure she gets it. I'm hoping we will have this case wrapped up soon, and we can figure out a suitable date for the party."

Phillip laughed. "You know she hates surprises. Are you sure you want to risk your life?"

Damien laughed. "I think this will be a surprise she likes." He unlocked the door. Gunner bounded towards them. The dog ran right past him and almost leaped into Phillip's arms. "What the heck?" Damien raised his hands.

"Hey buddy." Phillip dropped to one knee to get closer to the dog. "I haven't seen you in a long time. How you doing, big fella?"

Gunner howled, wiggling. He head-butted Phillip's chest.

"He seems really happy," Phillip said, standing.

"He's spoiled rotten. He also remembers you saved him. No wonder he loves you most." Damien looked up just as Dillon walked around the corner. Her eyes lit up at the sight of her director.

"Phillip, I didn't know you were coming over." She squinted at Damien. "Did you call him about the conversation?"

"Yes, but he doesn't know about the content of said conversation."

"What conversation?" Phillip asked, hugging his agent, who was more like his daughter. Which made being her boss extremely hard.

Damien headed towards the kitchen. "Want some coffee? It's why I needed you to come here. But I would like to wait for Captain Mackey."

"Oh boy, a full house. I just made a pot." Dillon followed Damien into the kitchen.

"Coffee sounds wonderful." Phillip sat at the table. He laughed when the cat took a chair. "What does he want?"

"Food." Damien shooed him down. "He always wants food. Him and Gunner." He pointed to Dillon. "It's her fault."

"He's just jealous." Dillon grabbed four mugs. "Is Joe coming too?"

Damien nodded as the doorbell rang. He ran to the front door to find Captain Mackey and Joe standing there. "Perfect timing. Come in. We have coffee."

Joe followed the captain in. "I'm guessing this will not be good news."

"All depends on how you look at it," Damien said.

In the kitchen, Dillon placed a bunch of muffins and scones, which Damien's mother had baked for them, on the table.

"Ooh muffins." Joe grabbed one, along with a cup of coffee, and leaned against the counter.

Damien grabbed a cup of coffee and stood next to his partner. "I have something you need to know." His eyes traveled between Joe, Phillip, and Captain Mackey. He told them about the conversation Jim had over-heard.

Director Sherman dragged a hand down his face. "How reliable is this detective?"

"Jim is a good cop. He can be trusted. He's really scared." Damien took a bite of a muffin.

Phillip turned toward the captain. "I'll let you tell Chief Rosenthal. But we need to come up with a plan. If Johnson finds out about Jim, he will kill him. I'm sure of that."

Damien told them about overhearing Cutter and one of the canteen workers. "It seems like everyone thinks I am under investigation. I hate that my men are having to deal with the rumors, but so far, the front is holding pretty damn good." He also told them about the stare-down with Lieutenant Ratcliff as he was leaving DC.

"Do you think he could be the other voice Jim heard?" Captain Mackey drank his coffee.

"I do not know. I don't see Ratcliff being dirty. Jim said that the other voice mentioned helping his little brother. I know Ratcliff had a younger brother who got into some trouble. But so did Detective Ardroin from Robbery. It could be either of them, or it could be someone else." Damien watched as Dillon sat silent.

"We need help." Joe grabbed a second muffin. "Your mom made these, didn't she?"

Damien nodded. "Yes. If you call her, she will make you a bunch."

"I'm calling later today." Joe laughed at Dillon's stare.

Phillip looked at Dillon. "What do you think about all this?"

"I think we have someone in DC who is up to his eyeballs in mud. I'm just not sure how we can find out who." Dillon refilled everyone's coffee cup.

"I have an idea." Damien glanced around the room.

"What?" Captain Mackey asked.

"We should bring Detective Travis in on this." Damien caught the look from Dillon. "Hear me out. He already knows based on what Jim said. And, he can find out information. He knows how to search and find things people think are hidden."

"I think it's a good idea." Joe chimed in. "Travis can be trusted, and he is a damn good detective. If it weren't for him, we never would have cracked the Metacruze case."

Captain Mackey looked at Phillip. "Do you feel comfortable bringing Travis on?"

Phillip pinched the bridge of his nose. "I don't see a way around it. We need someone on the inside who can get information without looking suspicious. This guy seems to fit the role. He helps all the units, right?"

"Yeah, he handles all the cyber shit. He and his team are the guys to go to whenever someone needs information, or a hard drive searched." Damien placed his coffee mug on the counter. "I think he would work. He can get into the other units and ask questions without anyone suspecting anything."

Captain Mackey finished his coffee. He stood. "Make it happen. Let him know today. Away from DC." He patted Phillip on the back. "I will speak with Rosenthal. You talk to your men involved and let's come up with something we can use to nail this fucker. I want the name of the dirty cop from DC. I hate dirty cops."

Phillip rose. "I think we can come up with something in the next few days. Let's shoot for next week. We can meet here and discuss how to proceed."

Dillon walked the men to the door. Captain Mackey left first. She waved as he drove off. She turned to see her director staring at her. "What?"

"Don't what me. How are you doing?" he asked her.

"I'm fine. I need to come over." She leaned against the doorway.

"Both Laura and I would like that. I know you were just over for dinner. But we would love to see more of you. And Damien." He smiled at her.

"I know. I will get better at this. I promise."

"There's nothing to get better at. Just know we love you, Dillon, and we are here for you." He reached out and took her in his arms. "I love having you as my agent. I get to see you every day. But it is the hardest part of the job. So many times, I want to hug you, and I know I can't. Not at work anyway." He squeezed her.

Dillon wrapped her arms around him. Her heart melted. The hard exterior seemed to fall away around him. "I love you guys, too. I'm pretty lucky to have you and Laura in my life."

He lifted her chin. "We are always here. If I ever have to choose you or this job, I will choose you. Just remember that." He kissed her cheek and hugged her one more time. "Stay safe." He started to leave, then turned around. "I suppose you are going to keep working with Damien and Joe on his current case?"

"If I can."

"When will you be cleared?"

"My last meeting with the psychologist has been moved to next week."

"Okay. You're not lead on this case. But you can work with them. Help them figure out things. That's it. I'm already letting you do too much without being cleared." Standing on the porch, he stared at her. "Call Laura. She needs to hear your voice."

"I will call tonight."

He chuckled. "I honestly don't know when it happened."

Her brow wrinkled. "When what happened?"

"When Laura and I became so attached to you. It was before your grandparent's murder. We used to stay up late worrying about you." He reached out, caressing her cheek. "I think I have always felt more for you than just a boss. Something about you."

She could see the moisture forming in his eyes. She took his hand in hers.

"Dillon, Laura and I just want to make sure you know how much we care about you. I, we—think of you like a daughter. You need to remember that when I'm grilling you."

She laughed. "I will try to keep that in mind. Especially when we are in the office."

He blinked, keeping the tears at bay. "Just call Laura."

"I will. I promise." She watched him walk to his car and drive away. When she turned around, Damien was standing there. "Well, that was some meeting," she said, closing the door.

"How you doing? You okay?"

"Yes. I'm fine." She locked the door. "What do you know about Corbin? Did you find anything out from Travis?"

As they entered the kitchen, they found Joe talking to Coach and sharing a muffin with him and Gunner.

"Stop. You are going to make them fatter than Dillon already has." Damien sat at the table. When Dillon sat, he told them what Travis had found out.

Dillon couldn't hide her smirk.

"What? What am I missing?" Joe asked.

"Your boy here funneled information to Travis in hopes he would find what he already knew." Dillon took Coach in her arms and snuggled him against her chest.

"Oh, using Dad's software, huh?" Joe laughed at his partner's stare.

"Well, it paid off." Damien stretched. "So, you two ready to grill this asshole. See if we can get him to shake loose and confess?"

"What's the plan?" Joe grabbed a soda pop from the refrigerator and a muffin for the road.

"I'm not sure. Let's just get in the SUV and figure it out on the way."

"Sounds good," Joe said.

Damien watched as Dillon put her weapon in her holster. With everything going on with DEA Johnson, he didn't think it was such a bad idea. He just hoped she didn't shoot anyone.

CHAPTER TWENTY-SIX

Damien pulled into the cycle shop parking lot. "No big party today."

Joe glanced around. "Hey," he pointed to the other side of the parking lot. "That's the truck." The nose of a black truck stuck out just past the building.

Dillon pulled up a few photos she had downloaded from the computer. "I need to walk over there, but the front end sure as hell looks like it." She held her phone out, showing Joe the photos. "I think we wait to show these to him."

Damien twisted, looking at her in the backseat. "What do you have in mind?"

She scooted towards the middle of the seat. "I think we should nudge. When will you get the search warrant? That would help a lot."

Damien opened his phone and texted Travis in ECD. "Let's see if we can get anything." His phone pinged. "Travis said he is waiting. ADA Flowers said it went through. She's just waiting for the paperwork."

"Great. Let's go in and try to catch him in a lie. As soon as you get word the warrant is valid, I say we get Travis and one of your detectives over to Corbin's place while we have a squad car pick Corbin up here. Then we can question him at DC." Dillon looked at each of them. "Sound good?"

"Sounds good to me. I think getting him on our turf works best," Joe said, opening the door.

Damien and Dillon followed him to the front of the store. He called dispatch requesting one squad car and advised them to have the officers wait in the parking lot for further instructions. He also requested no lights or sirens.

At the sound of the door chime, Corbin glanced up from the counter. "Detectives. What can I do for you?" He placed his palms down on the counter, leaning forward.

Several customers watched the interaction.

"Hey, Corbin," Damien stepped up to the counter. "Can we get a few moments with you? We have some follow-up questions."

"Uh, yeah. My sister isn't here. She's having a hard time with all of this." Corbin motioned for them to follow him to the back.

"I imagine she is," Dillon said.

"We will need to speak with her as well." Joe watched him as he shuffled a few chairs around in the small meeting room.

Corbin motioned for everyone to sit down. "I don't understand why you need to speak with her. She said she hadn't seen him before he was killed."

"It's part of our job. We have some follow-up questions for her." Joe smiled as he took a seat across from Corbin.

"We are waiting for some video to be analyzed," Dillon said.

Corbin's head whipped around. "What video?" he placed his arms on the table, then quickly brought them back, resting his hands in his lap. "I don't understand. Video from where?"

"Oh, a neighbor directly across from Frank's house has a security system. She was gracious enough to give us the last, what, twenty days of footage?" Dillon directed her question towards Damien.

"Yeah. That sounds about right," Damien said. "Imagine our luck."

Corbin shifted in his seat. He bit his bottom lip, twisting his head to each side, making a cracking sound. "What did you find on the surveillance? Anything interesting? I know my sister would like to know if you are any closer to finding Peter's killer."

The office door opened, and Chrissy walked in.

Corbin stood, rushing to her. "Chrissy, what are you doing here?" He pulled her close for a tight hug.

She pushed him back. "I needed a diversion. Timothy was up front. He told me you guys were here," she smiled at the detectives. "Please tell me you have some news."

Damien sat up, catching a nod from Joe. "Yes. We might have some information. We were just explaining to Corbin that we have home security surveillance from one of Frank's neighbors."

Chrissy moved to the table, taking a seat directly across from Damien. "Do you have anything? Can you see Peter?"

Dillon leaned into the table. "We do, and yes, we can see Peter." She turned her attention to Corbin. "First, we need some background. Can you tell us if you have ever been to Frank's house?"

Corbin sucked in his cheeks, biting the insides. His posture became rigid as his gaze darted to his sister. "No. I don't really know where Frank lived."

Dillon cocked her head to the side. "Chrissy, have you ever been to Frank's house?"

Chrissy struggled. She took a deep breath. "Yes. I really liked Frank."

Joe placed his elbows on the table. "Corbin, I'm confused. When we were here the other day, you seemed surprised Chrissy knew who Frank was. Why?"

Corbin fixed his stare on Joe. He spoke in a low, firm voice. "You must have made a mistake."

Joe shook his head. "Nope. No mistake. When Chrissy first mentioned Frank, you were surprised and even commented on clarifying she knew Frank. Can you tell us why?"

Corbin flinched back. "Um, no. No. You are making a mistake. I must have been referring to something else. I'm sure you have made a mistake."

Joe spoke when Damien's phone pinged. He showed the message to Dillon first, then stretched his arm out so Joe could see the warrants had come through.

"Corbin," Dillon said.

Corbin turned slowly towards the agent. Not taking his stare off Joe until the last minute. "What?"

"I asked you earlier, just a few moments ago, if you had ever been to Frank's house, and you said no."

"That's right." Corbin sat smugly in his chair.

She pulled her phone out and pulled up the photos from the security system. "Okay, I just needed to clarify. Also, your black truck out there. Do you drive it regularly?"

Corbin dragged his hand down his face. "Why do you care when or how much I drive my truck? It's registered to the cycle shop. So yeah, I drive it regularly."

"Okay. You just said you had never driven to Frank's home, and you had never been in the neighborhood before." She lifted her phone, making sure that Chrissy could see the picture. "Could you explain why your black truck was seen in Frank's neighborhood?"

Corbin pushed his chair away from the table. "I was never there."

Damien stood. "We have some more questions for you. But we need you to come with us to the station."

Joe stood, then made his way around the back of the conference table, positioning himself to help Corbin leave the room.

Chrissy rose. "I'm sure you guys have made a mistake. Corbin, tell them they made a mistake."

Corbin took his sister in a hug. "It's not my truck. I'll get this straightened out." His nostrils flared as Joe came closer to him. "Are you going to arrest me?"

Joe shrugged. "Not at all, Corbin. We just need to get some answers, and the best way to do that is at our headquarters. Once we get it straightened out and make sure it isn't your truck, then we can move on and find Peter's killer."

Damien had moved to the door of the office. "Chrissy, you are welcome to go with us. He will have to go in the squad car to District Central, but you can follow behind them."

"Yes. I want to. I want to be in the questioning. I'm sure I can help clear this up." Chrissy took her brother's hand. "Don't argue. They aren't arresting you. They just need to clear up a few things. Do this for me."

Corbin kissed her on the cheek. "I will. Make sure you follow us."

Dillon held open the door as Damien walked out first and then Corbin, followed by Joe and Chrissy. She tapped Chrissy on the shoulder. "Could you bring the registration for the truck?"

Chrissy glanced between Dillon and Corbin. "Corbin?"

"Um, it's in the truck. Just drive the truck." He threw her the keys just before they entered the main shop area.

Dillon smiled. "That's a great idea." She smiled at Damien, who raised an eyebrow at her.

Once in the parking lot, two police officers exited their car. "Lieutenant Kaine."

"Hey, Charlie. We need you to give Corbin a ride to DC. Take him and his sister into one of the interview rooms." Damien motioned for the officer to handcuff Corbin. He glanced down at his shoes and realized he was wearing the same boots from the other day. "Corbin, handcuffing you is procedure. We are not arresting you." Damien gave him a slight push towards the squad car. He patted him down. The only thing he had was his wallet. Damien placed it back in his pants pocket.

"Is handcuffing him really necessary?" Chrissy asked, glancing around the lot at the customers and employees gathering to watch.

"It is." Dillon pointed to the truck. "Just follow the squad car. They will direct you where to park in the garage." She walked over to the squad car after they placed Corbin in the backseat. She leaned into the officer. "Make sure they park on the west side, near evidence processing. But don't tell her. We have a warrant for the vehicle."

The officer nodded without responding.

When Chrissy pulled the truck out from the far side of the building, the officer entered the cruiser and left the parking lot.

Dillon stood with Joe and Damien. "I told him to have her park near the evidence processing area."

Damien walked to his SUV. "That's perfect. He's also wearing the shoes from the other night. When we get there, I will get the warrants printed, and we will get a crime scene tech to come and collect what evidence we need." He started the SUV.

"I can't wait to arrest this fucker." Joe popped a piece of gum into his mouth, placing the pack back into the console.

"Can you not buy your own gum?" Damien asked.

"No. Why would I? You always have some." Joe flashed a Cheshire cat grin at him.

CHAPTER TWENTY-SEVEN

Wednesday 11:30 a.m.

Damien pulled into the garage at DC. He could see Corbin's truck parked just outside the processing bay. "Let's head up to my office and get the warrants. From there, I will text CST Roger Newberry and see who he can have collect everything."

As the three of them walked into the basement area, several officers made quick eye contact with Damien and then averted their stare.

Dillon noticed several people speaking in whispers as they walked to the elevator. When the elevator doors shut, she cocked her head to the side. "What's up with everyone?"

Damien stared with a fixed look of concentration at his phone, checking for a text or missed call. "I'm not sure." His voice strained as his gaze shifted between Joe and Dillon. "I have a feeling something bad is about to happen."

Joe's eyebrows drew together. "No. Nothing bad is going to happen. You're overreacting."

Damien shook his head. "Then why was everyone staring and whispering at me and Dillon?" he asked.

As the doors to the elevator opened, Joe stepped out. "They weren't. You guys are just imagining things."

Entering VCU, all of Damien's detectives gathered in the center of the pen. Several other officers and detectives from other units were standing around talking.

The minute they saw the three of them, all conversations stopped.

Detective Hall rubbed his chin, moving his hand to the back of his neck. "Damien, are you okay?"

Damien shrugged. "Why wouldn't I be okay?"

Detective Hall's eyes widened. "You haven't heard the news?"

Joe stood at his desk. "Heard what news?"

"Um." Detective Hall stared at his partner, Detective Alvarez.

She shook her head. "I think you need to speak with Captain Mackey."

Damien's eyes shifted around. "Why would I need to speak with

Captain Mackey? What's going on, Hall?" he glanced around, making eye contact with a few of his detectives. "C'mon, guys. What's going on?"

Detective Jamal Harris stepped closer. "It's bad news. Really bad news."

Dillon placed her hands on her hips. "This is crap, guys. If you know something, then tell us."

Joe sat on the corner of his desk. "Jenkins, Hall, what's up? What do you guys know?"

Damien folded his arms across his chest. "Tell me." He waited.

Captain Mackey walked around the corner.

Dillon turned around, following the stares of the other detectives. Her brow furrowed when she saw her director.

"Damien. I need you and Dillon to meet us in the conference room." Captain Mackey stood on the outside of the pen. He waved his hands to the other detectives in the area. "I need you guys to do your job. This doesn't concern you." He turned towards Joe. "I need you to gather everything on your current case. The one you and Damien are working on, and come to the conference room."

Damien sighed, looking at Joe. He tilted his head downward, looking up through squinted eyes. "Do you still think I'm imagining things?" Taking Dillon's hand, he led the way to the conference room.

Dillon squeezed his hand, tightening her grip. "It's going to be okay," she said, leaning into him.

When Damien entered the empty conference room, he shut the door and spun around to face her. "What the hell is going on?" he said in a hushed tone.

"I don't know." Her voice was raspy and low. "What the fuck is Phillip doing here? Do you think it has to do with DEA Johnson?"

Damien's eyes darted towards the door. "I don't know. But everyone was acting like we have done something. Do you think Camilla could have said something?"

"I guess. It makes sense. Especially if she made it out to be more than what actually happened."

He pulled her close to him. "I'm worried," he said, kissing the top of her head. "This doesn't feel right."

Dillon wrapped her arms around him. "I'm right here with you." She looked up. "Look at me. Whatever we have to face, we will face it together."

Damien hugged her tighter. He was about to speak when the door opened and Captain Mackey walked in.

Director Sherman gave a slight nod to Dillon as he sat in a chair. "Dillon, we need you and Damien to take a seat."

Joe walked into the conference room, closing the door. "I have our current case file right here, Captain."

"Thank you." Captain Mackey took the file from Joe and read some notes. "Do you have anybody in custody or for questioning yet?"

Joe cocked his head to the side, glancing over at Damien.

"Don't look at Damien. I asked you a question." Captain Mackey waited for a response.

"We brought in the brother only a few moments ago. He's downstairs in interrogation," Joe said.

Captain Mackey closed the file, placing it in front of Joe. He turned his attention to Dillon and his best lieutenant. "Damien, when was the last time you spoke with Camilla?"

"She came by here the other day. Stood out in the pen trying to get us to open an investigation." Damien nodded in Dillon's direction. "Was that yesterday or the day before?"

"Yesterday." Dillon squared up, locking her stare on her boss. "Philip, what's going on?"

Captain Mackey hesitated. He closed his eyes for a tense second. "Damien, they found Camilla early this morning in a state park. She's been murdered."

Dillon gasped at the news. She reached over and took Damien's hand in hers.

Damien's eyes bulged. All of his body movement froze, even his breathing. He tried to say something, but his throat felt as if it had seized shut.

"I'm so sorry." Captain Mackey reached over and patted his forearm. "I know this is hard news to hear."

No tears rolled down Damien's face. Two lumps in his throat made it next to impossible for him to swallow. "Can you tell me anything?" he asked in a shaky, disbelieving voice. His gaze wandered around the room, unable to settle on one person.

"I can't tell you anything. The only thing I'm willing to say is where she was found. Channahon State Park." Captain Mackey sat back in his chair.

Dillon narrowed her focus, squinting at her boss and Captain Mackey. "Why can't you tell us anything else?

"I'm sorry it has to be like this, but we need you and Dillon to tell us where you were yesterday evening. Between the hours of 11 p.m. And 1 a.m."

Damien's shoulders drooped. He scooted his chair back, placing his elbows on his knees and resting his head in his hands. He didn't respond.

"Damien," Captain Mackey spoke.

Damien took a long breath in through his nose and breathed it out through his mouth. "Are you asking me for an alibi, Sir?"

Captain Mackey stared at his lieutenant. "Yes."

Damien let out a sardonic laugh, looking at Phillip. "I guess you are also wanting an alibi?"

Phillip's face tightened. "Everyone knows how contentious your relationship with Camilla was."

Damien's skin tingled. He tamped down the anger. "You guys, and I'm assuming every one of my men, think I can murder her because of our contentious relationship."

Dillon glared at her director. On some level, she knew this was her director asking for this, but it still cut deep. "We were at our home."

"Together." Damien sneered at them. "I guess we are each other's alibi."

"Can you prove you stayed at your house?" Captain Mackey asked.

"I don't fucking believe this. Camilla came and said she thought she was being stalked. Everyone heard her." Damien dragged his hand down his face.

Dillon spoke up. "You can check our security. It was set just before 9 p.m. It wasn't disengaged until 6 a.m. this morning. We sure as hell weren't at a state park last night."

Joe shifted in his seat. "Let's get Travis over to Damien's house. Let him comb over his security system."

Captain Mackey scrutinized his detective. He glanced over at Director Sherman. "Make it happen. I want him over there now." The captain sighed. "Listen, you, of all people, should know this is part of the drill. You would be the first suspect on any law enforcement's radar." Captain Mackey sent a sideways glance towards Director Phillips.

Damien shook his head. "Wow. Okay. Maybe if I was a stranger. I guess working for you for the last six years means nothing."

Dillon scrutinized her boss. "You guys really think we killed her?"

"Whether we think you killed her is kind of irrelevant," Director Phillips said.

"Um, no, it isn't irrelevant." Dillon looked down at her hands in her lap.

Damien's eyes widened. "Wait, that's why you brought Joe in." His gaze moved around the table. "You're going to suspend us."

"Damien, until we can confirm you had nothing to do with Camilla's death, we can't have you around other open cases or anywhere near Camilla's murder." Captain Mackey turned to Joe. "You can finish this case you have now." He pointed to the folder. "How close are you to closing it?"

"I think we can wrap this up in a few hours. Maybe a day," Joe said.

"Then get it done." Captain Mackey turned towards Damien and Dillon. "I need you two to go home."

Damien's pulse pounded against his temple. A radiating pain formed at the base of his skull. "Are you going to make us turn in our badges and guns? "

"No. I'm not asking you for your badge and gun. I need you to stay away from DC and any open cases until we can get this straightened out." Captain Mackey leaned back in his chair. "I know this is hard, Damien. But I need you to work with us."

Damien stood. "I'm going to go get my things from the office. Joe, you know what to do on this case," he said as he stepped towards the door. "Tell Travis to come over anytime."

Joe nodded. "Okay. Don't worry about this case. I'll close it. I got it covered."

Director Phillips and Captain Mackey both stood.

"Damien, you'll be back to work as soon as we can clear you. As soon as we can prove you two had nothing to do with Camilla's death," Captain Mackey said.

Damien squinted at his boss. "I'm surprised we have to prove we didn't kill her."

Captain Mackey looked at Philip. "I'm assuming you do not want Dillon anywhere near us or the FED building until this is cleared."

"Yes. Dillon, I know it's hard to swallow. But as long as there's any way somebody can accuse you of inappropriate behavior, we need to keep you away from cases." Director Sherman waited for her to respond.

"I get it." Dillon turned to Damien. "I'm ready to go."

"There is one more thing, Dillon." Director Sherman took a step towards her. "We will bring in a new profiler." His face softened at her expression. He reached out, touching her upper arm. "Listen, the new profiler isn't replacing you. He's going to help clear you guys, and he can also get the investigation started into Camilla's death. Once we can show you two had nothing to do with it, we will reinstate you."

Captain Mackey folded his hands in front of him. "Joe can handle this case. I will step in to make sure VCU runs smoothly. Just give us some time, Damien."

Damien nodded as he opened the conference room door. He glanced over at the pen, catching the odd stare from a few of his men. After grabbing some items from his office, he headed back to the pen. Standing in front of his men, he took a deep breath. "I'm being relieved of my position. Joe will handle the current case we were working on. Captain Mackey will step in as head of this unit until I can come back."

He made eye contact with each of his Detectives. "For the record, I did not kill Camilla. Nor did Dillon. We neither hired somebody to do it nor did we have a hand in planning her murder. I know you all have witnessed the countless times she and I have argued. But I would never resort to killing her."

Detective Hall took a step closer to him. "None of us think you had anything to do with her death. We will do whatever we need to help clear you, Damien."

Detective Mike Cooper stayed at the end of his desk. "Whatever you need, Damien, we will do it." He glanced at the conference room doorway, making sure no ears were listening. "We can bring files and whatever else you need to your house. You just say the word. We can run an investigation and clear you."

Damien smiled at his crew. "I appreciate that. I don't want any of you doing anything to get yourselves in trouble. We have to get past it. I know this will blow over.

Dillon turned her head towards the conference room when she heard her director and Captain Mackey exit. "Let's get out of here." She grabbed Damien's hand and headed towards the elevator.

Damien turned to Joe. "You rode with me. Hitch a ride with Travis to my house."

"Will do. I'll call when we are headed that way," Joe said.

Captain Mackey watched as Damien left. He turned towards the VCU detectives. "I expect you all to work and get your cases closed. I will be up in my office. Do not hesitate if you need something. I'm going to put Joe as point on the unit." He faced Joe. "Do not get a big head. You are the point of contact. Is that understood?"

Joe smiled. "Understood, Captain."

The VCU detectives watched Captain Mackey and Director Sherman leave the area.

Detective Cooper motioned to Joe. "Whatever you need. With your current case, just pull one of us. I think we also need to get together at Damien's. We can bring whatever he needs to help clear him and Dillon."

Joe sat at his desk. "We'll figure out what's going on as soon as we can. I can say from the meeting in the conference room, they just want to keep his hands clean. They don't think he killed Camilla, but they can't have him working any cases. We all know that. I don't fucking like it, but I understand." He rummaged through one of his desk drawers, hoping to find what he needed.

Detective Alvarez sat on the corner of his desk. "What do you need on the case you guys were working on?"

Joe took a deep breath when he found a large evidence bag. "I could use you down in interrogation. Dillon's presence seemed to throw our suspect off. I think having you in interrogation will help rattle him." He folded the paper bag and placed it and a few strips of evidence tape in the folder as well.

"Just tell me when." Detective Alvarez sat at her desk. "You know how much I love rattling assholes."

Joe texted CST Rodger Newberry to make sure he had somebody on the truck and to coordinate with Travis on warrants and searching Corbin's house. He texted Travis next.

I need to know if one of those warrants covers the clothes he is wearing?

"I'm not sure. Give me a second."

Joe read through some notes, checking to see what Travis had emailed Damien about the camera footage. They had Corbin's truck on several videos over the course of several weeks, putting him at or near Frank's house before the murder and on the day of the murder. His phone pinged.

"Hey, the warrant covers anything found in his house, vehicle, or at the shop. Only clothes covered if he is arrested."

"Okay. You are going to need to go through Damien's security system. I need to hitch a ride with you, if you don't mind. We can go after I interrogate Corbin."

"No problem hitching a ride. But why am I going through his security system?"

Joe winced. Travis didn't know everything yet.

"I'll explain on the way over. I may need an hour."

"No worries. I will hang around here. Just text me when you are ready to go."

Joe sent a thumbs-up emoji. Wiping a bead of sweat from his brow with his sleeve, he made a few notes on the case file. "Hey, Alvarez, you ready?"

She stood. "Heck yeah. Do you have a plan?" she asked as she took her weapon from her desk drawer and placed it in the holster on her hip.

"Yeah. I'll explain as we walk." Once in the elevator, he glanced at his phone. "I got a text from Roger. He's processing our suspect's truck and found blood and what he thinks might be brain matter on the pedal. It needs to be tested. He also found some blood on the steering wheel. Just a smudge."

"What else?" Alvarez put a piece of gum in her mouth. She offered a piece to Joe.

He shook his head no. "At the moment, that's it."

"How are you going to use it?"

The elevator doors opened. As they walked down the hallway, a few people stared at Joe. He rolled his eyes but kept his mouth shut. "Corbin, our prime suspect, will be in here with his sister. She has no clue we think Corbin killed our victim, her fiancé."

He stopped outside of the interrogation room. "I don't have an explicit warrant to force him to give us his shoes. We suspect he was wearing these when he killed Peter. I'm going to get him to give them to me voluntarily. I'm going to hand them to you." He waved an evidence bag. "Put them in here, seal, and sign the tag, then take them outside. Lock them up in one of the evidence lockers. When you come back in, go with whatever I say."

She giggled. "I always wanted to be an actress."

CHAPTER TWENTY-EIGHT

Before Joe opened the door to Interrogation 1, he flipped on the speaker. He and Detective Alvarez listened to Corbin and his sister talking as they watched through the one-way glass.

"Chrissy, I promise I don't know why they want to talk to me."

Chrissy shook her head. "You have to have some idea. Why would they think you had something to do with his death? Did you?

Corbin flinched back. "No. No, I didn't. They are focusing on me because they have no one else. They have nothing on me. I wish you would stop thinking I had something to do with Peter's death." He reached out and took her hand in his. "Chrissy, I would never hurt you. You know that."

Chrissy's head hung down. "They have pictures of your truck at Frank's house."

"That isn't my truck. I promise. I would never hurt Peter."

Joe watched Chrissy's body language.

She removed her hand from her brother's, clasping them together in her lap. "I don't know. Corbin. Something doesn't feel right."

"Chrissy."

Joe raised an eyebrow at Alvarez. "Show time," he said as he flipped on the recording system before he opened the door and walked into the room.

Corbin sat up straight. "Where's my truck?"

Joe sat down, placing the file he brought with him on the table. "They're processing it. Shouldn't take too much longer. Before we move forward, I want to read you your rights. This is procedure." Joe read Corbin his rights. "Do you understand these rights?"

Corbin nodded.

"I need you to answer verbally, Corbin," Joe said.

"Yes. I understand my rights. I thought you were just wanting to look at my truck's registration." Corbin gave a side glance to Detective Alverez. "Who are you?"

"I'm Detective Alverez."

Corbin's eyes narrowed. "What happened to the FBI agent?"

"She had another case." Joe stared at the man.

"Don't you need a warrant or something to go through my truck?"

Corbin asked.

"We have one." Joe slid a copy of the warrant over to Corbin.

He lifted the piece of paper and read it. "Why?"

"Why what?" Joe asked.

"Why are you searching my vehicle?"

"Since we have a truck resembling yours, we need to rule yours out. This is typical. Please don't worry about it." Joe smiled. "There is a way for you to clear this up really quick." Joe directed his statement towards Chrissy.

She glanced between the two detectives. "How?"

Detective Alvarez leaned into the table. "If Corbin wouldn't mind giving us his boots," she glanced down, nodding towards his feet, "that would help a lot. We could rule out his shoe from the print we found at the scene."

Chrissy turned towards her brother. "Give them your shoes."

Corbin hesitated. "I don't understand."

Joe pulled the evidence bag from inside the folder. "It's pretty routine. We found several shoe prints at the scene." He shrugged as he glanced at Alvarez. "It is a parking lot. But if we can rule out your shoes and show they don't have the same tread as some of the shoe prints we found, you could walk out of here in a super short amount of time."

Chrissy patted her brother's hand. "Give them your shoes. I want this to be over."

Corbin shifted in his seat. "What if I don't want to?"

Joe shrugged. "We can get a warrant, which might take hours. You will have to stay here until we get it, though."

Detective Alvarez whistled. "You don't want to stay here." She glanced at Joe, then leaned into Corbin. "The longer you stay here, the guiltier you look."

"Detective." Joe nudged her.

"What? Just because you don't want to tell him the truth doesn't mean he shouldn't know." She softened her look as she moved her chair a little closer to the end of the table, near Corbin, putting a little distance between her and Joe. "Hey, I'm just going to say it. You are not under arrest. Don't give them a reason to hold you here. And we can hold you for forty-eight hours."

Joe snarled slightly as he sighed. "Chrissy, we want to rule out Corbin as quickly as we can. We always have to look closely at family first." He opened the evidence bag. "I promise you they go right in here. We seal it. Detective Alvarez will sign the seal. And it will go down the hall to where your truck is." Joe glanced at his watch. "I bet we have you walking out of here faster than you think."

Corbin bit the inside of his mouth and chewed on his inner cheek. "I don't know. Maybe I need a lawyer."

"Corbin. Do it. Please. I want to go home. You may be here for longer than two days if we have to find a lawyer. That's wasted time on you when they could be looking for Peter's killer. If they are concentrating on you, they won't look for the actual killer." Chrissy's eyes pleaded with her brother.

Corbin stared at his shoes. Finally, he agreed and handed them to Joe.

Joe placed them in the bag and sealed it. He signed the seal and handed it to Alvarez, who also signed it before stepping out of the room. Joe pretended to make a note on a piece of paper in the folder.

"What are you writing?" Corbin asked.

"Just letting my superiors know how helpful you have been." He finished scribbling as Alvarez walked back in.

"Okay. Corbin. You said this wasn't your truck." Joe pulled one photo from the folder, placing it in front of Chrissy.

Chrissy stared at the photo. She gave a quick glance to her brother, then back at the picture.

Joe placed another photo of the same truck in front of Chrissy again. "This photo was taken a few weeks before that one. They look like your truck."

"Well, it isn't my truck." He pushed the photos across the table.

Joe pulled the last few photos of Corbin's truck, showing Peter walking to the passenger side. The last photo showed him getting into the truck. "The problem, Corbin, is how many trucks look like yours and how many would Peter have known the driver well enough to get into the truck?"

When Chrissy saw the photos, she let out a small gasp. She reached out, touching the image of Peter. Her other hand dabbed her lips. Turning towards her brother, she squinted at him. "Is this you?"

He shook his head. "No. That is not me or my truck," he said as his finger tapped one photo. "You guys are trying to frame me because someone else has a similar truck. Corbin gathered all the photos, piled them up, and pushed the stack across the desk.

Joe's phone pinged. He lifted an eyebrow at Detective Alvarez.

Corbin saw the interaction. "What? What is going on?"

CHAPTER TWENTY-NINE

Damien walked into the living room.

Gunner and Coach stood dead center, looking for an explanation why they were home so early.

He scratched the big dog's ears as he walked past him, heading towards the kitchen.

Dillon removed her weapon and keys and placed them in the bowl next to the front door. She scooped up the cat as she headed towards the kitchen. Leaning against the doorway, she watched Damien chug a beer. The sadness and hurt in his eyes broke her heart. "I know it seems like they're blaming us, but I can't believe they actually think we killed her."

Damien reached into the fridge and grabbed another beer. He threw his empty bottle in the trash can next to him. "Seems to me they think we did it. I understand removing us from her case until they can square our movements, but I sure as hell don't understand being removed completely from our positions. It makes no fucking sense to me."

Dillon buried her face in the cat's fur. "Can you text Travis? I want him to come out here as soon as he can. He needs to go through our security system. Other than each other, it's all we have."

Damien sat at the table. He pulled his phone from his back pocket and typed a message to Travis. Within a few moments, his phone pinged with a response. "Looks like Joe is having him bring him over here later. I guess he can do it then."

Dillon sat across from him. Coach snuggled against her, not wanting to be put down. "We need to find out what happened to her. I can't believe they wouldn't tell us anything."

"How are we going to do that?" Damien peeled the corners of the beer label.

Dillon frowned. She snapped her fingers. "Call Dr. Forsythe. Ask him to get us the records."

Damien stared blankly at her.

"What? You know he would help us."

"I don't want to put him in a position that might get him in trouble."

"I will call then." She pulled out her phone to dial the ME.

"Stop. I'll do it." Damien groaned as he dialed the doc's number. "Hey Doc. It's Damien." He tapped the front of the phone, putting it on speaker. "I'm here with Dillon."

"Hey guys. What's up?"

"Um, have you heard anything regarding me and Dillon?"

"No. Should I?"

Damien sighed. "Was your office pulled in on the murder at Channahon State Park?"

"Beth went up to get the body of a young woman. That's all I know. I was on a conference call when our office was notified we would take over the case."

"You haven't spoken with Captain Mackey yet? Or the FBI?"

"No. Why would I need to speak with them? What's going on, Damien?"

Damien tugged on the ends of his hair. "The body found at the park is Camilla."

There was a long pause of silence on the phone.

"Oh, Damien. I'm so sorry. I know things have been over for some time between you two, but I know she used to be an important part of your life. I'm confused why Captain Mackey would need to speak with me."

"They removed me and Dillon from working the case. Actually, they removed me from working any case at DC." Damien's words hung thick in the air. The base of his skull pounded.

"You're kidding, right?" Dr. Forsythe huffed into the phone.

"I wish. Listen, I'm going to ask a favor. Could you send me copies of everything on her case? Dillon and I can't sit around here doing nothing." Damien motioned for Gunner to come to his side. The big dog sulked over. Damien scratched his ears, reassuring him he loved him as much as Coach.

"Oh, man."

Damien's shoulders sank. "I know I shouldn't ask. Please. No one will know."

"Hell, I'm not worried about that. Are they waiting to clear you, or are you suspended indefinitely?"

"Just waiting to prove we didn't do it. You won't find a trace of Dillon or me anywhere near Camilla's body. That I can promise you."

"Okay. I'll do it." He chuckled into the phone. "If I lose my job, you will have to supplement my income."

"Deal," Dillon said. "I promise you I will take care of you."

Dr. Forsythe laughed. "Good. How about if I come by later this evening?"

"Great. We will have dinner." Dillon nodded at Damien.

"Yeah. Doc. Come hungry." Damien sat silent for a moment. "Hey, thanks , Bernard."

"Damien, I know you didn't kill her. I also know you need this. I'll see you later. Look for me after 6:30 p.m."

"Okay. See you then." Damien disconnected the phone call. He stared at Dillon. Her eyes were closed as she hugged the cat. This bothered her as much as him. Maybe they could at least work this case on the side. Then, when they were reinstated, they would have a head start on solving it. "We are going to need help with this."

"What are you going to have your crew do? I'm assuming that is who you are referring to when you say we need help.

"I'm not sure yet." Damien threw the second empty beer bottle away. "What the heck are we going to do for dinner?"

"Don't we have something in the freezer from your mom?"

Damien shrugged. "Let me look." Scanning the contents, he sifted through several frozen meals. "Actually, we have enough to feed a small army." He pulled out a few containers. "Okay, we have two lasagnas, two rigatoni dishes, and two ravioli dishes." He looked at a few more containers. "We have some kind of pepper dish. How about rigatoni or ravioli?"

Dillon put down the cat and looked in the pantry. "Ravioli. We have two loaves of bread we can bake. I'd say we have a meal."

"We have some wine, too. Joe and Travis may eat too." Damien stared at the freezer. "You think we should make a third dish?"

Dillon shrugged. "Those will be enough. Even for McFattbutt." She laughed at herself.

Damien pulled his phone from his pocket, fiddled with it, then placed it back in his pocket. He grabbed a diet soda and another beer. "I need something to do," he said, heading for the office.

Dillon trailed after him. She opened his beer and took a long pull. "What can you do?" She set the bottle on his desk.

"I don't know. But I can't just sit here. I need to find out what I can on Camilla." Damien booted up his computer. He placed his weapon and holster on his desk.

"Do you think you should do that?" she sat at her desk.

"Probably not." He typed out a message to Joe. When his phone pinged back, his brow wrinkled.

"What's up?" Dillon asked. "Who texted you?"

"Joe. I asked him how the case was going. He wants me to call him in ten minutes. He also said he's about to nail Corbin."

CHAPTER THIRTY

Joe leaned into Detective Alvarez. He whispered in her ear.

She shook her head. "That's not good."

Corbin's eyes darted between the two detectives. "What? I demand to know what is going on."

Chrissy wiped the moisture from her cheek. "Please. Is there something we need to know?"

Joe leaned back in his chair. "They found blood in your truck. On the steering wheel." He tilted his head down, narrowing his eyes as he stared at Corbin. "Any idea how the blood got there?"

Corbin chuckled. "Dude, I cut myself all the time at the shop. Sometimes I don't even realize it until I get home and the blood has dripped all over my steering wheel." He clasped his hands on the desk.

Chrissy reached over and placed her hand on his arm.

"Has Peter ever been in your truck?" Joe asked.

Corbin's brow furrowed. "I don't think so. There would be no reason for him to be in my truck."

Detective Alvarez watched Chrissy. She removed her hand from her brother's arm and leaned away from him. Alvarez sent a sideways glance to Joe.

Joe cocked his head to the side. "Is there something wrong, Chrissy?"

Chrissy looked up with a distant stare, not responding right away.

"Chrissy." Corbin took her hand in his.

She yanked it back. Still not answering the question, Joe asked.

"If you know something, Chrissy, now would be a good time to tell us," Detective Alvarez said in a soft tone.

"Corbin, Peter has been in your truck. Why would you lie?" Chrissy waited for him to respond.

Corbin let out a nervous laugh. "He hasn't been it recently. But sure, I've given him a ride before."

Joe nodded. "Why didn't you just say that?"

He shook his head, shrugging at the same time. "I thought you were referencing those pictures."

"I see." Joe flipped through the papers in the folder. "Did you like Peter?"

Corbin sat back in his chair. He placed his hands in his lap. "Why are you asking me if I liked Peter?"

"I can see the conversations between you and Peter via your social media, and you say some pretty nasty things to him." Joe closed the folder.

Chrissy folded her arms across her chest. "I told you earlier, Corbin has always been protective over me. I'm not sure why you are asking again."

"Chrissy, how long did you date Hershel Marcum?" Joe asked.

A quick smile flashed across her face, replaced just as quickly by a flash of sadness. "We dated for almost a year. He died in a car wreck. We had just decided to get married but hadn't told anyone." She smiled at her brother. "Except for Corbin. I had to share it with someone."

"Did you like Hershel?" Joe asked Corbin.

"Yeah. Why wouldn't I? He was an NFL player. Took us to a couple of games." Corbin shifted in his chair.

"Did it bother you he was black?" Joe scribbled a note in the folder.

"No. What? Now I'm a racist?" Corbin huffed out a breath.

"Did you want your sister to marry him?" Detective Alvarez asked.

"I think my sister was too young to be in his kind of spotlight." Corbin reached over and took her hand. "I would hate for her to have gotten hurt."

Detective Alvarez spoke in a soft, calm voice towards Chrissy. "Maybe there was another reason Corbin didn't like Peter. More than just being protective." She faced Corbin. "Did Peter do something to make you not like him? Or do something to make you get angry with him?"

He flinched in his seat. "No."

"How well did you know Frank, Chrissy?" Joe asked. He watched Corbin's reaction to Frank's name.

Chrissy's look softened. "Frank was fantastic to Peter. Helped him a lot."

Detective Alvarez scooted her chair closer to Corbin. "You didn't like Frank, did you?"

"What? No." Corbin shifted in his chair. Scooting back from the table. "I've never met him."

"You're reacting as if you knew Frank and didn't like him," Joe said. His phone rang. "Hang on." He turned from the table and stood, moving towards the far side of the room.

"Yeah," Joe looked at Corbin.

"You asked me to call in ten," Damien said.

"What do you have, Roger?"

"Roger? Oh, you're in interrogation."

"Yes. Oh. Are you sure? On the pedal. Wow. Okay. Anything else?"

"I hope you nail this guy," Damien said.

"I think we are about to. Send me the report. Thanks, Roger." Joe clicked off the call.

"What is going on? I need to know." Corbin's eyes darted between the detectives. "Why are you asking me about Frank, and why are you bringing up Hershel?"

"That was our lead crime scene tech. They found blood and brain matter on the pedals of your vehicle." Joe waited before continuing.

Chrissy sat stiffly. "What do you mean, brain matter?" She glanced at her brother. "What are they talking about?"

Corbin waved his hands in the air. "How the hell should I know?"

Chrissy's shoulders slumped forward. "Please, tell me what is going on. What have you found out?"

Joe pulled his chair next to her, taking her hands in his. "The crime scene crew found blood and brain matter embedded in the peddles of your brother's vehicle." He squeezed her hands. "Whoever killed Peter bashed his skull in." He caught Corbin's stare.

"It wasn't me, man. You can't blame this on me. How do you even know it's Peter's, huh?" Corbin's knee bounced up and down.

Joe focused on Chrissy. "Did you ever tell Corbin about the relationship between Frank and Peter?" Joe asked.

"No. I never had a reason to. I don't understand what all this has to do with Peter's murder." Chrissy's eyes filled with moisture. "Please. Tell me what's going on."

"During the autopsy, they found a small piece of leather caught between Peter's teeth." Joe's eyes darted to Corbin, then focused on Chrissy. "It matched a tear in the leather on Corbin's boots. The ones we took from him. There was also blood on the boots." Joe lifted his gaze, glancing at Alvarez. "The blood matched Peter's."

Chrissy froze. She stared blankly at Joe. It didn't register what he said. Blood. Boots. Peter. Everything swirled around in her head. She closed her eyes as she put everything together.

Detective Alverez glared at Corbin. "Why did you kill him?"

Corbin stood, knocking his chair over. "I didn't kill him." He turned towards his sister. "Chrissy, you know I would never kill Peter. I would never hurt Peter."

Chrissy's body trembled. "This, this isn't right. You have made a mistake." She glanced from Detective Alvarez to Joe. "No. Please tell me you made a mistake."

"I'm sorry, Chrissy. We didn't make a mistake. We have DNA proof that Corbin's boot was used to cause massive injuries to Peter. What we are not sure of is why." Joe moved closer to Corbin.

Corbin grabbed his sister's chair, forcing her to turn and look at him. "Chrissy. I didn't do this."

Chrissy stood. She took her brother's hand in hers. "I need to know the truth. Did you kill Peter? I will protect you and hire the best lawyer if this is all a mistake. I need to know the truth."

Corbin reached out and put a strand of hair behind her ear. "I love you so much. Ever since Dad died, I have taken on his role in your life. I promised him I would protect you. I did it to save you."

Chrissy's body froze. "You did what to save me? Did you kill Peter?"

"He would have left you for Frank. He loved him more than you." Corbin made eye contact with both detectives. "Peter spent endless hours over there. I saw them hugging and sitting on the porch with their arms around each other."

Corbin lifted his sister's chin. "You were too naïve to see it. Peter was gay, and he was having an affair with Frank. He...."

Chrissy pushed him in the chest with both her hands. "I can't believe you."

Corbin held her by her arms. "Chrissy, I did you a favor."

"My gosh. You are so stupid. Peter wasn't gay, and neither was Frank." Chrissy pushed him away. "How could you kill Peter?"

"I saw them!" Corbin pulled at the ends of his hair. "I saw them hanging out together. I followed them at different times. I—I saw them shopping, with their arms around each other like fucking lovers." Corbin moved towards his sister.

"I saw them sitting on Frank's stoop. Frank often had his arm draped around Peter. They laughed and acted like they were dating. How about all those nights he spent over there?" Corbin waited for her to respond.

"Nights? What nights?" she asked.

Joe and Detective Alvarez held their positions, letting this play out.

Corbin wagged his forefinger at her. "See, you didn't even know. He spent the night there. I saw him leaving in the mornings. They hugged in the doorway. It was disgusting. To watch, knowing he would come over to our house and sit there like nothing was going on."

Chrissy's head dropped to her chest. "I knew about all those nights he spent over there." Tears flowed down her cheek.

Corbin's eyes widened. "I don't understand. If you knew, why would you still marry him?"

Chrissy faced the detectives, no longer able to look at her brother. "Frank had cancer. All those nights Peter stayed over there, he helped him after chemo." She turned back to her brother. Her nostrils flared as she squeezed her hands into fists. "Frank was like a father to Peter. He loved him. Like. A. Father."

Corbin shook his head. "No. No. That's not true. What about all the fights you had?"

"Peter wanted to move up the date of the wedding." Chrissy cried out. "I said no because everything was already set and paid for." She turned towards the detectives. "He asked me so many times. I kept saying no. I wished I had just said yes. He just wanted Frank there. He loved him so much."

Corbin took a step back. A heaviness settled in his gut. "Chrissy. I—I thought he was gay. I thought he and Frank were having an affair." His shaky voice squeaked as his gaze wandered.

Chrissy's arms hung at her side. Her fists shook as she clenched her jaw. "Did you kill Hershel?"

Corbin averted his gaze. "Why are you asking me about Hershel?"

"You always hated he was black. Now, knowing you killed Peter because you thought he was gay. I know you killed Hershel, too." Chrissy's chest rose rapidly.

"No. I didn't kill Hershel. Chrissy. Come on." Corbin took a few steps towards his sister.

"You killed them both." Chrissy's eyes narrowed into slits. She slapped him across his face.

Detective Alvarez stood closest to Corbin. She moved within arm's reach.

Joe stepped closer to Chrissy. "Corbin, we need you to face the wall and put your hands behind your back."

Corbin reached for his sister.

She pushed him, hitting his chest with her closed fists. "I hate you. You killed Peter. And I know you killed Hershel. I hate you." She continued hitting his chest, screaming at him.

Joe pulled her away from her brother. "Chrissy. It's okay."

She turned to Joe. Burying her face in his chest and wept.

Detective Alverez spun Corbin around and pushed him up against the wall as she handcuffed him and read him his rights again. "Do you understand these rights I have just read to you?"

"Yes." He wiggled against the restraints. He tried to get to his sister. "Chrissy? Please. I did this to protect you. You deserve better than Hershel and Peter. I saved you."

Chrissy spun around, wiping her face with her hand. "You didn't save me. You only wanted to control me. I should've seen it. But I was too blind. Well, now I see you for what you are. A bigot and a murderer. You're a monster. I hate you." She turned her back on him as Alvarez walked him out the door.

"Chrissy, I did it for you. I love you. Remember that, Chrissy. I did it for you." Corbin yelled as the interrogation room door closed.

Joe reached out to the young woman. "Hey, let me have an officer drive you home."

Chrissy wrapped her arms around her waist and cried. "I don't understand why he would do this. He's my brother. I don't even know what to tell my mom. She's going to be devastated."

"Tell her the truth. You can get past this. It will be hard. But you will." Joe pulled a card from his wallet and handed it to her. "Listen, it's going to get rough. This is a number for a counselor. She helps people who have gone through tragedies like this. Call her."

Chrissy took the card, following Joe out of the room.

Joe flagged an officer over. "I need you to take her home, please."

The officer nodded and escorted Chrissy out of the building.

Detective Alverez walked up alongside him. "He's being fingerprinted."

Joe stepped into the room just outside the interrogation room he had just vacated. He switched off the recording and typed some notes on a computer corresponding to the interrogation room session. He emailed himself a copy of the video before heading up to VCU.

Detective Alvarez fell into step with him. "That went pretty darn good. Did Roger really call?"

"No. It was Damien. I texted him earlier and asked him to call me while we were in there."

"Well played." She held the door to VCU. As they neared the empty pen, she stopped. "Whatever we need to do to clear Damien, just let us know."

"I will. I'm heading over there in a few with Travis. We might need to call everyone and have dinner. You know, just the crew hanging out." Joe winked.

"Sounds like a plan."

Travis walked up to them. "Hey, you ready?"

Joe grabbed his jacket. "Yeah. Hey, Alvarez, thanks for helping me nail that bastard."

"It's what I live for."

As Travis and Joe walked towards the elevator, Travis typed a message to Officer Katie Baker.

Joe peered over his shoulder. "I knew it."

Travis glanced up at the Irishman. "You better not say a word."

Joe laughed. "I don't have to. Everyone knows you two are seeing each other."

Travis' mouth hung open. "How? We have been super careful."

Joe laughed at Travis' wide eyes and open mouth. "Dude, this place is filled with detectives. Did you really think you could hide it?"

CHAPTER THIRTY-ONE

Damien paced around the kitchen.

Dillon watched him out of the corner of her eye as she finished the last touches on reheating two pasta dishes. She checked on the bread and grabbed two cold bottles of wine from the fridge, one white and one red. After setting the table, she crossed her arms over her chest. "Will you stop? What is bothering you? Besides the obvious."

He shook his head, continuing to pace. "I need everything on Camilla. I also need to know if any other murders like this have happened."

Dillon cocked her head to the side. "You think other women were murdered? And did you come to this conclusion by pulling something out of your ass?"

Damien frowned, rolling his eyes. "No. I'm just hoping Camilla wasn't killed for being—Camilla."

Dillon hooted in laughter. "Of course, Camilla was killed for being Camilla. Why else would she be killed?"

"I'm hoping she is part of a major serial killer plot and not just killed because she is—was—a class A bitch." He plopped into a chair at the table. "I know that sounded horrible. I just think it would be easier for her parents to swallow the murder of their daughter if it wasn't because she was such a shit."

Dillon stepped behind him, placing her arms around his neck. She rested her chin on his shoulder, placing her cheek to next to his. "I know how much you cared for Camilla. I also know how much she hurt you. That you are concerned about her family shows me why I fell in love with you. And why Camilla regretted losing you." She kissed the top of his head. "Everyone should be here...."

The doorbell rang.

"Speak of the devil." Dillon headed to the door.

Damien and Gunner followed her.

Coach's ear twitched while he lay on the sofa, but he made no effort to move.

Dillon checked the drop-down screen on the security system before opening the door. "It's Joe and Travis."

Damien let them in. "Hey. Thanks for coming, Travis." He stepped back as they entered.

Joe gave Dillon a kiss on the cheek. "How you guys holding up?"

Gunner wiggled, waiting for someone to pet him. His tail whipped Travis' leg as he groaned and head-butted Joe in the thigh.

Joe reached down and loved on the big dog. "Hey buddy." He scratched his ears. "Oh, you like this, huh?" he scratched for a few more minutes. As soon as he stopped, he watched as the dog made his way to Travis.

"Good. I guess. I mean, I—we—haven't been accused of murder before, so I'm not really sure," Dillon said.

Travis pointed to the security panel on the wall. "Is that the system?" He placed a small black bag on the coffee table.

Damien nodded. "This is the main console." He grabbed the remote for the TV hanging on the wall and fiddled with it. Within a few minutes, the screen lit up with several camera views. He handed another remote to Travis.

"You can use this remote to access the system. I have already unlocked it, so you can download every recording as far back as forty-five days. Anything more, and you can get videos from my father's security company. They are housed on his server." Damien stuck his hands in his jean pockets.

It took no time for Travis to run through the commands on the screen and pull up things he needed. "This system is sweet."

Damien chuckled at his excitement. "My dad had it specially designed for much larger estates. But it will work anywhere." He looked over at Joe. "How's the crew?"

"First, no one thinks for one minute you killed Camilla or had a hand in her death. Second, they all want to help."

The doorbell rang again. A camera view on the screen showed Dr. Forsythe standing at the door.

"Hey, Doc, thank you for coming over." Damien stepped to the side, letting Bernard enter.

Travis glanced up. "I have all the files, videos, and all the times the system was engaged and disengaged. I will go through everything and give Captain Mackey the information."

"You have everything? Are you sure?" Dillon asked.

"Yeah. This system is really easy to download all the information. I placed it on a jump drive. As soon as I correlate everything for the time in question, I'm sure they will clear you and Damien for duty again." Travis packed up his tools.

"You don't have to go, Travis. We have food for everyone," Damien said.

Travis checked his watch. "Um, thanks. I need to go."

Damien smirked at Joe's big smile. "Okay."

Travis followed his stare. "Why are you smiling?" he asked Joe, as his nostrils flared.

Joe laughed. "He has a date."

Dr. Forsythe watched the interaction between the men. Not knowing Travis, except for a few brief encounters at Division Central, he remained silent.

"I bet I know who the date is with." Dillon pinched her lips together, trying not to laugh.

Travis' shoulders sagged under the stares. "I have plans with Katie."

"Our Katie?" Damien asked.

Joe nodded. "Yup."

"Oh." Damien looked over at Dillon.

"He thought he was hiding it," Joe said, scooping up Coach off the sofa.

"I'm going to go." Travis headed towards the front door.

Dillon giggled at how uncomfortable Travis was. Remembering her own embarrassment every time someone found out she and Damien were dating. "Dr. Forsythe, come to the kitchen with me."

Damien followed Travis to the door, opening it. "Listen, Travis. We are going to need to speak with you about Jim and what he heard in the bathroom. Until then, make sure you don't mention anything to anyone."

Travis stood on the porch. "Is there something wrong?"

"No. I promise. Just keep quiet about what happened. Hopefully, this situation involving Camilla will straighten out in a few days. That's when I will need you to come to the house again. We can't discuss what we need to discuss at DC." Damien leaned into him. "I promise, it is nothing bad."

"No worries. I know you guys will be back to normal in no time." Travis turned to leave, then turned around. "I heard there is a new profiler coming in over the next day or so."

"Yeah, the captain and Dillon's director are having one come in. We've been told he will help clear us, and give space between us and the case." Damien shrugged. "At least that's what I've been told."

"I'm sure that's all it is. Damien, whatever you need, I will do it. I think it's pretty shitty what they are doing to you, just to save face."

"Thanks, man. I will more than likely take you up on that offer."

"Let me know when and where." Travis headed to his car. "I'll talk to you guys later."

Damien closed the door. He listened to the laughter coming from the kitchen. For a split second, calmness surrounded him. However, with every step towards gleeful sounds, anxiety crept over him.

CHAPTER THIRTY-TWO

Dr. Forsythe beamed a smile at Damien as he walked into the kitchen. "It smells delicious."

Dillon placed one of the pans of ravioli in the center of the table. She set down a platter with sliced bread and a small dish of butter. "Let's dig in. We can talk while we eat."

Joe's phone pinged. He quickly replied before placing his phone on the table.

"Is everything okay?" Damien asked as he lifted several large stuffed ravioli onto Dr. Forsythe's plate. He continued filling Joe's plate and Dillon's before his own.

"Yeah. Taylor is running late again." Joe took a bite of his pasta. "Oh, this is so good."

"We will make sure you and the doc have some leftovers to take home," Dillon said.

Dr. Forsythe echoed Joe's praises. "Your mother is such an excellent cook."

"How do you know I didn't cook this?" Damien asked.

"Please. We all know she cooked this." Dr. Forsythe continued to eat, spreading butter on a piece of crusty bread.

An awkward silence fell over them. Damien picked at his food. He stopped eating and took several sips of wine. "Joe, tell me about the Corbin interview."

"I had Alvarez help. We used his sister to put pressure on him. When I had you call, I made him think we found blood on his shoes. Matching it to Peter." Joe dabbed his bread in the sauce on his plate. "We got him to confess."

Joe was about to take a bite of his bread, stopping the delicious morsel inches from his mouth. "He killed Peter because he thought he was gay and having an affair with Frank. What he didn't know was his sister knew all about Frank. When she realized what her brother did, she questioned him about Hershel."

"What did the brother say?" Damien asked.

Swallowing his bite, Joe continued. "He said he didn't do it, but his sister said he always had a problem with Hershel being black. There's your motive. Can anyone prove it? I don't think so."

Damien glanced at Dillon. "I'm glad you got his ass. Frank can rest in peace."

Dr. Forsythe looked around the table. "This was the young man from the parking lot, correct?"

"Yes," Joe answered.

"Okay. I can't wait anymore. I noticed you brought nothing with you. File wise," Damien said.

"Beth hadn't returned by the time I'd left. I figured we could use this meeting as a strategy meeting." He took a sip of wine. "I called Captain Mackey."

Damien sat up straight. His fork stopped short of his mouth. "And?"

The doctor finished his bite. He placed his fork on the side of his plate and took a gulp of water. "I asked him what was happening concerning Camilla's death."

"And what did he say?" Damien snapped back.

"Dude," Joe chimed in. "Chill the fuck out. Give the man a chance to speak."

Damien snarled at Joe. "Shut up."

"You are wound way too tight. You're not going down for this. And I know you want to get back to DC and get back to work. But you have to chill out." Joe poured some more wine into his and Damien's glass.

Damien focused his attention on his plate as he gathered his thoughts. "I'm sorry. I don't mean to sound impatient or—or angry at you. I'm not."

"You have experienced a significant loss. And I don't think you have had time to process this." Dr. Forsythe rested his elbows on the table. "Captain Mackey had little in the way of answers. He expressed he doesn't think you or Dillon killed Camilla. And whether you choose to believe this, he hated pulling you off duty. He knows what this job means to you."

Bernard turned towards Dillon. "His sentiments carried over to you too, my dear. It is not lost on him or your team how this is hitting the two of you."

Damien took a bite of ravioli. Having something in his mouth kept him from saying something he might regret.

"Have you had any reports of another woman killed, like Camilla?

Anything pop up from around the state? Maybe some other Jane Does?" Joe asked.

"I'm running a search. After I spoke with you and Dillon, my assistant culled any reports. I should have something regarding those inquiries tomorrow." Bernard Forsythe buttered another piece of bread as he spoke. "I know it isn't what you were hoping to hear. But give me a few days, and let's see what this new profiler is going to do."

Joe glanced over at Dillon. "I know you think you are being replaced. That isn't the case."

"From what I have gathered from the captain, your director knows this profiler. He says he is one of the best out there. He has an uncanny ability to see patterns left by the killer. Your director thinks he will help clear you and Damien by showing an underlying pattern between other victims." Dr. Forsythe took a drink of wine.

"I don't think I'm being replaced." She glanced at the dog on the floor as she gathered her thoughts. "I don't like losing control. I can't help but wonder what if this profiler is really good? Maybe they will replace me."

"Not by this guy." Bernard reached over and took Dillon's hand in hers. "This guy runs a unit out of Arizona. He has to go back there." He chuckled at her glare.

"Wow. Funny Doc." Dillon snuck a piece of food to both Gunner and Coach.

"Do you know his name?" Joe asked.

Bernard held up his finger as he chewed. "Derek Reed."

"Oh, I know him." She gulped a sip of wine. "He is a great profiler, and I know he doesn't want to leave Arizona."

Damien snapped his fingers. "Is that the same post they wanted you to take before you came here?"

"Yes. I was slated for it, then Jason Freestone happened." She blew out a breath. "I do not want to have to deal with Jason ever again."

"You and me both." Joe snagged the last piece of bread on the tray. "This is so good." He smeared a large dollop of butter on it, then used it to sop up the remaining sauce on his plate.

Dillon sipped her wine. "Agent Reed runs a cold case unit called the Legacy Unit," she set down her glass. She glanced at Bernard. "He has an unbelievable talent of seeing connections."

Damien's brow furrowed. "What do you mean?"

"I can't explain it. I know he and his crew have solved some really old cold cases. It's like—I don't know. Like he speaks to the dead or something. He has closed some cases no one else had solved," Dillon said.

"As soon as I have some information, I will send it to you." Dr. Forsythe shook his head. "No. I will bring you copies here. No emailing files." He glanced at all three of them. "I know you guys are very cautious, but you can't let anyone know you are working on this case on the side."

Joe nodded as he handed his plate to Dillon, who was clearing the table.

Doc stood. "Let me help." He stepped over to the sink and began rinsing the dishes before placing them in the dishwasher.

"Thank you, Bernard." Dillon stuck her tongue out at Joe.

Joe waved her off. "I know the team wants to help," he said, glancing at Damien. "I think we should let them."

Damien leaned back in his seat.

Coach snagged Dillon's vacated chair and scoured the table. He looked at Damien's plate, which had yet to be removed. Slowly, he reached his paw over and grabbed a piece of sausage.

Damien watched as the furball ate it and came back for seconds just before Dillon picked it up. He wiggled his eyebrows at her. "So wifely." He dodged out of the way before she smacked him.

"You will pay for that later."

Damien poured the last of the wine into his glass. "I'm not sure what we should have them do. I don't want any of them getting in trouble."

"Stop. We can investigate. I was thinking we could all come over here one night. Maybe tomorrow," Joe glanced at the doc, "if Bernard gets some case information for us. Then we can dole out a case to each team...."

"You guys need to make VCU cases a priority," Damien said, cutting him off.

"This is a VCU priority case, you *effing eejit*." Joe reached out like he was going to smack Damien.

"Listen, the last thing I want is anyone getting wind of the team working on something with me, especially since I'm not allowed to work on cases. Don't *mettere la pulce nell'orecchio*," Damien said.

Dr. Forsythe turned around, laughing. "Don't put a bug in the eye?

What does that mean?"

Damien's brow wrinkled as he chuckled. "Bug in the eye?" he laughed as he realized what Bernard meant.

Bernard held a dish towel in his hand, pointing at Damien. "Don't make fun of your elders. I've been trying to brush up on my Italian, so I can understand you."

Damien sniggered as he took a sip of his wine.

Joe shook his head. "Not bug in the eye... flea in the ear. Don't cause suspicion."

Damien and Joe roared with laughter.

Dillon rolled her eyes at Dr. Forsythe. "I swear they're twelve years old."

CHAPTER THIRTY-THREE

Dillon lay curled up next to Damien on the sofa. Everyone had left with full bellies and food to go. "I need to call the lawyer tomorrow. Make sure he is getting Taylor's case ready. I think this needs to be dealt with yesterday."

Damien changed the TV channel to the local news. "I agree. I'm worried about her. Especially after Taylor updated us when she picked up Joe."

Dillon sat up, stretching her legs over his and propping herself up against the side of the sofa. She moved Coach and took his spot.

He huffed and growled, then settled down when she laid him on her stomach and scratched his ears.

"I will call Nicky tomorrow. I gave him all the information about Taylor a few weeks ago. He should have something we can use to get ahead of him." He pulled his phone from his pocket and texted his brother.

"I thought you were going to wait."

"Eh." He checked his watch, about to call. "Nicky sleeps with the chickens. Maybe I should wait," he said as he put his phone back in his pocket.

Dillon cocked her head to the side. "He does what?"

Damien glanced away from the TV. "He does what—what?"

"How much wine did you drink?" She stared into each eye. "Are you having a stroke?"

"I have no idea what you are talking about."

"You said your brother sleeps with chickens. Isn't that like against some agriculture law or something? To have chickens in the house. And why would your sister-in-law allow that?"

"Who the hell has chickens in the house?" he twisted to face her. "How much wine did you drink?"

Dillon giggled. "Okay. You said he sleeps with chickens."

Damien's brow wrinkled. Then he laughed. "It's an old Italian saying. If you go to bed early, or earlier than most, then we say, 'you sleep with the chickens.'"

"That is so stupid."

"Didn't you have any weird sayings when you were growing up?"

Gunner moved from the floor to take up space on the sofa next to Damien. He nudged Dillon's feet, forcing her to share Damien's lap with him.

Damien scratched his ears. His warm, soft skin eased his tension.

"I'm sure my grandfather did. I don't really remember if my dad or mom used to say anything." She shrugged. "I can guarantee if they did, it wasn't near as entertaining as your family."

Damien's phone pinged. He pulled it from his pocket. "I guess he is still awake. Nicky says he has quite a bit of information. He's been waiting for me to call about it."

Dillon yawned. She peaked at his phone and saw the time. "I think I drank just enough wine to make me sleepy. I'm going to go to bed with the chickens."

"Sleep."

"What?"

"Sleep with the chickens."

"Didn't I say that?"

"No. You said, 'go to bed with.' That implies something slightly more erotic. And gross."

Dillon laughed. "Well, maybe it's my fantasy."

Damien shook his head. "You need help."

She leaned in to him. "You are the only man or chicken in my fantasies." She kissed him, running her fingers through his hair as she stood. "You coming with me?"

Coach jumped off. Not happy with her disrupting his slumber.

"Do you mind if I check out what Nicky sent me? I just texted him to email it to me."

Gunner scooted around and took up more of Damien's lap.

"Not at all." She scooped up the cat up from the floor. She headed towards the stair, but stopped in the hallway. "Are you okay, Damien?"

"Yeah. I am. I'm not very sleepy. I need to occupy myself for a bit."

"Sure you don't want me to occupy you?"

He laughed. "We have all day for that."

A big smile spread across her face. "I'm sleeping in. After we wake up, let's go get something to eat."

"I like that idea. I guess there is a silver lining to being put on administrative leave." He saw her smile fade. "I'm okay. Sleeping in sounds great. I won't be long."

"I love you."

"I love you more."

He heard her sweet-talking to the cat as she walked upstairs. Remembering a text from Mrs. C., he quickly checked it, giggling at the picture of his elderly next-door neighbor and her dog. Mrs. C. was more of a *nonna* than a neighbor.

Mr. Pickles wore Bermuda shorts and a Hawaiian shirt. Dark sunglasses sat crooked on his nose, and a tropical-looking drink with an umbrella sat near his paws. "Wonder if Mrs. C. knows she's a pet photographer," he said out loud as he touched the screen.

Opening his photo app, he marked several photos for deletion. He had some dating as far back as three years ago. "Who does this?" he said. His breath stopped when he saw a picture of Camilla. She sat on the sofa, the same spot he sat in now. She held her glass of wine in the air.

Even with all the trouble and heartache she caused him, he didn't hate her. His thumb glided over her image. An immense sorrow slammed into him. Maybe he should've taken her stalking worries more seriously.

He dipped his chin towards his chest as his posture slumped. His bottom lip quivered as he tried to fight back the tears. "I'm sorry. I should've listened. I should've helped." Guilt slammed into him for letting his anger keep him from doing his job. He pulled Gunner close to his chest, burying his face in his fur. "I'm so sorry, Camilla. I'm so sorry." The tears flowed down his cheeks.

Gunner whimpered as he scooted closer, nuzzling his head against him.

CHAPTER THIRTY-FOUR

Thursday 7:00 a.m.

Joe walked into the VCU. His eyes drifted towards Damien's closed office door. He shook off the awkward feeling of being there without Damien. He checked the open cases on the digital board hanging on the wall.

Two cases had been closed yesterday evening and six remained open. There were several awaiting court dates. He gave Damien's office another sideways glance. "Why is his door closed?"

He twisted his head from side to side. His neck bones popped, echoing in the empty room. Fiddling with some papers on his desk, his attention kept coming back to the office door. Standing, he pushed his chair back. "Something is up."

He glanced down the hallway leading to other offices as he stood outside the door. Leaning in close, almost pressing his ear against it, Joe heard movement. Reaching out, barely touching the doorknob, he took a deep breath and rushed in. "What the fuck? Who the hell are you?"

A man glanced up from the desk.

Joe squinted. "Who are you?" he crossed his arms over his chest. "And why are you sitting at Damien's desk?"

"You must be Joe." The man stood. "I'm Derek Reed. FBI Special Agent Derek Reed." He extended his hand.

Joe took the man's hand. "Yeah. I'm Joe. Detective Joe Hagan."

"I need your help." Derek motioned for him to join him.

Joe stood, sizing up the agent. Tall, thin, but muscular. Kind of geeky looking. Joe also figured women probably thought he was attractive in a geeky way. He had wavy dark brown hair, which seemed too long for an FBI agent. "Help with what?"

"Please, sit. I'm here to clear your boss. And from what I can tell, your good friend." Derek folded his hands on the desk. "I'm here to help. I promise." He waited for the ex-football player to sit. Derek wondered if there were any doorways Detective Joe Hagan had to turn sideways to get through. "I bet you have some questions for me."

Joe reached into the jellybean jar. Separating the colors into groups, he put a handful of red ones in his mouth. He pulled the chair out and sat, staring at the agent. "Where are you from?"

"Arizona. I run the Legacy Unit out there." Derek took a sip of the coffee in his cup. "I made some," he motioned to a pot behind him. "Would you like some?"

Joe squinted at the pot. "That thing hasn't worked for a while."

Derek chuckled. "A fuse was burned out."

"Do you carry spare coffee maker fuses around with you? Just in case?"

"Not hardly." He took a sip of coffee. "I have the same brand at home. What most don't know is there is a small compartment on the base. It holds two extra fuses."

Joe smirked. "Seriously?"

"Yup."

"Well, shit. All this time, we've been drinking the crap Detective Hall makes every day." Joe shook his head. "He can't make coffee."

"Tell me what you can about Camilla and Damien." Derek took another sip of his coffee.

Joe sighed. "Damien and Camilla dated a long time ago. For several years." He bit the inside of his cheek.

"Just say it."

"I hated her. No one liked her." He leaned forward, placing his elbows on his knees. "Hell, Damien's cat didn't even like her."

"Did they have a nasty breakup?"

"Why are you asking about that?"

Derek sat up straight but softened his jaw. "I'm trying to get a clear understanding of their relationship."

Joe dragged a hand down his face. He tilted his head back. "Camilla was a handful. She wanted what Damien could do for her career. She's a cheater and a bitch."

"How did the relationship end?"

"Damien found her in a hotel room with her boss. She works, worked, for one of the most prominent law firms in the city." Joe placed another group of jellybeans in his mouth.

Derek watched as Joe's posture slumped. His hesitation to tell what he knew only reinforced his conclusion regarding their friendship.

"Ever since they broke up, she has tried one thing after another to get back into his life. Anything she could do to break him and Dillon, Agent McGrath, up, she tried it." Joe walked over to the little fridge in the corner. He grabbed a diet soda.

Sitting down, he opened it, taking a long guzzle. "Recently, she had been complaining about someone stalking her. We just thought it was another tactic. Another way to fuck up Damien's life." Joe glanced at his feet.

"Is that what the argument was about the other day?"

Joe nodded. "Yeah. She came in wanting us to open a case. It got heated."

Derek opened the file. "That's when she filed the stalking report?"

"Yes. I explained we couldn't do anything until she made a formal complaint. Not that we could've done anything, anyway. But it helped get her out of here." Joe took a sip of his soda. "I walked her down."

Derek tilted his head to the side. "Can you tell me what you two spoke about?"

"Not much. I asked her if she knew who might be after her. She said no." Joe stared at the agent. "She screwed a lot of men. Physically and otherwise. We all thought it could be a wife of one husband she'd had an affair with. She kept saying it was no one she knew."

"Did she tell you any details?" he held up the report. "This has nothing."

"No. She said it felt like someone was watching her. Sometimes she thought someone followed her when she went to the garage at her office. Or when she went across the street to the café during work."

Derek jotted some notes. "Did she say if it only happened at work?"

Joe shrugged. "I don't know. Maybe." He paused. "No. She mentioned she thought a van followed her a few times."

"By chance, did she give you a description?"

"She said an older van, like something a handyman would drive," Joe smirked. "By then, I tuned her out. She started bitching at the sergeant on duty, and I wanted to get the hell away from her."

"Tell me about Agent McGrath's relationship with her." Derek scribbled on his pad of paper.

"They hated each other." Joe chuckled. "Dillon didn't hold back any punches." He raised an eyebrow at him. "Dillon didn't need to protect Damien any more than Damien needed to protect Dillon. Camilla seethed with jealousy. She tried to intimidate Dillon, threatening to cause problems for her if she didn't walk away."

"How did Dillon react to Camilla's threats?"

"She threatened to shoot her."

Derek laughed.

"She then threatened to remove each of her fingers and feed them to her." Joe laughed. "I probably shouldn't have said that." He chuckled, shaking his head. "Dillon would never touch her. She would ram the force of the FBI down her throat. And by that, I mean, get search warrants and expose every dirty little secret."

Derek smiled at the detective. "Thank you for your honesty."

Joe crooned his neck. "What else do you have in that file?"

Derek handed the file to him. "Here, I need your help, so you might as well look at what we have so far."

Joe took the file and opened it.

Derek observed as Joe winced and inhaled when he saw the photograph of Camilla. His brow drew together as Joe made the sign of the cross. He continued to watch the detective as he scanned each piece of paper. When Joe came back to the photograph of Camilla, Derek could see his lips move, but he couldn't hear the words.

Joe felt the agent's stare as he said a small prayer for the dead and one for Damien. He knew his partner would see this photo and he wanted to make sure the saints and angels watched out for him.

"This isn't Damien," Joe said as he laid the file on the desk. "If Damien or Dillon were to have killed Camilla, they would just shoot her and walk away." He shrugged. "Dillon would punch her first, then shoot her." He motioned towards the photograph. "They wouldn't have done that."

"I don't think they would've either. But I still have to come up with some alternative theories. Do you remember any other cases resembling this?" Derek lifted his pen. "Anything?"

Joe took another handful of jellybeans. This time, he popped them all into his mouth. His knee bounced. "Dillon is the one you want to ask this. She's a walking encyclopedia of old cases."

"I will. For now, I need you to think. Did you ever have anything in this area that seems similar?"

"About a year ago. We had a case a where a young lady was murdered in the park. They pulled out the big guns on that one."

"Why?" Derek asked as he leaned forward.

"It turned out a person she knew murdered her. But the killer tried to make it look like a psychopath had done it." Joe's brow wrinkled. "I can't remember if there was a case or not. I think I remember Damien mentioned something about an earlier case." Joe snapped his fingers. "Wait, it wasn't Damien, it was Roger Newberry, head CST. He mentioned a previous case years ago, like ten-plus years ago. A serial killer used to leave the girls in the park."

Derek scribbled some notes.

"But those girls were raped and slit open like a fish." Joe chomped on another handful of jellybeans.

"Do you remember the case?"

Joe frowned. "No. But Dr. Forsythe would know. He was here during that time. At least I think he was."

"What are you working on?"

Joe cocked an eyebrow at him. "Why?"

"I could use your help. I'm not familiar with this area. Or anyone here."

"And people would be more receptive to speaking to you with me around," Joe said, raising an eyebrow at him.

Derek smiled. "That too."

"I'm available. I just need to leave someone in charge. I probably need to check with the captain, too."

Derek waved him off. "I already did. The captain said to put Detective Jamal Harris in charge of the unit."

"You already cleared this with the captain?" Joe stood as he asked the question.

"Yes."

"What if I said no?"

"I knew you wouldn't." Derek gathered his satchel and jacket. He grabbed the small rolling suitcase from behind the desk. "It's still cold here."

"Don't change the subject. I don't have to help."

"No. You don't. But I know you will. You want to clear your friends and solve Camilla's murder." Derek stood at the door before he pulled it open. "Am I wrong?"

"What is it with all you profilers? You guys learn how to get into people's heads in some class?" Joe waited for him before opening the door.

"Something like that." Derek opened the door.

"Did you come straight from the airport?"

"Yes. I need to find a hotel." Derek walked out into the VCU pen. All heads turned and stared at them. "I'm Agent Derek Reed." He raised his hands when the room went dead quiet. "I'm here to clear your boss and colleague. Joe has graciously agreed to drive me around the city."

Joe picked up his jacket off the back of his chair. "Jamal, you are in charge. If you guys need extra hands, use Officer Baker and Officer Hoffman. They can partner with you guys to help with the open cases."

Detective Hall ogled the agent. "Damien didn't kill Camilla."

Derek tuned towards the detective. "I believe you."

"Do you need to speak with us?" Detective Alvarez asked.

Derek had read about each of the team members on the flight over. Alvarez had come from Vice and still had a rough edge around her. He had no doubt she could kick his ass. "I might."

Detective Jamal Harris stepped forward. He extended his hand. When Derek took it, he squeezed a tad bit hard. "Damien didn't kill her. We will help in any way we can. But he and Dillon had nothing to do with her murder."

"Again, I believe you, just like I believe Detective Hall. I would appreciate all your help. After all, you know Damien and Dillon better than I do. I welcome all your insights." Derek turned towards Joe. "Are we ready?"

"Yeah." He led the way to the elevators. "Who do you think we should talk to first?"

"Who do you think we should talk to first?"

Joe hit the button for the garage level. He watched the quirky man. "Aren't you in charge of this?"

"Not at all. We are working together." Derek patted the front pocket of his jeans. He then searched the pockets of his jacket.

"Are you looking for something?"

"Gum."

Joe reached into his jacket pocket. "Here." He handed him a pack.

"Thanks. I forgot mine."

"We can stop and get you some. You seem like you might need it." Joe exited the elevator.

Derek followed him. "That would be great." Several people stopped as they walked down the hallway and gave him the once-over. He made eye contact with one individual wearing a DEA hat.

Before he went into the garage, he turned back and saw the man staring at him. Derek did not know who he was, but a chill ran up his spine. He had a bad feeling. Something niggled at him. A warning. He needed to warn someone, but he had no idea who.

CHAPTER THIRTY-FIVE

Thursday morning 5:30 a.m.

Dillon stretched, reaching for Damien. She found Gunner instead. "You're not who I was expecting."

Gunner cracked one eye at her, then yawned, rolling over to expose his belly for some morning scratches.

Dillon kissed the tip of his nose. Shivering as she crawled out from under the covers, she frowned, glancing at Damien's untouched side of the bed. Grabbing her warm, snuggly robe, she listened at the top of the stairs before descending.

Straining to hear anything, Dillon gripped the handrail. She was about to take her first step when Gunner ran past her, his bulky body clipping her calves. Her left knee gave out as she stumbled down the first few steps.

"Gunner!" Dillon held on to the banister with a death grip. "That dog is trying to kill me, and Coach probably told him to do it." She regained her composure and glanced at the foot of the stairs.

Coach sat staring at her.

"I knew you were behind this," Dillon said as she stepped off the last step. She scooped up the cat. "I suppose you want your stinky canned food?"

Gunner danced crazily at her feet.

"One second, you dumb dog." Dillon stopped when his expression changed.

Gunner sat with a distinguishable pout on his face.

"I'm sorry. I didn't mean to hurt your feelings." She scratched his ears and placed the cat on the floor. "You're not a dumb dog." Dillon peeked into the office.

Damien sat at his computer, engrossed in something on the screen.

"You didn't come to bed last night. Are you okay?" she leaned against the doorframe, waiting for him to respond. "Hello? Earth to Damien." He still didn't answer her. "I have a morning date with Fred. We are going to have crazy monkey sex in the driveway. Care to watch?"

"That's great."

She shook her head and headed towards the kitchen and the back door. After letting Gunner out into the fenced-in yard, she emptied a can of wet cat food into Coach's dish. "That should keep you happy for about an hour."

Dillon stood in front of the open fridge. "One of us has to go shopping soon." But there was enough for a good size breakfast. "I'll cook breakfast. Then we can go out for lunch." Before starting the meal, she let in the dog. The smell of bacon had both animals following her every move. Once the meal was complete, she loaded up two plates and some drinks on a tray and carried it to the office.

Damien glanced up at her. "When did you get up?"

She cocked her head to the side. "Oh, I don't know." She set the plate down on his desk. "Why didn't you come to bed last night?" His face looked puffy, and his hair was disheveled. Dark circles underneath his eyes gave him a sunken look. "Did you sleep at all last night?"

Damien munched on a piece of bacon. He stared at his computer screen, making some scribbled notes on a pad of paper.

"Damien?" she took a bite of her eggs, waiting for him to reply. Dillon broke off a piece of bacon and gave a bite to Gunner and Coach. "Hello?"

Damien glanced up as he ate a piece of toast. "I'm sorry. Listen, I think I found something."

Dillon pushed her plate to the side as she rolled her chair to his desk. Scooting it next to him, she peered over his shoulder. "What are you looking at?"

"Do you remember the case we had where the jogger was killed?"

Dillon shrugged. "No. I don't think so."

"Rachel. Rachel Burrows. She was murdered in one of the state parks."

"Oh yeah. Didn't it turn out to be her boyfriend's secretary who killed her?"

"Yes. About twelve years ago, there was a string of women murdered in state parks. At first, everyone thought Rachel's murder might be that same killer." He shuffled through some papers until he found what he was looking for. "For roughly five years, they found women all over this state and in Indiana at state parks. Then, ten years ago, the killings stopped. Poof. Nothing."

"Damien." Dillon read a piece of paper. "Is this what you did all night?" she laid it on his desk. "Search for serial killers who could've killed Camilla?"

"Yes. I mean, no. Just listen." He closed his eyes. "I know Camilla said she was being stalked. Well, what if the killer is back? They found her in a state park. Channahon State Park." He stared at Dillon. "I know. You think this is a stretch."

"I think you're sleep deprived. You want answers, and you will find them anywhere you can. I think you are too close to this."

"No," Damien said as he pushed his chair back. "I'm not wrong. I'm not searching for answers." He shrugged as he chuckled. "Okay. I am looking for answers, but not because I am too close to this. Just hear me out."

She raised her hands in defeat. "Okay. Convince me."

He typed in a command and put a bunch of pictures up on the big screen hanging on the wall. "These are the women killed over those years I just mentioned."

Dillon walked over to the screen, studying each of the pictures. "These women were brutally murdered." She nodded towards him. "Do you have any of the case files?"

"Yes. I pulled all of them from the National Incident-Based Reporting System. All the details are right here for each case. Well, I have what they uploaded into the system." He handed her a few sheets of paper. "I don't have the actual police files from the detectives who handled the cases."

"We don't even know how Camilla died." She laid the papers back on his desk.

"I know. That's why we need her file." Damien tapped on his keyboard.

"Don't."

"Don't what?"

"Don't get the files by ill-gotten means."

He laughed. "I'm not."

"Call Doc."

He glanced at the clock. "I already did. He said he would bring whatever he had tonight."

"Beth too?"

"Yeah."

Dillon bit the inside of her lip.

"Why does that seem to bother you?" Damien asked.

"It doesn't. I'm just wondering about another case."

"What other case?"

She frowned. "I don't know. She was working on a young girl the other day when we were there. I asked her for some information on it."

"Why did you do that?"

"I don't know. Something seemed familiar to me. But I can't place it."

CHAPTER THIRTY-SIX

Thursday 9 a.m.

Joe drove his truck into the parking lot of the medical examiner's facility. After he answered a text from Taylor, he turned towards his companion. "Give me just a minute." Joe typed out another message.

When are you leaving?

In about two hours. I'm heading home to pack.

Can someone go with you?

Yes. Charlotte is riding with me. We are going to our house first, then hers. Don't worry. I won't be alone.

Joe groaned as he typed.

I need you to text me when you get to the hotel. Are you flying?

Yes. Corporate jet.

Okay. I like that. Keep me informed. I love you.

I love you. make sure you love on Muffin.

That cat is so old. If she dies while you are gone, it's not my fault.

She is not going to die. I love you.

Love you, too.

Joe looked at Derek. "Sorry."

"No worries. Is everything okay?" Derek asked.

"Not really. But it's a very long story." Joe exited his truck. "C'mon, we will meet the doc and then see where we should go next."

Derek followed Joe into the lobby. He couldn't help but notice the receptionist's eyes light up at the sight of Joe, then quickly fade when she saw him.

"Hey, Maggie." Joe stepped up to the desk. "Can you let Dr. Forsythe know I'm here?"

"Sure, Detective Hagan." Maggie shot a side glance at the new guy. When she hung up the phone, she smiled at Joe. "Is Damien okay?"

"Yeah, he's fine," Joe said looking over his shoulder at two officers.

"Okay, that's good. Dr. Forsythe said to go on back." She handed Derek a visitor's pass.

"He's with the FBI, Maggie. And he's with me." Joe motioned for Derek to follow him. When the buzzer sounded, Joe pushed the large metal door open. Stepping through, he noticed the concerned look on Derek's face. "You okay?"

Derek stopped. He tilted his head to one side, placing his finger over his lips. After a moment, he looked at Joe. "Do you ever hear voices in here?"

"All the damn time." He walked down the corridor. Making a right at the first crossway. "I know Damien does too, but he likes to make me think I'm the crazy one."

"How long have you two been partners?"

"Oh man, going on six or seven years now."

"Both of you are Catholic." Derek chuckled at Joe's raised eyebrow. "I did some light reading on the plane."

"I bet. I bet you also know the answer to every question." Joe made another right.

Soft music filtered towards them.

"I know what is in the files. I don't know about the man; when he isn't the detective." Derek smiled as they stood outside two large swinging doors.

"I'll answer whatever you need. I want to get my friend cleared and get him back to work." Joe pushed through the doors. Dr. Parker and Dr. Forsythe peered up from a body on a table. "Hey, Docs."

Dr. Forsythe squinted at the stranger. "Who do you have with you, Joe?"

"Guys, this is FBI Special Agent Derek Reed." Joe turned towards Derek. "This is Dr. Beth Parker and Dr. Bernard Forsythe."

"Hi, nice to meet you both." Derek bent over a table. He stared at the body of a young woman who had her throat slit from ear to ear.

Dr. Forsythe watched the agent scrutinize the dead girl. Agent Reed walked to the head of the table, inspecting the wound. Dr. Forsythe saw Dillon do this same thing whenever she saw a victim. He knew she saw details most didn't see, and he knew this agent did the same. "Agent Reed. I've heard about you."

From his thin, lean stature, and well-tanned skin, Derek saw a runner standing before him. "Don't believe any of the bad stuff."

Beth smacked her forehead. "I know who you are."

Joe's brow wrinkled.

Derek leaned towards her over the table. "I didn't do it."

She laughed. "You solved those murders from the 80s. It was you."

"What murders?" Joe asked.

"Cory Thompson. He murdered four young girls in four different states during the 80s." Beth looked at Joe. "He would've gotten away with it too, had it not been for this guy solving the case."

Joe faced Derek. "How'd you solve such an old case?"

"I'll tell you about it later. I promise." He waved his hand over the dead girl. "Tell me about this girl. This isn't Camilla."

Dr. Forsythe paused. "How do you know it isn't Camilla?"

Derek wiggled his eyebrows. "I have my ways." He chuckled at himself. "I pulled her file from your system."

"Hmm." Dr. Forsythe folded down the sheet covering her body. "She bled out." He pointed to the gaping wound in her throat. "This killed her. She wasn't raped. He also left this mark on her." He pointed to a symbol carved in her abdomen.

Derek studied the carving. "May I have a glove?" he asked, shifting his stare between Dr. Forsythe and Dr. Parker.

"Yes." Dr. Parker handed him a glove.

After gloving his right hand, Derek let his finger trace the symbol. He bent closer, following the intricate pattern. Removing the glove, he pulled his small notepad from the back pocket of his jeans. Using the pen attached to the spiral edge, he drew the symbol.

When he finished, Derek looked up to see all eyes on him. "This symbol was carved with skill," he said, pointing to its edges. "Whoever did this took great care to make sure the lines and design were precise."

The doctor stepped back to another table. He motioned for everyone to follow him. "This is Camilla." Before he removed the sheet covering her, Dr. Forsythe lifted his gaze to Joe. "Are you ready for this?"

Joe nodded. He kept his arms crossed over his chest.

"Very well, then." Dr. Forsythe folded down the cover, revealing Camilla's face and upper torso.

Joe inhaled, making a hissing sound. "Damn."

"You sure you're okay?" Dr. Forsythe asked.

"Yes. Just." Joe closed his eyes. "Just a little weird."

Derek pulled the sheet down, exposing Camilla's abdomen. "She has the same mark."

Dr. Forsythe nodded. "Dr. Parker worked on the first girl. She brought it to my attention only a few moments before you walked in."

Joe's eyes lit up. "This alone clears Damien and Dillon." His gaze fell on each individual. Stopping at Derek. "Unless we are going to say they killed this other girl only to cover up their murder of Camilla."

Derek smirked. "I'm betting they didn't." He looked over at the first girl. "She is a lot younger than Camilla."

"Yes. I noticed," said Dr. Forsythe.

Derek studied the wounds on each girl. "The cuts are almost identical. No hesitation marks." He addressed both doctors. "Do you have the pictures from the scene for both murders? I left the folder with Camilla's pictures in my briefcase in Joe's car."

Dr. Forsythe grabbed two files from a nearby desk. "Here. I haven't received the tox results or anything from Trace yet. This is an incomplete file."

Derek looked at the photos.

"When Dr. Parker mentioned the symbol on both girls matching, I looked at the photos from each crime scene. Remember, the younger girl was murdered out of our jurisdiction.

"Our crime lab wasn't on scene. I had to get the files from the detective. They took a lot of pictures, but they were out of their league, which is why they called us. They collected all the evidence. I sent off the samples they collected, along with some more of our own."

Dr. Forsythe sat up on his stool. "From what I can see, unless Damien and Dillon are serial killers, they didn't kill Camilla. Nor did they kill this other girl."

Derek studied the pictures. Both women had been laid out in the same fashion. Arms outstretched, hair, and makeup similar. He kept looking from photo to photo.

Joe stared over his shoulder. Seeing Camilla in the photograph, he couldn't help but think how peaceful she looked. He brought his attention to the symbol carved into the younger girl's skin. "I don't remember having a case with this symbol on our victims."

Dr. Forsythe nodded in agreement. "I searched our files and even ran the description of the symbol through a known database used by the feds. I couldn't find anything resembling what you see here. I'm still looking, though."

Derek handed the pictures back to the doctor. "Could I get a copy of the second girl's picture? Along with Camilla's file. Just in case I don't have all the information."

"Sure." Dr. Forsythe gathered both files and all their contents. "Take these. I have copies of everything." He handed the folders to Derek. "When will you be talking to the captain?"

"I'm meeting with them in the morning to discuss what I have so far. I am going to dig a little into both cases. I'm sure with what we have here, Damien and Dillon will be back at work by tomorrow or the next day." Derek waved the folders. "Thank you for these."

Joe clapped his hands together. "If you have what you need, Agent Reed, I think we can head out of here."

Derek extended his hand to both doctors. "Thank you."

"You're welcome." Dr. Forsythe waited for the agent and Joe to leave the room. He raised his eyebrows as he looked at Beth. "I think I will bring some wine tonight when we go to Damien's house. It sounds like a celebration may be in order."

CHAPTER THIRTY-SEVEN

Joe peered over at Derek. "Do you want to go by Damien's house? Meet him and Dillon in person?"

"I would love to." Derek stared out the window. "I thought traffic in Phoenix was bad."

"Chicago traffic sucks. There are times I wonder why I stay." Joe made a right onto Lakeshore Drive. "This city, though, does something to you." He pointed to the lake. "This place is fantastic in the summer."

"We have skiing not too far from me. And a ton of lakes. Lots to do. But damn, it's hot in Arizona." Derek glanced over his shoulder into the back seat. "I need to find a hotel."

"You think, with what we found, you will be here longer than a day or two?"

Derek shook his head. "No. I really don't. They brought me in to distance everyone associated with Damien and Dillon. This way, it looks fair."

"I understand. This has crushed Damien, though. I know it has." Joe sat quietly for a few moments. "He and Camilla were over long ago. But she kept trying to get him back." He peered over at his passenger. "Not because she loved him, mind you. She was incapable of love."

"Then why did she want him back?"

"To stroke her ego." Joe made a series of turns and then got on the highway. "After a case, we had a few years back, Damien and I became poster children for the VCU. Then Camilla wanted him back. She figured he could do more for her career and standing in the city. Especially because of his father's connections."

Derek lifted the gum from the console. "May I?"

"Of course."

Derek took two pieces, placing one in the front pocket of his jeans and the other in his mouth. "Does Damien use his father's connections on a lot of cases?"

"When doing so doesn't go against policy." Joe flashed Derek a big smile.

"I bet." Derek chuckled. "I will not say anything. I've circumvented policy, maybe."

"I like you even more." Joe pulled off the freeway and turned down a main thoroughfare. "I didn't call them. He checked his watch. It's close to lunch. I'm going to stop up here and get us some sandwiches."

"Bribing them, huh?"

"Never. I would never do such a thing. I'm hurt you would even suggest it." Joe laughed as he and Derek exited the car.

CHAPTER THIRTY-EIGHT

Thursday 7 a.m.

Brycen walked into his kitchen. He grabbed two cups of coffee and headed to his living room. "Hey, Grandfather, how are you this morning?"

His grandfather stared at the TV. "I'm fine." He continued watching his show.

"That's good. Here." He moved a full cup of cold coffee and last night's untouched dinner plate out of the way. "I brought you some fresh coffee. Would you like me to fix you some breakfast?"

His grandfather's stoic expression never changed. "No. I'm not hungry."

Brycen sat next to him in the adjacent chair. "You need to eat." He saw the pictures scattered on the coffee table. There were only four that fit his project. The others he kept for sentimental reasons. "Do you like the project so far?"

"I'm not sure I would do it like this," he replied as he sat staring at the TV.

Brycen smiled. "I know. But I must do this my way. We talked about this." He shuffled the pictures around. He placed Camilla's picture front and center. "I know I need a few more. Maybe three or four. I can't decide on the total number. I think she should be in the middle." He pointed to Camilla's picture. "I think I only need three more. Something about the number seven seems to fit."

Brycen took the sentimental photos and set them to the side. That left three girls before Camilla. He positioned the pictures where their hands seemed as if they interlocked with the next picture. "Three more is all I need."

His grandfather grunted. "I think you made a mistake with the last one."

Brycen saw the flicker of amusement in his grandfather's eyes. Brycen's lip quivered. "I don't think so. I know she doesn't fit the other girls, but she is the centerpiece of my project."

"I've told you, do not get attached to them. That's what almost got me caught a long time ago. I told you, but you never listen."

Glancing at his watch, Brycen stood. "I don't want to discuss it. I am the one doing it now, and I will do it my way. I have to go to work. I will be home in time for dinner." He grabbed his wallet from the kitchen counter, then stepped back into the living room. "I'm making your favorite. Pork chops and mashed potatoes."

His grandfather, Terrance, continued watching his show, never once drinking his coffee.

"I love you, Grandfather." He walked out of the door when he turned and went back to his grandfather's chair. Brycen bent over and kissed the top of his head. "I'll see you tonight."

Inside his van, he checked the dating app on his phone. Two girls kept popping up. He picked the one who looked like she would fit his project the best. Her bio said she frequented a local sports bar called O'Malley's.

As he drove out of the driveway, he thought about his conversation with his grandfather. It bothered him that he didn't always support him. He knew it was hard for his grandfather to let go of the reins. But he still didn't have the right to tell him he was doing something wrong. "It's my way now, old man. And you will have to live with it."

Brycen couldn't stop the nagging feeling he had made a mistake taking Camilla. Once he had her in his van, though, he couldn't turn back. "I need to stop letting my grandfather get in my head. I know what I'm doing. He's an old man, and his time has passed."

He shifted his focus to the next girl and the prospect of adding her to his project. Her latest post said she would be at a popular club. He chuckled as he thought how easy it was to hunt his prey.

CHAPTER THIRTY-NINE

Back in the car, Derek took in the scenery as they drove towards Damien's house.

"Do you like pets?"

"Yes. I have a dear friend who gave me her dog. Lola. She goes everywhere with me. And the secretary in our unit always brings her Great Dane to the office." Derek's brow wrinkled at Joe's expression. "What?"

"The FBI allows her to bring her dog to the office?"

"My unit is separate from the main FBI building. We have our offices in an old Catholic church."

"That's so cool. I hate coming to DC. It would be so nice to have our own building." Joe turned down a long drive leading to Damien's condo.

Derek glanced at the property. "This looks like a nice place. It's like being in a city, but living in the country, but still close enough to not feel too country."

Joe pointed to his partner's building. "Each building has two townhomes. Damien bought out his neighbor. Eventually, he will expand his home to make it bigger."

"Sounds like a sweet deal. Does it have a yard?"

"Yeah. It isn't very wide. But it is as long as the building. Not much to care for."

Derek whistled. "I hate mowing. Thank goodness I have very little grass to worry about."

Joe exited the truck, carrying the sandwiches.

As he followed Joe up the stairs, Derek tucked the files from the ME's office under his arm. He shivered, regretting the fact he left his jacket in the truck. "It's a little chilly."

Joe laughed as he rang the bell. "You get used to it. This is warm compared to what March usually gives us. I should warn you, Gunner is a sweetheart, but he is big and klutzy."

"I'm guessing this is a dog?"

"Yeah. I'll fill you in on it later." As he finished his sentence, the door opened. "Woah. Dude. What the hell happened to you?" Joe asked as he entered Damien's home.

"Uh, I haven't slept. Why are you here? And who is this?" Damien closed the door behind the stranger.

Gunner bounded around the corner, knocking Dillon into the wall.

"Really, Gunner?" she regained her balance and continued into the living room.

Gunner wiggled his butt as he waited for Joe to pet him. Once he got the attention he sought, he uttered a low growl, eyeballing the newcomer with suspicion, yet wiggling in anticipation of scratches.

"Hey Joe." She stopped and stared at the man next to him. She raised an eyebrow. "I didn't know you were coming by so early. And bringing guests."

Derek reached down and let the dog sniff the back of his hand. When he got the okay, he scratched his ears. "You must be Gunner."

Joe laughed. "Chill out, guys. This is Agent Derek Reed. And he just cleared you two." He lifted the bags of food. "I brought food. Let's sit down in the kitchen and eat. We will fill you in on what we learned this morning at the ME's."

Derek extended his hand. "Nice to meet you. Sorry to barge in unannounced."

Damien shook it. "We are used to it. You cleared us?"

Dillon shook Derek's hand. "I know your work. Your profiling skills have always impressed me."

"Thank you. I'm nothing special." Derek followed them into the kitchen.

"You stopped Josiah Craig," Dillon said.

"It wasn't just me. I had a good team." Derek took a seat at the table, placing the files in front of him.

"Don't be so modest. I know from the reports you found him when no one else could. I remember people saying it's like you have a sixth sense or something," Dillon said.

Derek cleared his throat. "I wish I had a sixth sense. But in the end, I just followed a trail. I still didn't get there in time. The latest girl he had taken, well," he took a deep breath. "I didn't get there in time to save her."

"You still stopped him." Dillon touched his shoulder. Removing her hand just as quickly. "He was a nasty killer."

Derek nodded but said nothing.

"Explain what exactly 'you cleared us' means. Does it mean we can start working on Camilla's case?" Damien waited, staring at Joe, Derek, and the case files.

"Damien, give them a chance to speak." Dillon grabbed some plates and tea from the fridge. She offered Joe a diet soda. "Would you like tea, soda, or water?" she asked Agent Reed.

"Water is fine. Thank you." Derek waited for Joe to dole out the food.

"We just came from Bernard's." Joe looked at the wrinkles on Derek's forehead. "Dr. Forsythe."

"Oh, that's right." Derek unwrapped his sandwich. He took a long sip of water when Dillon placed his glass on the table.

Joe chewed his food, pointing at the files. "We can look at those after we eat. But it seems another girl, who came in a few days before Camilla, was murdered in another state park."

Dillon shot Damien a side glance.

Joe squinted at them. "What?" he waved his hand at them. "What have you been up to?"

Derek ate his sandwich. He noticed the big cat jump up and sit in one of the vacant chairs at the table. The cat watched and waited for the perfect moment.

"Where did the other chairs come from?" Joe asked.

"Storage. Figured we would need them later," Damien said.

"Explains why the table is bigger. You put in the middle leaf." Joe drank half his soda.

Dillon looked at Derek. "That's Coach," she said as she took a sip of tea. "He sits at the table and waits for food."

"He's a big fellow." Derek reached over and gave him a piece of pepperoni from his sandwich.

Not wanting to be left out, Gunner bolted over. Wiggling his butt and whining for his fair share.

"Great. Look what you've started." Damien glared at the cat.

Coach huffed and ignored him.

"Don't avoid my question. What have you been up to?" Joe asked.

Dillon shrugged. "We can discuss it later."

Joe scoffed. "Don't worry about him." He tilted his head towards Derek. "He won't rat you out."

Derek pretended to zip his lips. "I promise. Share what you know. Maybe I can help. Plus, I can report it tomorrow, and it will look like it came from me. My job is to clear you two or find you to be serial killers."

CHAPTER FORTY

Damien pointed at the folder. "Is one of those Camilla?"

"Yes," Derek said.

Damien sat back in his chair.

"He didn't sleep at all last night. He found something." Dillon broke off some bread for the cat and dog. "At first, I thought maybe he was grasping at tiny straws, but he may be onto something. Based on what you said about another girl."

"What did you find?" Joe asked.

"You remember when Rachel was murdered in the park?" Damien asked.

Joe nodded as he took another bite of his sandwich. "That's the case I mentioned earlier," he said to Derek.

Damien focused on the FBI Agent, but his gaze drifted to the folder. "About fifteen years ago, several women were found murdered in state parks all around Illinois and Indiana. But ten years ago, they stopped. Camilla said she was being stalked. Maybe the same killer is back."

"Do you have the other cases? The ones from fifteen years ago?" Derek asked.

"Yeah. I used the National Incident database. All the girls were killed in the same manner. They were raped, then slit from the groin to the throat. A stab wound in the rib cage immobilized them. Placed just right so they couldn't scream out." Damien guzzled his soda.

Joe frowned.

Derek finished his sandwich. "Camilla and those other women were killed in completely different manners."

Damien's lips pursed together. "Still. There may be a connection."

Derek leaned forward on his elbows. "Tell me about Camilla."

"What do you want to know?" Damien asked.

"Well, tell me her habits." Derek finished his glass of water.

"Would you like some more?" Dillon asked.

"No. Thank you." Derek gave Coach's head a scratch.

Joe stood. "Let's go to your office, pull up what we have, using the Incident database, and see if we can find other victims." He glanced at Derek. "This is needed for your report, anyway. And they expected me to shuffle you around and find answers."

Dillon smirked at the men. "Just don't tell them you got the information here."

Joe shook his head. "We hung out at Derek's hotel, using his laptop and talking to the doctor."

Derek smiled. "Exactly."

Joe grabbed another soda before following them into the office.

When Derek saw the large LCD screen on the wall, he whistled. "This is nice. Not the dead girls, the screen."

"Thanks." Damien sat at his computer. "Those are the victims of the serial killer I mentioned."

Joe and Derek sat in the extra office chairs.

Derek opened the file of the young girl and handed it to Dillon. "This is Tracy Welch. They found her in Starved Rock Park. But she wasn't taken in the park. She was last seen with her friends at a bar." He scanned the file. "Rockin' Robin's."

"It's a dance club. Mostly under thirty crowd. More like under twenty-five crowd, really." Joe popped the tab on his soda.

"Camilla wouldn't be caught dead in a place like that," Damien said.

"It's very possible Camilla and the other girl were killed by the same person. At least by the way they were dressed. Although the murders are similar, Camilla is much older than the other woman. She doesn't seem to fit the same profile.

"I mean, without other victims, I can't say what the victimology is, but Camilla and the other woman look nothing alike. I need to understand why a killer would veer so much from his intended victim. Please, tell me about her." Derek smiled as he sat and waited.

Dillon sat in her chair, watching the profiler. He had deep, dark green eyes. He had a strong jawline, but his eyes and mussed-up brown hair gave him a boyish look.

In contrast to Damien, Derek was tall and lean. Not very muscular, but not scrawny either. She focused on Damien. She realized he hadn't answered Derek's question. "Damien?"

"Camilla cared about Camilla. If you couldn't do something for her, she really had no need for you." Damien squirmed in his chair.

"She was mean and heartless." Dillon cut in. "She used people and thought everyone was supposed to be at her beck and call. When I came on the scene, she went into overdrive to get him back."

Damien chuckled. "I thought maybe Dillon was going to shoot her a few different times."

"Joe mentioned that," Derek said.

"Damien doesn't want to speak ill of the dead. So, I'll tell you," Dillon said. "Camilla was ruthless. She was a cheater. And when we heard she had been killed, we all thought it was a spouse of someone she slept with."

"She had a lot of affairs?" Derek asked as he pulled out his small spiral notebook.

"She did," Damien said. "It was why I broke off my engagement. I found out she was sleeping with her boss." His eyes cast downward. "And several other men."

Dillon made a micro-movement towards Damien, rolling her chair in his direction, but stopped. She scanned the file of the young girl. "This is the girl Beth was working on when we were at the morgue. This victim is twenty-two. From what the detectives gathered, she came from a small town up north. She and some friends came into town for the weekend."

"Yes. I haven't spoken with anyone, but I noticed in the file she left the club with a young man. You can see from the description that her friends didn't really know what the guy looked like," Derek said, watching Dillon study the photograph from the file. "What are you looking at?"

Dillon showed him the photo. "I noticed this mark on her abdomen when I was at the ME's office."

Derek opened Camilla's file. "The same mark is here."

Dillon's

"What is the mark?" Damien asked.

"It's a circle with a line down the middle. Three small chevron bars with a number directly under them on one side. On the other side of the line is the symbol for a female," Dillon looked up. "You know, like on a bathroom door. There is a number in the center of the girl." Dillon held the photo of the young girl out for Damien to see.

Dillon read on. "One witness said he looked like he was twenty-three or twenty-four, and another said he looked like he was in his thirties."

Damien typed on his keyboard. He searched the National Incident database again and typed in the young woman's name. "Her information hasn't been entered into the system yet."

Damien took Tracy's file from Dillon. "It says she was attending a junior college in her hometown. It could be she planned to meet someone down here."

Derek motioned towards the big screen. "Do those cases from years ago have any type of branding on the women?"

Damien typed out a few commands. He used his mouse to enlarge a few of the autopsy photos from several of the cases. "Here." He highlighted a mark on each body.

Derek stood and stared at each photo on the screen. Each woman had the same emblem carved on their abdomens. A circle with three chevron bars and a number. "Were these marks ever made public?"

Damien scrolled through the cases on his screen. He quickly peered at Derek, catching the sideways glance from Dillon. "I don't see any press releases from the cases mentioning the marks."

Dillon turned her chair towards the agent. "They wouldn't have mentioned this in the news, but when I was talking to Beth the other day at the morgue, I saw the symbol on our young victim, and it seemed familiar to me."

Derek's eyes narrowed in on her. His mouth opened, but he closed it before he asked his question. He pointed at the screen. "These chevrons are almost identical to the chevrons on our two victims. Except, these older ones are much more hastily done. Whereas the newer ones look like the killer took time to make sure the carvings were clean and concise."

Dillon rose, stepping closer to the big screen. She looked at each photo. "Are these all the photos from the cold case?"

Damien searched his computer screen. "It looks like it. I can do some more digging and see if we can find any more."

Derek nodded as he pulled his phone from his pocket. "If it looked familiar, could you have seen the case file?"

"I don't know. I don't remember this case. But after the academy, I spent some time studying a lot of cold cases. I could have seen it there. I just know this symbol seems very familiar." Dillon's lips tightened into a thin line.

"Hang on." Derek pushed a speed dial button and waited. "Kyle, I need you to do something for me. I'm going to text you some information. I need you to find any other cases with the same manner of death. Anything matching what I send you." He motioned for the file. "Okay, yeah, here. I will just tell you." He stood and stepped out of the room.

CHAPTER FORTY-ONE

Joe's phone pinged.

"How's Taylor?" Dillon asked.

"She just landed. She had to go on a last-minute trip with her director and a few other people." Joe put his phone in his pocket. "I'm glad she is out of the city, to be honest." He sighed. "I just hope nothing happens to Muffin."

"Is that cat still alive?" Dillon asked.

"Yup. She has to be the oldest cat in the world." Joe laughed.

"You know you need to get her a kitten. This way when Muffin dies, it will be easier on Taylor," Damien said.

"I know," Joe said.

"Anyway, the lawyer will appear in court tomorrow. He got an emergency hearing. He said he would call Taylor afterward," Dillon said.

"The sooner we can get her brother out of her life, the better," Joe said.

Damien snapped his fingers. "I have some information about her brother from Nicky. I'm sorry, man. I forgot to even look at it."

"She's going to be gone for a few days. I think they won't be back until late Saturday. Possibly even Sunday. We can go over it later, in between Camilla's case. Let's just get you back on the job first," Joe said.

Derek walked back in. "I have a guy who can find anything. He used to be a hacker."

"Really?" Dillon asked with a smirk. "Like no joke?"

"No joke. And don't repeat that. He will get back to me soon." Derek handed the younger victim's file back to Damien. He studied the cold case victims' photos. "These are much more brutal than Camilla and Tracy." He moved closer to the screen, looking over each picture.

Dillon stood next to him. "The first killer subdued them, rendering them unable to yell for help. To cry out, but he didn't want them unconscious." She paused for a moment.

Derek admired the profile of Dillon's face. Her features were perfect. She had porcelain-like skin, yet it had the right amount of color. There was no makeup on her. She didn't need it.

Dillon turned towards him, then glanced around the room. "The latest killer did the same thing, just not in the same manner. Both killers wanted their victims conscious. One wanted them to feel the pain, and one didn't. This means the latest victims had to have been given a drug to subdue them, yet keep them somewhat aware of what was happening." She studied the marks on the bodies of the women. "Can you put the photos from Camilla and Tracy's file on the board?" she asked Damien.

"Sure," Damien said. "Let me scan the photos in manually. Save me from searching the ME's database." He motioned for her to hand him Camilla's file. As he opened it, he exhaled a sharp breath.

Dillon's head snapped around towards the sound. "Are you okay?"

He exhaled slowly. "Yeah," he said, staring at the photo.

"I'm sorry. I should have thought about you seeing her picture. I forgot you hadn't seen her file yet," Dillon said.

"I'm okay. I can separate it." Damien swallowed. His throat burned. He pushed down the rush of emotions. "Here are the autopsy photos." He scanned the two pictures. Moving the images around, he dropped the newest victims in the center of the screen. "Here. Look at the symbols." Damien zoomed in on each image.

Derek and Dillon stepped closer to the screen.

Dillon took a pointer from a tray at the base of one TV. She nodded towards Damien. "Put all the pictures of the cold case victims on the other screen."

Damien moved the pictures to the second LCD screen on the wall.

"Now, can you put them in order of their deaths?"

He did what she asked. "Okay," Damien said. "Here they are in order."

Dillon stepped closer. "Focus on the carvings. Can you blow just that section up on each?"

It took Damien a few minutes to go through the files. "Here," he said as he clicked his mouse.

"Look." Dillon pointed to each picture. "The numbers end with thirteen."

Damien tightened the focus on Camilla and Tracy's photos, showing only the carved emblem.

Dillon pointed to their photos. "Look at the numbers under the chevrons."

Derek stepped to the other side of the screen. "Holy shit."

Damien zoomed in on Camilla's abdomen and then on Tracy's. "The numbers under the chevrons are sixteen and seventeen."

Dillon's eyes lit up. "Look at the numbers on the other side of the carving. Camilla is number four, and Tracy is number three."

Joe stood. "Wait, a minute. That means there are two other girls unaccounted for."

"Yes, it does." Derek sat in his chair.

Joe's eyes widened. "Well, shit. This right here is all we need to get you two back on the case. Let's go tell the captain."

"Tomorrow," Derek said.

Joe's excitement bubble deflated.

Damien chuckled at his partner. "Remember, you aren't even supposed to be here, and we aren't supposed to be helping you."

"Crap. Okay. I get it," Joe said, sulking.

Dillon moved to her desk. "I'm searching the FBI database for past cases. They have a section covering symbols."

"Dr. Forsythe said he did that but found nothing." Derek stated.

"I know I have seen that first symbol—no, not the first one, but something very close to it. I just can't remember where." Dillon grunted as she continued searching.

Joe sat in his chair. "If the cases are connected, any ideas how?"

Derek leaned forward, putting his elbows on his knees. He started to speak but stopped himself. Opening his mouth again, he stopped himself once more.

"What?" Joe asked. "Just spit it out."

"There isn't enough information yet to answer your question." Derek sighed. "I don't like guessing."

Dillon spun around in her chair. "Here's the thing. The numbers under the chevrons on the newest victims show a continuation of the previous murders. That's not a coincidence. It is deliberate."

"The murders are so different. The first murders were done with anger and rage. But Camilla and Tracy were murdered with care. The killer took the time to pose them and dress them," Derek said. "Why would this killer give any kind of credit to the previous killer and not kill them the same way? Why is he dressing and posing them? We need to find the other victims."

Dillon sighed. "Maybe your guy will find something we haven't found. But my guess is victims one and two weren't killed in this area."

Damien rubbed his temples. His head thrashed with pain. The lack of sleep and dealing with Camilla's murder was taking a toll on him. "I can run a few searches and see if something comes up in another state."

"Let's assume a drug was used on the latest victims. It still doesn't explain why the new killer is paying homage to his predecessor. The connection could be family, acquaintance, or admiration of the work," Joe said.

Derek ran his fingers through his hair. "If we knew those answers, we could solve the case." He nodded in Joe's direction. "Do you think there is a hotel near here?"

Joe's brow wrinkled. "I don't know. I can see on my phone."

"We have an extra room. Why don't you stay here?" Dillon asked.

"Oh, I couldn't impose," Derek said, waving his hands.

"No imposition at all," Damien said. "Really, we could use your help."

"If you're sure." Derek's gaze moved from Damien to Dillon.

"We're sure," Dillon said. "The room is made up and ready. You might have to share it with Gunner. He seems to think it's his bedroom."

Derek laughed. "I have to share my bed regularly with a boxer named Lola. She is a bed hog."

CHAPTER FORTY-TWO

Detective Jim Fogle stood in line at the canteen. The lunch crowd was heavy today. It seemed like everyone was eating in instead of going out. Jim nodded at Travis when he walked in with Officer Katie Baker.

As he turned back towards the line, DEA Agent Johnson walked in. *What the hell? Why is this guy always here?* Jim twisted his head from side to side, cracking the bones in his neck to ease the tension. His heart rate sped up. He blew out a sharp breath, calming his nerves.

Five men were with the agent. Two were from Burglary, Lieutenant Thomlinson and Detective Ardroin. One was Cutter from the evidence locker, Lieutenant Ratcliff from Narcotics, and the last guy was the lieutenant from Vice. Jim couldn't remember his name.

He listened to their animated conversation as they walked towards the line. One man spoke as Jim picked out a few items from the food line. His heart pounded against his chest. It was the second man from the restroom. He gathered his nerves and turned to the group. Smiling, he nodded at DEA Johnson. He glanced at Cutter. "Hey, Cutter. How's the evidence locker?"

"Boring. But at least I don't have to worry about being shot." Cutter elbowed the man next to him.

"You're a wuss." The man said.

Jim feigned laughter. The man who just spoke was the other man from the bathroom with Johnson.

"Dude, you okay?" DEA Agent Johnson asked Jim. "You look like you're about to pass out."

Jim wiped the sweat from his brow. "I think there's a bug going around." He grabbed his tray and walked to the cashier.

"Hope you didn't give it to us." Agent Johnson laughed as he watched the detective walk away.

Jim halfway chuckled, waving as he walked to the cashier. His hands shook as he handed her some money. Moving to the back of the cafeteria, he sat at a corner table. "Stay calm. Relax." He took a few deep breaths before making a call.

CHAPTER FORTY-THREE

Thursday afternoon

Brycen came back from lunch. They had placed a sign in the building's lobby letting the employees know there would be a memorial gathering for Camilla at four in the atrium.

Someone had purchased a beautiful flower arrangement. Brycen smirked as he read the notice. "I don't think anyone considers Camilla a good person."

"What did you say, Brycen?"

Brycen jumped, turning towards the sound of his name. "Oh, hey, Mark."

"Kind of jumpy, aren't you?" Mark followed Brycen to the elevator.

"I was thinking about Camilla. I can't believe she's dead." Brycen hit the button for the tenth floor.

Mark laughed. "I can't believe someone actually thinks anyone here cares about going to a memorial for Camilla." The doors opened on another floor, and a few people got on. Mark leaned over to Brycen, covering his mouth with his hand. "I'm not surprised she was murdered. I just wonder which wife did it."

Brycen smiled at his co-worker. "Sixty-four-million-dollar question."

They exited on the tenth floor and walked down the hallway, stopping midway.

Brycen's brow wrinkled. "Did they send you here to fix this pipe in the ceiling?"

Mark shook his head. "No. I need to get on up to the roof. Seems there is a small leak. I'm going to look and see if it's coming from the new AC unit installed the other day."

"Crap. You know Jeff installed it, right?"

Mark sighed. "Yes. And I told Darryl not to let him do it. But he insisted he was ready. Plus, we were shorthanded on Monday."

Brycen walked a few feet away and unlocked a maintenance closet. He pulled out a ladder and left the door open. "Do you know anything about Camilla's death?"

Mark glanced over his shoulder. "All I know is George Dunlap collapsed when he heard the news. They had to call an ambulance."

"You're kidding?"

"Nope. You know he and Camilla have been an item for years now."

Brycen stopped what he was doing. "No. I didn't know. Isn't he married?"

Mark threw back his head and laughed. "Every man she slept with was married. Rumor has it her boyfriend from a long time ago found her and Dunlap in a hotel room."

Brycen straightened up. "What boyfriend?"

"I'm not sure of his name. But he was the detective who found the bodies of several girls on a farm downstate. His picture was everywhere."

Brycen's throat seized. He tried to swallow several times, but his mouth was too dry. "I—I don't understand. She dated a detective, like a private detective?"

"No. A homicide detective. Some dude from Division Central. He and his partner were all over the news for a long time." Mark snapped his fingers. "I think about a year ago, I'm not sure. Anyway, this FBI Agent came to Camilla's office." Mark started laughing.

"What is so funny?" Brycen hoped Mark hadn't heard the slight quiver in his voice.

"The scuttlebutt around here was she was the new girlfriend of the detective. All I know is I heard it was the one time Camilla had her ass handed to her. Marcy, the receptionist in Camilla's office, overheard the entire incident."

Brycen held tight to the ladder to keep Mark from seeing his shaking hands. "Let me get this straight. Camilla used to date a homicide detective who is now dating an FBI agent?"

Mark raised an eyebrow at his friend. "Yeah. I mean, I don't know. Why do you care?"

Brycen shrugged as he opened the ladder. "I don't. I guess I'm stunned, that's all. How lucky for her family, they have a connection with a homicide detective. I bet her murder gets solved quickly."

"I don't know about how quickly it gets solved. But I bet they pull out all the stops for her. I feel sorry for whoever killed her. They picked the wrong person to kill." Mark checked his watch. "Shit, I need to get going. Let's go have a few beers later."

Brycen waved at him as he walked away. "Sure." He let out the breath he held. Inhaling deeply threw his nose and exhaling slowly through his mouth. He thought about everything he did at the scene.

Closing his eyes, he replayed it in his mind. "Shit," he said, standing in the hallway. "Why did I not know she dated a homicide detective? A fucking homicide cop." He smashed his hand against the ladder.

Brycen focused on his breathing. His mind raced as he fought to get his emotions under control. Breathing slowly, he raised his hand, repeatedly touching his chin. His left foot tapped on the floor. He closed his eyes and thought of the other night. Going over every movement, he found nothing wrong with his actions before, during, or after he killed Camilla. "Relax. It's okay."

He opened his eyes when he heard the elevator doors open. Walking up the ladder, he removed one of the ceiling tiles and muttered under his breath to himself. "Calm down. You didn't leave any trace of yourself behind. Relax, Brycen. Just relax."

CHAPTER FORTY-FOUR

Dr. Beth Parker pulled up the sheet and covered Tracy Welch. Dr. Forsythe had a meeting and asked her if she would do the autopsies on her and Camilla.

Beth needed a few minutes before moving to the second autopsy. Usually, she had no problem performing her duties as an ME. But when working on such a young woman, she had to work a little harder to separate her emotions.

Memories of her younger sister crashed into her like a tidal wave. Murdered when she was in college, Beth never reconciled not being able to help the detectives solve her case. A case she still works on all these years later, hoping to find her sister's killer.

Closing her eyes, she let out a slow breath. She placed the palms of her hands on the table, supporting her weight. After a moment, she took in a deep, cleansing breath and opened her eyes. Exhaling, she focused on the task and moved to the table containing Camilla's body.

"Okay, sweetie," she said as she grabbed a camera from the little metal table beside her. Beth took photos before she started any autopsy. After one of her first cases ended with charges being dismissed and the killer going free, she made sure she had a record of what the body looked like before she put scalpel to the skin. As she snapped a few wide-angle photos, she zoomed in on certain areas.

She concentrated on the most likely places the killer would have touched his victim. Starting with the mark carved into Camilla's torso, Beth zoomed in with the lens. After taking several photos from different angles, she placed the camera on the standing table.

Using a small ruler, Beth noted the diameter and deepness of each pass made with the blade. She cleaned out the wound track, swabbing the inside and surface area, hoping to find any evidence left by the killer.

As she examined the carving, she noticed how precise the cuts were. Every line cut seemed to be an identical match to the mark left on Tracy. Beth reached over her head and pulled a microphone hanging from the ceiling towards her. "Case number 321450. Knife wounds made by the killer have clean edges with no apparent hesitation marks. At the deepest point, the carving reached a depth of .393 inches. The carving was done postmortem."

Beth made a few more notes on her pad, then moved to the wound on the neck. Again, making notes and measuring the depth, she recorded her case notes. She swabbed the neck and the surrounding area as she moved the overhead light to illuminate the area at a different angle. Bending, she noted the makeup on Camilla's face.

She stepped over to Tracy and did a quick comparison. The killer had used more makeup on his younger victim than on Camilla. Glancing between the two women, her brow wrinkled.

"That's odd," Beth said. She quickly looked at Tracy's lips, then focused on Camilla's. There was a difference in the pigment's sheen. The center of Camilla's lips had a dull appearance when compared to Tracy's lips.

She grabbed the camera and adjusted the light. "I can't believe it." Her hands trembled as she took several photos. With her pulse racing, she tapped down her excitement. Looking through the picture on the camera screen, she zoomed in.

Comparing the photograph to Camilla's lips, she couldn't believe what she saw. She grabbed a DNA swab and gently dragged it over the center of Camilla's top and bottom lips. She sealed the swab in an evidence box and marked it for priority testing.

CHAPTER FORTY-FIVE

Jim sat in the corner with his back against the wall, watching the group of men. He pushed the call button on his phone. "I'm sorry to call you."

"It's okay. I told you to. What's going on?" Damien asked.

"I'm in the canteen. I'm eating lunch. DEA Johnson came in with five other men. I heard them talking. One man with them was the second guy in the bathroom."

Damien motioned for Joe and Dillon. "Hey, I'm going to put you on speaker. Okay, Jim. Joe and Dillon are with me."

"Okay."

"You said the other man from the bathroom was in the canteen," Damien said.

"Are you sure?" Joe asked.

"Yes. I couldn't believe it. I never would have thought it would be him."

"Can anyone hear you?" Damien asked.

"No. I'm in the corner. I'm watching them now. They aren't near me. But DEA Johnson keeps looking in my direction. I think he knows."

"Calm down, Jim. He doesn't know. You haven't told anyone, have you?" Damien asked.

"No. No, I haven't. But he keeps looking at me."

"Okay, who are the other men with Johnson?" Dillon asked.

"Cutter, Lieutenant Thomlinson, Detective Ardroin, Lieutenant Ratcliff, and the Lieutenant from Vice."

"Lieutenant Diego?" Damien's voice rose an octave.

"No, not Diego. The new dude."

Damien nodded. "I know who you're talking about."

Dillon glanced at Joe, shrugging.

Joe scooted next to her. "He transferred in from Rockaway. I can't remember his name. He didn't come over until after the Metacruze case."

"Oh. Okay," she said.

"Listen, Jim, can you get over to my house?" Damien asked.

"I think so. I can come after my shift today. I get off at six."

"What about Travis? Does he get off at six too?" Damien asked.

"Yeah. Yeah, he does. Wait, a second."

Damien and the others listened to a muffled conversation.

"Jim?" Damien said into the phone. "Jim, are you there?"

"Yeah, I'm here. There's an argument. It looks like DEA Johnson said something to Katie. Travis isn't happy."

A loud crash in the background made everyone jump.

"Jim, what the hell is going on?" Joe yelled at the phone.

"Fuck, I got to go. Travis just punched the hell out of Johnson. I'll be over after my shift."

"Jim?" Damien yelled into the phone. "Shit. Call someone in our group and see if they know what the hell is going on," he said motioning towards Joe.

Joe stood. "I will. I'm going to step out so they don't hear you or Dillon."

Damien let out a long breath. He dragged a hand down his face and let his chin drop to his chest. "Shit."

Derek peered over at Dillon. "I'm guessing Johnson is an asshole?"

Dillon raised an eyebrow at him. "Of epic proportion." She leaned her head back against her chair. "We have a problem with him. He has a problem with us. We have been instructed to stay clear of him."

"Oh, I see. I have someone like that in my life." Derek stood, stretching. "Where is the bathroom?"

"To the right." Damien pointed towards the door.

Gunner followed Derek out of the office.

"Gunner, leave the man alone." Dillon whistled for him. She heard Derek tell him he was going to the bathroom and would be right back.

Gunner ran back into the office in a huff.

"C'mon, boy. Let's go outside for a few minutes." Damien led the dog out the back door and waited on the patio.

Joe came out and stood with him. "Hall said Johnson told Katie he heard she was making detective. Then he asked her if she had to sleep with you to get the promotion."

"What the fuck is wrong with that guy? *Vorrei davvero ucciderlo.*" Damien's nostrils flared.

"Don't say that around anyone else. If he ends up dead, you and

Dillon and now Travis will be at the top of that list." Joe leaned against a patio post. He smiled as Gunner ran by, chasing a bird.

"What else did you find out?"

"Hall said Captain Rolland was in the cafeteria and heard the statement. He told Johnson to leave DC. Johnson was claiming he was going to press assault charges." Joe snickered. "Hall and Alvarez were in the canteen. Hall said Captain Rolland told Johnson if he even thought of doing that, he would file sexual harassment charges against him."

"What did Johnson say?"

Joe laughed. "Nothing. Hall said he left with his tail tucked between his legs."

Damien turned towards his friend. "Listen, go back. Check in with everyone. Let the captain know you dropped off Reed at a hotel, and you planned to go back and get him later and go over some of the evidence. Then find Jim and make sure he gets over here later. Along with Travis."

Joe squinted at him. "What about Derek being here?"

Damien exhaled slowly. He watched Gunner run about before he spoke. "I can't explain it, but I trust this guy. I don't think he will say anything about this, and I feel like he can help."

Joe huffed. "I mean, he seems like a good guy, but I don't know about trusting him."

Damien smiled at him. "I see. *Fidarsi è bene non fidarsi è meglio.*"

"Trust is earned."

"I know. But there's something about him. *Porta con sé i morti.*"

Joe shook his head. "Don't start with carrying the dead. I know you are upset about Camilla. Don't carry that shit. You didn't do anything to cause her death."

Damien didn't look at his friend. The weight of her death covered him like wool on a sheep. He felt the tears fill his eyes. Squeezing them together, he tried to stop the overflow.

Joe reached over and gripped Damien's shoulder. "Let her go. Let it go. If you don't, it will eat you from the inside."

Damien took a deep breath through his nose and slowly blew it out of his mouth. "I know." He looked Joe in the eye. "I need to find her killer. I owe her that."

"Fine. I'll give you that." Joe whistled for the dog.

As they walked into the small room just off the kitchen, they heard laughter in the living room.

Damien glanced between the two FBI agents. "What is so funny?"

Dillon giggled. "Derek was telling me about his hacker and when he was arrested at the FBI office as a suspect."

Derek smiled at their confused expressions. "He looks like a surfer. He doesn't look like he should even be an FBI agent. The police thought he had broken into our building. They almost shot him. Which isn't funny. But the rest of it was."

"I want to hear this story." Damien nodded towards Joe. "He's going to go back to DC. Check on the Travis situation. I told him to bring Travis and Jim back with him."

Dillon gave a sideways glance at Derek. "You sure that's a good idea?"

"Yes." Damien sighed. "We will explain things later," he said to Derek.

"No worries. I can always stay in my room and give you some privacy." He motioned to Joe. "I need to get my bag out of your truck."

"Yeah. Follow me out." Joe opened the front door. "Figure out what you want for dinner, and I will bring it with me."

Damien shrugged. "That's good, or we have a shit ton of food in the freezer."

"Isn't the ME coming over later too?" Joe asked.

"Last I heard," Damien said.

"Okay. I'll be back soon." Joe walked out with Derek in tow.

Dillon moved closer to Damien. "You really think that's a good idea? Having everyone over with Derek here?"

Damien stared out the window. "I was telling Joe I trusted him," he said, spinning around. She had a long wisp of hair hanging in her face. He gently moved it behind her ear. "You are so beautiful."

She let her shoulders drop as she wrapped her arms around him. "I know this is hard. Don't shut me out. Okay?" she said, looking up at him.

"I won't. I promise."

Derek walked back in. "Are you two sure I won't be in the way?"

"Not at all." Dillon picked up the cat from the sofa. "I bet you are a little tired. You want to take a shower and relax a bit while we wait for everyone?"

"Man. A nice long shower sounds great." Derek shifted his satchel on his shoulder.

"Follow me. You can use the master bathroom." She winked at Damien. "It's really the only reason I stay with him." As they walked to the stairs, she pointed towards the spare room. "That's where you will be. You saw the bathroom already." Dillon turned towards him. "You want to take a minute and drop your stuff, and then I'll show you the master bath?"

"Yeah, give me a second." Derek walked into the spare room and set his bags on the bed. He grabbed a change of clothes and headed back out. "This will work," he said, chuckling. "What am I about to see here? Is this shower really that special?"

"Yes. Yes, it is," she said.

Damien took comfort in the easy banter between the two agents. Something he hadn't heard from Dillon in a long time. Things seemed to get back to normal. "And then this happens," he said as he plopped on the couch.

Exhaustion crept through his bones. Gunner sat next to him and got his ears scratched. Damien closed his eyes. He could hear his *Nonna's* voice in his head. Clear as day.

"Fidati del tuo istinto."

She used to say 'trust your gut'. When he first became a detective. She would always remind him to follow what his soul told him. Despite Joe's reluctance, his gut told him he could trust Derek.

CHAPTER FORTY-SIX

Travis paced the VCU. Katie had left, and he needed to calm down. He had never wanted to beat the hell out of someone like he did in the canteen.

"Dude," Alvarez said, "you are going to wear out our floor."

Detective Hall had filled in Detectives Cooper and Harris, who had missed the altercation.

"Well, hell. The one time we sneak out to get lunch, all the fun happens." Detective Cooper high-fived Hall.

"It was epic." Detective Hall bounced around like a boxer in the ring. "Pow! Travis knocked that fat cow to the floor."

Travis laughed at Hall. "I shouldn't have hit him."

"Fuck that," Detective Sheila Alvarez said. "You should have kept hitting him."

"No. I should have just let Katie report it," Travis said.

"Listen, he had it coming. No one is going to knock you for this." Alverez looked around the room at her squad. "Why is his fat ass always here, anyway? Doesn't he work for the DEA? He is always at this place."

Cooper rocked back and forth in his chair. "I think the guy is dirty. He's up to something. I don't have proof, but he is up to something."

Travis bit his bottom lip to keep from saying anything. He heard a noise behind him. As he turned around, he saw Detective Jim Fogle motioning for him to come to ECD. "Hey, I really appreciate you guys. Hall, Alverez, thanks for having my back down there."

"Any time, Travis." Hall continued to dance around like a boxer. "But know that I could whip your ass."

Alvarez laughed, slapping her knee. "Shit, you couldn't win a fight against a blind man. Sit your skinny ass down."

Travis left the two sparring in the center of the pen. As he got closer to the glass wall of ECD, he could see the whites of Jim's eyes. He keyed in the combo to the soundproof room. "What happened?"

Jim made sure the lock was secured and then turned his back to the VCU pen. "I know who the other guy in the bathroom was."

It took a few minutes for the conversation to register in his brain. "How? When?"

"I was in line in the canteen when Johnson and his cronies came in. I heard them talking, and I recognized the voice." Jim peered over both shoulders.

"No one can hear us." Travis took a seat across from him.

"I know. I can't help it. I started sweating when I heard his voice, and Johnson even asked me what was wrong. He said I looked sick."

"What did you do?"

"I fucking got away from them as quick as I could. I was sitting in the corner in the back when all hell went down with you and him." Jim crossed his arms, then uncrossed them. He kept looking towards the doorway.

"We need to call Damien."

"I did. Just before you hit Johnson. Fuck, man. He kept looking at me while I was eating. What if he knows?"

Travis leaned forward in his chair. "How could he know? Did you tell anyone else?"

Jim clenched his fists. His body stiffened. "No. I haven't breathed a word of this to anyone. But he kept glancing over at me. Why would he do that?"

"Listen, did you tell Damien while you were talking with him?"

Jim bit his nail as he shook his head. "No."

"Okay. I can call Damien, and we will find out what to do next. Who was the other voice?"

Jim opened his mouth to say the name when the phone rang.

Travis answered it, holding up his finger. "ECD."

"Travis, this is Joe. I'm on my way to DC. I was making sure you were in the ECD. Is Jim with you?"

"Yeah, he's right here." Travis mouthed Joe's name to Jim.

"Great. You two stay there."

The phone went dead.

Travis hung up the receiver. "Joe said not to leave."

"I'm not going anywhere. I might even stay in a hotel so he can't find me."

CHAPTER FORTY-SEVEN

Agent Johnson stood next to his car in the garage.

The man from the bathroom had followed him out of the canteen. "Why the hell would you say that?"

Johnson spun around, facing him. "Don't fucking come at me. These assholes can't take a joke."

"A joke? Are you serious? That wasn't a joke. That was an asshole thing to say. Not to mention you broke every sexual harassment policy this place has." He ran his hand through his hair, yanking on the ends. "I can't believe you. I told you not to bring attention to yourself."

Agent Johnson placed his hands on the hood of his car. He knew he'd messed up. He didn't need this and blamed Kaine for even putting him under the spotlight. His shoulders rolled forward. "This is all Kaine's fault."

His companion huffed in disbelief. "You must have some kind of mental problem. Are you now blaming Kaine? Maybe you need to get the hell out of town now. Take your money and drugs and get out of here."

Agent Johnson growled as he pushed himself off his car. He turned on his friend like a lion turns on his prey. "Don't tell me what to do. I will leave when I have everything I'm entitled to. I still need to finalize the drug deal. That will take another couple of weeks. And while I'm waiting, I will get my revenge on that fucking guinea. And then I will take out that bitch of an FBI agent. Both of them deserve to be buried in the desert."

"Whoa. I don't want any part of that. You want to kill them? That's on you. I helped cover your tracks here. And that is all I'm doing." The man backed away.

Johnson stepped closer to him and grabbed him by the collar. "You are in this too. You will do what I need, or I will make sure your little brother goes to a hole for the rest of his life. Do you understand?"

The man knocked his hands away. "Don't you ever threaten me or my family again. Do I make myself clear? I will take you down, even if it means I go to jail." He turned away and walked back towards the building.

"I would rethink your position if I were you, Lieutenant." Johnson stewed, watching the Lieutenant enter the building away from him. He opened his car door as Joe's truck drove into the garage.

Joe snickered as he drove past DEA Agent Johnson. The episode in the canteen would get Johnson into even more trouble. He parked several parking spots over. Once he exited his vehicle, he crossed to the other side of the garage so he wouldn't be tempted to finish what Travis had started.

"You scared?"

"Yeah, dickhead. I'm scared. Scared I might catch crabs from you."

"You need to warn your boy and his bitch girlfriend. I'm coming for them."

Joe stopped before he reached the building. He turned and faced Johnson. "Listen, you stinky little fart, you come anywhere near them, and they will never find your body."

"Are you threatening me?"

Joe laughed. "Not at all. That's a promise. Oh, hey, don't forget to ice that bruise on your cheek." He heard Johnson screaming obscenities as he walked into the building.

CHAPTER FORTY-EIGHT

Thursday afternoon

Joe sat on the corner of Hall's desk as he listened to him, and Detective Alvarez give all the details of what happened in the canteen. He updated them on what he could regarding Damien.

He glanced over his shoulder and saw Travis and Jim Fogle in the ECD office. "Okay, Harris, you and Cooper are on call, correct?"

"Yep. Get to spend the evening with this pecker." Harris laughed at Detective Cooper's reaction.

"You love me, and you know it." Cooper threw a tennis ball at his partner.

"That may be true, but I don't want to spend every waking moment with you. I have a life." Harris threw the ball back.

"You know you don't have a life. Your sorry ass sits at home just waiting for your life to begin," Alvarez said.

"Okay, you guys are pathetic." Joe glanced over his shoulder again. "I need to touch base with Travis, and then I will be out of the office helping Agent Reed."

Hall perked up. "Do you trust him?"

Joe looked at his friend. "I think so. He has found some evidence proving Damien and Dillon had nothing to do with Camilla's death. There's something about the guy. He isn't in it for the glory. Something else drives him. I'm not sure what it is." Joe stood. "I need to get moving. Don't repeat anything. We won't be telling the captain until we have more information."

Hall zipped his lips.

"We won't say anything," Harris said.

Joe listened to their banter as he walked towards ECD. The Electronic and Cyber division had a soundproof and airtight room. It had its own ventilation system separate from the rest of DC and was often cooler than the rest of the floor. Before he entered, he braced himself for the drop in temperature.

He used his keycard, but the lock didn't open. He pushed the intercom button. "You gonna let me in?"

Travis glanced up from a circuit board and moved to open the door. "Hey sorry. We shut down the key reader."

Joe stepped inside. "Afraid?"

Travis smirked. "Not at all. Wasn't sure if one of Johnson's cronies would try to pay us a visit." He smiled. "Jim is freaked out."

Jim spun his chair around. "If he finds out I know about the bathroom, I know he will kill me."

Joe sat next to him. "First, Travis, tell me about the incident in the canteen."

Travis explained what Johnson said and what led to him punching him. "He deserved it. I couldn't let him say what he did and not do something. Katie deserves better."

"I saw him in the garage. His cheek and eye were swelling. Just know, you need to avoid him at all costs. He will come after you and try to piss you off, enticing you to do something." Joe took a piece of gum from the open pack on the counter.

"I know. I'm ready. I plan on ignoring him."

Joe laughed. "Good luck. Hopefully, we will get his ass out of the way permanently." He turned to Jim. "Tell me about the conversation you heard."

Jim recounted the incident. "I couldn't believe it. When I heard the voice from the bathroom, I almost shit my pants. I know Johnson saw it too. Hell, he even asked me if I was about to pass out."

"Listen," Joe said. "We won't let anything happen to you. Johnson does not know you were in the bathroom. And he won't find out. No one will mention this." Joe shot a look at Travis.

"Dude, I haven't told a soul. Not even Katie. And that is hard for me," Travis said.

"I know. Man, I know. I'm still scared." Jim clasped his hands in his lap.

Joe sat and waited, giving the man space.

Travis moved closer. "Damien and Joe won't let anything happen to you." He half chuckled. "I'm sure I have distracted him, and he will come for me."

Joe smirked at Travis. "That's one hundred percent true."

Jim halfheartedly laughed at the remark. He looked at Joe. "It was Lieutenant Thomlinson."

Joe sat up straight. "Are you sure?"

"One hundred." He glanced between the two men. "Now, do you understand why I'm so freaking scared? How high up does this shit go?"

Joe pulled his phone and texted Damien. He stood, resting his hand on Jim's shoulder. "Come over to Damien's house after work." He turned towards Travis. "You need to be there, too."

They both nodded.

"Jim can ride with me. I'll bring you back later tonight." Travis stood.

"No. I'll just follow you out. I'm off tomorrow and the next day." Jim leaned forward, resting his elbows on his knees.

"Listen, Jim, you're going to be okay." Joe moved towards the door. "You both get off at 6 p.m.?"

They both nodded.

"Good. See you later." Joe walked out and headed out of VCU. Standing in the elevator, he texted Damien. When it stopped on the third floor, he exited before he realized he was on the wrong floor. As he stepped back, Lieutenant Thomlinson entered.

Joe smiled. "Hey, Lieutenant, how's it going?"

Thomlinson shrugged. "Okay. How's Damien?"

Joe grinned back. "Doing well." He waited a moment, then continued speaking. "Man, what the heck happened in the canteen today? Heard about Travis knocking the shit out of Dickhead Johnson."

Thomlinson's nostrils flared. He regained his composure. "What Johnson said to Officer Baker was completely out of line. I'm sorry she experienced it."

"You and he have been pretty tight," Joe said as the elevator doors opened.

Both men stepped out. They stopped right outside the entryway to the Robbery division.

Thomlinson put his hands in his pants pockets. "I know many people think he's an asshole. Hell, even I can admit he's an asshole, but he has helped me a few times."

Joe stepped away and started for the side entrance leading to the garage. He turned back and looked at the lieutenant. "Unfortunately, Johnson does nothing nice without a price. Hope you didn't have to pay too much for his kindness." Joe waved. "See ya. Lieutenant."

CHAPTER FORTY-NINE

Damien glanced up from his phone. "I don't believe this."

"What?" Dillon asked as she munched on a bowl of chips.

Gunner watched each chip leave the bowl and followed it to her mouth. Every time she didn't share, he moaned.

Dillon frowned at the dog. "I guess you want a chip?"

Gunner yipped at her, wagging his tail.

She held out the chip. "Easy." She then put the chip in her mouth and leaned down towards the dog.

Gunner stepped closer. He craned his neck, inching close to her. He placed his muzzle close enough to take the chip and not touch her. He chomped, wiggling his butt.

"Good boy." Dillon rubbed his head.

"Seriously? What is wrong with you?" Damien asked.

"What? I'm teaching him not to snatch the food from my hand or my mouth." She cooed at the dog. "You are such a good boy. Yes, you are."

"Did you even hear what I said?"

"No. I wasn't paying any attention to you." She batted her eyelashes at him.

He rolled his eyes. "It's Thomlinson."

Dillon leaned her head to one side. "What's Thomlinson?"

"This is why you should pay attention. Joe texted me. The second voice in the bathroom, the one Jim heard, was Thomlinson."

Dillon sat up straight. "No way. I was sure it was Detective Ardroin."

"Why would you think it was him?"

"That man is always around Johnson at DC. It's like he has to be up the man's ass." Dillon spun around in her chair. "This is going to piss off Captain Mackey."

"Hell yeah." Damien leaned back in his chair. "I knew Thomlinson's brother had some drug issues, but they had to be terrible for him to take help from Johnson."

Damien typed out a few commands on his computer.

"What are you doing?"

He smiled in her direction. "Research."

"I think you should call your captain, and I should call my director.

Put them on a conference call and tell them what we have." Dillon let Gunner lick the bowl, scarfing down a few crumbs.

"I will, but first I want to talk to Jim and Travis. We need Travis to help track Thomlinson." Damien stopped typing. "It must come from him, so it can go into the official record."

"I can't imagine helping DEA Johnson steal the drugs was worth the price."

"No kidding. Not only is his career over, but he may face jail time." Damien heard a noise in the hallway. He cocked his ear and listened as Agent Reed came down the stairs and entered his room.

"Why do you trust him?" Dillon asked, leaning closer to his desk.

"Why don't you?"

"I don't trust anyone. You know that." She laughed. "I kind of trust him. He has nothing to gain by keeping us shut out of DC."

Damien relaxed. He closed his eyes as he laid his head on the back of his chair. "Something about him. I can't put my finger on it." He shrugged. "I think he cares more for the dead than the living."

Dillon quit spinning and stared at him. "You think he is like you? *A morte ze le portame 'n spalla.*" She stumbled through the pronunciations.

"If I carry the dead on my shoulders, so do you. You need to work on your Italian."

"My Italian is fine." She laughed. "I agree with the other part, though. We both have that problem."

They heard the door across the hall open and close.

Derek walked in.

His boyish good looks struck Dillon. "Did you enjoy the shower?"

Derek flopped into a chair. His line of sight shifted between Damien and Dillon. "I'm not sure I would ever leave my house if I had that shower."

Damien barked out a laugh. "I hear you on that."

"Have you heard from your guy in Arizona?" Dillon asked as she stood.

"He texted me. He said he had a few things and was putting them together. I should have an email soon."

Dillon turned towards Damien. "I'm going to put in a few pasta dishes and get those baking." She spun her watch on her wrist. "An hour should be enough time to bake from frozen. Maybe a little more time. They should get it done about the time everyone shows up."

As she headed towards the kitchen, she turned at the opening of the doorway. "Text Joe and tell him to pick up a few loaves of bread from D' Amato's Bakery."

"I will." Damien typed out a text on his phone. When it pinged back, he looked up. "Travis and Jim should be here around 6:30."

"When are the Doc and Beth showing up?" she asked.

Damien shrugged. "I would assume around the same time. I can text them."

"No, don't bother. I will just bake the two largest dishes we have in the freezer." She whistled for Gunner to follow her out.

Damien eyed Derek.

Derek turned from the doorway to see Damien staring at him. "What?"

"What made you want to be a profiler?"

"I like puzzles."

"Nothing happened in your past to drive you to this profession?"

Derek leaned forward, placing his elbows on his knees. "You mean like Dillon's past?"

"Something like that."

Derek waited a beat before answering. "No real tragedy to speak of."

Damien cocked his head to the side. "You just like puzzles, huh?"

Derek winked at him. "Yeah. That about sums it up."

"What do you think about this killer?"

Derek leaned back. He folded his hands in his lap. "I think he's methodical. I think he is creating something."

"Creating something?"

Derek nodded. "Yeah. He isn't driven by rape or the murder itself, like the previous killings. Those were filled with anger. These new murders are so different."

Damien leaned forward on his desk, folding his hands in front of him. "Yet they are so similar."

"Similar because of the emblem left on the girl's torso and where the bodies were discovered." Derek glanced up at the photos, still on the big screen, pointing. "The first killer stalked the girls in the park. Our new guy finds his victims elsewhere but kills them in the parks. He has a way to transport them. And he isn't worried about being caught. This tells me he's researched the areas. The first killer seemed to hang out and stalk, no pre-planning."

Damien closed his eyes. He opened them when Dillon walked back into the room.

"I have a few thoughts on this case." Dillon said as she sat at her desk. She handed both men one of the three beers she carried with her.

"Thanks," Derek said as he twisted off the top. Taking a few long gulps, he relaxed into his seat. "This is nice."

"What are your thoughts?" Damien asked as he took a long pull.

"Our first killer liked the chase or the ambush. The thrill of stalking his prey." Dillon stepped over to the screen. She motioned to Derek. "Do you agree?"

"Yes. I think that is a reasonable assumption." Derek drank his beer.

She did a double take.

"What?" Derek asked.

"That's odd to say. A reasonable assumption."

Derek squared up with Dillon, facing her. "It is an assumption. And based on what I see here, I think it is the right assumption."

"Hmm. Okay." Dillon continued. "Our new killer seems to be more concerned with the appearance of the victims themselves."

"Like he's making something?" Damien asked.

"Exactly." She finished her beer.

"That's what he just said." Damien pointed at Derek.

"It's very neat. Tidy." Derek put his empty beer bottle in the closest trash can.

"What does that tell us?" Damien asked.

Dillon held up her finger and went to the kitchen. She came back with several more beers in her hand.

Derek stared at the photos on the TV screens. He opened his beer and took a sip, facing Dillon. "The first killer is confident in his abilities. He knows with the right strike, he can render his victims unable to call out for help. He's angry, and he hates women."

He set his beer down on the corner of Dillon's desk. He turned towards Damien. "I think the second killer is not sure of his abilities. He uses a drug to render them unconscious, yet aware but unable to fight back. I think he is younger than the first killer." Derek stopped and turned towards the screen. He stared at the two new victims.

"Well? Is that it?" Damien asked.

"No." He faced the detective. "This new killer isn't angry at all. He takes care of the women. He doesn't defile them by raping them like his predecessor." Derek stood and moved towards the middle of the screen. "No. This killer covets what he sees. He wants a certain look."

Derek moved closer to the screen. "Can you blow up the two pictures of Camilla and Tracy? I want to see them next to each other."

Damien pulled the two pictures and placed them front and center on the screen. "There. What do you see?"

Derek studied the pictures. He stepped closer and examined each one. "No. No. That can't be."

"Can't be what?" Dillon asked, standing. She walked over to where he stood and stared at the screen.

"Can you overlay the pictures putting Camilla's right hand next to Tracy's left hand?" Derek asked Damien.

"Sure." He moved the pictures until the hands were almost on top of each other. "Holy shit."

Dillon's jaw dropped. "We need to find the other victims."

"Yeah, we need to see if they fit." Derek stepped back and took his beer from the desk. "I know it's only two, but if you look at Tracy's right hand, it is positioned just like Camilla's. The other victims will be posed to fit."

Dillon crossed her arms over her chest. "Talk about taking fifth-grade art to new heights."

"Well, I thought he was making something. I wasn't expecting to see this," Derek said.

"We need to find the first two women. I wonder how many girls he needs before the paper doll chain is complete," Dillon said, taking a sip of her beer.

CHAPTER FIFTY

Thursday 4 p.m.

Brycen stood at the back of the atrium. Keeping his distance from the front, he picked a spot, allowing him to see and hear everything. Several of the big wigs gathered near the stage. Mr. Dunlap sat in the front row of seats. His face was visibly pale. Brycen laughed under his breath, glancing around, making sure no one heard him.

He was a little pissed about Camilla having so many affairs. Although most of them happened before he came to work here. But it didn't really matter in the end. She was his perfect muse, and why he started this project. That and to show his grandfather he could take over the family tradition.

Most everyone in the audience sat with smirks on their faces. He stared at the large photo sitting front and center on the makeshift stage. Camilla was more than beautiful. She really was almost perfect. Brycen thought about those last few moments with her.

Closing his eyes, he relived it, savoring the gentle kiss, he gave her. He smelled her perfume. The woman's scent was intoxicating. He jumped when he felt someone touch his arm, and turned to the person.

"Hey, what did I miss?" Mark asked.

"Not much. Stupid speeches. No one cares. Don't they know this?"

"I think they just wanted to look good for the news," Mark said.

Brycen peered around. "What news?"

Mark pointed towards the front of the atrium. "Channel Four."

Brycen stared toward Mark's finger. He hadn't noticed them when he entered. His gaze drifted around the atrium. A news crew had set up two cameras. One panned the audience while one focused on the front stage. "Hey, I need to run to my locker. When do you want to meet for that beer?"

"I'm heading out with a few buddies tonight. We are going over to O'Malley's and watch a few basketball games." Mark rubbed his hands together. "Getting ready for March Madness. You can meet us over there."

"Yeah, what time?" Brycen asked.

Mark glanced at his watch. "Probably around eight. Meet us there."

"I will." Brycen waved as he walked away. Glancing over his shoulder, he made sure nobody saw him leave. His watch said 4:45. Checking the

company app on his phone, he clocked out.

As he left the building, he thought about Camilla. Going over each step, he was confident he didn't leave any clues behind. He chastised himself for not knowing about the homicide detective.

But now he had to focus on his new girl. She frequented O'Malley's. this would be the perfect chance to see her. As much as he told himself he had covered his tracks, something niggled at him. He had to clear his mind and get ready for the newest addition to his project. Licking his lips, he smiled as he thought of her profile picture. A beautiful young woman who would help round out his collection.

Pulling into his home driveway, he entered his garage and waited for the door to shut. Before exiting his vehicle, he thought about what he should tell his grandfather. Maybe he would keep what he learned about Camilla to himself. At least for the time being. The last thing he wanted was to hear his grandfather say I told you so.

CHAPTER FIFTY-ONE

Joe sat in his truck. He removed his phone from his pocket and texted Taylor.

"Hey babe. Have you landed?"

"Yeah. Just got to my hotel room."

"I need you to not go out alone. Just in case."

"I hadn't planned on it. I hope this is over soon."

"Damien has some information that may help. We are going to go through it while you're gone. Should have something by the time you return."

"Okay. I need to go. We are meeting for dinner in a bit, and I want to freshen up. I love you, Joe."

"I love you."

Joe placed his phone in one of the drink cup holders. He put the keys in the ignition and was about to start the truck when Lieutenant Thomlinson stepped out of the building.

Parked close to where the lieutenant stood, Joe turned the key without starting the truck and lowered his windows enough to hear part of his phone call.

"I don't care. You need to leave. Go anywhere. Just get out of town. Promise me?"

Joe watched as the lieutenant paced. "Something is going down," he whispered out loud.

"Please, do this for me. Things are going to move fast and you aren't safe. Take the money I gave you and the ID and go. They will get you out of the country. You've been wanting to travel through Europe. Go now."

Someone walked out of the building.

Lieutenant Thomlinson turned around, facing the direction of Joe's truck.

Joe ducked down enough to hide from the lieutenant's line of sight.

"Just do it. I love you. Text me when you land, but do it on a phone you

buy in Europe. Ditch your phone now. Don't argue with me, just do it. Please. You're in danger. Remember, I love you." Lieutenant Thomlinson pocketed his phone.

Joe sat up in time to see Lieutenant Thomlinson walk back to the door. The man turned around and looked directly at him. Joe made eye contact. The lieutenant's posture slumped, and his eyes were wet and dull.

Thomlinson held his gaze.

Joe saw his lips move, mouthing several words. *What are you saying?* He turned on the ignition when Thomlinson walked into the building. As he pulled out of the garage, he drove past the glass door leading into the building. Lieutenant Thomlinson stood on the other side and watched him as he drove by. He mouthed the same words again.

A queasy feeling came over Joe. Something didn't feel right. None of this felt right. Pulling out into traffic, Joe ran the exchange through his brain. "What the hell did you say?" he said as a car drove past, honking his horn. "Fuck you, buddy. Shit!" Joe swerved over, barely missing a vehicle. He phoned Damien. "I'm on my way back. I think we have a problem."

CHAPTER FIFTY-TWO

Damien laid down the phone. "That was Joe. He's on his way back. Says he thinks we have a problem. He asked me to look up Thomlinson and see if I can find out anything about his family." He drank a few sips of beer before he started typing on his computer.

"Who's Thomlinson?" Derek asked. Gunner sat at his feet and Coach sat on his lap.

Dillon squinted at Damien.

"You don't have to tell me," Derek said.

"It's part of the problem with DEA Agent Johnson." Damien rocked back and forth in his chair. "We think someone in DC is dirty along with Johnson and we think that person helped cover tracks allowing Johnson to steal drugs from our evidence locker."

Derek raised an eyebrow at him. "And you guys think Thomlinson is the inside man?"

"It's looking that way," Dillon said.

"Does that agent wear a DEA hat all the time?" Derek asked.

"Yeah, why do you ask?" Damien finished his first beer and opened the second.

"I saw him in the hallway when Joe and I left DC. I got a weird vibe from him," Derek said.

"What kind of weird vibe?" Dillon asked.

"Not sure how to explain it, but I had a feeling something bad was going to happen." Derek watched as Dillon and Damien exchanged glances. "You don't have to tell me, but maybe I can help."

Damien placed his elbows on his desk. He stared at Dillon for a few moments, then turned towards the agent. "It seems Lieutenant Thomlinson is the one who helped Johnson steal the drugs. We are not sure how much he was involved. Did he take the drugs or just help cover it up? We don't know."

Dillon opened another beer. "Johnson has had it in for us ever since I got into the FBI unit here. I turned him down when he asked me out."

Derek spun around, facing her. "You spurned him?"

"I guess. I said no. I was dating Damien." Dillon sipped her beer.

"What has happened between you two?" Derek asked, looking at Damien.

"He hates me. Because of my family. Johnson thinks I got to where I am on the backs of my parent's success. Agent Johnson thinks he is the smartest guy in the room."

"It really started when your team and Vice covered the Metacruze case," Dillon said.

"What case is that?" Derek asked.

"DEA Johnson and his team had been working on the case. It crossed over to a case we had and ultimately Vice and VCU solved it. He was pissed," Damien explained.

"Let me get this straight," Derek said. "You spurned him," he faced Damien, "and you bested him at his own job. Is that correct?"

Damien laughed. "I guess that's about it."

Derek shifted in his seat, making Coach jump off his lap. "I think you two have much more to worry about than Johnson being dirty."

"Really?" Dillon asked.

"I think before he is finished with whatever plan he has for the drugs, he is going to come after you two."

Dillon smirked, glancing at Damien.

Damien chuckled.

"What am I missing?" Derek asked.

"We hope that happens," Dillon said as the doorbell rang.

CHAPTER FIFTY-THREE

Brycen entered his home. Removing his jacket, he heard the TV playing in the living room. The local news recapped the murder of Camilla, showing clips from the memorial service. He stopped, watching from the entryway.

As one camera panned the crowd, he didn't see himself in any of the shots. "Well, that's good." Walking into the living room, he placed his hand on his grandfather's shoulder. "Hey, Grandpa. How was your day?"

"It was okay."

"Great. I will have dinner ready shortly."

"Humph."

Brycen cleaned the plate and placed it in the dishwasher. After putting some butter in a pan with some onions, he removed the pork chops from the fridge. He seasoned them and placed them in a pan, searing both sides.

He prepared the instant mashed potatoes. Removing the pork chops, he added a little flour, cream, and extra butter to the pan, creating a gravy. He placed the pork chops back into the pan and let them simmer for a few more moments. Taking two plates from the cupboard, he filled them with the food, and placed both on a tray. Adding two drinks, he headed to the living room.

"Here, Grandpa." He set a plate on the small table next to his grandfather's chair. "I made some sweet tea. Your favorite." Brycen ate, watching the news. He glanced at his grandfather. "It's good, isn't it?"

"It's not bad."

"I have plans tonight with my friends. We're going to a bar." Brycen smiled at his grandfather. "I have another girl. I'm hoping she will be there tonight." He removed his phone from his pocket. Scrolling through a few photos, stopping on the one with the young woman's profile picture. "Here." He held his phone out for his grandfather to see.

His grandfather stared blankly at the picture.

Brycen jutted his chin out, sneering. "I thought you would like this one. I wanted to give you one I thought you would have done in your day. She also fits my project."

"I don't think you should. I think you should wait."

He turned towards his grandfather. "I'm calling the shots now. I know what I'm doing." Brycen finished his dinner. He picked up his plate. "I'll leave your plate here. I know you like to take your time eating."

Brycen cleaned up the kitchen before showering and changing. Before he walked out of his closet, he reached into a little box on the shelf. He removed a vial. Lifting it up to the light, he checked the amount of liquid inside. "This should be more than enough," he said, placing the vial in the front pocket of his jeans.

He walked back into the living room and sat next to his grandfather. "I'm going to be leaving soon," he said, reaching over and taking his grandfather's hand in his. "I wish we could do some of these girls together. I wish I could have seen you in your prime."

"I would never do it the way you are. You make it too complicated."

"Planning helps things go smoother. Look at the one girl from Virginia. You almost got caught." Brycen leaned in aggressively towards his grandfather. "I won't get caught."

"You have made a mistake. It just hasn't caught up to you yet."

"No, I haven't!" Brycen stood, pushing back his chair. "Stop saying that."

"You did. You made a mistake with Camilla. You should never have killed her."

Brycen watched as his grandfather's mouth curved slightly upward. "Stop. You always want to make me feel insecure compared to you. I'm better at this than you. I will prove it to you. I will be one of the most regarded artists of all time. When they see my work, they will know all these women had to die for the greater good. For art."

CHAPTER FIFTY-FOUR

Joe twisted the doorknob. When it opened, he stepped inside. "Yo!"

Gunner ran in, barking until he saw Joe. Wiggling his butt and whining, he stood on his hind legs.

"Hey buddy." Joe moved the bag of bread to his left hand, holding it out of reach. "Quit trying to steal the bread."

Dillon walked around the corner. "How did you get in?"

"It was open." Joe shut the door behind him. He bent over and kissed Dillon on the cheek. "It smells great in here."

She glanced at her watch. "Only about forty-five minutes and all the dishes should be ready. Thanks for getting these." She took the bread from him.

Joe rubbed his hands together. "You're welcome and I can't wait."

Dillon shook her head as she walked towards the office. "Look who just barged in."

"Hey, you left the door unlocked." Joe nodded at Derek. "Have you come up with anything new?"

"Our killer is taking art to a whole new level," Dillon said, walking in from the kitchen.

Joe's gaze darted around the room. "Come again?"

Derek smirked. He pointed to the LCD screen on the wall. "See the pictures?"

Joe glanced up. He twisted his head from side to side. "You serious?" he asked, pointing at the photos.

"Yep. He's creating a paper doll chain." Derek rocked back and forth in the chair. "It looks like he is using new victims to pay tribute to an earlier killer. We don't have anything else yet."

Derek shifted in his seat. "Tell me about Lieutenant Thomlinson."

Joe's eyes darted between Dillon and Damien.

"It's okay. Share it," Damien said.

Joe's eyes narrowed in on his partner before he shifted his focus on Derek.

Derek laughed. "Listen. I think I can help with this. Nothing will go any further than me. I promise." His face softened as he waited for Joe to start talking.

Joe recounted the experience in the garage. "I think something is going down."

"What do you think he said?" Dillon asked.

Joe leaned forward, resting his forearms on his knees, and clasped his hands together. "Man... he saw me. He knew I was looking right at him. Then when I drove by, he stood there waiting, and mouthed the same words. I feel like I know exactly what he said, but I can't... I don't know. I can't know for sure."

Derek straightened up. "Are you willing to try something?"

Joe raised his eyebrows at him. "What does this something entail?"

Derek laughed. "Close your eyes."

"Are you going to hypnotize me?"

"No. Not really. Okay, kind of. Trust me." Derek pulled his phone from his pocket and brought up a metronome app. "I want you to concentrate on the ticking noise." He pushed play and the click clack of the metronome filled the office.

Damien glanced at Dillon, who stared at Derek.

"Okay, close your eyes," Derek said.

"Man, if you make me cluck like a chicken, I will shoot you." Joe sighed and wiggled in his chair. He settled in and closed his eyes.

"Listen to the noise. Just relax. Concentrate only on the clicking noise." Derek waited a moment. "Now, think back to the garage. You can hear the conversation. Do you hear Lieutenant Thomlinson?"

"Yes. He's on the phone."

"He turns and sees you. He's looking right at you. You make eye contact."

Joe relaxed into the chair. His face softened. "He's staring at me."

"What does he do? Does he move his hands, place his phone in his pocket, or does he do something else?"

Joe's brow wrinkled.

"Don't think about it. Remember the conversation you heard. He finishes speaking on the phone. Thomlinson turns and stares at you. What is the next thing he does?"

The wrinkle across Joe's forehead dissipates. "He nods at me."

"Okay. Then what does he do?"

"He looks down at his phone, then looks back at me. It's quick."

Derek nodded. "What do you see next?"

"The man says something. Directly to me."

"Joe, it is dead silent around you. You hear no other noises. Concentrate on hearing what he says."

Joe clenched his fist. "I can't hear him. I can see his lips move."

"You can hear him. Read his lips. They are moving and he is telling you something. Concentrate on his lips as they move."

Joe's eyebrows squished together. "He's saying, I'm... I'm sorry. He's telling me he's sorry."

"That's good, Joe. What else is he mouthing to you?" Derek asked.

Joe leaned to the right. He tilted his head as if to hear better. "Thomlinson said I'm sorry. Then he said...."

"Listen to your breathing, Joe. Thomlinson said what?"

Taking a deep breath, Joe sunk into his chair. "I'm sorry. I'm so sorry." Joe shook his head. "No. Not I'm so sorry, but something like I shouldn't have or I had no choice. Yeah, he said he had no choice." His eyes popped open. He stared at Derek. "How did you do that?"

Derek laughed as he shut off the metronome app. "I didn't do anything. Just made you think about what you saw in the garage with no distractions."

Joe nodded in Damien's direction. "He said he was sorry and he shouldn't have and he had no choice. I can see it plain as day."

Damien turned towards Derek. "If he is sorry and said he had no choice, I'm assuming Johnson forced him to help him get the drugs."

Standing, Joe walked to the kitchen and grabbed a beer from the fridge. He came back to the office and remained standing as he popped the top. "When he said he was sorry, I felt something weird."

"What was the feeling you had? Was it sadness, worry, dread?" Derek asked.

Joe snapped his fingers. "Dread. I felt like something bad was going to happen. To Thomlinson. That's just too fucking weird." He sat in his chair.

"I can let the captain know about this later, after we speak with Jim and Travis." Damien glanced at his watch. "They should get here pretty quick." He glanced over at Dillon. "What's up with you?"

Dillon snapped her head around. "Huh?"

Derek and Joe looked at her.

"You got something on your mind?" Derek asked.

"Listening to the clicking noise made me think about the symbol. I know I have seen it before, and it wasn't on a dead person." Dillon stood. "I'm going to check on the food. And feed the fatties."

Gunner jumped up from his perch under her desk and followed her out of the room.

Joe turned towards Derek and Damien. "What's up with her?" he took a long sip of his beer.

"It's bugging her. When she knows she has seen something or knows something, it bothers her until she can figure it out. This whole situation is getting to her. To me." Damien logged back into his computer.

Joe turned towards Derek. "Are you going to leave right after you talk to the captain?"

Derek blinked his eyes. "I hadn't thought of it. I would assume once I cleared you guys, they would hand the case back to you." He leaned back in his chair, crossing his legs. "Then again. I can see them not wanting to look like they made a hasty decision. And keep you two off the case longer."

Joe snapped his fingers. "I think you should ask to stay on. Suggest they let Damien and Dillon help you. That way it can fall on you, but get them back where they belong."

Damien stared at his partner. He raised an eyebrow at him. "You trying to get a new partner?"

"Ha. Yeah. Of course. Any chance to get rid of your ass?" Joe laughed.

Damien looked over at Derek. "You know, if you stayed on for a few days, it might push them to let us back onto the case. You could say our familiarity with the city could help you."

"I know what they did by removing you seemed like a slap in the face. They just needed to show the public there was nothing fishy going on. But, if you don't mind having a house guest for a few extra nights, I think I can swing it. I may even pull rank if they give me a hard time."

"Pull rank on who?" Dillon asked as she walked back in with beers for everyone.

"We asked Derek if he could stay a few extra days and thought if he suggested you and I help him, it might get us back to the job sooner." Damien took the beer from her outstretched hand.

Dillon ogled the agent. "Why would you pull rank?"

"Only if they said no." Derek smiled as he opened his beer.

"I don't want you getting yourself into trouble. You do good work with your unit. Don't do anything to fuck that up." Dillon spun around in her chair.

"Not to worry. No one is stupid enough to take over my unit. We deal with very old murder cases. Most with no witnesses left to help. No evidence. It's amazing we solve anything," Derek said.

Dillon punched away on her computer. She searched every case she could think of. She found nothing. "I know there is something."

"What did you say?" Joe asked.

"This damn symbol. I know I have seen something with those damn chevrons. I just can't place it." Dillon started to ask a question when the doorbell rang.

Joe jumped up. "I got it." He walked to the front door. "Hey Travis." He popped his head out of the door. "Where is Jim?"

Travis glanced over his shoulder at the road leading to the house. "He should roll up any minute. I gave him the address, and he pulled it up on his phone. I think he left right after me."

Joe shrugged. "I guess he will get here soon." Closing the door, he heard a car pull in. He watched as Jim parked, glanced back at road, and quickly move towards the door. "Hey, what's wrong?"

Jim walked into the home. He peered out the window, searching the lane. "I know someone followed me."

Joe grabbed his shoulder. "Listen. No one knows you know anything besides us. You need to calm down."

Jim shook his head. "No. No. I didn't tell anyone."

"Then let's not worry. Okay?" Joe patted his back. "C'mon, follow me. You want a beer?"

Jim nodded. "That would be great."

Joe stepped into the kitchen and grabbed a beer for Jim. "This way." He led him down the hallway to the office.

Jim walked in, nodding at everyone. He glanced at Derek. His eyes widened when he looked over at Joe.

"It's okay, Jim. This is Special Agent Derek Reed. He is running a case for us while we are suspended. He is also going to help with the Johnson shit." Joe pointed to his empty chair. "Have a seat." Joe nodded in Travis' direction. "This is Travis, from ECD."

Damien turned towards Travis. "Tell me about the incident."

Travis recounted the events of earlier. "I don't think Johnson realizes the hornet's nest he stirred up."

"He doesn't give a rat's ass about it. He's just mad no one came to his defense." Dillon scooped up the cat as he strutted by. She placed him on her lap and scratched his ears.

Jim sat quietly in the chair.

Damien nodded in his direction. "Are you okay, Jim?"

"I don't like this. Do you think he knows I know something?" Jim's hand shook as he sipped his beer.

"He thinks someone followed him out of the garage and to here," Joe said.

"What car followed you?" Damien asked.

"I don't know. It was more of a sense that someone followed me." Jim shifted in his seat.

Dillon turned towards Joe. "Didn't Johnson leave DC earlier after the fight in the canteen?"

"Yeah. He left when I showed up." Joe sat on the edge of Dillon's desk. He reached over and squeezed Jim's shoulder. "DEA Johnson was gone before you left."

Jim nodded. "I know I sound like a freaking nut job. But he scares me. And now Thomlinson is involved. What if he finds out and tells Johnson I know something?"

"I don't think you should worry." Joe gave Damien a side glance. "I don't think Thomlinson was a willing participant."

Damien nodded. "Even though Thomlinson did help Johnson, we think Johnson used something against the lieutenant to force his help."

"Jim, quickly run through what happened in the bathroom for Derek," Dillon said.

Jim took a long breath and held it before releasing. He remembered the moment like it had happened yesterday. Recounting the bathroom conversation, he told them about other times he has seen Johnson since. "I just can't help but think he knows." Jim said, as his eyes darted from person to person.

Damien spun his chair to face Travis. "How hard would it be to track Johnson's movements? If you could?"

Travis leaned forward. "If I could get permission, I could put a tracker in his car. I could download something to his phone. He just needs to open a text from me, then I could embed a virus which would track his location and record his phone calls."

"How would you get him to open a text from you?" Dillon asked.

"I'm sure, him being the asshole he is, he couldn't resist opening a text from me. And I'm sure I could make him click on the image... especially if I call him a name and then send him a photo."

"Wouldn't that put you in harm's way, though?" Dillon asked.

"The dude is already pissed at me for knocking him on his big butt. If he comes after me, I will shoot first and ask questions later." Travis tilted his head back. "I think I could get him to open the picture or link if I just mention Damien."

Dillon laughed. "That would do it. He is so blinded by hate he wouldn't be able to resist."

Damien smirked at them. "I want to call the captain and the director and tell them what we have come up with. If we can get the okay to track him, we might bust his ass and keep the drugs from changing hands."

"We need to make sure we have all the paperwork in place first. If it isn't done by the book, he could skate on anything we find." Travis glanced at everyone in the room.

"What if he finds out I'm the one who started this whole thing? What if he finds out I was in the bathroom and overheard everything?" Jim set his beer on the edge of Dillon's desk. "He will come after me."

"Jim, we can put the focus on us." Dillon motioned between her and Damien. "We can make Johnson focus squarely on us. He won't have time for you."

Jim nodded as he stared at his hands.

Travis twisted his watch. "Listen, I have to go. I'm meeting Katie." He stood, moving towards the office door. "Jim, you want me to follow you home?"

Jim's eyes widened. "Yeah. I would."

Travis smiled. "Great." He saluted everyone in the room and nodded for Jim to follow.

"I really appreciate everything you guys are doing." Jim nodded, keeping a downward gaze as he followed Travis out.

Dillon walked behind them and stood at the doorway, watching as they drove away. She walked back to the office and leaned against the doorframe. "That guy is scared to death."

"I would be too." Joe said. "Johnson is a fucker, and he will take out anyone who gets in his way."

Derek sat quietly and listened to everything surrounding the DEA agent. He glanced at Damien, then over his shoulder at Dillon. "Do you think it's wise to have him focus on you guys?"

Damien smirked as the doorbell rang. "Better it be us than Jim. He doesn't stand a chance up against Johnson. At least we will be ready for him."

CHAPTER FIFTY-FIVE

Thursday 6:45 p.m.

Dillon went into the kitchen and removed the food out of the oven. She quickly placed the tray with several loaves of bread in and reduced the heat a few degrees.

"Can I help with anything?" Derek asked from the doorway.

Gunner stood next to him, leaning into him as the agent scratched his ears.

"Yeah," she pointed to a cabinet. "Grab six glasses and set them on the table for me."

Derek grabbed the glasses, and filled them with ice from the freezer. Setting them on the table, he turned towards Dillon. "Plates?"

"Over there." She pointed to another cabinet. She laughed at Derek's raised eyebrow. "He set the kitchen up. I have yet to go through and rearrange it."

"That explains so much." Derek chuckled as he spun around to find the cat in a chair. "I guess we need an extra plate."

Dillon placed the big bowl of salad on the table just as Damien and the others walked in. She walked over and picked up the cat. Giving him a big kiss, she set him on the floor. "Hey, guys. I hope you are hungry."

Beth inhaled. "It smells fantastic. I can't wait to eat."

Dr. Forsythe scooped up the cat while placing his bag on the floor against the wall. "How's my Coach today?"

Coach nuzzled his neck and face.

"Who's my favorite cat?" Dr. Forsythe scratched his ears, kissing his nose. "You are." He squinted at Dillon. "I think he is getting a little chunky."

"Fat. He's getting fat." Damien pointed to Dillon. "It's her fault."

Dillon grabbed the bread out of the oven and placed it on a cutting board. Slicing it, she placed the pieces in a bowl and covered it with a towel, keeping in the warmth. "Let's sit down and eat and discuss this case."

Beth hung her bag on the back of her chair.

Grabbing Gunner and Coach's food bowls, Dillon quickly filled them with dry kibbles. She watched as both went over to the bowls and sniffed, then turned and sat, waiting for the good stuff. "That's all you two are getting."

Coach's ears flattened.

Gunner whimpered and laid down on the floor, letting out a little huff.

Beth closed her eyes as she swallowed a sip of her wine. "This food is unbelievable."

Derek nodded in agreement. "This is fantastic. I'm going to be spoiled staying here."

"Damien's mom. She gets all the credit." Dillon took a bite of her bread.

"How have your parents been?" Dr. Forsythe asked. "I haven't seen them in a few weeks."

"They are doing well. They are taking the grandkids on a trip for spring break. Just the kids and grandma and grandpa." Damien took a sip of his water.

"How fun is that?" Dr. Forsythe placed some more salad on his plate. "I regret sometimes not having kids. I would love to have grandkids."

"I'm sure Nicky will let you have his anytime you want to play grandpa. They know you and love you, I might add." Damien winked at Bernard. He smiled at Dr. Parker. "He and my parents are quite close."

"Derek, are you married?" Damien asked.

"No. Don't ever plan on it either," Derek said.

Dillon lifted her wineglass, motioning for Damien to pour some from the open bottle on the table. "Thank you." Setting down her glass, she placed some salad on her plate. "Do you have any kids, Beth?"

Dr. Parker shook her head. "No. I traveled too much for my work. It would never have worked."

"I'm in no hurry for kids." Dillon raised an eyebrow at Damien when he gave her a sly grin.

"I can't wait to have kids," Joe said, taking a bite of bread.

"That's because you want any excuse to act like a kid." Dillon laughed at his glare.

"I can't stand it anymore. Let's get to the case." Damien pointed to the bag on the floor. "Does that have information?"

"Hold your horses," Bernard said. "What have you guys found? Anything?"

Dillon glanced around the table. "Derek?"

Derek swallowed his bite of food. "It looks like we have two different killers, from different time periods, but they seem to be connected. We aren't sure how, though. Or why."

Bernard's brow wrinkled. "Explain."

Damien took a sip of his wine. "When we are done, we will show you on the screen in the office, but we linked the two current murders to several from over ten years ago."

Bernard set his glass down. "What murders from years ago?"

"The state park murders," Joe said.

Dr. Bernard Forsythe placed his elbows on the table. "Are you sure?"

"Yes. The mark on Camilla and the other girl are very similar to marks left on the girls found in the state parks," Dillon answered. "Albeit they are not identical. The ones from ten years ago are very crude in design and execution. While the current murders are much more deliberate."

"The killer took his time making them. It looks like he is referring to the prior killings by continuing the chevron design and numbers on one side, while the killer is making his own mark on the other side of the symbol," Derek said. He lifted his glass of wine, stopping before he took a sip. "In my experience with cold cases, when they are connected to a more recent murder, focusing on the past case is usually the biggest help."

Bernard leaned back in his chair. "I wasn't here when those murders occurred. I'm not professionally acquainted with them, but I have read the files."

"What can you tell us about the old case?" Derek asked.

"As far as the investigation reports, the victims were taken by surprise at the parks they were murdered in," he said.

"Was there any sign the previous killer stalked his victims prior to the attack?" Derek asked.

"No. The killer waited and pretty much blitz attacked his victim. The reports found no evidence of stalking," Bernard said.

Dillon held her glass in her hands. She took a sip of her wine, holding her glass to her lips. "What did the reports say about the carving? Anything at all?"

"I can send you guys the reports I have, but as far as I recall, they came to the same conclusions you have. They were crudely and hastily done. There were no other murders reported having the same skin carving. It appears this emblem is specific to these murders." Bernard took a piece of bread and a second helping of pasta.

Joe poured more wine into his glass. "We need to research the old cases."

Damien looked at Bernard. "Do you have any notes from the detectives on the cases? Or just the general files?"

"I have what was uploaded." Bernard saw the slight nod Damien gave Dillon. "And I'm gathering you already have the same information."

Damien smirked at his friend. "I might."

Derek smiled. "I have a feeling you are more like my agent Kyle than you know. He often gathers information he shouldn't."

Dillon chuckled at the agent. "You don't know the half of it."

"If you don't mind, I will put in the request to your captain. I can tell them I would like to work with you and the VCU team and if we play our cards right, we can solve two cases at once." Derek took a bite of food. "I don't want you to think I'm trying to take control, but if I put in the request, I can get my team in on it and between all of us, we can get answers."

Damien pushed his plate to the middle of the table. "I want to call the director and the captain now. I think having all of us here, including Beth and Bernard, will help."

Bernard smiled at Beth. "Welcome to the club."

She laughed. "I like this club. Especially if food is provided."

Coach jumped up on Dillon's lap. He reached his paw out and snagged a piece of meat from her plate.

"Seriously, cat." Dillon pulled her plate a little closer. She dropped a piece of bread on the floor for Gunner.

"See why they are getting fat." Damien said as he scoffed at her.

"Tell them about what you found on Camilla," Bernard said, motioning towards Beth.

"Oh, I don't have any results yet, but we may have something." Beth adjusted herself in her chair. "When I did the postmortem on Tracy, I noticed a difference in the makeup used on her lips versus that on Camilla's."

Joe's brow wrinkled. "You mean like a different color?"

Beth shook her head. "At first, I thought it was the lighting giving the lips a different sheen. But when I looked closer, I found an imprint."

Damien sat up straight. "An imprint? I don't understand."

Dillon leaned into the table. "You mean like something touched Camilla's lips?"

"Yes." She reached around and grabbed her bag. Beth retrieved a folder. She pulled out two photos and laid them on the table so the others could see.

"You can clearly see what looks like an imprint of a pair of lips." Beth pointed to the dull shading on Camilla's lips.

Joe lifted the photos, holding them side by side. "That definitely looks like a pair of lips."

Dillon took the photos from Joe's hand. She held them where she and Damien could compare them to each other.

"If the killer kissed Camilla and not the other victim or victims, what does that tell us?" Damien's gaze shifted from Dillon to Derek.

Derek glanced around the table. "It tells me our killer not only knew Camilla, but had an attachment to her."

"I agree with Derek," Dillon said. "But I'll go even further. I think he coveted her. And we all know—you covet what you see."

CHAPTER FIFTY-SIX

Brycen parked in the lot next to the bar. Turning off the engine, he watched as several people wandered up and down the street, going in and out of other bars. This part of town was a popular place for the mid twenty crowds.

Looking at his phone, he checked the dating app. The girl who frequented this place popped up on his screen. Her bright blue eyes stared back at him. "You are perfect, aren't you?"

Scrolling through her pictures, a heart popped up on the screen. Brycen's pulse sped up. He glanced through the front window, searching the street as best he could. Checking the app again, it showed the heart was on the move.

Brycen exited his vehicle and checked the magnetic colored strip covering the logo. He adjusted it a bit, making sure the logo was covered. Walking towards the doorway of the bar, he checked the app again. His distance parameter showed his match to be within a quarter mile of him. As she got closer, the heart would change to a bright red. His heart was currently pink.

Walking towards the bar entrance, he stopped once more and glanced around. There were a lot of pretty girls out tonight. And if his perfect match didn't show, he had no doubts he could find a replacement.

Brycen opened the door and walked into O'Malley's. The scent of stale beer and fried food hit him. He scanned the tables and found his friend, Mark, from work. Waving as he walked towards the table, his phone pinged. He pulled it from his pocket and looked at the screen. The heart's color had shifted to a redder hue. Brycen looked towards the front door.

"Brycen," Mark yelled out over the crowd.

Hearing his name, Brycen turned around and walked towards the table, glancing back over his shoulder.

"Yo, dude, I was wondering when you were going to show up." Mark handed him a beer from a bucket on the table.

"Thanks," Brycen said, taking the beer. He quickly glanced at his phone. The heart's color had no pink, but had not turned bright red.

"Brycen, this is Doug, Carl, Patrick, and Monty." Mark pointed to each man as he introduced them.

"Hey, good to meet you guys. Eli, I didn't realize you were coming out too." Brycen said, sipping his beer.

"Couldn't resist a night out at O'Malley's," Eli said. He noticed Brycen's attention focused on the bar area and a group of women in line. "She's cute." Eli motioned to the young woman smiling in Brycen's direction.

Brycen gave her a half smile as he nodded in her direction. "Yeah. I guess."

Mark peered over his shoulder. "You guess? She's very cute," he said, grinning at Brycen.

Doug leaned to the side, getting a better view. "She is." He turned towards Brycen. "If you aren't interested, I am."

"Not interested." Brycen tipped his beer in his direction. "Go get her, tiger."

Doug laughed, slapping Brycen's shoulder. "Tiger," he laughed again, looking at Mark. "I like this guy."

"Did you catch any of the news?" Mark asked, leaning into Brycen.

"A little before I left."

"Well, did you see us on the screen?"

Brycen sat up. "No. I didn't. Are you sure I was on there?"

Mark's brow wrinkled. "Yeah, I'm sure. You and I were at the back. I guess one camera scanned the entire area and caught us." He slicked back his hair. "Maybe we can get famous over this."

"I don't want to be famous." Brycen's grip tightened around his beer bottle. He watched Doug as he spoke with the young women who had smiled at him.

"Did you ever spend time with Camilla?" Mark asked Brycen. "Hello, Yo, Brycen?"

Turning towards the sound of his name, Brycen smiled. "Yeah?"

"Did you ever spend time with Camilla?"

"Why would I spend time with her?" Brycen guzzled the last of his beer. He waved off his friend when he offered him another one. "No, thanks."

"I had to fix the vent in her office. She treated me like I was a piece of gum from the bottom of her shoe." Mark chuckled at his friend, Doug. "Douggie is laying on the charm."

Brycen watched Mark's friend. He had his arm wrapped around the woman and she leaned into him. His phone vibrated in his pocket. Pulling it out, his upper lip twitched. The app showed a bright red heart.

CHAPTER FIFTY-SEVEN

"I need you guys to be on the call." Damien said, looking at Bernard.

Dr. Forsythe's brow wrinkled. "Why do you need us?"

"I want you guys to tell them what you have discovered. I also want you to let them know about the second woman. I think we need to call them now, and tomorrow we can go into the VCU." Damien said.

Dr. Forsythe nodded at Beth. "I don't have anything yet. I am waiting for more information about other murders. But with the other victim from out of our jurisdiction, I think we can say Camilla's death is not a solitary event."

"Derek is waiting for his guy to get back to him. He may have some information about other girls as well." Damien drank his wine and stood. "Grab a drink and let's go into the office." He began placing dishes in the sink. "I will help clean this later."

Dillon nodded. "It can wait." She packaged up any leftovers and placed them in the refrigerator. Wrapping the bread, she placed it in a cabinet. "Don't look at me like that. I know you two will get it if I leave it anywhere else," she said to the cat and dog.

Coached huffed and ran ahead of her.

As Dillon entered the room, Coach sat in her chair, glaring at her. "That's my seat."

Gunner spun around a few times before laying in his bed. Sighing, his head fell over the side of the bed.

"Wow," Derek said, reaching down to pet him. "You have such a horrible life."

"They are so spoiled. The two of them." Dillon lifted the cat off her chair and placed him on her lap.

Joe took a seat near Damien, while Beth and Bernard sat in the other two empty chairs.

Beth turned towards Derek. "What information are you waiting for?"

Derek's brow squished together before he realized what she was referring to. "I have an IT guy who can find most anything. I asked him to hunt down any cases similar to Camilla's and Tracy's murders. Specifically, anything with the emblem or something like it."

Beth nodded. "I sent off the swab from Camilla's lips to Trace. I asked them to rush the DNA. If we are lucky, we could get results in a day or two."

Damien sighed as he pulled his phone from his pocket. "Before we call the captain and the director, let me show you guys everything we have found." He logged in to his computer and made sure all the pictures were on the main screen on the wall.

"Here are all the photos of the women killed over ten years ago." He pointed to the screen. Damien explained the emblem and how the new killer was somehow connected but they weren't sure in what capacity. "If we can find other women killed with the new emblem carved on them, we may figure out how, when, and where the killer is picking his victims."

"Yes, but we all agree Camilla was the odd man out. No matter how many other victims we find. She will be the key," Dillon said.

"I agree with Dillon," Derek said. "I bet when we find other murdered women, I think they will all resemble Tracy. Young, in their twenties. I bet most will have last been at clubs or hangouts where the younger crowd frequents."

Dr. Forsythe stared at all the photos of the young women killed years before. "These women are older. Not college age. Also, I remember from the files the victims were never stalked in their daily life. So, this killer was an opportunist."

Dillon nodded. "I agree. I think this new killer is a planner. He has a specific woman in mind for his art project...."

Beth cut her off. "I'm sorry. What do you mean art project?"

Dillon glanced at Damien.

He typed out a few commands on his keyboard. "This is Tracy." He took Camilla's photo and overlaid next to the first one. "Look," he said, pointing to the TV screen.

Dr. Forsythe and Beth stared at the screen.

"What are we looking at?" Beth asked.

"The killer posed them so their hands would connect. From the carving on their bodies, it seems there are several other victims in his paper doll chain," Derek said.

"Well, I'll be damned." Dr. Forsythe stood and moved closer to the screen. He studied Camilla's photo. "I think this information, along with what we have uncovered, should get you guys on the case ASAP. How about we make that call?"

Damien nodded. He dialed the captain's number. "Hey Captain, it's Damien. I need to conference you and the director in on a call. Can we do it in about ten minutes?" He nodded, giving the room a thumbs up. "Okay. I am going to call the director and get you both on the line. I will call you back in just a few minutes."

Hanging up, he glanced at Dillon. "You want to call him or me?"

Dillon shrugged. "You can do it."

Damien called him and then conferenced in the captain. "Can you both hear us?"

"Yes," Captain Mackey said.

"I hear you guys," said Director Sherman.

Damien gave a brief explanation, then handed the call over to Derek, who told them what they found. He had Dr. Forsythe and Dr. Parker give the details of their findings. When they had finished, Derek spoke again. "I believe it would be in the best interest of both DC and the FBI to let me lead this investigation with the help of Dillon, Damien, and Joe."

"I don't have a problem with Derek running the lead. I think this will also keep our hands clean, so to speak. With Damien and Dillon's connection to one of the victims I think this will give us enough space to keep the questions at bay."

"As long as Derek is the lead and remains on lead. I don't have a problem. Dillon is not one hundred percent back on the job, but I will let her work under Derek."

"Gee, thanks." Dillon rolled her eyes.

"Stop rolling your eyes at me. You know the drill. Technically, you have one more session and then the doctor can give you the release. I will let you run with this case. But you can't do anything else without the release," Director Sherman said.

"I have one scheduled for next week. Hopefully, this case will be closed by then," Dillon said.

"I want all of you in tomorrow. We will meet in my office. Director, you don't need to be at this one unless you want to," Captain Mackey said.

"What is happening on the Johnson front?" the director asked.

"Travis and Jim were here earlier. We need to get clearance for Travis to put a tracker on his phone. Do you want to discuss this tomorrow or right now?" Joe asked.

"Bring what you have with you tomorrow. We can discuss it then. How long can you stay out here, Derek?" Captain Mackey asked.

Derek sighed. "I can stay at least through next weekend. If the case goes any longer, I may need to arrange a few things. I will let my director know tonight about our plans," Derek said.

"Before we decide on Johnson, I want to make sure we are doing it by the book. I don't want to give him a chance to skate on anything because we didn't do it right," Director Sherman said. "I will have something by tomorrow morning regarding the tracer."

"Be at my office by 9 a.m. How quickly could Travis get the tracer on Johnson's phone?" Captain Mackey asked.

"As quickly as sending a text," Damien said.

"I need to make a call. Let me call you back." Captain Mackey hung up.

"I have a feeling I know who the captain is calling. I imagine you will have the go ahead on the tracer pretty quick. Dillon, I want you to keep me posted," Director Sherman said.

"Yes, sir."

Silence filled the room when the director disconnected the call.

"Can they ever say goodbye?" Dillon asked as she twirled around in her chair.

"I think you are required to do that when you reach a certain position," Joe said. "Or maybe when you reach a certain age."

Dillon chuckled. "I hate it."

Dr. Forsythe and Dr. Parker stood.

"I think we need to go. And I will get you any other cases I find," Dr. Forsythe said. "Although, I'm sure you guys will have information before me."

"As soon as I get the results on the DNA, I will call you with them. I'm going to push it first thing in the morning."

Damien followed them to the door.

Beth stepped out onto the porch. "Thank you for dinner. It was delicious."

"You're welcome. I'm sure it is the first of many," Damien said.

Bernard turned towards him. "I know how hard this case has been. You are going to need to talk about Camilla at some point. I'm always here. You can tell me anything. And you know it will stay between us."

"I know. I appreciate hearing it though. You're a good friend Bernard."

Dr. Forsythe hugged him. "We need to have lunch. Just you and me." He waved as he and Beth headed to his car.

Damien closed the door, locking it and walked back to the office. He leaned against the doorway. "I'm going to clean the kitchen."

Dillon looked up. "Want some help?"

"No. You guys keep digging for information. Derek, you think your guy Kyle has anything yet?"

"I can call him now," Derek said.

Damien walked into the kitchen. As he rinsed the dishes and placed them into the dishwasher, he thought about Camilla. If the killer knew her, and stalked her, like she said, then the killer had to be someone she worked with or someone who saw her every day and knew her schedule.

As he wiped the counters and the table, he concentrated on the people he met at her office. He ran through her closest co-workers, besides the men she slept with. His phone rang. Drying his hands, he answered. "Captain, what's going on?"

"You have the go ahead for Travis. I want you to call him now and get him to work his magic. Keep this between you, Dillon, and Joe. I don't think anyone else needs to know."

"I understand. I will call Travis now." Damien looked at the silent phone. "Damn, I really hate that." He dialed Travis.

"Hey, Damien, what's up?"

"I just got off the phone with Captain Mackey. Put the tracer on Johnson's phone."

"Sweet. I got the picture ready with the code embedded in it. As soon as he clicks on the attachment, it will download and work in the background. He won't even know it's there."

"Can you tell when he clicks on it?"

"Yeah, I will get a ping with the location the minute it downloads to his phone. If I don't get anything, I will resend it. I'm sure he will answer this text, though. He won't be able to resist."

"Okay. As soon as it is up and running, let me know. You are going to have to steer clear of him. Make sure you always take your weapon with you." Damien said.

"I always do. But I can stay clear of him. I have an army buddy. I can go to his house and stay out of the fray if need be. But I'm not worried about Johnson. I think confronting him at DC will also keep him from getting suspicious."

"Just don't do anything stupid."

"I won't. I promise."

"Let me know when it is set up. We will be in at 9 a.m. to see the captain tomorrow. I need to know if he clicks on it before then, if possible."

"Gotcha. See you in the morning," Travis said as he disconnected the call.

CHAPTER FIFTY-EIGHT

DEA Johnson drove back to DC and sat in the parking lot. Parked right in front of the doorway, he waited for Lieutenant Thomlinson to come out. It was well past quitting time, and he was sure he hadn't missed him. "Where the hell are you?"

He had phoned him several times after their last encounter, but he never answered. Calling again, the call went straight to voicemail. "I know you are fucking ignoring me." His teeth ground against each other as he forcibly bit down. He tapped his foot against the floorboard. Glancing at his watch, he tapped the face.

Leaning his head back against the seat, he closed his eyes for a few minutes. He had the drugs, and he had already been in contact with the cartel. Originally, his plan was to sell the drugs and just get the hell out of town. But Thomlinson knew too much and he couldn't leave with any loose ends. "It's time to clean up a little. Then I can get on with life." Pulling his phone from his pocket, he texted a friend.

I need the passport and paperwork ASAP. The weekend at the latest.

Not sure I can get it by then. May need a few extra days. Supply problem.

I can't wait. Get it as quick as you can. I'll give you a bonus.

I'll try. I'll be in contact.

Johnson placed his phone on his dash. "Can't anyone do a fucking job anymore?" He lit a cigarette, inhaling deeply, his body relaxed. He checked his watch again. When his phone pinged, the tension returned.

Picking it up from the console, he opened his text messages. "What the fuck?" he clicked on the message from Travis. He had sent a photo with a message under it, but he couldn't read it all without clicking on it.

Clicking the image, the entire message opened. Under the image of a big fat donkey, the message was in all capital letters.

No wonder Dillon chose Damien over you. Who would want to date this when they had a stallion?

Johnson texted back.

Funny asshole. You don't even know what a naked woman looks like, you fucking skinny little prick. Fuck off.

Johnson tossed his phone onto the passenger seat. "Maybe after I put

Thomlinson in his place, I should do the same with that prick." As much as he wanted nothing more than to fuck up the snot-nosed brat, he was smart enough to know if anything happened to the ECD geek, he would be the first person they'd look at. "I don't need that kind of heat now."

Glancing at his watch, Johnson was about to drive out when Lieutenant Thomlinson stepped out into the garage. He watched the lieutenant speak with the guard and then walk to his vehicle. Johnson let the lieutenant drive out of the garage before he followed.

CHAPTER FIFTY-NINE

Taylor sat in the bathtub. She had brought some candles with her, knowing she had a spa room reserved. She was exhausted after the day of meetings. While the others in her group went out to eat with some of the other meeting attendees, she opted to go back to her hotel room.

Ordering from the restaurant on site, she ordered a carafe of wine to be delivered to her room. Sitting in the warm bath with a full belly and a full glass of wine, Taylor relaxed. Soft music played through her phone speaker.

Humming the tune, she took a long sip of wine, savoring the taste. Just as she took another sip, her phone rang. Fumbling with her drink, she finally answered it. "Hello?"

"Do you actually think you can take me to court?"

"You have left me with no choice." She held the phone away from her ear as she clicked on the app to record the phone call.

"You don't get choices. You are a woman. You should not even be working. Dad set you up for the marriage and you ran."

"We aren't living in the dark ages. You don't have any say over me. Just like Dad didn't."

"Prisha, you can't speak like that."

"Quit calling me that. It is the name Dad gave me; you know I go by Taylor."

"No. That is American. You are not American."

"Adnon, I was born in America. I am American. Why are you calling me?"

"I will come for you. I have someone who has promised me great wealth for your hand in marriage."

Taylor's jaw hung open, digesting what he had said. "You're fucking crazy. I'm not marrying anyone. There is someone in my life. I am going to marry him."

"No. No, you are not. You will do what I say."

"Adnon, I will call my lawyer in the morning and getting a restraining order against you. If you come anywhere near me, you will go to jail."

"Prisha, I will get what I want. If I have to get rid of the man you are living in sin with, I will. I will need to purify you. But once that is done, you can be married."

"Adnon, I gave you the chance to have the money from our parents. But now I will fight for what is mine. Dad deserved what he got, for all the abuse he put mom through."

"Don't say that. I will get the money and if you do not marry this man, I will kill you."

"If you come anywhere near me, I will shoot you." Taylor hung up the phone. Her hands trembled as she set it on the side of the tub. She knew her brother would sell her off to the highest bidder, and if he couldn't, he would make sure no one else could have her. She had to kill her brother before he killed her.

CHAPTER SIXTY

Brycen turned around and looked towards the door. His phone vibrated in his hand. Looking at the screen, a bright red heart pulsed. Her app should do the same thing.

Watching the entrance, his eyes widened when she walked in. Her long hair cascaded over her shoulders. The dress she wore hung just above the knees. He smiled inwardly, as he thought he wouldn't have to redress her. She would fit perfectly as she was.

He stood and followed her to the bar. Standing behind her and her friends, he listened to her giggle as she looked at the dating app. Brycen was about to say something when a younger man approached the group.

The app didn't display her name, only a username. Brycen waited, listening to the college guy trying to impress the women. One of the young ladies in the group stepped closer to the guy. She leaned into him, touching his arm as she spoke.

Brycen got closer to her. "Hi."

She spun around and smiled. Her brow drew together as she tilted her head to the side. "Hi. Do I know you?"

He held up his phone. "Just a guy 22"

Her eyes widened. "No way." She opened the app on her phone. She held it next to his. Both phone screens turned black, and then a large heart filled the screens. "I knew you looked familiar. I'm Candy Girl."

"Nice to finally meet you." Brycen leaned towards her. "Can I get you something to drink?"

The young woman nodded and stood on her toes to reach his ear. "I'll take a diet soda."

Brycen lifted one of his eyebrows at her. "Not drinking?"

"I don't drink alcohol. I usually drive. Tonight, I rode with my friend."

"Give me a minute," Brycen said, stepping up to the bar. As he waited for the drinks, he glanced over his left shoulder. The young woman was more beautiful in person.

Pleasantly surprised she didn't wear a lot of makeup. Not like most women her age who caked it on. No. She didn't need it. Brycen looked around the bar. He glanced up and checked the corners for cameras. One was above the cash register. Not wanting to risk being seen putting a few drops from the vial into her drink, Brycen waited.

Turning around, he held out her drink. "One diet soda."

"Thank you." Her fingers gently grazed his.

Brycen nodded for her to follow him. He walked away from where his friends from work sat. The risk of Mark seeing him with her made Brycen rethink if his grandfather was right. Maybe he should wait.

But after seeing her in the flesh, walking away and waiting for another day seemed too hard to do. Brycen found a small table in the back. "Will this work?"

"Yeah." She lifted her head, making sure she could see her friends.

"Is there anything wrong?" Brycen asked.

She shook her head. "Not really. I don't want my friends to leave without me. Otherwise, I will have to take a cab."

"I can give you a ride home." Brycen smiled at her.

"I don't know if that is a good idea. I don't really know you."

Brycen held out his hand. "Hi, I'm Brycen. I live with my grandfather. I take care of him. I work at Twenty-Four Plaza Drive."

"Nice to meet you, Brycen. I'm Lilly," she said, shaking his hand.

"See. Now you know me." Brycen winked at her.

Lilly stared at her phone. Her friend sent her a text making sure she was still in the bar. Lilly typed out her response.

"Is everything okay?" Brycen asked.

Lilly put her phone in her pocket. "Yes. My friend wanted to make sure I was still in the bar. I told her not to leave without me." As she glanced around the bar, she stepped closer to Brycen. "Oh, no."

"What?"

"A guy I went out on a few dates with is here. He acted like we were getting married. Took me forever to get him to quit calling me."

Brycen leaned a little to the right. "I think he saw you. Here he comes."

Lilly groaned as the man came closer to their table.

"Lilly?" he asked as he stepped next to her. "You look great."

"Thank you, Todd. How have you been?"

"Great. I miss you." Todd's gaze shifted to the man next to her. "And who is this?"

Lilly's eyes widened as she looked at Brycen.

Brycen put his arm around her waist before he spoke. "Hey, nice to meet you."

Todd shook his hand. He stared at Lilly. "Is this your boyfriend?"

Lilly twisted her head and smiled at Brycen, but didn't respond.

"We have known each other since grade school," Brycen said. "We only just dated." He pulled Lilly into the crux of his arm.

A gorgeous blonde walked over to Todd. "I was wondering when you would show up."

Lilly watched as the snobby lady grabbed Todd by the hand.

"I'll talk to you later," Todd said as he left their table.

Lilly leaned her head back. "Oh man. He totally killed my vibe." She raised up on her tippy toes, searching for her friend. Her shoulders sank when she saw they were gone. "Oh, no."

"What is it?" Brycen asked.

"I can't find Gianna." Lilly continued to search for her.

Brycen reached over and took her hand. "I promise, I'm a good guy. Let me give you a ride home."

"You don't even know where I live."

Brycen shrugged. "It doesn't matter."

Lilly bit her bottom lip as she glanced around the bar area. Todd kept staring at her, even as the woman nibbled on his ear. "I don't want to stay any longer, but I need to go to the restroom." She left her drink on the table.

Brycen flagged down a waitress and asked if she could bring him a to go cup from behind the bar. Within minutes, she returned. Brycen thanked her. He reached into his pocket, grabbing the vial, and used his thumb and forefinger to open the lid before removing it from his jeans.

Palming the vial, he lifted the lid and straw off the to go cup. As he poured her soda into the cup, he added three small drops of the drug. Quickly replacing the lid and returning it to his pocket as Lily walked back to the table. "Is everything okay?"

Lilly's brow wrinkled as she stared at the to go cup.

"I figured you were getting ready to leave, and I thought you might want to take your soda with you. I had the waitress put it in here." Brycen held out the Styrofoam cup.

"Thank you." Lilly took several sips.

"Hey, if you want to go but don't want me to give you a ride, at least let me stand outside with you while you wait for someone to pick you up."

Lilly sighed in relief. "Would you?"

"Yeah, no problem." Brycen reached out and took her hand. "Let's go outside where it is quieter to order your ride."

When they stepped outside, the crowd had thinned, and a light mist of rain had fallen. "Hey, my work van is right there. Let's get in it while we wait."

Lilly shivered in the damp, cold air. "I would like that." She glanced down at her dress. "I didn't dress for this weather."

"C'mon. I'll turn on the heat."

As she walked beside him, she stumbled, falling into him. "I'm sorry."

Brycen gripped her hand tighter. "It's okay. Are you alright?"

"Yeah. Just feeling a little dizzy." Lilly fell against him. "I don't under-stand."

Brycen unlocked the passenger door. "There is a bug going around. Maybe it's hitting you. People I work with complained about dizziness and headaches before they got really sick." He helped her up into the van.

Walking around to the driver's side, he scanned the parking lot. Not a soul in sight. He bit the inside of his cheek to keep from smiling. Climbing up into the driver's seat, he started the vehicle. "Did you call for a ride?"

Lilly rested her head against the seat. "Not yet. I don't think I could see my phone to do it. Things seem out of focus." She turned towards the sound of his voice. Her vision blurred, as if she looked through a magnifying glass. Lilly felt as if her body and mind had separated. She heard Brycen, but his words were garbled. She tried to lift her arms, but they felt as if weights held them down.

Brycen chuckled when she tried to speak. "I bet you are feeling a little disorientated. No matter how much you scream, no one will hear you."

Lilly mumbled as she slumped to the side.

Brycen caught her before she fell over. He reached around her and pulled the seatbelt across her body. Putting the van in drive, he headed out of the parking lot.

Lilly groaned.

"It's okay, Lilly. You're going to be fine. Just enjoy the ride."

Her ears echoed as if she were in a wind tunnel. Her eyes lids felt heavy, but she was sure they were open. Lilly saw flashes of bright lights. "Am I going home?" She tried to turn her head, but she couldn't move it. "Did I say that out loud?"

Brycen smiled as he hit the highway. The state park he wanted was roughly twenty-five minutes outside the city limits. He glanced over at her. Licking his lips, he couldn't wait to get started.

CHAPTER SIXTY-ONE

Damien stepped into the office. "We got the go ahead for Travis. He is putting the tracer on Johnson's phone tonight."

Dillon smirked. "I would love to see his face when he gets the text."

Joe laughed. "Wouldn't we all?"

"Did you guys come up with anything?" Damien pointed to Derek's empty chair. "Where did he go?"

"Calling his guy back in Arizona. He needs to let his team know he will be here for a few days," Joe said.

Damien stared at his watch. "I feel like I haven't slept in a year."

Dillon stood, walking towards him. "You need to take a hot bath, then go to bed." She hugged him.

Joe placed his phone back in his pocket. "Adnon called Taylor to-night."

Dillon spun around and faced him. "What did he say to her?"

Joe read through the texts. "Looks like he threatened to sell her to the highest bidder if she continued to live with me and didn't marry some dude he has picked out."

"Did she record the call?" Dillon asked.

"Yeah, she did." Joe laughed. "She wrote—tell Dillon I recorded the call."

"Good girl. We have enough to get a restraining order now." Dillon made a scribbled note on her desk pad. "Tell her to send the file to this email address." She handed him the piece of paper.

Joe typed it out. "She will get it to you as soon as she figures out how." He laughed, shaking his head. "As smart as she is, she can't figure out anything on her phone. I'll have to help her. You will get it by tonight."

"That's fine. I will forward it on to the lawyer. He can play it in court tomorrow," Dillon said. "This will really help."

Joe stood. "I'm going to go home. How about if I drive over here in the morning, leave my car and we can all go into DC together?"

"Sounds good. Be here by 7:30 and I'll cook eggs." Dillon stood stretching. "I'm going to take Gunner out before I go upstairs."

Damien followed her and Joe out of the office.

Joe kissed her cheek as he headed for the door. "Tomorrow night I'm eating over here."

"Thanks for the notice," Dillon called out as she headed out the back door in the kitchen.

Damien stepped out onto the porch. "I'm glad about getting back to work. Although the sting of being accused of killing my ex-girlfriend will take some time to go away."

"Listen, it was all done to cover their asses in the news. Don't carry it around with you." Joe walked to his truck. "I will be here in the morning. Get some sleep. You look like shit."

"Fuck you," Damien said as he closed the door. He set the alarm system, reminding himself to tell Derek about it. As he headed down the hallway, he checked the cat's bowl on the counter. It still had food in it. It was the only place Gunner couldn't get to Coach's food.

Back in the office, he stared at the TV screen, still filled with pictures of the dead women. The level of depravity people had still amazed him all these years later as a homicide detective.

Derek entered right before Dillon walked in. "Hey, Kyle is still running searches. He said he would call me in the morning with his findings before we go to see the captain."

"No worries," Damien said as he shut down his laptop. "I'm beat, anyway."

"The time difference has caught up to me. I will sleep like a baby." Derek flopped down in the chair. "I really appreciate you letting me stay here. Much nicer than a hotel."

"My pleasure. I like having you here so I can get as much information first hand as possible," Damien said.

"So, you are just using me?" Derek asked.

"Of course." Damien laughed at the evil eye he gave him. "We will head out around 8:15."

Derek stretched. "I'm off to bed, anyway. My head is pounding."

"You need some headache medicine?"

"Who has a headache?" Dillon asked as she stepped through the office doorway.

"He does," Damien said, pointing at Derek.

"I got something if you need it," she said.

He shook his head. "I'm good. I brought some things with me. I will leave my door open. You said Gunner likes to sleep in there."

"Oh," Dillon laughed. "He's already lying on the bed."

Derek chuckled. "I'll go move him. Good night."

"Good night," Damien called out. "Derek, I set our security system. Don't open any doors to the outside or you will set it off."

"You don't have to worry. As soon as my head hits the pillow, I will be out." He walked down the hallway to his bedroom.

Dillon giggled when she heard him talking to Gunner. "I have a feeling Gunner is going to be spoiled. He's going to want to sleep with us after this."

Damien gave his head a firm shake. "No. Our bed isn't big enough for him, Coach, and us."

She followed him up the stairs. "Let's buy a bigger bed."

"We have the biggest bed on the market. What, are we going to put two king-size beds together?"

"Sounds great. Or there is a place in the city that custom builds mattresses to specific sizes."

Damien stopped at the entrance to the bedroom. "You have already researched this, haven't you?"

"Maybe." She winked at him as she walked through the master bedroom to the bathroom.

Removing his clothes, he heard the water filling the tub. A hot bath might just be what he needs. Taking everything off except his underwear, he made his way to the bathroom. Before he walked in, he went back to the bedroom door and closed it, but didn't latch it, allowing Coach's fat ass to get into the room.

Stepping into the bathroom, steam rose from the tub. "How hot is that water?"

Dillon looked at the tub and then at him. "Hot enough. I don't think you will boil to death."

"How your skin hasn't melted off your body with as hot as you get the water, I will never know." He removed his underwear and stepped over the edge of the tub. Dipping his foot in slowly, he let out a whistle. "That is hot."

"Quit being a baby and get in," Dillon said as she removed her clothes and stepped into the tub, big enough to have two or three other people in it with them. "I think I love you because of this tub."

Damien sucked in a deep breath as he lowered himself into the water. "If I die from heat stroke, they will think you tried to boil me alive."

Dillon sat across from him. She stretched out her legs as she sunk lower into the water. "This is heaven." Closing her eyes, she let her body relax.

Damien watched her face as she let go of all her cares and worry. He saw her face soften as her head tilted back and rested against the tub. "I still can't believe what's happened."

Dillon opened one eye, then closed it. "I know it's been hard on you. You can't shut me out, though. I get you might need a few days to really process this. But I don't want you to hold this inside."

His laughter filled the room.

"What the fuck is wrong with you? Why are you laughing?"

"You are telling me not to keep it inside. A tad bit hypocritical, isn't it?"

Dillon tried to be angry, but he was spot on. "I know I'm not the best person to give this advice, but you of all people should give me credit for at least wanting you to not do what I do."

Damien snickered. "Okay."

Dillon sat up and ogled him. "Okay what?"

"What do you mean, okay what?" Damien sank down in the water and wet his hair.

"Your tone. What are you really saying?"

"Alright. You haven't been talking much to me about everything you've been going through. And you have done a great job of avoiding dealing with your emotions."

"How can you say that? I've dealt with my emotions."

Damien frowned. "With sex."

Dillon's eyes widened. Then her mouth twitched. "I haven't heard you complaining."

"Of course, I'm not going to complain. But there is only so much sex can do for you. You need to get it out, too."

Dillon lifted herself up on to her knees and shuffled to him. As she came closer, she eased herself onto his lap, straddling his legs. She softly kissed his lips. "You are the best medicine. I promise, I will talk to you or someone if I need to. Let me process this my way, and I will let you process Camilla yours."

Leaning forward, her breasts brushed against his chest. Her hard nipples almost scraping him as she pressed herself against him. Damien swallowed her kiss, devouring her tongue. His erection grew and his desire overwhelmed him.

She stopped kissing him and gently slid herself over him. Dillon took in a sharp breath when he filled her. Placing her arms on his shoulders, she wrapped herself around him, pushing out any open space between them.

Damien closed his eyes and let the rhythm of her hips ease the tension his body had held on to for the last two days. Her slow and methodical movement brought him closer to climax.

He gently reached up and placed his hands on her face, pulling her lips towards his. As he kissed her, he could feel her body vibrate. "I love you," he whispered in between their dueling tongues.

She couldn't get her brain to make her mouth say anything. Her legs quivered ever so slightly at first. As the tingling feeling intensified, so did her breathing. Her breaths came in shorter and shorter pants. She had to quit kissing him.

Damien held her tight as her body trembled. He let her set the pace. His hands roamed down her torso. As he felt the curve of her ass, his breathing came in shorter pants. He cupped his hands on her butt and helped keep the rhythm. She became unable to make her hips move. Damien felt her trembling increase as her orgasm exploded. Her grip on his shoulders tightened as she leaned back and moaned.

Her cries of extasy sent him over the edge. At the moment of release, all the pain and fear he'd felt the last few days lifted off him. He grunted and pulled her close to him. He tried to stop himself, but the emotions overtook him. Tears filled his eyes as he buried his face in her neck.

Dillon knew instantly the change in him. It was as if she felt his pain pass through her body. She pushed him back, allowing her to look at his face. "Baby, I'm so sorry."

He couldn't muster the ability to speak. Pulling her to him, he buried his face again.

"I'm here." Dillon stroked the sides of his head, letting her fingers run through his wet locks. She waited, giving him the time he needed.

The tears flowed as he held on to Dillon. The emotions he felt confused him. Camilla had been a force in his life for so long. And yet, he was almost joyful knowing she wouldn't be there to hound him any longer. The happiness her death brought bothered him. It only pushed the guilt deeper into his soul. He wondered if he could ever forgive

himself for not taking her stalking claims more seriously and for not being one hundred percent sad she was dead.

CHAPTER SIXTY-TWO

Brycen drove into Waterfall Glen Forest Preserve. The main entrance to the park was located off Northgate Road. But Brycen was going to a more remote parking lot. He had scoped out the area over several days and knew one of the more remote gates remained unlocked.

Driving up to the gate, Brycen used the front bumper of the van to push open the small, rickety gate. It easily swung wide enough to let him drive through. Maneuvering down the narrow driving path, he took his time. Wanting to leave as little evidence behind as possible.

When he came to the clearing, he drove behind a large line of trees. Exiting, he stepped towards the back of the van and grabbed what he needed from the crate. He removed a large green tarp and threw it over the top of the van. This would give him some camouflage keeping his vehicle from being seen unless someone walked right up on it.

He lifted Lilly from the passenger seat. She was still sedated, and he didn't want to give her too much of the drug. He probably had about fifteen to twenty minutes before she came out of it. The original three drops seemed to be enough to keep her under control.

Carrying her over his shoulder, he headed towards his destination. This path wasn't too well traveled, but there was enough foot traffic that her body would be found in a day or so. Especially with the weekend coming up and more people setting out to enjoy the great weather Illinois offered this time of year.

Lilly felt as if she floated. She had the distinct impression her arms were swinging, but she couldn't tell for sure. Her eyes were open, at least she thought they were. The swaying made her nauseous. She had the overwhelming desire to throw up, but she couldn't get her body to cooperate. Lilly couldn't even swallow.

Reaching the path, he laid Lilly on the ground. She stirred and moaned but didn't move enough to make him concerned. He looked at his phone and the last picture of Camilla. Needing to make sure their hands lined up perfectly, he used the picture as a reference.

Once he had Lilly in the right position, Brycen set to work. He gently placed the tip of the lipstick on her lips and added a little more color to them. Using one of the face wipes from the package, he removed any mascara and eyeliner from under her eyes.

"What are you doing?" her voice sounded as if she spoke in slow motion. She could feel something rubbing against her face. "You have to help me. Brycen? Are you there?"

"I think you are ready," he said as he straddled her. Making sure not to put all his weight on her chest, he braced himself on his knees. He smoothed down her hair and made one last check of the position of her arms.

Lilly felt a heavy pressure on her chest. Her vision looked distorted, but she was positive someone or something stared down at her. "I need help. Can you help me?" The words echoed in her head.

She squirmed, trying to move. Her arms felt heavy and as if they were pinned at her side. A feeling of being trapped overwhelmed her. The pounding in her head increased in intensity as her pulse raced. "Please, if you can hear me, help me. I need help. I can't move." She screamed, begging the mysterious shadow to help her.

Brycen felt a slight movement from her. "I'm sorry we didn't get to spend time together. I would've liked to get to know you. We could have been good friends under different circumstances.

He wanted to listen to her soft, rhythmic breathing for a few more moments. But he feared the drug may wear off. "Sleep well, my sweet." Brycen removed the blade from its sheath and drug it across her throat.

He watched as the skin ripped open, exposing the soft pink flesh. Blood gushed from the gaping wound and the crimson pool formed against her outstretched arms.

Making sure to not move her, he carved the emblem into her abdomen. He put number sixteen for his grandfather, and number five for him, taking great care. Something his grandfather never cared enough to do.

He rose, standing over her. He removed his phone from his pocket. Snapping a few pictures, he scanned them, making sure they would work. "I wish all of them were this easy."

He thought about his grandfather's reaction as he walked to his vehicle.

The anticipation of telling him how easy tonight went had him giddy as a schoolboy. "This should prove to you I know what I'm doing."

Deep down inside, he believed his grandfather was jealous. Jealous of the killer he had become. His grandfather was frail and had to watch from the sidelines now. Brycen understood how hard that was. He had done it all his life while his parents were alive. Always feeling like his father never truly loved him and making him feel inadequate.

Because of this, Brycen gave the old man a break. It must be hard for him to live in the shadow of his grandson. To watch him complete what he never finished. There was no sense in kicking a man when he's down.

Removing the tarp from the top of the van, he threw it in the back. Backing out slowly until he could turn around, he made sure to not disturb any more of the surrounding. As he drove onto the highway, he tapped the steering wheel to the beat of the music. He had a few more targets to get to and then his project would be complete. Then it would be time to move on.

He needed a change of scenery and he thought his grandfather could use the change as well. Plus, Brycen wanted to start a new project, one all his own. Something he didn't have to share with his grandfather. A project showing his creativity and one he would get all the credit for.

CHAPTER SIXTY-THREE

Friday 9:00 a.m.

Captain Mackey listened to Agent Derek Reed explain what they had discovered. He watched Damien from the corner of his eye. The young man looked like he hadn't slept in several days.

"I believe if you allow Damien, Joe, and Dillon to work with me," Derek said as he shifted his gaze between the captain and Dillon's director, "we can make some fast headway on this case. I have cleared it with my boss and my team. I just want to make sure I'm not stepping on any toes."

Director Sherman walked to the large window.

"Are you sure you are up to covering this case?" Captain Mackey asked Damien.

"Do you think I am up to covering this case?" Damien replied.

"Damien. Don't take an attitude with me. You know we had to pull you, both of you, from the case," Captain Mackey said. He ogled his best detective. "You also look like shit. Have you slept at all?"

Damien glanced down at his folded hands. He bit the inside of his lip, giving him a chance to calm down. "Yes, I have slept. And yes, I think I can approach this case like any other case."

"What if Joe worked with Agent Reed? This would give you a chance to get your bearings."

Damien glanced at Joe before answering the captain. "I want to see this case through."

Derek straightened his posture. "I will be point on this. That will ease any extra pressure on Damien. It will also allow for Dillon to get back into the swing of working after such a long time off."

Joe spoke up. "I think this is a great idea. Captain, you know Damien has never let his personal issues come into play when he has worked a case."

"Stop. You are so full of shit. I can't even count how many times all of you have let your personal feelings dictate how you proceeded." Captain Mackey spun around in his chair and faced the window. "Director

Sherman, what do you think? Are you having any second thoughts after the discussion last night and now?"

Director Sherman turned towards the others. "I think it's a horrible idea."

"Director...." Dillon said.

"Stop. I only said it was a horrible idea. I didn't say you couldn't do it." Director Sherman looked at Captain Mackey. "We both know between the four of them, they will figure out who killed Camilla and if we can close a twelve-year-old serial killer case, that will go a long way to helping both of our images."

Captain Mackey saw Damien's nostrils flare. "Don't even think of saying it. You and I both know if there is a case that will instill confidence in the public and make us look good, that goes a hell of a long way in the community."

"I wasn't going to say anything," Damien said.

"Sure, you weren't." Captain Mackey leaned back in his chair. "Here's what I want. Director, you can chime in too." He rested his elbows on his desk. "You will be in charge," he said, pointing at Derek. "And only you."

Captain Mackey pointed at Joe, Damien, and Dillon. "You three will run all your movements by him. If he says it is a good idea, you can do it. I don't want any of you running off half-cocked and fuck this investigation up."

He held up his hand when Joe spoke. "There will be a lot riding on your backs. Once the public gets wind of this case being linked to the other women killed years ago, there will be a media frenzy. I don't want you to mention the other case until you have concrete evidence of the connection."

"Or, better yet, don't say anything until you have an arrest," Director Sherman said.

"I like that idea even better." The captain focused on Derek. "We both want daily updates from you. I don't want any surprises."

"I understand. I will use my team out in Arizona. They are running some checks for me. I can absolutely guarantee their silence on the case," Derek said. "This will also keep the information out of the public."

Director Sherman moved to the side of the captain's desk. "I know about you and your team. I'm not worried one bit about their involvement."

"Let's talk about DEA Johnson," Captain Mackey said.

"Travis put the tracer on his phone yesterday. He texted me late last night and let me know Johnson took the bait," Damien said.

"That's good." Captain Mackey turned towards the director. "What is happening on your end of this?"

"We are working with the head of DEA. There are a few officers who are helping gather information on some of Johnson's movements over the last several months."

"How far away are you from arresting him?" the captain asked.

"It's hard to say. We have a lot of damming information. Is it enough to sustain and indictment and sentence? I don't know. If this trace can give us something concrete, like where the drugs are, then we will have enough," Director Sherman said.

Captain Mackey stared at Damien. "I want you to update me on the situation. Anything and everything you get; I want to know about it. I will pass it on to the director. Under no circumstances do I want you or Dillon doing anything to push Johnson. Do I make myself clear?"

Damien nodded. "Yes, sir."

Dillon smiled as she nodded in agreement.

"Agent McGrath, do not provoke him either. Stay away from him. He has made some serious threats against both of you, and I don't want to give him a chance to act on those threats."

"Oh, you do care about me." She smiled at her director.

"Don't push it." Director Sherman squinted at her.

"I promise I won't. Am I to assume I can work this case like a normal agent, or am I still on some weird status?" Dillon asked.

"You're still on weird status until you have your appointment next week. But you can carry your weapon," the director said. "I will not put that in writing. As far as anyone else is concerned, you are just helping. When you get clearance next week, then we can put it in your official file."

"Thank you, sir," she said.

"Don't thank me yet," he said.

Damien stood.

Everyone else followed suit.

"I will keep both of you updated," Derek said as he stepped aside, letting the other go out of the office before him.

They remained silent until they reached the elevator.

Once the doors shut, Joe slapped his thigh. "Hot dog. The team is back together."

Damien smiled, but he didn't feel the same excitement his partner did.

"What's your problem?" Joe asked.

"I feel like this is a test. I can't explain it. But if it goes south, I have the sneaking suspicion it will be my ass on the line." Damien leaned back against the wall.

When the doors opened, Damien led the way to his office. As he walked into the VCU pen, cheers erupted.

"Damien!" Detective Hall yelled out as he stood and hugged his lieutenant. "Man, you back to work?"

Damien laughed at the hug. "Yeah, and quit getting handsy with me."

Detective Alvarez stood and hugged Dillon. "Are you working too?"

"In a limited capacity, but yeah, I'm back," she said.

Officer Katie Baker walked up to the group. "It's good to see you guys."

"I heard about Johnson. He hasn't given you any more trouble, has he?" Joe asked.

"Not at all." She glanced over her shoulder at Travis, who was in the ECD room. "Not after he laid his ass out."

"You let me know if he does." Damien turned towards his team. "You guys have met Agent Reed. He will be in charge of Camilla's murder case. Both Joe and I, along with Dillon, will assist him."

Detective Jamal Harris eyeballed his boss. "What does that mean for us?"

"I am back as the Lieutenant of this unit," Damien said.

"Okay. Good. I thought for a moment you had been demoted," Jamal said.

"No. No demotion. But I want to put all my attention to this case, so I already spoke with the captain and you will be in charge of the day to day here in the VCU."

Jamal nodded. "I got you covered."

"Of course, if you have questions, call me. If I'm not here, or available, ask the captain." Damien glanced up at the case board. "If you need help on a case, pull in Katie to work with someone. She is about to make grade so she can handle it."

Katie smiled.

Alvarez winked at Katie. "If she is coming into this unit, I can always be her partner."

Detective Hall spun towards her. He frowned. "You don't love me anymore?"

Alvarez laughed. "No. I never loved you."

Hall clutched at his heart. "I think it's breaking."

"I have no idea where Katie will go. As for now, she can work with anyone here." Damien looked at her. "If you have questions or run into something, Detective Harris is your point. If you need me, run it through him first."

"Yes, Lieutenant." Katie shifted her weight.

"I'm going to speak with Travis, and then...." He motioned to Derek. "Do you want to work from here or at my house?"

Derek thought about it. "Based on what the captain said, I think your house will work best."

Damien nodded in agreement. He faced Detective Harris. "We will work from my home." He looked everyone in the eye. "You are welcome to come to my home or call me for any reason. We must keep some information from getting out, and working at my house will help with that."

"I have things covered here. You don't have to worry," Detective Harris said.

Damien waved for Derek and the others to follow him to ECD. When he keyed in the code for the door, a blast of freezing cold air hit him in the face. "Hey Travis. What do you have on Johnson so far?"

Travis lifted his phone off the desk and opened the app. "I tracked him driving around town yesterday. I need to look up a few of the places, but right now, it doesn't look like he went anywhere important. A few houses, and the store. That's it."

Joe sat on the corner of a desk. "Where is Jim?"

Travis shrugged. "I'm not sure. He might not work today. I didn't check his schedule. Been tracking down some information on a few other cases."

Damien walked to a nearby wall where the schedule hung. "He's off today. Which is probably a good idea. He was really rattled yesterday."

"The dude is scared to death Johnson will find out he was in the bathroom. I kept telling him, unless he blabs it, Johnson will never know," Travis said.

Dillon sat in a chair.

Travis glanced around the room. "I take it you guys are back to work?"

Damien shrugged. "Yeah," he pointed at Derek. "He's in charge of the Camilla investigation."

Travis smiled. "I know your guy, Kyle. It didn't register until this morning."

Derek's brow wrinkled. "Do I even want to know how you know him?"

Travis laughed. "No. You don't. He's a good guy. One of the best hackers I've ever known."

Joe crossed his arms. "Were you a hacker, Travis?"

"Let's just say I have a colorful past. And that doesn't leave this room." Travis winked.

"Not a problem. My lips are sealed," Joe said.

"Listen, we will work from my home. If you find out anything, let me know," Damien said. As he turned to leave, he paused. "Have you seen Thomlinson today?"

Travis shook his head. "No. I haven't. Why?"

"No real reason. Just wondered what his demeanor was like," Damien said.

"I have heard no one mention him. At least not for anything to do with Johnson," Travis said.

"Okay. Keep me posted if you hear anything regarding him," Damien said as he opened the door. Entering the VCU pen, he stood for a few minutes.

"What's wrong?" Dillon asked.

Derek looked at him. "What are you thinking?"

Damien's brow wrinkled. "I don't know. It's probably nothing." He led the way to the elevator. "Let's get out of here. I don't want to run into Johnson today."

Stepping into the lift, several phones beeped.

Dillon pulled hers out of her pocket. "Shit."

Derek stared at the message. He looked up. "You guys get the same message?"

Joe frowned. "I didn't get a message."

Damien smirked at his partner, then answered Derek. "If your message says to meet Bernard at the Waterfall Glen Forest Preserve, then yeah. We all got the same message."

Joe stepped out of the elevator. "What's at the reserve?"

"Another dead woman," Dillon said.

"Well, shit," Joe said. "I still don't understand why I can't get a text too."

Damien snickered as they walked out into the garage. "If you are getting texts, then your ass is also on the line, and the first to be blamed."

"You know, I don't need to get any texts," Joe said, smiling.

"That's what I thought," Damien said.

CHAPTER SIXTY-FOUR

Friday 8:00 a.m.

Brycen brought a fresh cup of coffee to his grandfather after removing the untouched dinner plate from the night before. "Here, Grandad." He set the mug on the little table. Picking up the remote, he found his grandfather's favorite morning show and put it on.

"I have some toast coming up in a few moments. Is there anything else you want for breakfast?"

His grandfather stared at the TV, mumbling no.

"I wanted to tell you about last night, but you seemed too tired." Brycen sat in the chair next to him. "Lilly, that's her name. She was very nice. I used the app to meet up with her. She wore the perfect outfit. I didn't have to even change her."

Brycen's grandfather huffed. "I don't think this is the best way to do it."

"What? Use the app?"

"Yes. What about leaving traces?"

Brycen dismissed him with a wave. "They can't trace me. I haven't used my real name or anything." He stood when he heard the toaster ding. "Things differ from back in your day. Now we have technology. No need for me to stand around in a park and attack some girl. This is why your kills only took place during certain times of the year."

Walking into the kitchen, Brycen thought about what his grandfather said. He shook his head and sighed. "Can you imagine how long it would take me to complete my project if I waited in a dark alley or park for the right girl to come along?" he yelled out as he buttered the toast.

"Grandfather, you are going to have to realize things just aren't the same as they were back in your day." Brycen set the toast on the table and saw the look on his grandfather's face. "You don't have to be mad. I'm doing things my way. I am going to finish what you started and finish my project."

Brycen sat in the chair. He turned up the volume on the TV. Covering the weather, Brycen pointed at the screen. "See. There is a cold front coming in over the next few days. No one in their right mind will want to go hang out at a park and run. Get with the times."

"You are making a mistake. Just wait and see. They can track you

through your fancy app," his grandfather said.

"No, they can't. Do you realize how many dating apps there are? First, they have to figure out which one I'm on, then they have to sift through thousands of users to find me." Brycen stood and moved to the side of his grandfather's chair.

"You watch. I won't get caught. Unlike you, who almost went to jail for a very long time. That won't happen to me. It's time you recognize I have surpassed you." He kneeled down in front of him. "I love you, Grandfather. I want you to be proud of me. Someday you will see what I am doing for your legacy and mine.

Brycen kissed the top of his head. "I will be back this evening. I think I will pick up some Chinese for us tonight. We need to celebrate."

CHAPTER SIXTY-FIVE

Friday 10 a.m.

Damien drove into the park. He followed the directions of the police officer who had been posted at the remote entrance. Pulling into the parking lot, he saw the crime scene van along with the coroner's van.

Exiting the vehicle, Derek took in the area. He motioned to Damien. "This isn't the main entrance, is it?"

"No. There are a lot of entrances leading to different trails. Some are running paths, some are hiking trails, and some are for horses. I think there are about six different entrances in total." Damien walked down the path.

"It looks like he drove this way." Dillon stepped around fresh tire tracks. A portion of the track had been blocked off while the crime scene techs worked on taking pictures of the tire treads.

As they came to a clearing, several broken branches littered the ground under a canopy of trees.

Derek stepped over to one of the tech guys. "When you get the measurements for this area, do you think I can get them from you?" he held out one of his cards.

"Sure. They have instructed me to send everything to you and Damien," the tech said.

Derek twisted his head, looking at Damien. "You guys work quickly."

Dillon laughed. "They have us on a short leash."

Damien shook his head. "I'm sure the captain and the director had the techs and Dr. Forsythe know we are in the loop now."

"Always finding the good in everyone," Joe said.

"Shut the hell up." Damien continued down the path. Another area had fresh footprints in the soft soil.

As Derek walked up to the tech who had a measuring tape next to the imprint, he noticed the prints going back to where the killer must have parked differed from one's leading away from the area. "It's clear he carried the victim from a vehicle." Derek pointed to the two impressions. "One set of prints is embedded deeper into the soil."

"That would lend to our victim being drugged or incapacitated,"

Damien said as they continued down the path.

Entering an open area, Damien walked to Dr. Forsythe. "Hey, Doc."

"Damien," Bernard smiled at the others. "Hello all."

"Where is Beth?" Dillon asked.

"She is looking at another case we had." Bernard chuckled. "Nothing to do with this. She is also trying to get the DNA results from Camilla's lips."

"Nice. I hope she can get them ASAP," Damien said.

Standing over the dead girl, Derek stared at her face. She didn't have much makeup on, but he wasn't sure the killer did this or if she wore little. "Do you have an ID on her?"

Dr. Forsythe pointed to a case. "Her belongings are there."

Derek took a pair of gloves from the case and put them on before he lifted the bag containing the wallet. In her driver's license photo, she had little make-up on.

He turned to the others. "Her name is Lilly Carver. It seems the killer didn't do much where her makeup was concerned. Looking at this, it seems she didn't wear much." Derek looked at Dr. Forsythe. "Do you remember seeing a photo of Tracy while she was alive? Like maybe her driver's license photo?"

Dr. Forsythe shook his head. "No. But I can get Charlie here to send you everything they have."

Charlie nodded. "Everything from Camilla and the other victim has been entered into the system. I can email you copies."

"Thank you." Derek pointed to Damien. "Send them to him."

The tech pulled out a tablet from the case. He typed out a few commands, then smiled at Damien. "I sent everything we have so far. If you find you need anything, let me know. I can hunt it down."

Damien raised his eyebrow at Charlie, as he cocked his head to the side. "What's with being so helpful?"

Dr. Forsythe laughed. "I threatened my team this morning."

Charlie laughed. "He did. He said this case was a priority, so he wanted to make sure we gave you everything as quickly as possible. Now, I have no control over Trace. But I will do my best to help get the information from them."

Joe laughed. "I'll get it from them."

"You need to play nice with Trace," Dr. Forsythe said.

"Sometimes they need a kick in the pants." Joe motioned as if he was kicking someone.

Derek walked around the body. Seeing a body in the crime scene was the best way to get a feeling for the killer. "You haven't found any other clothes?"

Dr. Forsythe sighed. "Not yet. I have the techs searching the area."

"But he left Camilla's clothes at the crime scene. He brought clothes for her. I remember looking at the photos the cops took at Tracy's scene, her clothes were also left behind." Derek said. "He didn't dress her."

Dillon eyeballed the profiler. "What are you thinking?"

Derek frowned. "This seems very neat. No extra clothes. No extra make up or redone make up. I'm not sure, but this has a different feel to it. He didn't have to do as much with this victim."

Dillon put on a pair of gloves and kneeled down next to the body. "Did you find the dress like this, or did you raise it?"

The tech raised his hand. "I raised it. I wanted to take pictures of the emblem. I have pictures of what it looked like before I moved it." He held out the camera.

Dillon scrolled through the photos on the camera screen. "I need these photos as soon as you get them on the system."

"You got it." Charlie took the camera back.

Dillon moved the garment a little, giving her a better view of the emblem. The number under the chevron was sixteen, the other number was five. The carving was perfectly done. "No hesitation marks, nothing indicating this killer had to think about what he was doing. It came naturally." She stared at the men. "We need to find the first two victims."

Joe squatted next to her. "I wonder how many this guy wants to kill."

"Unless they hit on the national database, we may never find the first two," Damien said.

Derek looked at Charlie, the tech. "Did you find a cell phone?"

Charlie shook his head. "No. No phone."

Damien motioned to Dr. Forsythe. "Do you know if Tracy's phone was found at the scene?"

Dr. Forsythe sighed, wiping his brow with the back of his gloved hand. "I need to check the records."

"Let's assume Tracy's phone was not found. Why would he take their phones?" Damien asked.

Dillon removed her gloves, wadding them up and placing them in a small trash bag on top of a case. "Maybe he talked to them. Texted them. Maybe something on their phone could give him away."

"We know he left Camilla's phone behind. They found it near her car. I don't think he needed to contact her that way." Derek removed his gloves, placing them in the same bag. "I believe he saw her or knew her. Which makes me think he worked with her or went to her place of business regularly."

"And if that is the case, how did he know the other girls? They clearly didn't work or run in the same circles as Camilla. Hell, Tracy didn't even live in this area. How is he finding them?" Joe asked.

"Get us everything you can, Doc. As quickly as you can," Damien said.

"Will do," Dr. Forsythe said.

"Maybe a chat room?" Damien suggested as they walked down the path to the lot.

"Maybe a chat room what?" Joe asked.

"Maybe they met in some kind of chat room. On-line community. Maybe even a gaming community." Damien paused on the trail next to the spot where the killer's vehicle was assumed to have been parked. "Have you figured out the height of the vehicle?" he asked the crime scene tech.

He pulled a notepad from the inside of his jumper. Flipping through the pages, he found what he needed. "From the foliage breakage and some branches, it looks like the vehicle was taller than most."

"Like a truck tall?" Joe asked.

The tech walked around the area towards a tree. "I don't think so. If I had to guess, I'd say more like a van." He pointed towards the branches that hung low on either side of the clearing. "You can see a uniform disturbance in this area. If it were a truck, I would expect the branches to only be broken in this area."

He used his flashlight to show how far back the broken branches were from the area where the front of the vehicle was parked. "You can see the broken branches go back further than what the cab of a truck would do."

"Will you make sure I get photos of this? Include your estimations for height and length of the vehicle as well," Damien said.

"Didn't you tell me Camilla mentioned she thought she saw a van following her a few times?" Derek asked Joe.

Joe scratched his head. "When... oh wait, yeah. She mentioned it when she was filling out the stalking incident with the sergeant."

"We might have just figured out a killer drives a van. Although I don't like to make assumptions, I think it fits," Derek said.

As Damien drove out of the lot, he glanced back at Derek. "Have you requested the girl's cell phone usage?"

"I just texted Kyle. I gave him each victim's name and told him to find the information for me. He should have it in a few hours," Derek said.

"We could also use Travis," Joe said.

"I have no problem using Travis. However, since we are working on keeping this under wraps as long as possible, and as I told the captain, I am going to use my team as much as I can. This also gives the appearance of DC and you guys not having influence over the gathering of evidence."

Damien stared at the road as he drove. "You're right."

Joe laughed. "Yeah, like I'm pretty damn sure the public doesn't need to know there is a serial killer on the loose, and we have no fucking idea who it is."

CHAPTER SIXTY-SIX

Brycen walked into work. He kept his head down as he headed towards the basement. Stepping into the elevator, he saw Mark enter the building and wave at him.

"Hold the door." Mark called at as he jogged towards the bank of elevators.

Brycen kept his finger on the button. "Hey, Mark."

Mark leaned against the railing. "Dude," he wiggled his finger at him. "I saw the girl you were talking to last night. She was hot."

Brycen's breath hitched as he swallowed a mouthful of spit. "What girl?"

"Don't be coy. The one you were talking to at the bar and then the table. I noticed you walk outside with her." Mark winked at him as they walked down the hallway. "Did you know her?"

"Yeah. Kind of." Brycen headed into the break room. The morning news played with the sound muted. He made a cup of coffee and read through the day's assignments.

He saw something out of the corner of his eye as Mark headed to the office in the back. Glancing at the TV Brycen nearly dropped his mug. "Shit." He stared at the picture of the park where he dumped Lilly. The news was reporting there was a crime scene van spotted there, but they didn't have any information yet about what might have happened. "Damn it," Brycen muttered.

He searched for the remote control. Lifting magazines and old newspapers off the table, he finally found it and quickly changed the channel to sports before anyone else came in. His hand trembled as he placed his mug in the sink. Nausea crested over him. The news won't take long to find out about Lilly and someone might report her missing. How many others saw him with her? Surely no one would remember him. Except for Mark. Brycen knew the minute Mark saw the girl; he would mention it. "This isn't good. Shit. Think."

"Hey, man. Who you talking to?" Mark asked, walking back into the room.

"Just myself." Brycen stuck his hands in his jacket pocket. "What are the assignments for the day?"

"Looks like you and me are on the tenth-floor roof. We need to get the

wiring fixed on the new unit." Mark made a cup of coffee. "I requested you to help me. I didn't want to be paired with Jeff. He's an idiot."

Brycen nodded. "When do you want to head up?"

"Let me drink this really quick." He lifted his cup of coffee. "You can get the tools we need set up. There was a note to check the other units as well. This way, as spring rolls in, everything will be ready to go."

"I can do that."

"Watch out for the cables. Jeff unhooked a bunch of them from the cable locks when he installed the new unit. I was up there yesterday. We are going to need to lock those back down."

"I'll grab some of the heavy-duty cable locks and anchors."

"I'll meet you up there shortly."

"Take your time," Brycen said as he stepped out of the break room and headed towards the roof.

CHAPTER SIXTY-SEVEN

Gunner ran to the front door. His head tilted from side to side as he heard keys jingling. He growled until the door opened. Once he saw who it was, he spun around in circles.

"You are so excited. Did we leave you alone too long?" Dillon scratched his ears before heading towards the backdoor. "Let's go potty, Gunner."

The dog raced ahead of her, whining at the door.

"How about if I reheat leftovers for lunch?" Dillon called out to the others.

Damien walked into the kitchen. "Sounds good." He kissed her cheek and grabbed a few bottles of water from the fridge, along with a bag of chips.

"Really? You can't wait fifteen minutes?" she asked him.

"No." Damien kissed her cheek again, then headed towards the office.

Derek grabbed his laptop and sat on the edge of Dillon's desk.

Joe texted something on his phone.

Damien noticed the concerned look on his face. "What's going on, Joe?"

"Taylor. Her brother keeps harassing her by text."

"Do you know if she has heard from the lawyer yet?" Damien asked.

Joe nodded. "He called her this morning before court. He is supposed to call as soon as it is over."

Derek glanced up. "This is about the restraining order, right?"

Joe nodded. "Yeah. He is a real piece of work. Since he is out of state, there may be some problem getting the order. But if she has enough proof of harassment, it will be easier."

"Keep me posted on the situation. I may have someone who can help," Derek said.

"I would appreciate all the help I can get. I bought the house from my landlords." Joe looked at Damien. "I meant to tell you guys. I just forgot."

"Wow. That's great." Damien turned on his computer.

"I didn't want to jinx it, and then I just forgot about it until it went through about a week ago. The last thing I want is for this guy to fuck this up and make us have to move or something." Joe pocketed his phone.

"We will keep that from happening," Damien said. "We need to speak with Lilly's family."

Derek nodded. "I know. I hate that part." He read through his emails. "Kyle got us something."

Damien sat up straight. "What did he find?"

Derek pointed to the board on the wall. "I'll send you the file. Put the pictures up there."

Damien clicked on the email and sent the photos to the LCD screen.

Derek stood in front of the screen. "He said he found three girls who fit our current killers, MO." As the pictures filled the screen, he studied the photos. He pointed to one. "This victim looks like she fits the age group, but if you look at the other two, this one doesn't seem to fit the daisy chain pattern."

Dillon walked into the office. "Hey, lunch...," her voice trailed off when she noticed the girls on the screen. "Who are these?"

Derek glanced over his shoulder at her. "Kyle found three more victims."

She stepped up next to him. "That one fits but doesn't." Dillon pointed to the first victim on the screen.

"What if she was the first?" Joe asked.

Derek and Dillon spun around and faced him.

"That would make sense," Dillon moved closer to the TV screen. "Without any notes from the crime scene, I have to think something went wrong and he couldn't pose her the way he wanted, or maybe he was about to be caught."

"It explains why the crime scene is messy." Derek glanced at the notes from Kyle. "My guy got some of the case notes. There was no carving on the body."

Pointing to the other two pictures. "The emblem was carved on the others," Derek said, turning to face everyone. "If she was his first victim, with the scene looking so messy, that would explain why no emblem. He didn't' have time. These other two girls are listed as one and two, with the emblem." He stepped to the side of the screen. "These two are posed, but they aren't as neat as Tracy, Camilla, and now Lilly."

Dillon clapped her hands. "Let's get the food while it's hot and we can discuss this more. Did he find anything else?" she asked as she led the way to the kitchen.

"Nothing else about our current killer. He said he may have found something resembling the emblem, but he's not sure." Derek took a plate and filled it with food. He grabbed a bottle of water from the fridge and sat at the table.

The others followed suit and joined him.

Coach waddled in and sat in the doorway, yawning and stretching.

"I see he never misses a chance to get food," Derek said, as he laughed at the grumpy look on the cat's face.

"Just look at his big butt. You can tell he never misses a chance to eat," Damien said.

Coach weaved in between the legs of the chairs, meowing at everyone.

Gunner sat and stared at the table.

"You two are pathetic," Joe said as he gave both a piece of bread.

"You're not helping," Damien said.

"Continue what you were going to say about what Kyle found," Dillon said.

Derek swallowed his food. "Yeah, right. He said he found something about a carving on the victim, but the victim isn't dead and it's a rape case. He isn't sure if it even has anything to do with our current case or our earlier killer. He can't seem to find a picture of it."

"There's nothing in the case records?" Dillon asked.

"No. He's digging a little more to see if it fits with our theory and what we suspect," Derek said. "At least now we have victims one and two." He took a sip of water. "Also, he found out Lilly's parents are overseas. Traveling on some kind of cruise. I think he said they were at sea for the next three days. They also don't live in this area."

Damien held up his finger as he took a drink. "Don't contact them on the ship."

Derek squinted at him.

"Seriously. Have your guy find out when they come back and what port of call, then you can have an FBI agent from the local field office meet them. Hopefully, by the time they return, we will have more answers for them." Damien took a bite of food.

"I think that will work." Derek texted a message to Kyle.

Dillon removed her phone from her pocket. "I'm going to text Beth and see if anything came back from Trace on the lipstick imprint." She placed her phone on the table.

Joe took another piece of bread from the basket in the center of the table. "I've been thinking about how the killer is meeting or contacting his intended victims."

He took a bite of food, sharing the bread with Gunner and Coach. "Besides Camilla, who we know he abducted from the garage, the others had to feel comfortable talking to him so he could get close enough to drug them. According to the file on Tracy, she didn't have any needle marks. And neither did Camilla."

Dillon picked up her phone and texted Beth again.

"Who you texting?" Joe asked.

"Beth. I'm asking her if they found out what the killer used to subdue the girls." She set her phone down and took a bite of bread. "Whatever he is giving them, he has to either put it in their drink or somehow get them to ingest it. On Camilla, he used chloroform to subdue her first because he took her from the garage. We didn't find any bruising from being hit or struck unconscious."

Dillon's phone pinged. "She wants me to call. I'm going to go to the office. I will be right back." She stood and stepped out of the kitchen into the hallway.

Damien considered all the evidence they had so far. Which was pretty much nothing. "We have so little to go on. No evidence at the scenes. No forensics. It's like we are looking for a needle in a huge haystack."

"Let's take what we do know. First, our current killer is using something to incapacitate the victims long enough to get them to the place he kills them. He must have a vehicle that people haven't paid much attention to." Derek took a gulp of water. "A nondescript work van."

"He is then giving them something to render them unconscious. Except for the young girl on the screen in the office. He had to hit her to knock her out. The bruising on her face didn't fit with the picture he is creating," Joe said.

"That's right," Derek said. "That's why I think she was his very first victim. Not only did it teach him what to do, but how to do it so he doesn't get caught. I'm going to have Kyle contact the person on the case and see if it tells us anything."

"Where did she get killed?" Damien asked as he put his plate in the sink.

Derek stood, placing his plate in the sink as well. "They found her in a park in Indiana."

"That's close enough to still be close to home." Damien leaned against the counter. "I think he is staying in this area. Maybe she was his first because she is far away."

Joe stood and stretched. He lifted Coach. letting him lick his plate, and threw a piece of bread to Gunner. "Did you have Kyle look through the victim's phone records yet?"

Derek nodded. "Yeah. He's putting it together."

Damien cleared the remaining dishes and put the bread on top of the fridge. "Let's go see what Dillon has."

CHAPTER SIXTY-EIGHT

Dillon wasn't in the office when they walked in.

Damien's brow wrinkled. Gunner had followed them in, and Coach went to the sofa when they all left the kitchen. He knew she wasn't messing with the pets. He sat at his computer and placed the photos from the murders over ten years ago on the screen.

"Something is nagging me," Derek said. He stared at the screen. "Can you tell me where the murders started?" He pointed to the LCD.

"Sure." Damien scanned the notes from all the murders. "It looks like four were done in Virginia. "Then the remaining ones were done in this area."

Derek sat in the chair. "Where in Virginia?"

Damien had to look at the screen. "Give me a second." He scrolled through the notes. "In and around the Chesapeake area."

"I think Kyle said this other case took place in the same area. Anyway, I'm distracted. Something brought our first killer here." Derek stared at the screen. He turned around as Dillon walked back into the room. "Did she have anything?"

"Yeah. Nothing on the DNA yet. But they discovered Tracy and Camilla had been drugged with ketamine," Dillon said as she sat behind her desk. "We can assume our killer used ketamine on Lilly, too."

"Ketamine?" Joe said. "They didn't find any needle marks."

"Ketamine can be administered orally in liquid form. It has a slower reaction time than if you injected it into a vein. But the effects last just as long. Sometimes dosing can get dicey when you administer by mouth." Derek glanced over at the screen. "This would give the killer time to get his victims into position with very little resistance."

"Derek was just asking about where the first few girls were murdered back ten years ago," Damien said.

"They weren't all murdered here?" Dillon asked.

"No. I guess I had assumed they all happened here," Damien said.

"Where did the first ones take place?" Dillon asked.

"Virginia," Joe said.

Dillon stared at Joe. Her gaze going distant.

"Hello? Dillon?" Joe called out to her, waving his hand.

Dillon turned on her desktop and started typing.

Joe tilted his head towards Damien. "What is wrong with her?"

Damien sighed. "I have no idea."

Dillon looked up to find everyone staring at her. "What?"

"What are you searching for?" Damien asked.

"Something about Virginia. I'm searching my notes from when I was in the academy." Dillon scanned through the files.

"What about Virginia?" Derek asked.

"I'm not sure. I remember doing some research on a case out there, but I can't quite place it."

"Does it have anything to do with this case?" Damien asked. She was about to answer him when his cell phone rang. "Damien."

"It's Jamal."

"Hey, what's up? Something wrong Jamal?"

Joe's head whipped around.

Dillon peeked out from around her desk.

"No. But a call came in regarding a suspicious death at Camilla's firm. Before one of us went out there, I thought I would see if you wanted to take it. I don't know if it has anything to do with your case or not, but since it is at her workplace, I thought it might be of some value to you guys."

Damien stood. "We will take it. Text me everything you have so far. I will keep you in the loop. Thanks Jamal. Make sure no one touches the scene before we get there."

"No problem. I'll let the captain know, too."

Damien put on his jacket. "We have a suspicious death at Camilla's workplace."

Dillon grabbed her jacket from the back of her chair.

Derek ran across the hall to his bedroom and grabbed his jacket and gun off the bed.

Dillon clipped her gun to her jeans before walking out onto the porch. She smiled at Joe. "I haven't been to this place since we three went there a while ago."

Joe snickered, glancing over his shoulder at Dillon as they entered Damien's SUV. "I remember that. You almost made the receptionist pee her pants."

Dillon rolled her lips together to keep from smiling. "I could've shot

Camilla that day." She peered over at Derek.

Derek half-heartedly chuckled. "I can see you threatening her." He leaned forward, touching the back of Damien's seat. "What is the suspicious death?"

Damien tapped his phone and handed it to Joe. "Read that text for me."

Joe scanned the phone and the text from Detective Harris. "Looks like a maintenance worker fell off the roof."

Damien cocked his head to the side. "How?"

Joe shrugged. "I guess we will find out when we get there. It seems a little weird, though."

"How so?" Damien asked.

"With Camilla being abducted in her garage, and no video from security, and now someone else dies. Seems like this place has some bad juju," Joe said as he took a piece of gum from the middle console.

Derek patted his pockets. "Can I have a few pieces?"

Joe held the package out for him.

Derek took three sticks of gum and gave it back to him. "Thanks." He placed a piece in his mouth and pocketed the other two. He removed his phone from his pocket and made a call. "Hey Kyle."

"What's up?"

"Have you got any more information for me?"

"Yeah, I was about to call you."

Derek sat and listened as Kyle told him what he found. Removing his notepad from his pocket, he scribbled some notes. "Okay. Can you find who they were talking to?"

He nodded as he made a few more notes. "Get a warrant if you have to. We need everything pertaining to the accounts for both girls. Also, see if you can trace Lilly's whereabouts for the last twenty-four hours." He hung up his phone.

Dillon stared at him. "Well?"

"Kyle traced Tracy's phone number and records and searched her social media history. Tracy was on a dating app. She mentioned it a few times in her public posts."

"Dating app?" Joe turned around to look at Derek. "Which app?"

"Red Heart Lovers," Derek replied.

"Did he find anything on the first two girls? Were they using an app?" Dillon asked.

Derek searched his notes. "No app. But they were both from towns near each other. Danville and Urbana. He's still searching Lilly's phone records."

"Again, near the Indiana border," Damien said as he pulled into the parking garage of Camilla's work place. "Our killer was in the area for something, then came here. The other killer was in Virginia, then came here. That's not a coincidence."

"No. I don't think so. Until we have a name or someone in the crosshairs, we can't connect them." Derek exited the vehicle.

"Why did you park in here instead of in front?" Joe asked.

"I wanted to look at the area where Camilla was taken." Damien stood and stared at a parking spot. He glanced around, looking over the garage area.

"What are you looking at?" Joe asked.

"Travis had the videos from the garage sent to him after Camilla's death, but there was nothing on them. It looked like the system had a glitch in it."

"Or our killer made the glitch happen," Joe said as he stood next to Damien.

Derek also surveyed the area. "If the killer could make the security system go offline, then he has a working knowledge of this business."

Dillon touched her fingertip to her nose. "And that means he is here a lot. Like a worker."

"I think so. But again, we have nothing to go on but an assumption. I don't want to rule anything out." Derek held the door to the building. "However, it seems like too much of a stretch for the killer not to be connected to this place. He had to see Camilla every day, which would help with knowing her schedule and stalking her."

Walking into the building, an officer rushed over to Damien.

"You can't come in here."

Damien held up his badge. "Lieutenant Kaine."

"Oh, excuse me, Lieutenant." He pointed to the area out in front of the building. "You can find the ME out front."

Damien nodded and led the others to the front of the building.

Roger Newberry, the head Crime Scene Tech, glanced up at them. "Hey, Kaine. I was wondering if you would be at this scene."

"Hey, Roger. It's good to see you." Damien looked at the broken body of a young man.

Dr. Forsythe smiled up at the crew. "Well, hello. I haven't seen you for a few hours." The doctor chuckled.

"That long?" Damien moved around the body. "Do you guys know how he landed here?" He looked up at the rooftop about ten stories up.

Dr. Forsythe pointed to the roof. "That roof has all the ACs for the entire building. According to the head maintenance guy, it was easier than putting everything on the very top of the building. I think there are twenty-two floors in total. Made it easier to filter the air mid-way than from the top down."

"Less stress on the system," Joe said, walking around the brain matter seeping from the guy's cracked head. "Man, that had to hurt."

"What do you think happened?" Dillon asked.

Dr. Forsythe stood. "For him to get this far from the building, I think he had to have been pushed or thrown off. But the guy who was working with him said he tripped over some cables." He raised an eyebrow at Damien. "I need to do some measurements. And while it seems plausible, I think our victim here is too far from the building."

Damien glanced up at the rooftop. He walked over and stood next to the building. Taking a few steps, he made some mental notes. "He seems a little too far out. But if he tripped over the cables, the forward motion could propel him further than just falling off."

"Let's go up and see the roof," Derek said. "While I'm here, I want to ask some of Camilla's co-workers some questions."

Damien looked over at Dillon. "What if you and Joe do that? Me and Dillon will go up to the roof. Then we can interview the man who was working with," he pointed to the dead man on the concrete.

"Mark. Mark Tanner," Roger said as he handed the bagged wallet to Damien.

Damien looked at the driver's license photo through the bag. "Good looking kid." He handed it back to Roger. "Anything you get forward it to me."

Dr. Forsythe stood up and stretched. "You think it is related to Camilla's death?"

"Not sure. Seems like this place either has a curse or a bucket full of coincidences." Damien smirked. "We all think it seems odd."

"I do to." Dr. Forsythe went back to gathering samples. "I will make sure you get my full report." He snapped his fingers. "Call Beth. She may have gotten the DNA results."

Dillon nodded. "I will." She grabbed a pair of gloves from the open kit.

They all headed into the building.

"What floor did Camilla work on?" Derek asked as they stepped into the elevator.

"The fourteenth," Joe said as he pushed the buttons for both floors.

Dillon and Damien stepped off the lift at their floor.

"When you two are done, come here. We will wait for you," Damien said.

"You got it." Joe waved as the doors shut.

Dillon walked down the hallway leading to the roof access.

A police officer stood guard at the door. "You can't exit this way."

She held up her FBI credentials. "We are here for this case."

"Sorry, Agent."

"No worries. Can you tell me what you know?" she asked him.

"I was the first on scene. I had my partner stay down on the ground. When I got up here, the coworker who was with the deceased was visibly upset."

"Did he tell you what happened?" Damien asked.

"He said they were fixing an AC unit. The dead guy tripped and lost his balance, falling forward right off the side." The officer's brow drew together as his face tightened.

"What is it, Officer?" Dillon asked.

"I'm not a detective. I shouldn't be commenting on the scene."

"Comment. Tell me what you thought." Damien waited for his response.

The officer took a slight step back. "I had the distinct impression the guy wasn't being honest. Nothing he said or did. Just an impression I got as he told me what happened. It seemed too perfect."

"Okay. Stay out here until we are done." Dillon held open the door out onto the roof.

"I will, Agent."

Damien walked out onto the roof. The area around the AC units was littered with tools. He saw scuff marks in the area of some cables. He pulled out his phone and dialed Roger Newberry's number.

"Kaine, where are you?"

"I'm on the roof. Have you already taken photos up here?" Damien asked.

"Yeah. I gathered anything I thought might be evidence and took photos of the area."

"Okay. What do you think about the scuff marks up here?"

Roger hesitated on the phone.

"Roger?"

"I'm here. I'm looking through my camera. Hang on."

Damien watched Dillon as she moved around the area outside of the police tape.

"Alright. You are referring to the dark marks around the cables, right?"

"Yeah. Do those look like scuff marks from someone tripping to you?"

"It's hard to say. Looking at the area around those large cables, I can see someone getting caught up in them and losing their balance. However, when I see where the body landed, something isn't adding up."

"Thanks." Damien disconnected the call and placed his phone in his front jeans pocket. "I'm not buying the guy's account."

Dillon glanced over the side of the building. "This edge isn't very tall." She leaned back and mentally measured the rise of the edge. "What? Maybe twelve to fifteen inches."

"I think it's a good guess." Damien stepped up next to her. "Our dead guy had to almost be running to stumble over the edge with enough momentum to get that far away. I find it hard to believe."

"Stand in front of the edge for me." Dillon stepped under the rope.

"Why?"

"I need you to catch me."

"What?"

As soon as he said it, Dillon stumbled over the cables and fell almost into Damien's arms.

Joe and Derek stepped out onto the roof at the same moment.

"Seriously, you guys can't keep your hands off each other?" Joe asked, laughing at the pair.

"Shut up." Damien lifted Dillon onto her feet.

Dillon stepped back in the middle of the cables. "Okay, let's try this." She moved back near the AC unit in question. She took one glove from her pocket and put it on her right hand. She was pretending to fix something. Seeing a tool near the edge of the building, she picked up another tool roughly the same size.

This time, she moved faster. She walked with a hurried step and tripped over the cable closest to the edge of the building. Had Damien not been there, she might have gone over the side. The tool in her hand landed near the other one, but not as close to the edge.

"Okay. If our dead guy was moving fast, maybe distracted, he could have gone over the edge. But he still wouldn't have landed as far away from the building," Joe said.

Derek leaned over the edge. "He had to be pushed while in motion or thrown over the edge."

Joe shook his head. "Look at where Dillon's tool landed. What if the other guy was coming at Mark with the tool? They scuffled." He pointed to the black marks on the roof. "As they are wrestling, our guy throws Mark over the edge."

Dillon replaced the tool where she found it, and put the glove in her jacket pocket.

"Why would his co-worker kill him, though?" Damien asked. "We are going to have to interview him and then do some digging into these two." He removed his phone from his pocket and texted Travis.

"I'm going to have Travis hunt down everything on our victim. We will start there. Let's go interview the guy who was up here with Mark." Damien glanced one more time at the edge of the building. He faced Derek and Joe. "The cop on the door said he had the impression the guy working with our dead guy, was lying."

Derek's brow wrinkled. He stood near the edge of the building and stared at the AC unit.

"How did the questioning of Camilla's co-workers go?" Dillon asked Derek. When he didn't respond, she glanced at Joe.

"Weird." Joe stepped away from the side of the building.

"Derek?" Dillon said his name.

"What? Did I miss something?" Derek asked.

Damien cocked his head to the side. "We were wondering how the questioning went?"

"Weird." Derek looked up. "Sorry, I was thinking about our dead guy. As for Camilla's workers, it seemed like they were instructed to not say anything bad."

Joe nodded as they huddled on the rooftop. "Yeah. I know the receptionist hated her, but she didn't say one bad word." He shivered. "Let's go inside."

They all followed him into the hallway.

Damien looked at the officer. "Let your partner know, when the ME leaves, you guys can leave the scene. Get back to your shift."

"Okay. I appreciate it."

"The guy who was with our dead guy up here, did he touch anything after you spoke with him?" Derek asked the officer.

The officer shook his head. "I don't believe so. When I came up here, he was standing near the edge. He looked dazed and confused."

"He didn't touch any of the tools on the roof?" Derek asked.

"No. He didn't."

"Okay, thank you." Derek stood at the elevator.

"Why did you ask that?" Joe inquired.

Damien stepped into the lift and held the door until everyone got on. He hit the button for the basement and leaned against the railing. "Yeah, why did you ask that?"

"After watching Dillon do her little test, the tools didn't look like they were in the right place. If you were holding a tool and tripped, you would think the forward motion would make you drop whatever was in your hand so you could catch yourself," Derek said.

"I'll text Roger and make sure he bags the tools," Damien said.

"Make sure he looks for fingerprints. Let's see if we can tell who held what tool last. If Mark didn't drop the tool to catch himself, maybe he dropped the tool to stop whoever was pushing him off the side."

"Roger said he will. He's almost finished down on the ground." Damien pocketed his phone as the doors opened.

"Back to Camilla. The receptionist said she complained about the maintenance workers here. Said they were always in places they weren't supposed to be. And she complained about someone following her," Joe said as they walked down the hallway to the maintenance area.

Stepping into the large break room, Damien could see a distraught man in an office. He nodded towards Joe. "That's got to be our worker."

Joe eyeballed the man as they neared the office. "He seems upset."

Opening the door, a man looked up from the desk. "May I help you?"

"I'm Lieutenant Damien Kaine, and this is Detective Joe Hagan, and FBI Agents McGrath and Reed."

The gentleman stood. "Nice to meet you all. This is Brycen Cartwright and I'm Mr. Dennison."

Damien extended his hand to Brycen. "Mr. Cartwright, we need to ask you some questions."

"Sure." Brycen looked over at his boss. "Can he stay?"

Damien looked over his shoulder at the others. "Absolutely. Can we move out into the break room?"

Brycen's boss stood. "Let's go out there. More room." As he exited the office, he told the workers to leave. "We just need some privacy. You guys can come back in a bit." He held the door as they filed out. Once they left, he locked the door. "This will give us the privacy we need."

Removing his notepad from the back pocket of his pants, Derek took a seat nearest to Brycen. "Can you start from the beginning and tell us what happened?"

Brycen rubbed his hands together. He took a deep breath before speaking.

"Take your time, Mr. Cartwright." Derek smiled at him.

"Um, Mark had gone up to the roof first. I had to grab a few tools and followed close behind him. When I got up there, we were messing with the AC unit. Mark stood." Brycen rocked back and forth.

"It's okay," Damien said as he gave a side glance to Derek. "How long were you up there before the accident?"

Brycen rubbed his temples. "Um, I don't know. A few hours. We took a break and then we went back to work."

"Okay. Tell us what happened." Derek said.

Brycen wrung his hands, squirming in his seat. "Mark stood and the next thing I knew, he was tumbling over the edge of the building."

Derek laid his pen on the table. "I'm not following how Mark stumbled if he was standing near the AC unit."

Dillon stood near the doorway. She saw a few guys outside in the hallway and excused herself from the room.

Damien watched as she left and spoke with the workers out in the hallway.

"I'm not sure what happened. I had my back to him, and I had the plate off the unit. I wasn't paying attention. I know he stood up, walked around the unit to check the outlet, and next thing I heard was him screaming as he went over the edge." Brycen's eyes darted around. "I swear I tried to get up to help him, but I wasn't fast enough."

"Were you and Mark good friends?" Derek asked.

Brycen flinched back. "Why are you asking that?"

"I'm just trying to get an idea of Mark's state of mind," Derek said.

"Mark wasn't suicidal," Mr. Dennison interjected.

"No one said Mark was suicidal," Joe said.

"No. We are not implying he was. We just want to know if Mark was careful when he worked." Derek smiled at Brycen. "If you were friends with Mark, you could give us some insight into his demeanor."

Joe scooted his chair a little closer to Brycen's. "Did you ever hang out with Mark outside of work?"

"Yeah. We would go for beers once in a while." Brycen scooted his chair away from the table.

"Have you been out lately with him?" Derek asked.

Brycen's lip twitched. "No. Not recently."

"Was Mark careless when he worked?" Derek asked.

"No. It was one reason he was so mad Jeff had been allowed to put in the AC unit. Mark was always getting on to us about minor safety issues." Brycen sheepishly lifted his eyes towards his boss.

"Then what distracted Mark so much he wouldn't pay attention to his surroundings? Especially if he was such a stickler for being safe. Was he on his phone?" Derek stared at the man.

Brycen shook, frowning. "No. I know the cables up there were messed up when Jeff installed the unit. Mark must have tripped over the cables." His eyes darted between Derek and Joe. "Didn't he?"

Damien glanced at Joe, then turned towards Brycen. "Did you or him straighten up the cables before you started working?"

"Um, I—I don't think so." He fidgeted with the sleeve of his jacket. "I didn't. Maybe Mark did."

"Then how did he trip over the cables if they had been straightened up?" Derek asked.

"I don't know. I just assumed he must have." He wiped his forehead with his hand. "I don't know why you are blaming me."

Derek straightened in his chair. "No one is blaming you."

"I was up there working. Mark stood and asked me something. I answered, and I heard him scream. I looked up, and he was going over the edge of the building." Brycen rocked back and forth as his body trembled. "I'm so sorry I couldn't do more." Tears filled his eyes. "He was my friend. I tried to save him." He stared at the men in the room. "I tried to save him."

Derek watched as the man broke down in sobs. He glanced at Damien, raising an eyebrow.

Mr. Dennison stood, pushing his chair back. "I think it would be best to let Mr. Cartwright go home. He has told you all he knows. It seems like a very unfortunate accident has occurred."

CHAPTER SIXTY-NINE

Dillon smiled at the men. "Hey, can I ask you a few questions?"

One of the guys nodded. "Sure. What do you want to know?"

"Tell me about Mark and Brycen. Were they good friends? Did they hang out after work?" she asked.

"Yeah," one man said as he crossed his arms. "They went out last night to O'Malley's."

"Do you know who else went?" Dillon asked.

"Me. I was with them. Mark had invited him to meet us out there."

"Who are you?" Dillon removed a small notepad from her back pocket.

"Eli."

"Eli?"

"Eli Smalls. Me, Mark, and a few other guys who don't work here met at O'Malley's. We stayed until it closed."

"Did Brycen stay the whole time?"

Eli paused for a few moments. "No. I was hitting on a girl. When I came back to the table, Mark said he left with a girl."

Dillon tilted her head. "Do you know the girl he left with?"

Eli shook his head. "No. I would recognize her if I saw her again. But I don't know who she was. I do know, Brycen was acting really weird today."

"What do you mean?"

Shrugging his shoulders, Eli sighed. "I came in this morning and the news was on. I stepped out to speak with someone. When I came in, Brycen had changed it to sports."

Dillon smirked at him. "Not a crime to change the channel."

Eli chuckled. "No. But he turned the TV off and placed the remote in the basket on the counter. No one ever does that. We always leave it on the table. And we always leave the news on."

He walked down the hallway, putting him out of earshot of the lounge, and nodded for Dillon to follow him. "Mr. Dennison gets a little cranky when we change the channel." He glanced over her shoulder. "Brycen is just odd. But after he turned off the TV, he was really jumpy around Mark. I overheard them talking while I was waiting for an elevator.

"Mark kept asking about the girl he took home last night. Brycen said he didn't leave with her. But Mark kept insisting he did. Said he saw him walk out with her and never return. Mark was giving him shit about it."

Dillon scribbled in her book. "What makes that such a big deal?"

"I had the impression Brycen didn't want anyone to know he had left with a girl. Or maybe that girl. I don't know, but the vibe coming off Brycen was odd."

"Do you know anything about Brycen?" Dillon asked.

"Not much. He keeps to himself. I know he had a crush on that lady who was murdered. I used to see him always on her floor. You know, Brycen used to service the coffee makers in this building."

Eli laughed. "He had a business with his grandfather. I know he helped Mr. Dennison one day when he was here, so he offered Brycen a full-time job. All I know is his parents died when he was young and his grandfather moved here to raise him."

"To go from a coffee maker repair guy to a HVAC maintenance worker is a big leap," Dillon said.

"Oh, Brycen went to HVAC school. Not sure where. Not in Chicago. Somewhere south of here. I think. He talked about it one day in the break room. Mr. Dennison put him on an internship. That's how he got the job here."

Dillon glanced over her shoulder when the door to the break room opened. "Thanks for your time." She handed Eli a card. "If you think of anything, call me. Please." Dillon watched as Eli pretended to be on his phone when Brycen walked past him.

As Brycen opened the side door to the stairwell, he glanced back at Eli. Dillon noticed Eli turned towards the wall. When Brycen left the hallway, Eli turned and went in the opposite direction.

Damien walked over to Dillon. "Did you get any information?"

"Not sure." She followed as they headed towards the elevator. "Eli was out with Brycen and Mark last night."

Derek spun around just as the elevator doors opened. "Brycen didn't mention that."

"He said Brycen was acting weird with Mark this morning. Mark was bugging him about a girl he left the bar with last night." Dillon waited until the door closed to continue. She glanced at the three men. "He said

Brycen had a crush on Camilla."

Damien cocked his head to the side. "Why?"

Joe snickered as the doors opened. Stepping out into the lobby, he turned towards the group. "Bad taste in women."

Derek chuckled.

Dillon barked out a laugh as they walked to the SUV. "Very bad taste."

CHAPTER SEVENTY

Dr. Parker's computer dinged with a message. She finished washing her hands and sat at her desk. "Let's see what we have." She opened the DNA results from Camilla's lips. "This doesn't make sense."

She scanned the file and then called Trace. "Hey, Margarite. This is Beth in the ME's office. Are you sure the DNA I sent you is correct?"

"Yes, ma'am. I ran it twice to make sure."

"That makes no sense."

"I know. I thought there may have been a cross contamination some-where or someone made a mistake. But there is no mistake."

"You are telling me my DNA sample matches an old case from 1989 in Virginia?"

"That's right. Find who the DNA in the system belongs to, and you will have a relative of your killer."

"Okay. Thanks." Beth hung up the phone. She wrote the case number down and where it was located and texted it to Dillon.

CHAPTER SEVENTY-ONE

Late Friday afternoon

Dillon sat in the back seat of the SUV. Joe explained how he and Taylor bought the house from his landlords. He was explaining how they were going to make it a two story and make the top floor the master suite area and an extra bedroom. As she sat, staring out the window, her phone pinged. Casually glancing at her screen, she sat upright. "Holy shit."

Derek glanced over at her. "What's going on?"

Damien turned down the radio and looked at her through the rearview mirror. "What is?"

"Beth got a hit on the DNA. It is connected to a case from 1989. A case out of Virginia. The case is sealed." Dillon scrolled through the file notes Beth forwarded.

"What is it?" Damien asked.

"Yeah, don't make us wait until we get home," Joe said.

Dillon looked at Derek. "Contact your guy, Kyle. Have him look at this case." She held out her phone, allowing him to type out the case number.

"This shouldn't take him long," Derek said as he typed.

Dillon nodded. The wheels in her head spun out of control. "Beth said there were matches to alleles in the DNA of this case. Our killer is related to someone in the system."

Derek looked at his phone. "Kyle has the case information. He's emailing it to me. He thinks this may be the case he was trying to get information on, but couldn't find it."

Damien sped up as they got closer to the exit leading to his home. "I need to update the captain about what we have so far."

"Let's see what Kyle has first. Get all our information together," Derek said.

Dillon entered the house, ignoring Gunner as she headed for her desk.

Damien scratched the dog's head. "Let's go outside for a bit." He led the dog to the back door and let him out into the yard. Grabbing a few sodas and a few bottles of water, he walked into the office.

Derek took a bottle of water. "Thank you." He sat with his laptop on his knees. "I'm looking at the file from Kyle. The case is sealed, because the victim was under eighteen." He glanced up at Dillon.

Dillon scrolled through her files. "Holy shit. I know this case. I can't believe I didn't think of it earlier."

Damien handed her a soda.

She popped the top on it and guzzled. "There was a rape victim. Early 1989. I couldn't get it opened, but the notes said she had been raped and the rapist was caught."

Dillon smiled as she glanced around the room. "Virginia was one of the first states to use DNA in rape cases. In 1999 they digitized all their DNA samples. And this was one of those first cases. I remember I wanted to find out about it, but they wouldn't let me get into the file."

Derek called Kyle. "Hey, can you get me any more information on this case? Derek nodded into the phone. "Yeah, I will square it. Get me whatever you can. I know I'm giving you permission. Get it to me as quick as you can."

He hung up his phone, glancing at his watch. "It will take him a bit. But this late on Friday afternoon, we would have to wait for the bureaucracy to get the file information. We need it now, not a year from now."

"Tell us what you remember about the case, Dillon," Damien said.

"There wasn't much in the file. A few notes, but there was a picture of an emblem. A very crude one. When I first saw Tracy on the table, I thought I had seen the emblem before. It was this case." She looked at Derek. "Didn't you say Kyle found an emblem during one of his searches? And he thought it looked like the other ones?"

"He did. He found mentions of a something being carved on a rape victim, with descriptions of it, but he couldn't find any pictures." Derek said.

Joe chugged his soda, then opened the water. His phone rang. "Hey babe." He stood and stepped out of the office.

Damien's phone rang. "What the hell?" he looked at Derek and Dillon. "It's the captain." He quickly answered it. "Hey Captain. What's going on?" He nodded into the phone. "Okay. We will head over there right now. I'm bringing Agent Reed. He is aware of the case."

Dillon watched as Damien paced behind his desk. She lifted her head in Joe's direction as he walked in with Gunner. "Have you gotten any texts from the VCU crew?"

He shook his head. "Nothing."

Damien hung up the phone. "Son of a bitch."

"What happened?" Joe asked.

"Thomlinson was found dead in his house." Damien stared at the floor. His shoulders sagged as the weight of the last week slammed into him. He lifted his gaze to Dillon and then shifted to Joe. "You know Johnson had everything to do with this."

"What does the captain want us to do?" Joe asked as he leaned against Dillon's desk.

"He is calling Travis to find out if he has him on the tracker going anywhere near Thomlinson's house. If he does," Damien looked over at Dillon. "Agents from your office will pick him up for questioning. We have been instructed to stay away from the case. They don't want to give Johnson anything to say we framed him."

Joe dragged a hand down his face. "This is shit. We can't let this guy get away with this. Thomlinson shouldn't have done what he did, but he didn't deserve to be murdered."

"They will find something. The good thing is, Johnson doesn't have a clue what we know. And if he went to Thomlinson's house, it will be on the tracker." Damien sat at his desk. He rubbed his face. "I feel like we got a bunch of little bites of shit, but nothing is getting us closer to a damn thing."

"There is nothing we can do for Thomlinson. Let's concentrate on our serial killer." Dillon leaned back in her chair. "I'm not even concerned about the damn dead guy at Camilla's place. Other than, I think our Brycen is involved."

"Alright." Damien ran his hand through his hair. "Setting our serial killer case aside for a few minutes. What are your thoughts on our dead guy from Camilla's work?"

Derek leaned back in his chair. "I think Brycen was involved, just like Dillon said. But I can't figure out why. What beef did he have with his co-worker? Especially if they were just out having a beer? And why would Brycen lie about it?"

Damien checked his email. "Travis sent me some information on our dead guy, Mark Chambers." He scanned the report. "Mark doesn't seem to have anything in his file. Never in trouble. Not even a ticket."

"Did you have him check Brycen out?" Derek asked.

"No. I didn't know about Brycen." Damien typed out a few commands on his keyboard. "I can get the information on Brycen."

"Eli did mention Brycen was jumpy around Mark. He kept asking about a girl Brycen left the bar with last night. Eli said he just figured Mark was giving him shit," Dillon said.

Derek stared at her. "That's not a reason to kill someone. There must be something else."

Damien keyed up his computer. He sighed as he started the search for information on Brycen Cartwright. "As for Brycen killing Mark, we have nothing. It looks like an accident and as far as I can tell, we don't have a shred of evidence to back up our suspicion that he threw Mark over the edge of the building. We don't even have a clue why he would throw Mark off the roof. And like Derek said, leaving the bar with a girl isn't a reason."

Derek read through his emails. Kyle searched Lilly's phone number. "Hey guys. It looks like Lilly was using the same dating app as Tracy."

"That's how our killer is getting his victims." Joe sat in the empty chair. "How do we track that?"

Derek pinched the bridge of his nose. "I told Kyle to get what he could from the company and told him to get a warrant if he needed." He typed out a text. "This should get us records from the app company. Tying two dead girls to a dating app should be enough to get user information."

"You don't have to use your real name to open an account on Red Hearts. How will we track the killer?" Joe asked.

Derek gave him a sly grin. "All Kyle needs is an IP address. If he can get the user's IP address, he can find him."

"What about the case from Virginia?" Dillon asked. She looked at Damien. "Can you get anything?"

Damien looked at Derek. "I could. If you want me to."

Derek squinted at the lieutenant. "I'm guessing you can get information by illicit means."

Damien laughed. "That sounds so bad when you say it like that."

CHAPTER SEVENTY-TWO

Brycen pulled the van into the driveway. He jumped out and ran into the house. Running into the living room, he turned on the news. Sitting in the seat next to his grandfather, he didn't even look over at him.

"You seem a little stressed."

Brycen ignored him.

"Let me guess. You have gotten yourself in a bit of a pickle."

Turning towards his grandfather, he glared at him. "Actually, I fixed a problem. I'm not stupid, you know."

"I never said you were. But you are making mistakes. I never made these mistakes."

Brycen's nostrils flared. "I read your diaries. You made plenty of mistakes. There wasn't the science there is now. That's the only reason you didn't get caught. But you almost did, didn't you?"

His grandfather huffed at him. "That girl wanted it."

"Then why did she turn you in?"

"Because she is a bitch like all women. Your mother was the queen of them."

Brycen stood. "Don't talk about her like that."

"Are you kidding me? You knew a long time ago what she was and what she did to your dad. That's why you did what you did." His grandfather sneered. "That was the only smart thing you ever did."

"I didn't do anything. It was an accident." Brycen's eyes filled with tears.

"Accident. Son, I saw the reports. They just couldn't pin it on you. You are smart. I will give you that. But you made a mistake. You should never have killed Camilla. I told you not to do it."

Brycen removed his phone. "I will have Chinese food delivered."

His grandfather continued looking at the TV. "You do that."

CHAPTER SEVENTY-THREE

Friday 7 p.m.

Damien stepped out of the shower. The hot water felt good against his skin. Thomlinson weighed heavily on his mind. He had texted Jim Fogle and made sure he was okay.

Jim said he was at his family's house in the southern part of the state. Damien thought it was a good idea for him to be out of the city. When Dillon asked him to get the information on the sealed case out of Virginia, he almost did it. Even Derek agreed. In the end, they opted to wait for Kyle to get it. He put on a pair of sweats and a T-shirt and headed back downstairs. "They aren't back yet?"

Joe looked up from his phone. "Nope. Maybe they are headed to Vegas."

Damien laughed. "I doubt that. Although I think we are all in need of a vacation."

"No shit. As soon as Taylor gets this shit figured out with her brother. I want to get the hell out of here. We should all go together."

Damien's eyes widened. "What about a cruise?"

"Too many people."

"Yeah. True." Damien sat at his desk.

Coach was sprawled out across it.

He picked him up and placed him in his lap. "How about a private yacht? We could do one of those private cruises in the Caribbean. Or somewhere it's warm."

"You paying the bill? That shit is pricey as hell." Joe raised an eyebrow at him.

Damien laughed. "Yes. We would pay for it. You just can't get us thrown in some jail."

"I would never get us thrown in jail."

"Right." Damien heard the garage door open. He walked out into the living room. "It's about time."

Dillon smiled and kissed him. "I had to show him the city."

"I will never ride with her again." Derek carried the food into the kitchen. "Do you ever ride with her?"

"No. She drives too fast." Damien unpacked the Chinese food. "I thought you were getting subs?"

"We changed our minds." She grabbed the two twelve packs of beer and placed them in the fridge. "Thought we could all use one of these." She held out four from the pack.

Joe took one and twisted off the top. He took a long pull. "This is nice."

They sat at the table. Everyone filled their plates.

Dillon quickly filled the cat's dish with canned food and gave Gunner a few treats on top of his food. She sat back down and guzzled her beer. "How's Taylor?" she asked Joe.

He swallowed his bite of food, holding up his finger. "She's good. They are having to do a lot of training. She's tired of it. Tomorrow and Sunday are the last two days. She is hoping to be home Sunday night."

"Does she have any more news on the case?" Dillon asked.

Joe shook his head. "Nope. All in limbo. The lawyer wasn't able to call her after the court hearing." He took a bite of his egg roll. "I'm sure the lawyer will have it under control."

Damien looked at Derek. "Do you have a girlfriend?"

Derek shook his head. "No. I had someone in my life for a bit. My work keeps me too busy." He got another beer from the fridge. "Anyone need one?"

Joe raised his hand. "I'll take one."

Derek handed him a second beer. "This is some great food. We have one Chinese restaurant that's worth going to. Best egg rolls on the planet. Although these are a close second."

"We eat out way too much." Damien grinned in Dillon's direction.

"Don't look at me like that. I'm learning how to cook." She pointed her fork at him like she was going to stab him.

"Damien and I were talking about how we should go on vacation together. You know the four of us." Joe wiggled his eyebrows at her.

"We do need a vacation. And I don't mean medical leave. That time didn't count as a vacation." Dillon turned towards Derek. "When was the last time you took a vacation?"

Derek laughed. "It was forced medical leave. After the Josiah Craig case."

She stopped eating. "I remember. I heard you were injured pretty bad."

"What happened?" Joe asked.

Derek really didn't want to go back to the case. But he didn't see a way around answering him. "Josiah snuck up on me. Damn near crushed my head in when he hit me with a piece of wood. He then tied me up and broke my cheek, my nose, and several ribs. Then he raped a girl in front of me and killed her. If all that wasn't enough, he shot himself in the head inches from me."

Everyone stared at him.

"Holy shit," Joe said.

"I knew you had been hurt. I didn't know about the other stuff," Dillon said.

"Not many do. I was placed on medical leave and drove out to Tennessee, where my family lives." Derek took a bite of an egg roll.

"I bet it was nice to see them after the case," Damien said.

"I never made it. I stumbled across an old case and ended up chasing a serial killer from the 80s." Derek swallowed, then took a sip of beer.

"Wait, is that the case Beth mentioned?" Joe asked.

"Yes. It's the same case."

"Cory...." Joe snapped his fingers.

"Thompson," Dillon said.

Derek nodded. "You know the case."

"I heard about it. It was amazing how you linked him to the murders." She put some extra rice on her plate.

"I was in the right place at the right time." Derek sighed. "I think giving those parents closure on their daughters and finding out exactly what happened to them is why I do this job."

Damien's mind flooded with memories of the first case he ever worked with Dillon. It was how he met her. Jason Freestone. One of the country's worst serial killers. He remembered telling the parents of the girls found on Jason's property what had happened to their daughters.

He held back some of the information. Damien still believed he did the right thing. There are just some things parents shouldn't know. When his brain let go of the memory, he looked up to see Dillon staring at him.

Joe and Derek were laughing.

He had no idea how long he hadn't been paying attention. But it was long enough for her to notice. Damien stared into her whiskey-colored eyes. The love he had for this woman transcended anything he ever had with Camilla. The best thing that ever happened to him was the worst case of his career. Damien got up and grabbed another beer. "Anyone?" he asked as he lifted his.

Joe held up his hand. "Me."

"You staying here?" Damien asked as he handed it to him.

"Yeah. I figured we would work on the case late. I made sure to ask the neighbor to check on Muffin and feed her. She will stay and pet her for a while. Plus, I don't want to go home," Joe said.

"Are you scared?" Dillon asked with a pouty face.

"No. But it is lonely." He pretended to cry as he winked at her.

CHAPTER SEVENTY-FOUR

Saturday 7 a.m.

Eli sat on the sofa watching the news. He really wanted the scores from the college basketball games. ESPN probably had a round up show replaying, but he also wanted the weather. Getting out of the apartment would do him good. Especially after Mark's death.

The vision of seeing him on the pavement played over and over in his mind. When he was at work, it had been easy to keep his thoughts at bay. Now, with nothing to really occupy himself, he couldn't stop thinking about him.

Not paying attention to the news, he almost missed the story. "Wait, a second." He grabbed the remote and rewound the live play. "Crap," he said when he went too far back. As the TV started playing, he stared at the face of the girl. She had been at the bar with them.

"No fucking way. That's the girl." Eli remembered her. It was her friend he had hit on. She had become all worried about the girl with Brycen. When they couldn't find her in the bar, the girls left to go look for her.

He dug into the front pocket of his jeans. "C'mon. I know I kept it." Eli rose and walked over to his jacket. He checked his pockets. When he couldn't find the card, he remembered his wallet.

Opening it up, he found the card. "I can't fucking believe this." He dialed the number and waited. "Agent McGrath? This is Eli from Mark's work. I know who the girl is Brycen left with. Yes, yes, I'm sure. I'm looking at her. She's missing. Her picture is on the news."

CHAPTER SEVENTY-FIVE

Saturday 6:30 a.m.

The pounding in Joe's head woke him up. He blinked several times, trying to focus. He tried to move, but his chest ached as if it was being crushed. "Shit. I can't breathe. I'm dying." He tried to sit up, but was greeted with a growl.

"What the heck?" Reaching up, his hand brushed against something soft and furry. "Coach? Man, you're crushing me." Joe moved the hefty furball to the end of the sofa as he sat up.

He glanced at his phone on the coffee table. "Crap." His head drooped to his chest. Joe tried to swallow, but his tongue stuck to the top of his mouth. Rising, he had to get his balance. He stretched, working the kinks out of his back.

"They need a bigger and more comfortable couch." Joe looked over at Coach, who had sprawled out. "I guess it works for you." He walked down the hallway. Derek and Gunner were sound asleep in the spare room.

Entering the kitchen, the smell of coffee filled the air. "Yes." He grabbed a coffee mug from the cupboard and filled it. "Dear woman, at least you had the sense to set up the coffee maker up."

Damien walked in, scratching his head. "Whose bright idea was it to drink all that whiskey and beer?"

"Yours."

"No. I said we should go over the case and next thing I know, we are playing cards." Damien filled a cup and added two sugars.

Joe laughed. "Derek told some damn funny stories. I think my sides are still hurting."

"I want to meet his team. They sound like a great group to work with." Damien leaned against the counter. "I know we should have worked on the case more. But I think my brain needed the break."

"We were waiting for information from Kyle. Hopefully, he will have some today." Joe heard a noise behind him and turned around to find Dillon standing there. "Well, my, my, my. Don't you look like crap."

Dillon pushed him out of the way. "I need coffee."

Gunner ran in and sat in front of the door.

"Let's go out, boy." Damien opened the door and watched as he did his business and bolted back in. "Too cold, huh?" he shut the door, locking it. He filled his bowl with food and also filled Coach's bowl.

Derek stepped into the bathroom in the hallway. He brushed his teeth and walked into the kitchen.

Everyone turned and stared.

"What?" he asked as he filled a mug with coffee.

"How do you not look like shit?" Dillon asked. "And why are you so... awake?"

Derek laughed. "I didn't drink all the whiskey."

Dillon was about to say something when her phone rang. She trotted to the office to get it.

Damien glanced at Joe. "I wonder who is calling her this time of the morning?"

"It can't be good. No one in their right mind is up this early on a Saturday." Joe opened the fridge and grabbed some eggs.

Damien took a pan out and put a few pats of butter in it. "Make enough for everyone. I think we have bacon." He opened the fridge and found it.

Derek sat at the table. "You two look like a happily married couple."

"Haha," Joe said as he scrambled the eggs.

About the time everything was done, Dillon walked back in.

Damien glanced over and saw her expression. "What is it?"

Her eyes darted around. "You guys will never believe this."

"What?" they all said in unison.

"That was Eli, the guy I spoke with while you spoke with Brycen. He remembered the girl that was at the bar. The one he said Mark kept harassing Brycen about." Dillon bounced on her toes.

Damien's brow wrinkled. "And this is important, because?" he asked, setting the orange juice on the table.

"It's important because the girl he saw Brycen talking to, and who he thinks left with him, is Lilly." Dillon sat at the table and took the plate Damien held out to her. "She's been reported as missing. Her picture was on the news."

Derek's cup of coffee stopped just before his lips. "Lilly, our dead Lilly?"

"The same one." She took a bite of bacon. "As soon as the news connects the missing girl to the crime scene vans in the park, this will hit the airways."

"Wait. Are you telling me Brycen is our killer?" Joe asked.

"I don't know. But it would make sense why Brycen killed Mark." Dillon took a piece of toast from a plate in the center of the table.

Joe took a sip of his orange juice. "Brycen Cartwright can't be our killer. It doesn't make any sense."

"Is Eli positive? Lilly was at the bar last night and left with Brycen?" Derek asked.

"He was hitting on her friend. Eli didn't know it until this morning. But when Mark said he had left and then her girlfriends got worried and they left, Brycen was gone, too. He thinks that's why Mark was ragging on him," Dillon said.

"That explains why Brycen killed Mark. Mark knew he was at the bar with Lilly. I bet that's what Brycen saw on the news. The crime scene vans in the park. That's why he turned off the TV." Derek sat back in his chair. "I need to see what Kyle has found. I'll be right back." He rose and went to his bedroom.

Damien finished his eggs and bacon. He placed his plate in the sink and filled his coffee cup. "I need to call the captain."

Dillon grabbed his arm. "Wait. Let's see what we can find out about Brycen. We need more than just him being at a bar with her."

Damien pulled on the ends of his hair. "We need to move on this."

"Damien," Joe said as he stepped up to fill his coffee cup. "Take a breath. We need to get everything first."

"Okay. I hear you. I just want this case to be over." Damien walked into the office.

Derek came out of the bedroom. "Let me get some more coffee. I will meet you all in the office."

Dillon sat at her desk.

Joe sat in one of the empty chairs with his eyes closed.

"How's Muffin?" Damien asked as he booted up his computer and continued the search he started the night before on Brycen Cartwright. Logging on to his dad's secure server, he pulled up the young man's life. At least what was public information.

"She's good. The neighbor texted me earlier when she went over before work."

"Good. Okay. Cartwright's parents were killed in the house fire. It looks like they suspected him of having set the fire."

Dillon squinted at him. "How do you know that?"

"I am reading a newspaper article."

"Are you sure? You didn't get into the sealed record?" Dillon asked him.

Derek walked in. "You don't need to worry about that."

Damien cocked his head to the side. "Huh?"

"Kyle got into the record. Brycen's juvenile record. It's true though. Brycen was the primary suspect in the arson, but they couldn't get enough evidence together. He didn't go to a foster home, as the papers reported." Derek took a sip of his coffee. "They put him in a psychiatric hospital. He stayed there until a family member took custody of him."

"How long was he in the hospital?" Joe asked.

Derek referenced his notepad. "Several years. Until his teen years. They didn't have enough evidence to charge him, but they had enough to have him committed to the hospital. It looks like he was almost catatonic after the fire."

"What family member took him in?" Damien asked.

"His aunt. On his mother's side. Brycen stayed there for about a year. She suffered a stroke. After that, Kyle couldn't find anything. We know he went somewhere because he never went back into the system. Kyle is working on finding out where Brycen went after the aunt's house." Derek sipped his coffee.

"Shit. This doesn't really give us anything to arrest him on. With his connection to Lilly, the most it might give us is a reason to question him." Damien leaned forward, placing his arms on his desk. He held the cup of warm coffee in his hands. "I think we should go question him. Use Lilly and the bar to get some information."

Derek stepped up to the large whiteboard under the LCD screen. He started making a list. "We know Lilly and Tracy used the same dating app. We know victims one and two were killed down near Indiana. Eli can place Brycen at the bar with Lilly. Do we know what kind of vehicle Brycen drives?"

Damien typed on his keyboard. "I can get that."

"Eli also said Brycen used to fix and maintain the coffee machines. He mentioned Brycen and his grandfather had some kind of business together. At some point, Brycen's grandfather came into his life," Dillon said. She snapped her fingers. "Shit. I forgot. Eli said Brycen had gone to HVAC school. He never graduated. But that's how he got the job at Camilla's company. Some kind of internship."

Damien stared at Derek. "Could that be who Brycen went to live with after his aunt?" he scoured some files on his computer. "I'm searching to see where Brycen might have gone to HVAC school."

"Yeah. He could be." Derek dialed Kyle's number. "Hey, I'm going to put you on speakerphone."

"Hey, everyone," Kyle said through the phone.

"What do you have?" Derek asked.

"Okay. I have a lot of information. I tracked Lilly to a bar in your area. O'Malley's."

Dillon's eyes widened.

"Kyle, are you sure you can place her at that bar?" Damien asked.

"Yeah. I used her phone and tracked it via cell towers. I can also place it within the state park she was found in, just before it goes offline."

"This is great. What else do you have?" Derek made a note on the board.

"I'm running a program that tells me if Lilly and the other victim who were using the dating app talked to the same person. The company has given me some information, but they are dragging their heels. I may have gone around them."

"Kyle, stay within the lines." Derek tilted his head back as he sighed.

"I did. I only took what the warrant specified." Kyle paused. "Okay, it took some digging, but I was able to get the name attached to the DNA sample in the system. It wasn't readily available. Looks like when the state of Virginia first loaded the samples onto their database, there were some legal issues regarding certain cases, and this case was one of them.

"Since the victim was a minor, and no charges were actually brought against the man, there were some questions whether they should list his DNA in the system. Somehow, it got put in there. I just had to match the codes from the sample to the DNA listing. Our guy is named Terrance Wallace. He's sixty-eight years old."

Dillon shook her head. "We haven't come across anyone named Wallace."

"I did some digging. Wallace was in the military. He was discharged with a general discharge. He had attempted to rape a young woman who worked on the base he was at. They couldn't prove anything because he claimed she led him on. The army discharged him. He was an E6 – staff sergeant."

"That's where the chevrons come from," Dillon said.

"But what connection to Brycen Cartwright does he have?" Damien asked.

Kyle giggled into the phone. "This is why I love this job. Terrence was Brycen's grandfather on his mother's side."

"Holy shit," Joe said. "That's the case."

"We still need more. We need this to stick. Where is Terrance now?" Derek asked.

"That I don't have. He moved from Virginia to the Illinois area. Looks like he has property just outside of Chicago. But there has been no activity on any of his accounts, except for one bank account. He is still receiving his social security. I can see regular payments to the mortgage lender. Looks like several years ago he refinanced his home."

"Kyle, did you break any banking laws?" Derek asked.

"I skimmed them. Almost above board." Kyle laughed into the speaker. "It's okay. It will hold up in court."

"What else do you have?" Derek asked.

"Your boy Brycen went to an HVAC school out of high school in southern Illinois. Near the Indiana border. At some point, though, he took over his grandfather's coffee machine servicing company."

"Damn," Dillon said. "He's a tad bit faster than you." She pointed to Damien.

"Pfft." Damien typed on his computer. "I found Terrance had a van registered to the coffee business." He stared at everyone in the room. "A van is what the tech thought was used in the park and Camilla said she saw a van following her."

"Kyle, how long will it take for you to get the address of the IP user who was on the dating app and contacted Lilly and Tracy?" Derek asked.

"That could take a few hours. Maybe even a few days. Like I said, the company isn't really cooperating. George is calling them this morning and putting the screws to them. But I wouldn't hold my breath getting it today. For sure by Monday. Unless...."

"Unless what?" Derek asked.

"Unless I hack their system. I could easily bypass their security wall.

Get the information."

Derek thought about agreeing, however, that may compromise the case and throw everything out of court. "No. We do that as a last resort. For now, keep working on it." Derek disconnected the call. "Call the captain. I'm going to call your director, Dillon." He stepped out of the office.

Joe stood and looked at the LCD screen. "Do you know what is going to happen when this shit comes out?"

"Oh yeah. I know exactly what is going to happen. When it comes out, I am connected to the case via Camilla." Damien looked at Dillon. "We may get more exposure than we want."

CHAPTER SEVENTY-SIX

Saturday mid-morning

Damien hung up the phone. "The captain wants us to interview Brycen in his home," Damien said as Derek walked back into the office. "He wants us to see if we can get anything out of him, then bring him and his grandfather to DC."

"He will assume we know something the minute we pull up in front of his grandfather's house," Derek said as he sat. "Your director said he is deferring to the captain for this," he said to Dillon.

Joe stood and stretched. "Let's get over there. Ask some questions and see if we can rattle him. At least we can get him and his grandfather in for questioning."

Damien nodded as he stood. "I think we need to just get over there."

"Let me get my gun and wallet." Derek walked out of the room.

Dillon walked to the front door and grabbed her gun and ID from the little table. "I'm ready. I really want to see him in his home and look at the grandfather as we ask him questions. By my calculations, I think we will have roughly twenty-four hours before all of this hits the airways."

"I want to be out in front of it too, when it does." Damien locked up as they all headed towards the SUV.

Dillon watched as the neighborhood got older. The houses decreased in size, but the yards got bigger. She never understood why anyone would live in a big house with no yard.

"Let's approach this like we are closing the case where Mark is concerned. If we get him at ease, then we can ask about Lilly," Joe said.

"We need to make him feel like he is doing us a favor. I don't think we should go in guns blazing. If we had a positive match of DNA on Brycen, we could arrest him on the spot. We don't even have anything against the grandfather for the other murders." Derek took a piece of gum from the front pocket of his jeans.

Silence fell over the SUV. The air was thick and sticky. Solving murders from over a decade ago seemed surreal. Damien hoped it would end with answers. But it seemed with every new piece of evidence they had more questions.

He pulled onto Brycen's street. The houses were modest but not very well kept. As he neared the property, Damien scoped out the area. "I'm going to drive by and make a U-turn. Then I can park in front of the house."

Derek noticed the van in the driveway. "That looks like the van from the coffee business."

"At least we know he is home." Joe took a piece of gum from the console. "Want some?" he asked Derek.

"No, thank you," Derek said.

As Damien parked, he thought he saw a curtain move. "I think Brycen knows we are here."

"I caught that movement, too." Joe pointed to one of the living room windows. "I think he is watching us now."

Brycen ran from window to window. "Why are they here?"

"I told you—you messed up."

Brycen whipped around and faced his grandfather. "I didn't mess up. I didn't make a mistake."

"You did. But you knew that. The moment you took Camilla. You knew you had messed up. You just didn't want to face it."

"Shut up. That's not true."

Exiting the vehicle, they crept towards the door. Damien put his finger over his lips as they stepped close to the home. "I can hear him arguing with someone."

Dillon leaned in to everyone. "Maybe he's arguing with his grandfather."

Derek touched his finger to his nose. He stepped up on the porch, listening before he rang the doorbell.

They waited, staggered on the stoop. They could hear the arguing through the walls.

"Quit saying I messed up."

"You did. I told you not to take her. If you had only listened to me."

Brycen glared at his grandfather. "You're just like mom. She used to tell me what a mistake I was. She always pointed out everything I did wrong. Just like you have done all these years."

Derek leaned into Damien. "It sounds like a heated argument." He rang the bell. "Hello? Brycen? This is agent Reed. We want to clear up a few things concerning Mark's accident. Could you speak with us?"

Brycen shuffled from right to left, hitting the sides of his head. "I can't come to the door right now. Can you come back tomorrow?"

"It will only take a few minutes. We are closing the case as an accident, but we need to clarify a few things. It's really just so the family can't sue you or the company." Derek glanced at the others. He leaned into Joe. "See if you can find a window you can look through."

Joe quietly stepped off the porch and snooped around the windows.

Brycen's grandfather laughed.

"What is so funny?"

"You. You have no idea what to do. Stand and fight, son. Don't let them take you. Do you want to be someone's bitch in prison?"

"They can't put me in jail. They don't have anything."

"Why do you think they are here? Brycen, get the gun."

Brycen shook as he stood near the window. "No. You heard them. They just want to ask a few questions."

"You are so stupid."

Derek motioned for Joe to come back to the front. He huddled everyone. "Did you hear that?"

Damien nodded. "We want him alive."

"Don't shoot to kill unless you have to." Dillon checked her weapon.

"I think we ought to save the taxpayers money," Joe said.

Derek rapped his knuckles on the door. "Mr. Cartwright, I need you to open the door. We really just want to talk."

Brycen ran to the bedroom and grabbed his grandfather's forty-five. He cocked the weapon, loading the chamber. "What should I do?"

His grandfather laughed. "Let them in. If they arrest you, shoot yourself."

Brycen didn't want to go to prison, but he didn't think he could kill himself. The door rattled when the agent pounded on it again. "Okay. I'm coming. Hang on."

Derek looked at the others. "Get ready. I'm not sure what is going to happen."

"Grandfather, I didn't mean to mess up."

"Let them in, Son. You know what to do."

Brycen opened the door and stepped back. The storm door was still locked. He stared out through the dirty glass at the agents. "What do you want?"

"We just need a few questions answered." Damien half waved at Brycen.

"I can do it here. What do you want to know?"

"It really would be better if you would just let us in." Derek took a half step closer to the storm door. He saw Brycen move to the side where he couldn't see his face, but he could hear him.

"Grandfather, I'm scared. I don't want to go to prison. They will put me in the same hospital as before."

"Brycen, you know what to do. I've told you this would be your out. And since you messed up, you have to pay the price. If only you would have listened to me. You're so stupid."

"No, I'm not. Quit saying that."

Derek turned towards the others. "I can't see him. He could have a weapon." He tried the handle of the storm door. It was locked, but it was also flimsy. He yanked down on the handle and broke it. "Brycen, we are coming in."

"You are stupid. You couldn't even kill your parents right. Everyone knew you did it. They couldn't prove it. And now you have ruined it for both of us."

"Stop. It wasn't my fault."

"Your dad was an idiot. And he passed it to you. I thought I could help you, but you're nothing but a retard. A damn retard."

"STOP!" Brycen lifted the gun.

Derek used the door to protect himself as best he could. He peeked around it. Brycen faced a man in a chair, holding a gun on him. The back of the chair faced Derek. All he saw was the man's head. He couldn't see Brycen's face. "Brycen. Don't shoot your grandfather. Let us help you."

"Do it. Put the gun to your head and pull the trigger. Do us all a favor," his grandfather said.

Damien's eyebrow wrinkled. He looked at Dillon. "Is this kid's grandfather actually telling him to shoot himself?"

Dillon cocked her head. "It sounds like it." She strained to hear the muffled cries.

Brycen stared at his grandfather's face. "I did all this for you. I only ever wanted to make you proud of me."

Derek was about to step out from the cover of the door when he heard the gunshot. He pushed open the door, followed by Damien, Joe, and Dillon. All with their guns out.

Derek kept his weapon trained on the crumpled body on the floor. "Brycen?" He called out as he moved slowly towards the back of the chair. The hair on his arms stood on end. He was close enough he could see what was left of Brycen's head. Brain matter splattered on the wall in front of him.

Dillon and Joe swept the other side of the home, making sure no one else was there.

"Clear on this end," Joe said as they returned to the living room.

Damien made his way around the chair, keeping his weapon trained on the grandfather. "Terrance, we know you killed all those women in the parks." As he came closer to the chair, Damien made eye contact with Derek. "Tell me that's not what I think it is."

As Derek stepped around towards the front of the chair. Facing the grandfather, he lowered his weapon. "It's worse."

"What the hell is going on?" Dillon holstered her weapon when Damien and Derek lowered theirs.

"Yeah," Joe said as he walked towards the men. "What the heck?"

As each one saw the chair. Their mouths dropped open.

"Who was he talking to if no one else was here?" Joe asked, staring at the grandfather.

"Himself. Maybe he took on his grandfather's personality. It's what kept him functioning." Derek said.

"How long do you think he has been dead?" Damien asked.

Dillon squatted down and looked at the mummified remains of Terrance Wallace. The State Park Serial Killer. "Gathering by the way the flesh has pulled back during the mummification process. At least a few years."

Joe stood in the center of the room. "You mean to tell me this fucker has been living with this dead body all this time? And talking to him like he's alive? Even holding conversations with him?"

"At some point, Brycen split with reality," Derek said. "I'm going to call the director and the captain. They will need to get a crew down here." He stepped into the kitchen as he made the calls.

Dillon saw something on the bookshelf behind Brycen's body. She walked over to it.

"Watch your step." Damien pointed to the brain matter.

"I am." Maneuvering around the scene, she studied the spines of several books. "These look like diaries." She pointed to the black and blue books. "Each one is labeled by year. Starting in 1990." Dillon looked at Damien. "These could be his." She pointed to the grandfather.

She stepped to her left towards a closed door. She unholstered her weapon. Using her sleeve to cover her hand, she twisted the doorknob. When the door opened, she used her elbow to flip the light switch. When she saw the room was clear, she holstered her weapon and continued.

The room was small. One wall had blown up pictures of the women Brycen killed. Victims one, two, and three were on one side, then Camilla was in the middle. On the opposite of Camilla was the latest victim, Lilly. There were two more places marked out, denoting spots for two more pictures. The far wall was covered in pictures of Camilla.

"Damien, I think you better come in here." Dillon stared at all the photographs of Camilla. There were several of her in the parking garage, getting in and out of her vehicle. There were almost twenty of her at her home. Some looked as though they had been taken between the slats of her blinds.

"What do you have?" When Damien stepped into the room, a small gasp escaped his lips. "Oh, no."

Dillon moved to stand next to him. "Do not blame yourself. We had no reason to think she was being stalked."

"She told us. Several times."

"Doesn't matter. She made a lot of shit up, too." Dillon reached out and took his hand in hers. "You couldn't have stopped it."

Joe walked into the room. "Hey—holy shit." Joe's jaw hung open. "He wasn't just stalking her. He was in love with her."

Derek called out as he came to the doorway. "What the hell, I was looking for you guys."

Damien stared at the two spots on the wall next to Camilla's photo of her dead body. "He had two more victims to add to his chain. Camilla was the centerpiece."

Derek watched as Damien took it all in. He knew seeing this was hard on him. He also knew the best thing was for him to see it. "The captain and director are on their way here. So is Roger Newberry and either Beth or Dr. Forsythe."

"Make sure they bag the diaries on the shelf by Brycen's body. I'm thinking they're the grandfather's. They could answer a lot of questions."

CHAPTER SEVENTY-SEVEN

Sunday morning

"You have everything?" Damien asked Derek as he loaded his bag into Dillon's car.

Derek cringed at the thought of riding with her to the airport. "I can just call a cab."

Damien laughed. "She promised me she would drive slowly. Right Dillon?"

"Scout's honor." She winked at Derek. "Come on, you big baby. Get in."

"I thought you liked me. But you don't. I can see that now." Derek said to Damien and Joe as he held open the door to Dillon's car.

"This is the initiation you have to go through." Damien laughed as Derek flipped them off.

"I don't like this club," Derek said. "If I make it to the airport, I'll catch the press conference on my phone. You guys are lucky you don't have to do it."

"The captain and Director Shepherd are handling the news. I'm sure it will be spun in a way that we all come out smelling like roses," Damien said.

"Ha. Good luck with that." Derek sat in the car. He closed the door and locked his seatbelt in place. "Please, drive slow."

Dillon revved the engine of her Carrera. "I would never do anything to put my car in danger."

"What about me?" Derek gripped the dashboard as she peeled out of the drive.

Damien laughed as he shut the door and headed towards the kitchen. "She's going to scare the crap out of him." Damien grabbed a couple of beers from the fridge.

"Yup. He may never come back here again." Joe took the beer Damien held out.

Damien motioned for him to follow him to the office. "I am very grateful we don't have to do the news briefing." He turned on his computer.

"No shit. What about Thomlinson?" Joe asked as he sat at Dillon's desk.

"The captain is having the FBI investigate his death. He doesn't want anyone from DC involved. This way DEA Johnson can't use it to get off on any of the charges."

"Do you think they will arrest him soon?"

Damien shrugged as he drank his beer. "I have no idea. I don't think they have enough. The tracer said he was there. But they need physical evidence." He opened his secure email. "I know I have been telling you I would go through the file Nicky sent me."

"Have you looked at it at all?" Joe asked as he propped his feet up on the corner of Dillon's desk.

"No. I haven't." Damien read through the file. "Is she coming home today or tomorrow?"

"Today sometime. She texted me an hour ago. Said she would leave there and getting on the plane around 3 p.m. At least that is what her boss told her."

"Good. I know you want her to be home." Damien scanned the file. "It looks like Adnon has a huge bank account. Do you know what he did for a living?"

Joe shook his head as he drank his beer. He burped really loud. "Not a damn clue. But if he has that much money, why is he going after Taylor's money from the inheritance?"

"Probably wants to control her. It looks like he was married. Did you know that?"

"Who? Adnon? He was married?" Joe frowned. "I am sure Taylor didn't know he was married. She hasn't spoken or heard from him in years." He took another long sip of his beer. "How long was he married?"

Damien continued reading. "Um, looks like he was married to a wealthy Indian woman, and that is where he got all his money. After she died."

"Seriously? Does it say how?"

Damien looked at Joe.

"What?" Joe asked.

"Nicky found some headlines about her death. There had been complaints that Adnon had cheated and she was divorcing him. Looks like a car killed her. They never found the driver of the vehicle that struck her."

"Get the fuck out." Joe leaned forward, placing his feet on the floor. "This guy is so damn scary." Joe finished his beer. "I'm glad he doesn't live here."

Damien continued to read. "Wait. Where do you think he lives?"

Joe shrugged. "I assumed he was still living where her parents lived. Since the court hasn't divided the estate yet. Why do you ask?"

"Nicky tracked his movements over the last year. He moved around a lot. It looks like he was in the city where his mother and father lived. But Nicky shows him in Illinois."

"What? You've got to be joking?" Joe stood. "Where in Illinois?"

Damien read through the satellite tracking data from Adnon's cell phone. "He's right here in the city."

"This city? Chicago?"

"Yeah. In Chicago."

Joe fell into the chair. "If Taylor finds out, she will freak. But I can't let her go about her daily activities without her knowing. This guy wants her dead."

"Listen, we can get protection for her. Now that we know Adnon is in the city, my dad can keep her safe."

"Shit, you and I both know Taylor won't go for that."

"She will have to. At least until this is settled in court."

"This guy isn't going to wait until court. Hell, even if he does, he doesn't care about court. He is in the city for one reason. And it isn't to split a fucking inheritance. He wants to get Taylor."

"Joe, you are always telling me we need to breathe and get as much information as we can before we act. Now I need you to do the same thing. Let's get all the details so we know what we are dealing with. We need to find out if he is acting alone or if he has some help. Let's do this the right way." Damien texted his brother.

"I'm going to get Nicky to let my dad know what's going on. We will get security for both of you. I need to get that phone for her. This way, we can track her." Damien's phone pinged. "We will go over this week and set up a security detail. Get the phone and set up a plan."

Joe stood pacing, shaking his head. "That's fine. I am willing to get as much information as we can. And I'm willing to put a security detail on Taylor. But if you think I'm going to sit around and wait for this fucker to do something and then react. You have another thing coming. I will kill him myself if I have to."

Sign up for my <u>newsletter</u> and get updates on when my next book is coming out, freebies, and pictures of my evil cat, Pumpkin.

Links to books:
<u>The Damien Kaine Series</u>
<u>The Derek Reed Series</u>
<u>Other Books</u>

ABOUT THE AUTHOR

Victoria M. Patton lives with her husband of twenty-five years, two dogs—Bogart and Georgie, and two cats—Squeakers and Pumpkin.

Her years in the Coast Guard doing Search and Rescue/Law Enforcement and her BS in Forensic Chemistry helps her figure out the best way to hide all the bodies, and then write thrilling stories to keep you up at night. If she has any free time, she drinks copious amounts of whiskey and binge watches Hulu and Acorn TV.

Check out her blog Whiskey and Writing where she tries to help new authors navigate the indie publishing world. If all else fails, she provides great whiskey recipes.

Email her at: victoria@victoriampatton.com.
Check out her author website at www.victoriampatton.com. Be sure to join her Email List for updates on her latest book.
Follow her at Facebook @WhsikeyandWriting
Twitter @victoriampatton and on Pinterest.

Please leave a review wherever you purchased this book.

Links to all my books:
[The Damien Kaine Series](#)
[The Derek Reed Series](#)
[Other Books](#)

ABOUT THE AUTHOR

Victoria M. Patton is forced to share her home with a husband, 2 dogs, and 4 cats. The strays just seem to find their house. Her kids are grown. One is in college, and the other is living on his own. She is almost an empty nester.

Her time in the Coast Guard performing Search and Rescue/Law Enforcement duties, and her BS in Forensic Chemistry help her figure out the best way to hide all the bodies and write amazing stories about the murders. If she has any free time, she drinks copious amounts of whiskey and binge watches YouTube TV, BritBox, and Tubi. She is on most social media outlets, type in her name, you'll find her.

To learn more about her and sign up for her monthly email visit her websites:

www.whiskeyandwriting.com
www.victoriampatton.com